EP

The following text should be
under the title 'The Tourist'
before the line starting: 'whole classical era barely exists anymore.'

Everybody wants to see the future, but of course they can't. They get turned back at the border. 'Go away,' the customs people tell them. 'You can't come in. Go home.' Often you'll get people on TV who say they snuck across. Some claim it's wonderful and some claim it's a nightmare, so in that way it's like before there was time travel at all.

But the past is different. I would have liked to have gone early, when it was first opened up. Nowadays whenever you go, you're liable to be caught in the same pan-cultural snarl: We just can't keep our hands off, and as a result, Cuba has invaded prehistoric Texas, the Empire of Ashok has become a Chinese client state, and Napoleon is in some kind of indirect communication with Genghis Khan. They plan to attack Russia in some vast temporal pincer movement. In the meantime, Burger Chef has opened restaurants in Edo, Samarkand and Thebes, and a friend of mine who ventured by mistake into the Thirty Years War, where you'd think no one in their right mind would ever want to go, said that even Dessau in 1626 was full of fat Australians drinking boilermakers and complaining that the 17th century just wasn't the same since Carnage Travel ('Explore the bloodsoaked fields of Europe!') organized its packaged tours. They weren't even going to show up at the bridgehead the next day; my friend went, and reported that the Danish forces were practically outnumbered by Japanese tourists, who stampeded the horses with their fleets of buses, and would have changed the course of history had there been anything left to change. Wallenstein, the Imperial commander, didn't even bother to show up till four o'clock; he was dead drunk in the back of a Range Rover, and it was only due to contractual obligations that he appeared at all, the Hapsburg government (in collaboration with a New York public relations firm) having organized the whole event as a kind of theme park. Casualties (my friend wrote) after seven hours of fighting were still zero, except for an Italian who had cut his finger changing lenses – an improvement, I suppose, over the original battle, when the waters had flowed red with Danish blood.

And that period is less travelled than most. The. . .

Voyager

EDITED BY DAVID PRINGLE

The Best of Interzone

HarperCollins*Publishers*

Voyager
An Imprint of HarperCollins*Publishers*
77–85 Fulham Palace Road,
Hammersmith, London W6 8JB

The *Voyager* World Wide Web site address is
http://www.harpercollins.co.uk/voyager

A Paperback Original 1997
1 3 5 7 9 8 6 4 2

A catalogue record for this book
is available from the British Library

ISBN 0 00 648243 0

Set in Sabon

Printed and bound in Great Britain by
Caledonian International Book Manufacturing Ltd, Glasgow

The stories appearing in *The Best of Interzone* were previously published as follows:

Greg Egan: 'Mitochondrial Eve', Interzone 92, Feb 95; J G Ballard: 'The Message from Mars', Interzone 58, April 1992; Garry Kilworth: 'The Sculptor', Interzone 60, June 1992; Richard Calder: 'The Allure', Interzone 40, Oct 1990; Nicola Griffith: 'Song of Bullfrogs, Cry of Geese', Interzone 48, June 1991; Ian Lee: 'Pigs, Mostly', Interzone 50, Aug 1991; Paul Park: 'The Tourist', Interzone 80, Feb 1994; Stephen Baxter: 'George and the Comet', Interzone 53, Nov 1991; Geoff Ryman: 'Warmth', Interzone 100, Oct 1995; Ian R MacLeod: 'The Family Football', Interzone 53, Nov 1991; Ian Watson: 'Ahead!', Interzone 95, May 1995; Molly Brown: 'Bad Timing', Interzone 54, Dec 1991; Paul Di Filippo: 'World Wars III', Interzone 55, Mar 1992; Timons Esaias: 'Norbert and the System', Interzone 73, July 1993; John Meaney: 'Sharp Tang', Interzone 82, April 1994; David Garnett: 'Off the Track', Interzone 63, Sep 1992; Brian Aldiss: 'The Eye-Opener', Interzone 74, Aug 1993; Ben Jeapes: 'The Data Class', Interzone 80, Feb 1994; Eric Brown: 'Downtime in the MKCR', Interzone 83, May 1994; Graham Joyce & Peter Hamilton: 'Eat Reecebread', Interzone 86, Aug 1994; Brian Stableford: 'The Unkindness of Ravens', Interzone 90, Dec 1994; Thomas M Disch: 'The Man Who Read a Book', Interzone 87, Sep 94; Kim Newman: 'Slow News Day', Interzone 90, Dec 1994; David Langford: 'The Net of Babel', Interzone 92, Feb 1995; Sean McMullen: 'A Ring of Green Fire', Interzone 89, Nov 1994; Mary Gentle: 'Human Waste', Interzone 85, July 1994; Eugene Byrne: 'Cyril the Cyberpig', Interzone 66, Dec 1992.

CONTENTS

INTRODUCTION

Interzone will be fifteen years old in the spring of 1997. Here, in brief, is the story of how the magazine began.

The decision was taken in the summer of 1981. Having grown tired of waiting for someone else to do it, we aimed to create a new British science fiction magazine virtually out of thin air. A group of us had organized an sf convention in Leeds, Yorkshire, over Easter weekend, 1981; and after all the bills had been paid we discovered that the event had yielded an unexpected profit of about £1,300. We decided to use the money to help launch a new professional sf magazine, believing that gatherings of science fiction enthusiasts are meaningless events unless they do something to promote the form of writing which is the reason for us all coming together in the first place.

There was no British sf magazine in existence in 1981, nowhere for a new writer to publish his or her short stories and receive fair payment for them. The legendary *New Worlds* had been created by a group of eager sf fans way back in 1946. It survived for 24 years and helped launch the careers of Brian Aldiss, John Brunner, J. G. Ballard, Michael Moorcock and many other writers – so we felt it was worthwhile to attempt something similar for the 1980s and 1990s.

Simon Ounsley and I, with other helpers in Leeds, set about planning the shape of the magazine: it would be digest-size, perfect-bound, with large print on thick paper; about 112 pages, comprising stories, reviews and articles; we would pay £20 per 1,000 words for fiction, and use all our personal contacts with authors in order to obtain a good line-up of names for our first issue. We had no illusions about paying ourselves for the work involved: this would be a voluntary spare-time activity. Most likely, the convention surplus would not even cover the costs of the first issue.

Meanwhile, down in London, Malcolm Edwards was then a freelance writer, working part-time as sf adviser to Victor Gollancz Ltd. I knew him quite well from the days when we had worked together at the SF Foundation, North East London Polytechnic, in 1978–79. In 1981 Malcolm prepared some costings for a prospective science fiction magazine, possibly to be published by the British SF Association. Although his initial scheme came to nothing, the exercise stimulated him to begin laying alternative plans for an A4, 32-page publication which would contain nothing but fiction. It would pay £40 per 1,000 words – a rate equal to, or greater than, the amounts paid by most American sf magazines at the time. The publication would be funded mainly by advance subscriptions. Malcolm was prepared to do the bulk of the work on such a magazine, but he was daunted by the prospect of reading hundreds of manuscripts, so he invited various people to become his assistant editors. That is how John Clute, Colin Greenland and others came into the project. But news of our intentions in Leeds had reached Malcolm, and he thought it would be foolish to have two new sf magazines appearing at the same time, competing for the same writers and the same market, so he wrote to me and proposed that we pool our resources – an offer we decided to accept.

The proposed magazine still did not have a name, and there were obvious problems over the choice of an editor-in-chief. We decided to form a collective of eight equal co-editors, not realizing at the time that we would be criticized severely for this somewhat eccentric decision – by writers, by readers, even by the *Times Literary Supplement*. The format we picked was the one Malcolm had planned. The magazine would be a quarterly, costing £1.25. It would depend entirely on its high-quality fiction, and there would be little or no illustration and non-fiction. In addition to the sf writers of our acquaintance, we would approach such leading authors as Martin Amis, Angela Carter, Salman Rushdie and D. M. Thomas in an effort to solicit wide-ranging material. (Of these, only the late Angela Carter was to respond, with two excellent stories – bless her memory.) We were now thinking in terms of a literary magazine, open to imaginative fiction in general as well as science fiction in particular.

We agonized over the matter of a name for the magazine. We wanted something which sounded sf but not blatantly so, something to jog the imagination but not lead it into any narrow channel. Eventually I decided to ransack the novels of William Burroughs in search of a suitable word or phrase. In *The Naked Lunch* he describes an imaginary city called Interzone: 'The Composite City where all human potentials are spread out in a vast silent market.' Wonderful! I suggested it to the others arguing that we didn't want a title with nostalgic overtones: this was to be a city magazine, hard-edged. After a week or two everyone seemed to agree it was a good name, and the magazine was duly christened.

Now came the task of launching the publication. Malcolm's fund-raising idea had been to solicit advance subscriptions from the membership of the British SF Association and various conventions. This we pursued. We contacted numerous authors and extracted promises of material from them; we then used their names to entice subscribers. Every member of the BSFA received a leaflet from us, and we inserted adverts in various fanzines and journals: 'What is *Interzone*? It is the title of an exciting new British sf magazine to be launched next Spring ... The magazine is being undertaken for the good of British sf, and for the good of sf in general ... The *real* 1980s start here!'

Malcolm Edwards did the lion's share of the preparatory work, becoming managing editor in all but name. His was the magazine's main address, with my Leeds address as an alternative. The advance subscriptions started to flow in. By February 1982 we had over 600. The first issue would cost us about £1,000 to typeset and print; payments to authors would amount to another £1,200. With our charter subscriptions, plus the remains of the convention money, minus advance publicity costs, we would be well in hand. Of our more than 600 charter subscribers well over half were BSFA members, and this success was partly due to a marketing ploy which offered a free limited-edition booklet to all those who subscribed before the end of January 1982. In the summer of 1981, I had approached J. G. Ballard for an original story to appear in the first issue. He didn't have one, but as it happened he had just completed a 13,000-word novelette, 'News from the Sun', which was due to appear in the literary magazine *Ambit*, and we were permitted to use this fine story as our special offer to entice subscribers. (The *Interzone* edition of 'News from the Sun', signed by the author, is now a collector's item; a few years ago, a second-hand book-dealer told me that he bought a copy for £50 and promptly sold it for £75.)

Other authors were now coming up with material. We obtained good stories from Angela Carter, M. John Harrison, John Sladek and Keith Roberts. Michael Moorcock had no short stories available, but he did offer us a novel, *The Brothel in Rosenstrasse*, from which we carved out an extract for use in our first issue. We decided that *Interzone*'s premier issue had to be filled with 'name' writers. Our advance subscribers were already committed, but we feared that no one else would buy an unknown magazine unless the cover could boast an array of well-known names.

What else should go on the cover we had no idea – none of the eight editors had much in the way of design experience. Malcolm sought out a professional designer who would also do the paste-up of the magazine for us. Philippa Bramson designed the layout of issue one; she created the headings and had them specially typeset; she devised the cover with its airbrushed logo and its motif of a black sun with a blazing yellow corona (which Angela Carter was to describe, rather unkindly, as looking like a fried egg).

Philippa and her successors as designer were to be *Interzone*'s only paid employees for quite some time. In the first six years of the magazine's existence none of the editors received any pay. At first we didn't even reimburse ourselves for out-of-pocket expenses. Thus, although none of us sank large sums of our own money into the magazine we all invested in it to a small degree. (And we succeeded in keeping the finances on a sound footing, never relying on loans or overdrafts.)

By the early months of 1982 we were already receiving a considerable influx of unsolicited manuscripts. Most of these came from unknown writers. Scores of beginners were eager to submit material to a magazine they had not even seen. Many of the manuscripts came from the USA – stimulated no doubt by that great American institution, the Creative Writing Class – but there were British hopefuls too. We were building up quite a slush-pile. Most of the submissions went to Malcolm's address in London, but a not inconsiderable number came to me in Leeds. At Malcolm's end, Roz Kaveney acted as the principal sieve (she is a phenomenally fast reader). Reading submissions proved very time-consuming, and simultaneously we were discovering how many other chores were involved in the editing and publishing of a magazine. Apart from making editorial judgements and physically producing the magazine, there were such matters as publicity, promotion, distribution and sales to worry about.

Distribution was a particular headache. We contacted several major distributors but none of them showed any interest in the magazine. Only Titan, the company which owned Forbidden Planet Bookshop, said that they would definitely take a quantity from us. We failed to find a newstrade distributor, so our modest dreams of selling 1,000 copies direct to subscribers, plus 1,000 to sf book-shops via Titan, and perhaps 3,000 through newsagents, proved over-sanguine. The print run for our first issue was 3,500 copies (which subsequently fell to a low point of 2,500 with issue five), and it was only in 1988, after long years of effort, that we were able to advance substantially beyond that initial print order.

Some copies of our first issue were distributed by hand to bookshops in Leeds and London. The subscribers' copies were mailed, with all the labels hand-written; the remainder languished in Malcolm's house and mine, to be sold gradually as back-issues. (We were able to declare issue one finally out of print in 1988, after six years on sale.)

That first issue brought a mixed response. We received one or two favourable mentions in the press and there was praise for most of the stories, but people criticized the magazine's thinness, its lack of illustrations and its dearth of non-fiction content. Sales were sluggish, and Titan cut their order for subsequent issues.

And yet, for all that, we were not disheartened. We knew we could do better, and we knew it would take time to establish readers' confidence. We felt we had created something from nothing: at last there was a new British science-fiction magazine. A long period of growth and con-solidation was just beginning . . .

In 1982, I moved to Brighton, Sussex, and met the artist Ian Miller, who became our Art Editor for a year or two. We succeeded in gaining Arts Council support for the magazine – a small annual grant which I am pleased to say has continued to the present day. After issue four, in 1983, Malcolm Edwards resigned, due to pressure of other publishing work. Other co-editors gradually fell by the wayside until, by 1985, the magazine was edited jointly by Simon Ounsley and me.

That same year, our first anthology was published, by J. M. Dent & Sons, and other books followed. John Clute and Malcolm Edwards were happy to accept the honorary posts of Advisory Editors. We took on Lee Montgomerie as an Associate Editor, and she is now Deputy Editor and my principal helper. In 1988, when the magazine moved from quarterly to bi-monthly publication, Simon relinquished his half-ownership and I took on full financial responsibility. Around the same time, we finally gained limited newstrade distribution. In 1990, we increased the frequency again, doubling output from six issues a year to twelve.

In the 110 issues to August 1996 *Interzone* featured new stories by well over 200 different writers (not to mention many non-fiction contributors and artists). About two-thirds of these writers have been British, with Americans making up the majority of the remainder. A scattering have been from other countries, including several Australians and Canadians and occasional writers from nations as diverse as the Czech Republic, Japan and the Philippines. Of these 200 plus authors, over half have been new writers; that is to say, they have published their first or second stories with us, and we feel they are our discoveries – or, at any rate, that we have helped nurture them from early points in their careers.

A substantial number of the new writers have gone on to publish books; in many cases, their initial acceptance by book publishers came as a direct result of their work being seen in *Interzone*. Indeed, editors and agents often ask us for writers' addresses. These newer writers, many of them now well established, include Sarah Ash, Stephen Baxter, Stephen Blanchard, Michael Blumlein, Scott Bradfield, Keith Brooke, Eric Brown, Molly Brown, Christopher Burns, Richard Calder, Greg Egan, Neil Ferguson, Nicola Griffith, Simon Ings, Richard Kadrey, Paul J. McAuley, Ian R. MacLeod, Jamil Nasir, Kim Newman, Rachel Pollack, Nicholas Royle, Geoff Ryman, Alex Stewart, Charles Stross and David Wishart. Not all of the foregoing, let it be noted, have developed into 'genre' writers – several, such as Blanchard, Bradfield, Burns, Royle and Wishart, are pursuing careers as mainstream novelists.

By no means everybody is represented in this anthology (which would be more accurately titled 'Some of the Best from Interzone's Past Five Years' but, within the necessary space constraints, I have tried to give a fair sampling of good stories not hitherto reprinted in authors' collections or in other anthologies.

Although it remains a small magazine, with just 2,000 subscribers worldwide, *Interzone* is now recognized as a major sf publication. In 1995, it received a Hugo Award from the members of the World SF Convention held in Glasgow – the first time that any British magazine has been so honoured since these awards began in the 1950s. Here are a couple of recent comments on the magazine from eminent American well-wishers, remarks which make us feel it has all been worthwhile:

'I was one of the first fifteen people in the US to subscribe to *Interzone* . . . because I truly believe that without a short fiction market the genre will calcify. The existence of *Interzone* has brought British sf back from its deathbed. The fact that there is another major national tradition of sf helps us no end here in the US' – Bruce Sterling, interview in *Locus*: The Newspaper of the Science Fiction Field (May 1996).

*   *   *

'Without *Interzone*, the already depressed British sf publishing scene would become a wasteland, and there would be no place left for new British writers to develop their craft . . . *Interzone* is and has been vital to the evolution of science fiction in the eighties and nineties, and I personally hope that it continues to be so for many years to come' – Gardner Dozois, from the introduction to his *The Year's Best Science Fiction*, Thirteenth Annual Collection (New York, St Martin's Press, 1996).

Heartened, we look forward to the next fifteen years, and to taking the magazine well into the 21st century.

David Pringle
EDITOR OF *INTERZONE*

MITOCHONDRIAL EVE

Greg Egan

With hindsight, I can date the beginning of my involvement in the Ancestor Wars precisely: *Saturday, June 2, 2007.* That was the night Lena dragged me along to the Children of Eve to be mitotyped. We'd been out to dinner, it was almost midnight, but the sequencing bureau was open 24 hours.

'Don't you want to discover your place in the human family?' she asked, fixing her green eyes on me, smiling but earnest. 'Don't you want to find out exactly where you belong on the Great Tree?'

The honest answer would have been: *What sane person could possibly care?* We'd only known each other for five or six weeks, though; I wasn't yet comfortable enough with our relationship to be so blunt.

'It's very late,' I said cautiously. 'And you know I have to work tomorrow.' I was still fighting my way up through post-doctoral qualifications in physics, supporting myself by tutoring undergraduates and doing all the tedious menial tasks which tenured academics demanded of their slaves. Lena was a communications engineer – and at 25, the same age as me, she'd had real paid jobs for almost four years.

'You always have to work. Come on, Paul! It'll take fifteen minutes.'

Arguing the point would have taken twice as long. So I told myself that it could do no harm, and I followed her north through the gleaming city streets.

It was a mild winter night; the rain had stopped, the air

was still. The Children owned a sleek, imposing building in the heart of Sydney, prime real estate, an ostentatious display of the movement's wealth. ONE WORLD, ONE FAMILY proclaimed the luminous sign above the entrance. There were bureaus in over a hundred cities (although Eve took on various 'culturally appropriate' names in different places, from Sakti in parts of India, to Ele'ele in Samoa) and I'd heard that the Children were working on street-corner vending-machine sequencers, to recruit members even more widely.

In the foyer, a holographic bust of Mitochondrial Eve herself, mounted on a marble pedestal, gazed proudly over our heads. The artist had rendered our hypothetical ten-thousand-times-great grandmother as a strikingly beautiful woman. A subjective judgment, certainly – but her lean, symmetrical features, her radiant health, her purposeful stare, didn't really strike me as amenable to subtleties of interpretation. The aesthetic buttons being pushed were labelled, unmistakably: *warrior*, *queen*, *goddess*. And I had to admit that I felt a certain bizarre, involuntary swelling of pride at the sight of her . . . as if her regal bearing and fierce eyes somehow 'ennobled' me and all her descendants . . . as if the 'character' of the entire species, our potential for virtue, somehow depended on having at least one ancestor who could have starred in a Leni Riefenstahl documentary.

This Eve was black, of course, having lived in sub-Saharan Africa some 200,000 years ago – but almost everything else about her was guesswork. I'd heard palaeontologists quibble about the too-modern features, not really compatible with any of the sparse fossil evidence for her contemporaries' appearance. Still, if the Children had chosen as their symbol of universal humanity a few fissured brown skull fragments from the Omo River in Ethiopia, the movement would surely have vanished without a trace. And perhaps it was simply mean-spirited of

2

me to think of their Eve's beauty as a sign of fascism. The Children had already persuaded over two million people to acknowledge, explicitly, a common ancestry which transcended their own superficial differences in appearance; this all-inclusive ethos seemed to undercut any argument linking their obsession with *pedigree* to anything unsavoury.

I turned to Lena. 'You know the Mormons baptized her posthumously, last year?'

She shrugged the appropriation off lightly. 'Who cares? This Eve belongs to everyone, equally. Every culture, every religion, every philosophy. Anyone can claim her as their own; it doesn't diminish her at all.' She regarded the bust admiringly, almost reverently.

I thought: *She sat through four hours of Marx Brothers films with me last week – bored witless, but uncomplaining. So I can do this for her, can't I?* It seemed like a simple matter of give and take – and it wasn't as if I was being pressured into an embarrassing haircut, or a tattoo.

We walked through into the sequencing lounge.

We were alone, but a disembodied voice broke through the ambience of endangered amphibians and asked us to wait. The room was plushly carpeted, with a circular sofa in the middle. Artwork from around the world decorated the walls, from an uncredited Arnhem Land dot painting to a Francis Bacon print. The explanatory text below was a worry: dire Jungian psychobabble about 'universal primal imagery' and 'the collective unconscious.' I groaned aloud – but when Lena asked what was wrong, I just shook my head innocently.

A man in white trousers and a short white tunic emerged from a camouflaged door, wheeling a trolley packed with impressively minimalist equipment, reminiscent of expensive Scandinavian audio gear. He greeted us both as 'cousin,' and I struggled to keep a straight face. The badge on his tunic bore his name, Cousin Andre, a small reflection hologram of Eve, and a sequence of letters and numbers which identified his mitotype. Lena took charge, explaining that she was a member, and she'd brought me along to be sequenced.

After paying the fee – a hundred dollars, blowing my recreation budget for the next three months – I let Cousin Andre prick my thumb and squeeze a drop of blood onto a white absorbent pad, which he fed into one of the machines on the trolley. A sequence of delicate whirring sounds ensued, conveying a reassuring sense of precision engineering at work. Which was odd, because I'd seen ads for similar devices in *Nature* which boasted of no moving parts at all.

While we waited for the results, the room dimmed and a large hologram appeared, projected from the wall in front of us: a micrograph of a single living cell. From my own blood? More likely, not from anyone's – just a convincing photorealist animation.

'Every cell in your body,' Cousin Andre explained, 'contains hundreds or thousands of mitochondria: tiny power plants which extract energy from carbohydrates.' The image zoomed in on a translucent organelle, rod-shaped with rounded ends – rather like a drug capsule. 'The majority of the DNA in any cell is in the nucleus, and comes from both parents – but there's also DNA in the mitochondria, inherited from the mother alone. So it's easier to use mitochondrial DNA to trace your ancestry.'

He didn't elaborate, but I'd heard the theory in full several times, starting with high-school biology. Thanks to recombination – the random interchange of stretches of DNA between paired chromosomes, in the lead-up to the creation of sperm or ova – every chromosome carried genes from tens of thousands of different ancestors, stitched together seamlessly. From a palaeogenetic perspective, analysing nuclear DNA was like trying to make sense of 'fossils' which had been forged by cementing together assorted bone fragments from 10,000 different individuals.

Mitochondrial DNA came, not in paired chromosomes, but in tiny loops called plasmids. There were hundreds of plasmids in every cell, but they were all identical, and they all derived from the ovum alone. Mutations aside – one every 4,000 years or so – your mitochondrial DNA was exactly the same as that of your mother, your maternal grandmother, great-grandmother, and so on. It was also exactly the same as that of your siblings, your maternal first cousins, second cousins, third cousins ... until different mutations striking the plasmid on its way down through something like 200 generations finally imposed some variation. But with 16,000 DNA base pairs in the plasmid, even the 50 or so point mutations since Eve herself didn't amount to much.

The hologram dissolved from the micrograph into a multicoloured diagram of branching lines, a giant family tree starting from a single apex labelled with the ubiquitous image of Eve. Each fork in the tree marked a mutation, splitting Eve's inheritance into two slightly different versions. At the bottom, the tips of the hundreds of branches showed a variety of faces, some men, some women – individuals or composites, I couldn't say, but each one presumably represented a different group of (roughly) 200th maternal cousins, all sharing a mitotype: their own modest variation on the common 200,000-year-old theme.

'And here you are,' said Cousin Andre. A stylized magnifying glass materialized in the foreground of the hologram, enlarging one of the tiny faces at the bottom of the tree. The uncanny resemblance to my own features was almost certainly due to a snapshot taken by a hidden camera; mitochondrial DNA had no effect whatsoever on appearance.

Lena reached into the hologram and began to trace my descent with one fingertip. 'You're a Child of Eve, Paul.

You know who you are, now. And no one can ever take that away from you.' I stared at the luminous tree, and felt a chill at the base of my spine – though it had more to do with the Children's proprietary claim over the entire species than any kind of awe in the presence of my ancestors.

Eve had been nothing special, no watershed in evolution; she was simply defined as the most recent common ancestor, by an unbroken female line, of every single living human. And no doubt she'd had thousands of female contemporaries, but time and chance – the random death of daughterless women, catastrophes of disease and climate – had eliminated every mitochondrial trace of them. There was no need to assume that her mitotype had conferred any special advantages (most variation was in junk DNA, anyway); statistical fluctuations alone meant that one maternal lineage would replace all the others, eventually.

Eve's existence was a logical necessity: some human (or hominid) of one era or another had to fit the bill. It was only the timing which was contentious.

The timing, and its implications.

A world globe some two metres wide appeared beside the Great Tree; it had a distinctive Earth-from-space look, with heavy white cumulus swirling over the oceans, but the sky above the continents was uniformly cloudless. The Tree quivered and began to rearrange itself, converting its original rectilinear form into something much more misshapen and organic – but flexing its geometry without altering any of the relationships it embodied. Then it draped itself over the surface of the globe. Lines of descent became migratory routes. Between eastern Africa and the Levant, the tracks were tightly bunched and parallel, like the lanes of some Palaeolithic freeway; elsewhere, less constrained by the geography, they radiated out in all directions.

A recent Eve favoured the 'Out of Africa' hypothesis: modern *Homo sapiens* had evolved from the earlier *Homo erectus* in one place only, and had then migrated throughout the world, out-competing and replacing the local *Homo erectus* everywhere they went – and developing localized racial characteristics only within the last 200,000 years. The single birthplace of the species was most likely Africa, because Africans showed the greatest (and hence oldest) mitochondrial variation; all other groups seemed to have diversified more recently from relatively small 'founder' populations.

There were rival theories, of course. More than a million years before *Homo sapiens* even existed, *Homo erectus* itself had spread as far as Java, acquiring its own regional differences in appearance – and *Homo erectus* fossils in Asia and Europe seemed to share at least some of the distinguishing characteristics of living Asians and Europeans. But 'Out of Africa' put that down to convergent evolution, not ancestry. If *Homo erectus* had turned into *Homo sapiens* independently in several places, then the mitochondrial difference between, say, modern Ethiopians and Javanese should have been five or ten times as great, marking their long separation since a much earlier Eve. And even if the scattered *Homo erectus* communities had not been totally isolated, but had interbred with successive waves of migrants over the past one or two million years – hybridizing with them to create modern humans, and yet somehow retaining their distinctive differences – then distinct mitochondrial lineages much older than 200,000 years probably should have survived, too.

One route on the globe flashed brighter than the rest. Cousin Andre explained, 'This is the path your own ancestors took. They left Ethiopia – or maybe Kenya or Tanzania – heading north, about one hundred and fifty thousand years ago. They spread slowly up through Sudan, Egypt, Israel, Palestine, Syria and Turkey while the interglacial stretched on. By the start of the last Ice Age, the eastern shore of the Black Sea was their home...' As he spoke, tiny pairs of footprints materialized along the route.

He traced the hypothetical migration through the Caucasus Mountains, and all the way to northern Europe – where the limits of the technique finally cut the story dead: some four millennia ago (give or take three), when my Germanic two-hundredish-great grandmother had given birth to a daughter with a single change in her mitochondrial junk DNA: the last recorded tick of the molecular clock.

Cousin Andre wasn't finished with me, though. 'As your ancestors moved into Europe, their relative genetic isolation, and the demands of the local climate, gradually led them to acquire the characteristics which are known as Caucasian. But the same route was travelled many times, by wave after wave of migrants, sometimes separated by thousands of years. And though, at every step along the way, the new travellers interbred with those who'd gone before, and came to resemble them ... dozens of separate maternal lines can still be traced back along the route – and then down through history again, along different paths.'

My very closest maternal cousins, he explained – those with exactly the same mitotype – were, not surprisingly, mostly Caucasians. And expanding the circle to include up to 30 base pair differences brought in about five per cent of all Caucasians – the five per cent with whom I shared a common maternal ancestor who'd lived some 120,000 years ago, probably in the Levant.

But a number of that woman's own cousins had apparently headed east, not north. Eventually, their descendants had made it all the way across Asia, down through Indochina, and then south through the archipelagos, travelling across land bridges exposed by the low ocean levels of the Ice Age, or making short sea voyages from island to island. They'd stopped just short of Australia.

So I was more closely related, maternally, to a small

group of New Guinean highlanders than I was to 95 per cent of Caucasians. The magnifying glass reappeared beside the globe, and showed me the face of one of my living 6000th cousins. The two of us were about as dissimilar to the naked eye as any two people on Earth; of the handful of nuclear genes which coded for attributes like pigmentation and facial bone structure, one set had been favoured in frozen northern Europe, and another in this equatorial jungle. But enough mitochondrial evidence had survived in both places to reveal that the local homogenization of appearance was just a veneer, a recent gloss over an ancient network of invisible family connections.

Lena turned to me triumphantly. 'You see? All the old myths about race, culture, and kinship – instantly refuted! These people's immediate ancestors lived in isolation for thousands of years, and didn't set eyes on a single white face until the 20th century. Yet they're nearer to you than I am!'

I nodded, smiling, trying to share her enthusiasm. It *was* fascinating to see the whole naïve concept of 'race' turned inside out like this – and I had to admire the Children's sheer audacity at claiming to be able to map hundred-thousand-year-old relationships with such precision. But I couldn't honestly say that my life had been transformed by the revelation that certain white total strangers were more distant cousins to me than certain black ones. Maybe there were die-hard racists who would have been shaken to the core by news like this . . . but it was hard to imagine them rushing along to the Children of Eve to be mitotyped.

The far end of the trolley beeped, and ejected a badge just like Cousin Andre's. He offered it to me; when I hesitated, Lena took it and pinned it proudly to my shirt.

Out on the street, Lena announced soberly, 'Eve is going to change the world. We're lucky; we'll live to see it happen. We've had a century of people being slaughtered for belonging to the wrong kinship groups – but soon, *every-*

one will understand that there are older, deeper blood ties which confound all their shallow historical prejudices.'

You mean ... like the Biblical Eve confounded all the prejudices of fundamentalist Christians? Or like the image of the Earth from space put an end to war and pollution? I tried diplomatic silence; Lena regarded me with consternation, as if she couldn't quite believe that I could harbour any doubts after my own unexpected *blood ties* had been revealed.

I said, 'Do you remember the Rwandan massacres?'

'Of course.'

'Weren't they more to do with a class system – which the Belgian colonists exacerbated for the sake of administrative convenience – than anything you could describe as enmity between *kinship groups*? And in the Balkans –'

Lena cut me off. 'Look, sure, any incident you can point to will have a convoluted history. I'm not denying that. But it doesn't mean that the solution has to be impossibly complicated, too. And if everyone involved had known what we know, had felt what we've *felt*' – she closed her eyes and smiled radiantly, an expression of pure contentment and tranquillity – 'that deep sense of belonging, through Eve, to a single family which encompasses all of humanity ... do you honestly imagine that they could have turned on each other like that?'

I should have protested, in tones of bewilderment: *What 'deep sense of belonging?' I felt nothing. And the only thing the Children of Eve are doing is preaching to the converted.*

What was the worst that could have happened? If we'd broken up, right there and then, over *the political significance of palaeogenetics*, then the relationship was obviously doomed from the start. And however much I hated confrontation, it was a fine line between tact and dishonesty, between accommodating our differences and concealing them.

And yet. The issue seemed far too arcane to be worth

fighting over – and though Lena clearly held some passionate views on it, I couldn't really see the topic arising again if I kept my big mouth shut, just this once.

I said, 'Maybe you're right.' I slipped an arm around her, and she turned and kissed me. It began to rain again, heavily, the downpour strangely calm in the still air. We ended up back at Lena's flat, saying very little for the rest of the night.

I was a coward and a fool, of course – but I had no way of knowing, then, just how much it would cost me.

A few weeks later, I found myself showing Lena around the basement of the UNSW physics department, where my own research equipment was crammed into one corner. It was late at night (again), and we were alone in the building; variously coloured fluorescent display screens hovered in the darkness, like distant icons for the other post-doctoral projects in some chilly academic cyberspace.

I couldn't find the chair I'd bought for myself (despite security measures escalating from a simple name tag to increasingly sophisticated computerized alarms, it was always being borrowed), so we stood on the cold bare concrete beside the apparatus, lit by a single fading ceiling panel, and I conjured up sequences of zeroes and ones which echoed the strangeness of the quantum world.

The infamous Einstein-Podolosky-Rosen correlation – the entanglement of two microscopic particles into a single quantum system – had been investigated experimentally for over twenty years, but it had only recently become possible to explore the effect with anything more complicated than pairs of photons or electrons. I was working with hydrogen atoms, produced when a single hydrogen molecule was dissociated with a pulse from an ultraviolet laser. Certain measurements carried out on the separated atoms showed statistical correlations which only made sense if a single wave function encompassing the two responded to the measurement process instantaneously – regardless of how far apart the individual atoms had travelled since their tangible molecular bonds were broken: metres, kilometres, light-years.

The phenomenon seemed to mock the whole concept of distance – but my own work had recently helped to dispel any notion that EPR might lead to a faster-than-light signalling device. The theory had always been clear on that point, though some people had hoped that a flaw in the equations would provide a loophole.

I explained to Lena, 'Take two machines stocked with EPR-correlated atoms, one on Earth and one on Mars, both capable of, say, measuring orbital angular momentum either vertically or horizontally. The results of the measurements would always be random ... but the machine on Mars could be made to emit data which either did, or didn't, mimic precisely the random data coming out of the machine on Earth at the very same time. And that mimicry could be switched on and off – instantaneously – by altering the type of measurements being made on Earth.'

'Like having two coins which are guaranteed to fall the same way as each other,' she suggested, 'so long as they're both being thrown right-handed. But if you start throwing the coin on Earth with your left hand, the correlation vanishes.'

'Yeah – that's a perfect analogy.' I realized belatedly that she'd probably heard this all before – quantum mechanics and information theory were the foundations of her own field, after all – but she was listening politely, so I continued. 'But even when the coins are magically agreeing on every single toss ... they're both still giving equal numbers of heads and tails, at random. So there's no way of encoding any message into the data. You can't even tell, from Mars, when the correlation starts and stops – not unless the data from Earth gets sent along for comparison, by some conventional means like a radio transmission –

defeating the whole point of the exercise. EPR itself communicates nothing.'

Lena contemplated this thoughtfully, though she was clearly unsurprised by the verdict.

She said, 'It communicates nothing between separated atoms – but if you bring them together, instead, it can still tell you what they've done in the past. You do a control experiment, don't you? You make the same measurements on atoms which were never paired?'

'Yeah, of course.' I pointed to the third and fourth columns of data on the screen; the process itself was going on silently as we spoke, inside an evacuated chamber in a small grey box concealed behind all the electronics. 'The results are completely uncorrelated.'

'So, basically, this machine can tell you whether or not two atoms have been bonded together?'

'Not individually; any individual match could just be chance. But given enough atoms with a common history – yes.' Lena was smiling conspiratorially. I said, 'What?'

'Just . . . humour me for a moment. What's the next stage? Heavier atoms?'

'Yes, but there's more. I'll split a hydrogen molecule, let the two separate hydrogen atoms combine with two fluorine atoms – any old ones, not correlated – then split both hydrogen fluoride molecules and make measurements *on the fluorine atoms* . . . to see if I can pick up an indirect correlation between them: a second-order effect inherited from the original hydrogen molecule.'

The truth was, I had little hope of getting funded to take the work that far. The basic experimental facts of EPR had been settled now, so there wasn't much of a case for pushing the measurement technology any further.

'In theory,' Lena asked innocently, 'could you do the same with something much larger? Like . . . DNA?'

I laughed. 'No.'

'I don't mean: could you do it, here, a week from

tomorrow? But – if two strands of DNA had been bonded together . . . would there be any correlation at all?'

I baulked at the idea, but confessed, 'There might be. I can't give you the answer off the top of my head; I'd have to borrow some software from the biochemists, and model the interaction precisely.'

Lena nodded, satisfied. 'I think you should do that.'

'*Why*? I'll never be able to try it, for real.'

'Not with this junkyard-grade equipment.'

I snorted. 'So tell me who's going to pay for something better?'

Lena glanced around the grim basement, as if she wanted to record a mental snapshot of the low point of my career – before everything changed completely. 'Who'd finance research into a means of detecting the quantum fingerprint of DNA bonding? Who'd pay for a chance of computing – not to the nearest few millennia, but to the nearest *cell division* – how long ago two mitochondrial plasmids were in contact?'

I was scandalized. *This* was the idealist who believed that the Children of Eve were the last great hope for world peace?

I said. 'They'd never fall for it.'

Lena stared at me blankly for a second, then shook her head, amused. 'I'm not talking about pulling a confidence trick – begging for a research grant on false pretences.'

'Well, good. But –?'

'I'm talking about taking the money – and doing a job that has to be done. Sequencing technology has been pushed as far as it can go – but our opponents still keep finding things to quibble about: the mitochondrial mutation rate, the method of choosing branch points for the most probable tree, the details of lineage loss and survival. Even the palaeogeneticists who are on our side keep changing their minds about everything. Eve's age goes up and down like the Hubble constant.'

'It can't be that bad, surely.'

Lena seized my arm; her excitement was electric, I felt it flow into me. Or maybe she'd just pinched a nerve.

'*This* could transform the whole field. No more guesswork, no more conjecture, no more assumptions – just a single, indisputable family tree, stretching back two hundred thousand years.'

'It may not even be possible –'

'But you'll find out? You'll look into it?'

I hesitated – but I couldn't think of a single good reason to refuse. 'Yes.'

Lena smiled. 'With quantum palaeogenetics ... you'll have the power to bring Eve to life for the world in a way that no one has ever done before.'

Six months later, the funds ran out for my work at the university: the research, the tutoring, everything. Lena offered to support me for three months while I put together a proposal to submit to the Children. We were already living together, already sharing expenses; somehow, that made it much easier to rationalize. And it was a bad time of year to be looking for work, I was going to be unemployed anyway ...

As it turned out, computer modelling suggested that a measurable correlation between segments of DNA could be picked out against the statistical noise – given enough plasmids to work with: more like a few litres of blood per person than a single drop. But I could already see that the technical problems would take years of work to properly assess, let alone overcome. Writing it all up was good practice for future corporate grant applications – but I never seriously expected anything to come of it.

Lena came with me to the meeting with William Sachs, the Children's West Pacific Research Director. He was in his late 50s, and *very* conservatively dressed, from the classic Benetton AIDS ISN'T NICE T-shirt to the Mambo World Peace surfing dove motif board shorts. A slightly younger version smiled down from a framed cover of *Wired*; he'd been guru of the month in April 2005.

'The university physics department will be contracted to provide overall supervision,' I explained nervously. 'There'll be independent audits of the scientific quality of the work every six months, so there's no possibility of the research running off the rails.'

'The EPR correlation,' mused Sachs, 'proves that all life is bound together holistically into a grand unified meta-organism, doesn't it?'

'No.' Lena kicked me hard under the desk.

But Sachs didn't seem to have heard me. 'You'll be listening in to Gaia's own theta rhythm. The secret harmony which underlies everything: synchronicity, morphic resonance, transmigration . . .' He sighed dreamily. 'I *adore* quantum mechanics. You know my Tai Chi master wrote a book about it? *Schrödinger's Lotus* – you must have read it. What a mind-fuck! And he's working on a sequel, *Heisenberg's Mandala* –'

Lena intervened before I could open my mouth again. 'Maybe . . . later generations will be able to trace the correlation as far as other species. But in the foreseeable future, even reaching as far as Eve will be a major technical challenge.'

Cousin William seemed to come back down to Earth. He picked up the printed copy of the application and turned to the budget details at the end, which were mostly Lena's work.

'Five million dollars is a lot of money.'

'Over ten years,' Lena said smoothly. 'And don't forget that there's a one hundred and twenty-five per cent tax deduction on R&D expenditure this financial year. By the time you factor in the notional patent rights –'

'You really believe the spin-offs will be valued this highly?'

'Just look at Teflon.'

16

'I'll have to take this to the board.'

When the good news came through by email, a fortnight later, I was almost physically sick.

I turned to Lena. 'What have I done? What if I spend ten years on this, and it all comes to nothing?'

She frowned, puzzled. 'There are no guarantees of success – but you've made that clear, you haven't been dishonest. Every great endeavour is plagued with uncertainties – but the Children have decided to accept the risks.'

In fact, I hadn't been agonizing over the morality of relieving rich idiots with a global motherhood fixation of large sums of money – and quite possibly having nothing to give them in return. I was more worried about what it would mean for my career if the research turned out to be a cul-de-sac, and produced no results worth publishing.

Lena said, 'It's all going to work out perfectly. I have faith in you, Paul.'

And that was the worst of it. She did.

We loved each other – and we were, both, using each other. But I was the one who kept on lying about what was soon to become the most important thing in our lives.

In the winter of 2010, Lena took three months off work to travel to Nigeria in the name of technology transfer. Her official role was to advise the new government on the modernization of the communications infrastructure – but she was also training a few hundred local operators for the Children's latest low cost sequencer. My EPR technique was still in its infancy – barely able to distinguish identical twins from total strangers – but the original mitochondrial DNA analysers had become extremely small, rugged and cheap.

Africa had proved highly resistant to the Children in the past, but it seemed that the movement had finally gained a foothold. Every time Lena called me from Lagos – her eyes shining with missionary zeal – I went and checked the Great Tree, trying to decide whether its scrambling of traditional notions of familial proximity would render the ex-combatants in the recent civil war more, or less, fraternal towards each other if the sequencing fad really took off. The factions were already so ethnically mixed, though, that it was impossible to come to a definite verdict; so far as I could tell, the war had been fought between alliances shaped as much by certain 21st-century acts of political patronage as by any invocation of ancient tribal loyalties.

Near the end of her stay, Lena called me in the early hours of the morning (my time), so angry she was almost in tears. 'I'm flying straight to London, Paul. I'll be there in three hours.'

I squinted at the bright screen, dazed by the tropical sunshine behind her. 'Why? What's happened?' I had visions of the Children undermining the fragile cease-fire, igniting some unspeakable ethnic holocaust – then flying out to have their wounds tended by the best microsurgeons in the world, while the country descended into chaos behind them.

Lena reached off-camera and hit a button, pasting a section of a news report into a corner of the transmission. The headline read: Y-CHROMOSOME ADAM STRIKES BACK! The picture below showed a near-naked, muscular, blond white man (curiously devoid of body hair – rather like Michelangelo's *David* in a bison-skin loin-cloth) aiming a spear at the reader with suitably balletic grace.

I groaned softly. It had only been a matter of time. In the cell divisions leading up to sperm production, most of the DNA of the Y chromosome underwent recombination with the X chromosome – but part of it remained aloof, unscrambled, passed down the purely paternal line with the same fidelity as mitochondrial DNA passed from mother to daughter. In fact, with more fidelity: mutations in nuclear DNA were much less frequent, which made it a much less useful molecular clock.

'They claim they've found a single male ancestor for all

northern Europeans – just twenty thousand years ago! And they're presenting this *bullshit* at a palaeogenetics conference in Cambridge tomorrow!' I scanned the article as Lena wailed; the news report was all tabloid hype, it was difficult to tell what the researchers were actually asserting. But a number of right wing groups who'd long been opposed to the Children of Eve had embraced the results with obvious glee.

I said, 'So why do you have to be there?'

'To defend Eve, of course! We can't let them get away with this!'

My head was throbbing. 'If it's bad science, let the experts refute it. It's not your problem.'

Lena was silent for a while, then protested bitterly, 'You *know* male lineages are lost faster than female ones. Thanks to polygyny, a single paternal line can dominate a population in far fewer generations than a female one.'

'So the claim might be right? There might have been a single, recent "northern European Adam"?'

'Maybe,' Lena admitted begrudgingly. 'But . . . *so what?* What's that supposed to prove? They haven't even *tried* to look for an Adam who's a father to the whole species!'

I wanted to reply: Of course it proves nothing, changes nothing. No sane person could possibly care. But . . . who made kinship such a big issue in the first place? Who did their best to propagate the notion that everything that matters depends on family ties?

It was far too late, though. Turning against the Children would have been sheer hypocrisy; I'd taken their money, I'd played along.

And I couldn't abandon Lena. If my love for her went no further than the things we agreed on, then that wasn't love at all.

I said numbly, 'I should make the three o'clock flight to London. I'll meet you at the conference.'

The tenth annual World Palaeogenetics Forum was being

held in a pyramid-shaped building in an astroturfed science park, far from the university campus. The placard-waving crowd made it easy to spot. HANDS OFF EVE! DIE, NAZI SCUM! NEANDERTHALS OUT! (*What?*) As the taxi drove away, my jet-lag caught up with me and my knees almost buckled. My aim was to find Lena as rapidly as possible and get us both out of harm's way. Eve could look after herself.

She was there, of course, gazing with serene dignity from a dozen T-shirts and banners. But the Children – and their marketing consultants – had recently been 'fine-tuning' her image, and this was the first chance I'd had to see the results of all their focus groups and consumer feedback workshops. The new Eve was slightly paler, her nose a little thinner, her eyes narrower. The changes were subtle, but they were clearly aimed at making her look more 'panracial' – more like some far-future common descendant, bearing traces of every modern human population, than a common ancestor who'd lived in one specific place: Africa.

And in spite of all my cynicism, this redesign made me queasier than any of the other cheap stunts the Children had pulled. It was as if they'd decided, after all, that they couldn't really imagine a world where everyone would accept an African Eve – but they were so committed to the idea that they were willing to keep bending the truth, for the sake of broadening her appeal, until . . . *what?* They gave her, not just a different name, but a different face in every country?

I made it into the lobby, merely spat on by two or three picketers. Inside, things were much quieter, but the academic palaeogeneticists were darting about furtively, avoiding eye contact. One poor woman had been cornered by a news crew; as I passed, the interviewer was insisting heatedly, 'But you must admit that violating the origin myths of indigenous Amazonians is a crime against humanity.' The outer wall of the pyramid was tinted blue, but more or less transparent, and I could see another crowd of demonstrators pressed against one of the panels, peering in. Plain-clothes security guards whispered into their wrist-phones, clearly afraid for their Masarini suits.

I'd tried to call Lena a dozen times since the airport, but some bottleneck in the Cambridge footprint had kept me on hold. She'd pulled strings and got us both listed on the attendance database – the only reason I'd been allowed through the front door – but that only proved that being inside the building was no guarantee of non-partisanship.

Suddenly, I heard shouting and grunting from nearby, then a chorus of cheers and the sound of heavy sheet plastic popping out of its frame. News reports had mentioned both pro-Eve demonstrators, and pro-Adam – the latter allegedly much more violent. I panicked and bolted down the nearest corridor – almost colliding with a wiry young man heading in the opposite direction. He was tall, white, blond, blue-eyed, radiating Teutonic menace . . . and part of me wanted to scream in outrage: I'd been reduced, against my will, to pure imbecilic racism.

Still, he was carrying a pool cue.

But as I backed away warily, his sleeveless T-shirt began flashing up the words: THE GODDESS IS AFOOT!

'So what are you?' he sneered. 'A Son of Adam?'

I shook my head slowly. *What am I*? I'm a *Homo sapiens*, you moron. Can't you recognize your own species?

I said, 'I'm a researcher with the Children of Eve.' At faculty cocktail parties, I was always 'an independent palaeogenetics research physicist,' but this didn't seem the time to split hairs.

'Yeah?' He grimaced with what I took at first to be disbelief, and advanced threateningly. 'So *you're* one of the fucking patriarchal, materialistic bastards who's trying to reify the Archetype of the Earth Mother and rein in her boundless spiritual powers?'

That left me too stupefied to see what was coming. He

jabbed me hard in the solar plexus with the pool cue; I fell to my knees, gasping with pain. I could hear the sound of boots in the lobby, and hoarsely chanted slogans.

The Goddess-worshipper grabbed me by one shoulder and wrenched me to my feet, grinning. 'No hard feelings, though. We're still on the same side, here – aren't we? So let's go beat up some Nazis!'

I tried to pull free, but it was already too late; the Sons of Adam had found us.

Lena came to visit me in hospital. 'I knew you should have stayed in Sydney.'

My jaw was wired; I couldn't answer back.

'You have to look after yourself; your work's more important than ever, now. Other groups will find their own Adams – and the whole unifying message of Eve will be swamped by the tribalism inherent in the idea of recent male ancestors. We can't let a few promiscuous Cro-Magnon men ruin everything.'

'Gmm mmm mmmn.'

'We have mitochondrial sequencing ... they have Y-chromosome sequencing. Sure, our molecular clock is already more accurate ... but we need a spectacular advantage, something anyone can grasp. Mutation rates, mitotypes: it's all too abstract for the person in the street. If we can construct exact family trees with EPR – starting with people's known relatives ... but extending that same sense of precise kinship across ten thousand generations, all the way back to Eve – then *that* will give us an immediacy, a credibility, that will leave the Sons of Adam for dead.'

She stroked my brow tenderly. 'You can win the Ancestor Wars for us, Paul. I know you can.'

'Mmm nnn,' I conceded.

I'd been ready to denounce both sides, resign from the EPR project – and even walk away from Lena, if it came to that.

Maybe it was more pride than love, more weakness than commitment, more inertia than loyalty. Whatever the reason, though, I couldn't do it. I couldn't leave her.

The only way forward was to try to finish what I'd started. To give the Children their watertight, absolute proof.

While the rival ancestor cults picketed and fire-bombed each other, rivers of blood flowed through my apparatus. The Children had supplied me with two-litre samples from no fewer than 50,000 members, worldwide; my lab would have put the most garish Hammer Horror film set to shame.

Trillions of plasmids were analysed. Electrons in a certain low-energy hybrid orbital – a quantum mixture of two different-shaped charge distributions, potentially stable for thousands of years – were induced by finely-tuned laser pulses to collapse into one particular state. And though every collapse was random, the orbital I'd chosen was – very slightly – correlated across paired strands of DNA. Quadrillions of measurements were accumulated, and compared. With enough plasmids measured for each individual, the faint signature of any shared ancestry could rise up through the statistical noise.

The mutations behind the Children's Great Tree no longer mattered; in fact, I was looking at stretches of the plasmid most likely to have stayed unblemished all the way back to Eve, since it was the intimate chemical contact of flawless DNA replication which gave the only real chance of a correlation. And as the glitches in the process were ironed out, and the data mounted up, results finally began to emerge.

The blood donors included many close family groups; I analysed the data blind, then passed the results to one of my research assistants, to be checked against the known relationships. Early in June 2013, I scored 100 per cent on sibling detection in a thousand samples; a few weeks later, I was doing the same on first and second cousins.

Soon, we hit the limits of the recorded genealogy; to provide another means of cross-checking, I started analysing nuclear genes as well. Even distant cousins were likely to have at least some genes from a common ancestor – and EPR could date that ancestor precisely.

News of the project spread, and I was deluged with crank mail and death threats. The lab was fortified; the Children hired bodyguards for everyone involved in the work, and their families.

The quantity of information just kept growing, but the Children – horrified by the thought that the Adams might out-do them with rival technology – kept voting me more and more money. I upgraded our supercomputers, twice. And though mitochondria alone could lead me to Eve, for book-keeping purposes I found myself tracing the nuclear genes of hundreds of thousands of ancestors, male and female.

In the spring of 2016, the database reached a kind of critical mass. We hadn't sampled more than the tiniest fraction of the world's population – but once it was possible to reach back just a few dozen generations, all the apparently separate lineages began to join up. Autosomal nuclear genes zigzagged heedlessly between the purely-maternal tree of the Eves and the purely-paternal tree of the Adams, filling in the gaps . . . until I found myself with genetic profiles of virtually everyone who'd been alive on the planet in the early ninth century (and left descendants down to the present). I had no names for any of these people, or even definite geographical locations – but I knew the place of every one of them on my own Great Tree, precisely.

I had a snapshot of the genetic diversity of the entire human species. From that point on there was no stopping the cascade, and I pursued the correlations back through the millennia.

*   *   *

By 2017, Lena's worst predictions had all come true. Dozens of different Adams had been proclaimed around the world – and the trend was to look for the common paternal lineage of smaller and smaller populations, converging on ever more recent ancestors. Many were now supposedly historical figures; rival Greek and Macedonian groups were fighting it out over who had the right to call themselves the Sons of Alexander the Great. Y-chromosomal ethnic classification had become government policy in three eastern European republics – and, allegedly, corporate policy in certain multinationals.

The smaller the populations analysed, of course – unless they were massively in-bred – the less likely it was that everyone targeted really would share a single Adam. So the first male ancestor to be identified became 'the father of his people' ... and anyone else became a kind of gene-polluting barbarian rapist, whose hideous taint could still be detected. And weeded out.

Every night, I lay awake into the early hours, trying to understand how I could have ended up at the centre of so much conflict over something so idiotic. I still couldn't bring myself to confess my true feelings to Lena, so I'd pace the house with the lights out, or lock myself in my study with the bullet-proof shutters closed and sort through the latest batch of hate mail, paper and electronic, hunting for evidence that anything I might discover about Eve would have the slightest positive effect on anyone who wasn't already a fanatical supporter of the Children. Hunting for some sign that there was hope of ever doing more than preaching to the converted.

I never did find the encouragement I was looking for – but there was one postcard which cheered me up, slightly. It was from the High Priest of the Church of the Sacred UFO, in Kansas City.

Dear Earth-dweller:

Please use your BRAIN! As anyone KNOWS in this SCIENTIFIC age, the origin of the races is now WELL UNDERSTOOD! Africans travelled here after the DELUGE from Mercury, Asians from Venus, Caucasians from Mars, and the people of the Pacific islands from assorted asteroids. If you don't have the NECESSARY OCCULT SKILLS to project rays from the continents to the ASTRAL PLANE to verify this, a simple analysis of TEMPERAMENT and APPEARANCE should make this obvious even to YOU!

But please don't put WORDS into MY mouth! Just because we're all from different PLANETS doesn't mean we can't still be FRIENDS.

Lena was deeply troubled. 'But how can you hold a media conference tomorrow, when Cousin William hasn't even seen the final results?' It was Sunday, January 28th, 2018. We'd said goodnight to the bodyguards and gone to bed in the reinforced concrete bunker the Children had installed for us after a nasty incident in one of the Baltic states.

I said, 'I'm an independent researcher. I'm free to publish data at any time. That's what it says in the contract. Any advances in the measurement technology have to go through the Children's lawyers – but not the palaeogenetic results.'

Lena tried another tack. 'But if this work hasn't been peer-reviewed –'

'It has. The paper's already been accepted by *Nature*; it will be published the day after the conference. In fact,' I smiled innocently, 'I'm really only doing it as a favour to the editor. She's hoping it will boost sales for the issue.'

Lena fell silent. I'd told her less and less about the work over the preceding six months; I'd let her assume that technical problems were holding up progress.

Finally she said, 'Won't you at least say if it's good news – or bad?'

I couldn't look her in the eye, but I shook my head. 'Nothing that happened two hundred thousand years ago is any kind of news at all.'

I'd hired a public auditorium for the media conference – far from the Children's office tower – paying for it myself, and arranging for independent security. Sachs and his fellow directors were not impressed, but short of kidnapping me there was little they could do to shut me up. There'd never been any suggestion of fabricating the results they wanted – but there'd always been an unspoken assumption that only *the right data* would ever be released with this much fanfare – and the Children would have ample opportunity to put their own spin on it, first.

Behind the podium, my hands were shaking. Over 2,000 journalists from across the planet had turned up – and many of them were wearing symbols of allegiance to one ancestor or another.

I cleared my throat and began. The EPR technique had become common knowledge; there was no need to explain it again. I said, simply, 'I'd like to show you what I've discovered about the origins of *Homo sapiens*.'

The lights went down and a giant hologram, some 30 metres high, appeared behind me. It was, I announced, a family tree – not a rough history of genes or mutations, but an exact generation-by-generation diagram of both female and male parentage for the entire human population – from the ninth century, back. A dense thicket in the shape of an inverted funnel. The audience remained silent, but there was an air of impatience; this tangle of a billion tiny lines was indecipherable – it told them absolutely nothing. But I waited, letting the impenetrable diagram rotate once, slowly.

'The Y-chromosome mutational clock,' I said, 'is wrong. I've traced the paternal ancestries of groups with similar

27

Y-types back hundreds of thousands of years – and they never converge on any one man.' A murmur of discontent began; I boosted the amplifier volume and drowned it out. '*Why not?* How can there be so little mutational diversity, if the DNA doesn't all spring from a single, recent source?' A second hologram appeared, a double-helix, a schematic of the Y-typing region. 'Because mutations happen, again and again, at *exactly the same sites*. Make two, or three – or fifty – copying errors in the same location, and it still only looks like it's one step away from the original.' The double helix hologram was divided and copied, divided and copied; the accumulated differences in each generation were highlighted. 'The proof-reading enzymes in our cells must have specific blind spots, specific weaknesses – like words that are easy to misspell. And there's still a chance of purely random errors, at any site at all – but only on a time scale of millions of years.

'All the Y-chromosome Adams,' I said, 'are fantasy. There are no individual fathers to any race, or tribe, or nation. Living northern Europeans, for a start, have over a thousand distinct paternal lineages dating to the late Ice Age – and those thousand ancestors, in turn, are the descendants of over two hundred different male African migrants.' Colours flashed up in the grey maze of the Tree, briefly highlighting the lineages.

A dozen journalists sprang to their feet and started shouting abuse. I waited for the security guards to escort them from the building.

I looked out across the crowd, searching for Lena, but I couldn't find her. I said, 'The same is true of mitochondrial DNA. The mutations overwrite themselves; the molecular clock is wrong. There was no Eve two hundred thousand years ago.' An uproar began, but I kept talking. '*Homo erectus* spread out of Africa – dozens of times, over two million years, the new migrants always interbreeding with the old ones, never replacing them.' A globe appeared, the entire Old World so heavily decorated with criss-crossing paths that it was impossible to glimpse a single square kilometre of ground. 'Homo sapiens arose everywhere, at once – maintained as one species, worldwide, partly because of migrant gene flow – and partly thanks to the parallel mutations which invalidate all the clocks: mutations taking place in a random order, but biased towards the same sites.' A hologram showed four stretches of DNA, accumulating mutations; at first, the four strands grew increasingly dissimilar, as the sparse random scatter struck them differently – but as more and more of the same vulnerable sites were hit, they all came to bear virtually the same scars.

'So modern racial differences are up to two million years old – inherited from the first Homo erectus migrants – but all of the subsequent evolution has marched in parallel, everywhere ... because Homo erectus never really had much choice. In a mere two million years, different climates could favour different genes for some superficial local adaptions – but everything leading to Homo sapiens was already latent in every migrant's DNA before they left Africa.'

There was a momentary hush from the Eve supporters – maybe because no one could decide anymore whether the picture I was painting was *unifying* or *divisive*. The truth was just too gloriously messy and complicated to serve any political purpose at all.

I continued. 'But if there was ever an Adam or an Eve, they were long before Homo sapiens, long before Homo erectus. Maybe they were ... Australopithecus –?' I displayed two stooped, hairy, ape-like figures. People started throwing their video cameras. I hit a button under the podium, raising a giant perspex shield in front of the stage.

'Burn all your *symbols!*' I shouted. 'Male and female, tribal and global. Give up your Fatherlands and your Earth Mothers – it's Childhood's End! Desecrate your ancestors, screw your cousins – just do what you think is right *because it's right.*'

The shield cracked. I ran for the stage exit.

The security guards had all vanished – but Lena was sitting in our armour-plated Volvo in the basement car park, with the engine running. She wound down the mirrored side window.

'I watched your little performance on the net.' She gazed at me calmly, but there was rage and pain in her eyes. I had no adrenaline left, no strength, no pride; I fell to my knees beside the car.

'I love you. Forgive me.'

'Get in,' she said. 'You've got a lot of explaining to do.'

THE MESSAGE FROM MARS

J. G. Ballard

The successful conclusion of NASA's Mars mission in 2008, signalled by the safe touch-down of the Zeus IV space vehicle at Edwards Air Force Base in California, marked an immense triumph for the agency. During the 1990s, after the failure of the Shuttle project, NASA's entire future was in jeopardy. The American public's lack of interest in the space programme, coupled with unsettling political events in the former Soviet bloc, led Congress to cut back its funding of astronautics. Successive US Presidents were distracted by the task of balancing the national budget, and their scientific advisers had long insisted that the exploration of the solar system could be achieved far more economically by unmanned vehicles.

But NASA's directors had always known that the scientific exploration of space was a small part of the agency's claim to existence. Manned flights alone could touch the public imagination and guarantee the huge funds needed to achieve them. The triumph of the Apollo landing on the moon in 1969 had shown that the road to the spiritual heart of America could be paved with dollar bills, but by the year 2000 that road seemed permanently closed. Struggling to keep the agency alive, the NASA chiefs found themselves reduced to the satellite mapping of mid-western drought areas, and were faced with the prospect of being absorbed into the Department of Agriculture.

However, at the last hour the agency was saved, and given the funds to embark on its greatest mission. The announcement in Peking on January 1, 2001, that a Chinese spacecraft had landed on the moon sent an uneasy tremor through the American nation. True, the Stars and Stripes had been planted on the moon more than 30 years earlier, but that event lay in a past millennium. Was the next millennium to be dominated by the peoples on the Asian side of the Pacific rim, spending their huge trade surpluses on spectacular projects that would seize the planet's imagination for the next century?

As the pictures of the Chinese astronauts, posing beside their pagoda-shaped space vehicle *The Temple of Lightness*, were relayed to the world's TV screens, news came that an Indonesian space crew and an unmanned Korean probe would soon land next to the Chinese.

Galvanized by all this, a no longer somnolent President Quayle addressed both houses of Congress. Within weeks NASA was assigned a multi-billion dollar emergency fund and ordered to launch a crash programme that would leapfrog the moon and land an American on Mars before the end of the decade.

NASA, as always, rose bravely to the challenge of the tax-dollar. Armies of elderly space-engineers were recruited from their Florida retirement homes. Fifty civilian and military test pilots were pressed into astronaut training. Within two years Zeus I, the unmanned prototype of the vast space vehicles that would later carry a five-man crew, had roared away from Cape Canaveral on a six-month reconnaissance voyage. It circled the Red Planet a dozen times and surveyed the likely landing zone, before returning successfully to Earth.

After two more unmanned flights, in 2005 and 2006, Zeus IV set off in November, 2007, guaranteeing President Quayle's third-term electoral landslide, which the five astronauts saluted from the flight-deck of the spacecraft. By now the Chinese, Indonesian and Korean lunar programmes had been forgotten. The world's eyes were fixed on the Zeus IV, and its five crew-members were soon more famous than any Hollywood superstar.

Wisely, NASA had selected an international crew, led by Colonel Dean Irwin of the USAF. Captain Clifford Horner and Commander John Merritt were former US Army and Navy test pilots, but the team was completed by a Russian doctor, Colonel Valentina Tsarev, and a Japanese computer specialist, Professor Hiroshi Kawahito.

During the two-month voyage to Mars the quirks and personalities of the five astronauts became as familiar as any face across a breakfast table. The Zeus IV was the largest spacecraft ever launched, and had the dimensions of a nuclear submarine. Its wide control rooms and observation decks, its crew facilities and non-denominational chapel (if a marriage was arranged, Colonel Irwin was authorized to conduct it) happily reminded TV viewers of the Starship Enterprise in the *Star Trek* TV series, still endlessly broadcast on a hundred networks. Everyone responded to the calm and dignified presence of Colonel Irwin, the deadpan humour of Captain Horner, the chirpy computer-speak of the mercurial Japanese, and the mothering but sometimes flirtatious eye of Dr Valentina. Millions of viewers rallied to their aid when the Zeus IV passed through an unexpected meteor storm, but the ultra-hard carbon fibre and ceramic hull, a byproduct of the most advanced tank armour, proved even more resilient than the designers had hoped. The inspection space-walks seemed like gracefully choreographed ballets – which of course they were, like every other activity shown to the TV audience – and confirmed that mankind had at last entered the second Space Age.

Two months to the day after leaving Cape Canaveral, the Zeus IV landed on Mars, whose sombre presence had loomed ever more threateningly for the previous weeks. Signals blackouts caused by the planet's magnetic fields added their own thrills and panics, skilfully orchestrated by NASA's PR specialists. But the landing was a triumph, celebrated by the hoisting of the Stars and Stripes and, behind it, the flag of the United Nations. Within an hour the crew of the Zeus IV was standing on Martian soil beside the spacecraft, intoning their carefully rehearsed 'Hymn to the Space Age.' From that moment no Congressman dared to deny the NASA chiefs anything they demanded.

For the next six weeks public interest in the Mars mission remained high, sustained by NASA's careful attention to the emotional needs of the world-wide audience. Life within the spacecraft was presented as a cross between a TV sitcom and a classroom course in elementary astronautics. The crew tolerantly went along with these charades. Dr Valentina was seen replacing a filling in Commander Merritt's mouth, and Professor Kawahito, the heart-throb of a billion Asian viewers, won a hard-fought chess tournament against the Zeus IV's combined on-board computers. Romance was in the air as Dr Valentina's cabin door remained tantalizingly ajar. The TV cameras followed the crew as they drove in their excursion vehicles across the fossil Martian seas, collecting rock samples and analysing the local atmosphere.

At the half-way stage of their mission the crew revealed a mild impatience with the media roles imposed on them, which the NASA psychologists attributed to a greater maturity brought on by a sense of planetary awe. To remind them of Earth, the astronauts were urged to watch episodes of *Dallas*, *Dynasty* and *The Flintstones*, and to take part in a series of Oval Office interviews with President Quayle. But their spirits lifted as the day of departure drew near. When the Zeus IV rose at last from the Martian surface the entire crew burst spontaneously into an unscripted cheer, in which some observers detected a small note of irony.

* * *

Ignoring this impromptu levity, NASA planned a lavish reception at Edwards Air Force Base, where the Zeus IV would land. Every Congressman and Governor in the United States would be present, along with President Quayle, the heads of state of 30 countries and a host of entertainment celebrities. An unending programme of media appearances awaited the astronauts – there would be triumphal parades through a dozen major cities, followed by a worldwide tour lasting a full six months. NASA had already appointed firms of literary agents and public relations experts to look after the commercial interests of the astronauts. There were sports sponsorships, book contracts and highly paid consultancies. The news of these deals was transmitted to the home-coming crew, who seemed gratified by the interest in their achievement, unaware that whenever they appeared on screen their images were accompanied by the cash totals now committed to them. Two days before the Zeus IV landed, NASA announced that three major Hollywood studios would collaborate on the most expensive film of all time, in which the astronauts would play themselves in a faithful recreation of the Martian voyage.

So, at 3.35 pm on April 29, 2008, the Zeus IV appeared in the California sky. Accompanied by six chase planes, the spacecraft swept down to a perfect landing, guided by its on-board computers to within 50 metres of President Quayle's reception podium. The stunned silence was broken by an immense cheer when two of the astronauts were glimpsed in the observation windows. The crowd surged forward, waiting for the hatches to open as soon as the landing checks were over.

Despite the warmth of this welcome, the astronauts were surprisingly reluctant to emerge from their craft. The decontamination teams were poised by the airlocks, ready to board the spaceship and evacuate its atmosphere for laboratory analysis. But the crew had overridden the computerized sequences and made no reply over the radio link to the urgent queries of the ground controllers. They had switched off the television cameras inside the craft, but could be seen through the observation windows, apparently tidying their cabins and changing into overalls. Dr Valentina was spotted in the galley, apparently sterilizing her surgical instruments. A rumour swept the review stands, where President Quayle, the Congress and invited heads of state sweltered in the sun, that one of the crew had been injured on re-entry, but it soon transpired that Dr Valentina was merely making soup. Even more strangely, Professor Kawahito was seen setting out six parallel chessboards, as if preparing for another tournament.

At this point, an hour after their arrival, the crew became irritated by the grimacing faces pressed against the observation windows, and the interior shutters abruptly closed. This dismissive gesture made the crowd even more restive, and the ground staff tried to force the main hatch. When they failed, the head of NASA's crash recovery team began to pound on the locks with a baseball bat borrowed from a youngster seated on his father's shoulders. The first whistles and jeers rose from the crowd, who jostled the scaffolding towers on which the impatient TV crews were waiting. A camera-man lost his footing and fell through the roof of a parked bus. Loud-speakers blared meaninglessly across the million or more spectators sitting on their cars around the perimeter of the airfield. The heads of state, diplomats and generals consulted their watches, while President Quayle, making involuntary putting movements with the portable microphone in his hands, beckoned in an unsettling way to his military aide carrying the briefcase of nuclear launch codes. The boos of the crowd were only drowned when a squadron of jet planes flew low over the field, releasing streams of red, white and blue smoke. Ordered away by the frantic control tower, the victory flight broke up in confusion as the pilots returned to their muster points in the sky, leaving a delirium of crazed smoke over the Zeus IV.

At last calm was restored when a company of military police took up positions around the spacecraft, forcing the crowds behind the VIP stands. Led by President Quayle, the dignitaries shuffled from their seats and hurried along the lines of red carpet to the refreshment tents. The TV cameras trained their lenses on the Zeus IV, watching for the smallest sign of movement.

As evening fell, the spectators beyond the airfield perimeter began to disperse. Powerful arclights bathed the spacecraft, and during the night a fresh attempt was made to contact the crew. But the messages in morse code tapped on the hull, like the laser beams shone at the darkened observation windows, failed to draw any response. No sound could be heard from the interior of the craft, as if the crew had settled in for the night, and a hundred theories began to circulate among the NASA chiefs and the teams of doctors and psychiatrists summoned to their aid.

Were the astronauts in the last stages of a fatal contagious disease? Had their brains been invaded by an alien parasite? Were they too emotionally exhausted by their voyage to face the reception awaiting them, or gripped by so strong a sense of humility that they longed only for silence and anonymity? Had an unexpected consequence of time dilation returned them psychological hours or days after their physical arrival? Had they, perhaps, died in a spiritual sense, or were they, for inexplicable reasons of their own, staging a mutiny?

Surrounded by the deserted stands and the silent bunting, the NASA chiefs made their decision. An hour before dawn two thermal lances played their fiery hoses against the heat-resistant plates of the spacecraft. But the carbon-ceramic hull of the Zeus IV had been forged in temperatures far beyond that of a thermal lance.

A controlled explosion was the only solution, despite the danger to the crew within. But as the demolition squad placed their charges against the ventral hatchway, the shutter of an observation window opened for the first time. Captured on film, the faces of Colonel Irwin and Commander Merritt looked down at the limpet mines, the detonators and fuse wire. They gazed calmly at the NASA officials and engineers gesticulating at them, and shook their heads, rejecting the world with a brief wave before closing the shutter for the last time.

Needless to say, NASA allowed nothing of this to leak to the public at large, and claimed that the crew had alerted their ground controllers to the possible dangers of a virulent interplanetary disease. NASA spokesmen confirmed that they had ordered the crew to isolate themselves until this mystery virus could be identified and destroyed. The Zeus IV was hitched to its tractor and moved to an empty hangar on a remote corner of the airbase, safe from the TV cameras and the thousands still camped around the perimeter fence.

Here, over the next weeks and months, teams of engineers and psychologists, astrophysicists and churchmen tried to free the crew from their self-imposed prison. Right from the start, as the doors of the hangar sealed the Zeus IV from the world, it was taken for granted that the astronauts' immolation was entirely voluntary. Nonetheless, an armed guard, backed by electronic security devices, kept careful watch on the craft. Sets of aircraft scales were manoeuvred under the landing wheels, so that the weight of the Zeus IV could be measured at all times, and instantly expose any attempt at escape.

As it happened, the spaceship's weight remained constant, never fluctuating by more than the accumulated dust on its hull. In all senses the Zeus IV constituted a sealed world, immune to any pressures from within or without. A controlled explosion strong enough to split the hull would also rupture the engines and disperse the craft's nuclear fuel supply, provoking a worldwide political outcry that would doom NASA forever. There was no way of starving the crew out – to deal with the possibility of the Zeus IV missing its rendezvous with Mars and stranding itself forever in deep space, a 200-ton stock of food had been placed aboard, enough to last the crew for 40 years. Its air, water and human wastes were recycled, and there were enough episodes of *Dallas* in the video-library to amuse the astronauts for all eternity.

The Zeus, in fact, no longer needed the Earth, and the NASA officials accepted that only psychological means would ever persuade the crew to leave their craft. They assumed that a profound spiritual crisis had afflicted the astronauts, and that until this resolved itself the rescuers' main task was to establish a channel of communication.

So began a long series of ruses, pleas and stratagems. The puzzled entreaties of relatives, whose tearful faces were projected onto the hangar roof, the prayers of churchmen, the offer of huge cash bribes, the calls to patriotism and even the threat of imprisonment, failed to prompt a single response. After two months, when public curiosity was still at fever pitch, the NASA teams admitted to themselves that the Zeus IV crew had probably not even heard these threats and promises.

Meanwhile an impatient President Quayle, aware that he was the butt of cartoonists and TV comedians, demanded firmer action. He ordered that pop music be played at full blast against the spacecraft's hull and, further, that the huge ship be rocked violently from side to side until the crew came to their senses. This regime was tried but discontinued after two hours, partly for reasons of sheer ludicrousness, and partly for fear of damaging the nuclear reactors.

More thoughtful opinion was aware that the crisis

afflicting the Zeus crew merited careful study in its own right, if mankind were ever to live permanently in space. A prominent theologian was invited to the Edwards airbase, and surveyed the claustrophobic hangar in which the Zeus was now entombed, draped like Gulliver in its cables and acoustic sensors. He wondered why the crew had bothered to return to Earth at all, knowing what they probably faced, when they might have stayed forever on the vast and empty landscapes of Mars. By returning at all, he ventured, they were making an important point, and acknowledged that they still saw their place among the human race.

So a patient vigil began. Concealed cameras watched for any signs of internal movement and electronic gauges mapped the smallest activities of the crew. After a further three months the daily pattern of life within the Zeus IV had been well established. The crew never spoke to each other, except when carrying out the daily maintenance checks of the spacecraft systems. All took regular exercise in the gymnasium, but otherwise stayed in their own quarters. No music was played and they never listened to radio or television. For all that anyone knew, they passed the days in sleep, meditation and prayer. The temperature remained at a steady 68°F, and the only constant sound was that of the circulation of air.

After six months the NASA psychiatrists concluded that the crew of the Zeus IV had suffered a traumatic mental collapse, probably brought on by oxygen starvation, and were now in a vegetative state. Relatives protested, but public interest began to wane. Congress refused to allocate funds for further Zeus missions, and NASA reluctantly committed itself to a future of instrumented spaceflights.

A year passed, and a second. A small guard and communications crew, including a duty psychologist and a clergyman, still maintained a vigil over the Zeus. The monitors recorded the faint movements of the crew, and the patterns of daily life which they had established within a few hours of their landing. A computerized analysis of their foot-treads identified each of the astronauts and revealed that they kept to their own quarters and seldom met, though all took part in the maintenance drills.

So the astronauts languished in their twilight world. A new President and the unfolding decades of peace led the public to forget about the Zeus IV, and its crew, if remembered at all, were assumed to be convalescing at a secret institution. In 2016, eight years after their return, there was a flurry of activity when a deranged security officer lit a large fire under the spacecraft, in an attempt to smoke out the crew. Four years later a Hollywood telepathist claimed to be in contact with the astronauts, reporting that they had met God on Mars and had been sworn to silence about the tragic future in store for the human race.

In 2025 the NASA headquarters in Houston were alerted to a small but sudden fall in the overall weight of the Zeus – 170 pounds had been wiped from the scales. Was the spacecraft preparing for take-off, perhaps employing an anti-gravity device which the crew had been constructing in the seventeen years since their return? However, the tread-pattern analysis confirmed that only four astronauts were now aboard the craft. Colonel Irwin was missing, and an exhaustive hunt began of the Edwards airbase. But the organic sediments in the trapped gases released from a discharge vent revealed what some engineers had already suspected. Colonel Irwin had died at the age of 62, and his remains had been vaporized and returned to the atmosphere. Four years later he was followed by the Japanese, Professor Kawahito, and the Zeus was lighter by a further 132 pounds. The food stocks aboard the Zeus would now last well beyond the deaths of the three astronauts still alive.

In 2035 NASA was dissolved, and its functions assigned

to the immensely wealthy universities which ran their own scientific space programmes. The Zeus IV was offered to the Smithsonian Institute in Washington, but the director declined, on the grounds that the museum could not accept exhibits that contained living organisms. The USAF had long wished to close the Edwards airbase, and responsibility for this huge desert expanse passed to the National Parks Bureau, which was eager to oversee one of the few areas of California not yet covered with tract housing. The armed guards around the Zeus IV had long gone, and two field officers supervised the elderly instruments that still kept watch over the spacecraft.

Captain Horner died in 2040, but the event was not noticed until the following year when a bored repairman catalogued the accumulated acoustic tapes and ran a computer analysis of tread-patterns and overall weight.

The news of this death, mentioned only in the National Parks Bureau's annual report, came to the attention of a Las Vegas entrepreneur who had opened the former Nevada atomic proving grounds to the tourist trade, mounting simulated A-bomb explosions. He leased the Zeus hangar from the Parks Bureau, and small parties of tourists trooped around the spacecraft, watching bemused as the rare tread-patterns crossed the sonar screens in the monitor room.

After three years of poor attendances the tours were discontinued, but a decade later a Tijuana circus proprietor sub-leased the site for his winter season. He demolished the now derelict hangar and constructed an inflatable astrodome with a huge arena floor. Helium-filled latex 'spacecraft' circled the Zeus IV, and the performance ended with a mass ascent of the huge vehicle by a team of topless women acrobats.

When the dome was removed the Zeus IV sat under the stars, attached to a small shack where a single technician of the Parks Bureau kept a desultory watch on the computer screens for an hour each day. The spaceship was now covered with graffiti and obscene slogans, and the initials of thousands of long-vanished tourists. With its undercarriage embedded in the desert sand, it resembled a steam locomotive of the nineteenth century, which many passers-by assumed it to be.

Tramps and hippies sheltered under its fins, and at one time the craft was incorporated into a small shanty village. In later years a desert preacher attracted a modest following, claiming that the Messiah had made his second coming and was trapped inside the Zeus. Another cultist claimed that the devil had taken up residence in the ancient structure. The housing drew ever closer, and eventually surrounded the Zeus, which briefly served as an illuminated landmark advertising an unsuccessful fast-food franchise.

In 2070, sixty-two years after its return from Mars, a young graduate student at Reno University erected a steel frame around the Zeus and attached a set of high-intensity magnetic probes to its hull. The computerized imaging equipment – later confiscated by the US Government – revealed the silent and eerie interior of the spacecraft, its empty flight decks and corridors.

An aged couple, Commander John Merritt and Dr Valentina Tsarev, now in their late eighties, sat in their small cabins, hands folded on their laps. There were no books or ornaments beside their simple beds. Despite their extreme age they were clearly alert, tidy and reasonably well nourished. Most mysteriously, across their eyes moved the continuous play of a keen and amused intelligence.

THE SCULPTOR

Garry Kilworth

Niccolò reached the pale of the Great Desert at noon on the third day. He dismounted and led his horse and seventeen pack camels towards the last water he would see for six weeks. There at the river's edge they drank. Some would have said that so many camels was an expensive luxury, but Niccolò knew the value of too many over too few. Only eight of them were carrying the statuettes. Of the remaining camels, two were loaded with his and his mount's personal supplies, three were carrying water, and three were loaded with fodder to feed the other camels. The last camel was packing fodder for the fodder-carriers but not for itself. It was possible that this camel, or one of the others, would die of starvation before he reached the Tower.

Niccolò had had to call a halt at seventeen. When he had consulted the sage, Cicaro, the old man had recommended that to ensure survival he take an endless string of camels with him. Distance, food-chains, energy levels, temperatures, humidities, moisture loss – when all the relevant information had been given to Cicaro, and the calculations made, the result was camels stretching into infinity. Impossibilities were not the concern of the sage. He merely applied his mathematics to the problem and gave you the answer.

At least they were flesh and blood. Towards the end of the journey Niccolò could begin eating them, if it became necessary. At that moment he found the thought distasteful, though he was no sentimentalist, and had refrained from even naming his horse. Niccolò knew, however, that when it came to the choice between starvation or butchering one of the beasts, whatever he promised himself now, he would use the knife without hesitation. He had eaten worms, even filled his stomach with *dirt*, when he had been without food. Man is a wretched creature when brought to the level of death. When he has shed his scruples he will eat his own brother, let alone a horse or a camel.

Yet there was a mystery there. Man also perplexes himself, Niccolò thought, as he filled his canteens from the river. When he and Arturo had almost run out of water in this very desert, they had fought like dogs for the last few mouthfuls, would have killed each other for them. Then rescue had come, at the last moment, preventing murder.

Yet, not two months afterwards, Arturo ironically committed suicide, hung himself in the back room of a way station, for love of a whore.

Why does a man fight tooth and nail to live one day, and kill himself the next? It was as if life was both precious and useless, not at the same time, but in different contexts. Life changed its values according to emotional colours. In the desert, dying of thirst, Arturo had only one thought in mind – to *live*. It had been a desperate, savage thought, instinctive.

Yet that instinct had vanished when Arturo had climbed on that ale barrel and tied a window sash around his neck. Why hadn't it sprung out from that place in which it was lurking, waiting to perform, to kill for life? Perhaps it is hopelessness that kills the instinct in its lair? In the desert, if he fought hard and callously enough, the water might eventually belong to him. The love of the lady though, no matter how savagely he battled, could never be his. If she withheld it, could not feel such for him, then he was helpless, because he could never in a million years wrench *love* from her grasp like a water bottle.

A craft came along the river, silently, the helmsman

apparently happy for the most part to let it follow the current. The cargo was sheltered from the sun by a palmleaf-thatched cabin, which covered the deck with an arch-shaped tunnel. The sail was down, unnecessary, even a hindrance in the fast flow.

As the boat went by, Niccolò was able to peer inside, through a window-hole in the thatch. A giant of a man sat in the dimness within: a clumsy-looking fellow, appearing too big for his craft, but a man with peace, contentment, captured in his huge form. He was knitting. His great hands working the wooden needles while his elbow occasionally twitched the tiller, as if he could steer sightlessly.

It seemed he knew the river so well – the meanders, the currents, the sandbars and rapids – had travelled this long watery snake for half a century – he needed no eyes. Maybe he could feel the flow and know to a nautical inch, a fraction of a fathom, where he was in time and space? Perhaps he navigated as he knitted woollen garments, both by feel, on his way to the sea.

Niccolò signalled to the man, and received a reply.

Afterwards he made camp by the river that wound beneath the star patterns visible in the clear sky. The campfire sent up showers of sparks, like wandering stars themselves, and though Niccolò did not know it they gave someone hope. A lost soul was out there, in the desert, and saw the glow in the heavens.

The following morning, Niccolò woke to the sound of camels grumbling, kicking their hobbled legs, shaking their traces. The horse took no part in this minor rebellion. A nobler creature (in its own mind), it held itself aloof from dissident camels. Niccolò fed the camels, then he and the horse ate together, apart from the other beasts.

Three days out into the desert, Niccolò came across the woman. Her lips were blistered and he had trouble forcing water past them. When she opened her eyes she said, 'I knew you would come. I saw your fire,' then she passed out again.

In the evening he revived her with some warm jasmine tea, and soon she was able to sit up, talk. She was not a particularly pretty woman. At a guess she was about the same age as he was, in her very early thirties. Her skin had been dried by the sun, was the colour of old paper, and though it was soft had a myriad of tiny wrinkles especially around the eyes and mouth. Her stature was slight: she could have been made of dry reeds. She wore only a thin cotton dress.

'What are you doing out here?' he asked her.

'Looking for water,' she said, sipping the tea, staring at him over the rim of the mug.

He gestured irritably.

'I can see that, but how did you get lost? Were you part of a caravan?'

She shook her head, slowly.

'I was searching for my mother's house.'

'Here, in the desert?'

Her brown eyes were soft in the firelight.

'It wasn't always a desert,' she said. 'I thought there might be something left – a few bricks, stones, something.'

Niccolò nodded. He guessed she was one of those who went out searching for their roots. Lost now, but lost before she even came into the desert. One of those who had been separated as a child from her family during the exodus, and had found out her father's name, where her parents had lived, and had gone looking to see if there was anything left.

He stared around him, his eyes sweeping over the low and level plain. Only a short three decades ago there had been a thriving community here, the suburbs of a city. On the very place where they were sitting buildings had stood, streets had run. The city had been so vast it took many days to travel by coach-and-six from its centre to the outskirts.

47

Now there was nothing but dust.

'I can't take you with me,' he said. 'I'm heading for the Tower...' He nodded towards the marvellous structure that dominated the eastern sky, taller than any mountain in the region, so tall its heights were often lost in the clouds. Since it was evening, lights had begun to encrust the Tower, like a sprinkling of early stars.

She said timidly, 'I can come with you.'

'No. I don't have the food or the water to carry a passenger. I have just enough for my own needs, and no more. I'll point you in the right direction. You can make the river in five, maybe six days, on foot. The first refugee camp is two days on from there.'

She looked at him with a shocked expression on her face.

'I'll die of thirst.'

'That's not my fault. I came across you by chance. I didn't have anything to do with your being here. You might make it. I'll give you a little water, as much as I can spare.'

'No,' she said firmly, hugging her legs and staring into the fire, 'you'll take me with you.'

He did not answer her, having nothing more to say. Niccolò of course did not want to send her out there, and he knew she was right, she probably *would* die, but he had no choice. His mission depended on him making the journey safely. To ensure success, he needed to do that alone, without any encumbrances. She would hold him back, drink his water, eat his food, spy on him, probe for his secrets. He would probably have to kill more than one camel to get to the Tower, if he took her along too. It was not in his plans.

Finally, he spoke.

'We must get some rest, we both need it.'

Niccolò gave her the sleeping bag and used a horse blanket himself. Once the sun was down, it was bitterly cold, the ground failing to retain the heat. She moved closer to him for warmth, and the fire blocked his retreat. He had not been with a woman for so long, he had almost forgotten how pyrotechnical the experience could be. Just before dawn she crawled under the blanket with him and said, 'Take me – please,' and though he knew that the words had a double-meaning, that he was committing himself to something he wished to avoid, he made love with her.

In the morning, he knew he could not send her on her way. He wanted her with him, in the cold desert nights, and afterwards, in his bleak life.

'You'll have to ride on one of the pack camels,' he said. 'Have you ever been on a camel?'

'No, but I'll manage.'

'What's your name?' he asked, almost as an after-thought, as he helped her up onto her perch. He had chosen one of the less vicious camels, one that did not bite just out of pure malice, though it was inclined to snap when it got testy at the end of a long hard day's walk.

'Romola,' she smiled. 'What's yours.'

'Niccolò. Now listen, Romola, we've got a long way to go, and your . . . you'll get a sore rump.'

'You can rub some cream into it, when we stop at night,' she said, staring into his eyes.

'We're not carrying any cream,' he said, practically, and swung himself into the worn leather saddle.

They moved out into the desert, towards the wonderful Tower, whose shadow would stretch out and almost reach them towards the evening. He and Arturo, eight years ago, had set out on a mission of murder, and had failed even to cross the desert. This time he was well prepared, but carrying a passenger. If anything happened, he would have to abandon her, for the mission was more important than either of them.

The city was still there, of course, he reminded himself.

It was vertical, instead of lying like a great pool over the surface of the continent. It was as if the houses had been sucked up to the clouds, like water in a waterspout, and now stood like a giant pillar supporting heaven. The city had become the Tower, a monument to artistic beauty and achievement: a profound and glorious testament to brilliant architecture. Perfect in its symmetry, most marvellous in its form, without parallel in all the previous accomplishments of man. It was grace and elegance, tastefulness and balance, to the finest degree possible this side of heaven. The angels could not have created a more magnificent testimonial to art, nor God Himself a splendour more pleasing to the eye.

And at its head, the great and despised architect and builder himself, its maker and resident.

The Tower had been started by the High Priest designate, da Vinci, when he was in his early twenties.

'We need to get closer to God,' he had told his contemporaries and the people, 'and away from the commerce and business of the streets. We have the cathedral's steeple of course, but think what a great monument to the city a tower would be! We could use the bricks and rubble from condemned buildings, to keep the cost of the construction low. The air is cleaner up there.'

Da Vinci was now truly a 'high priest' living at the top of the Tower, away from the people, protected by his army of clergy. It was said that oxygen had to be pumped to his chambers, night and day, in order to breathe up there. It was also very cold, and fires were maintained constantly, the fuel coming from the stored furniture of a million inhabitants of the old city.

He had begun the work, as he had promised, by using the debris from demolished houses, factories, government buildings, but gradually, as the fever for greatness took him, so he had urged his priests to find more materials elsewhere. Gravestones were used, walls were pillaged, wells were shorn of bricks. The people began to complain but da Vinci told them the wrath of God would descend upon any dissenter, and since he was God's instrument, he would see to it that the sentence was death.

By this time the Tower had become a citadel, within whose walls a private army grew. The Holy Guardians, as they were called, went forth daily to find more building materials, forcing people from their homes around the Tower, and tearing up whole streets to get at the slabs beneath.

Not all the citizens were unhappy about da Vinci's scheme, or he never would have got as far as he did. Many were caught up in his fervour, added fuel to his excitement and determination. The guild of building workers, for example, a strong group of men, were totally behind the idea of a Tower to God. It promised them work for many years to come.

Also the water-carriers, with their mule-pulled carts; the tool makers; the waggoners carrying supplies for the builders and the Holy Guardians; the weapon makers; the brick workers; the slate and marble miners. All these people put themselves behind da Vinci with undisguised enthusiasm.

Da Vinci began recruiting more youths, and maidens, as the Tower's demands for a larger workforce grew, and these came mainly from the city streets. When the guild could no longer find willing, strong people to join them, they sent out press gangs and got their labour that way. Eventually, they had to get workers from the farms, around the city, and the land was left to go to waste while the Tower grew, mighty and tall, above the face of the world.

Churches were among the last buildings to be stripped, but torn down they were, and their stained-glass windows and marble used to enhance da Vinci's now fabled monument. The High Priest strived for perfection in his quest for beauty. Inferior materials were torn out, removed, shipped down to the ocean in barges and cast into the waves. No blemish was too small to be overlooked and allowed to remain. Every part of the Tower, every aspect deserved the utmost attention, deserved to meet perfection at its completion.

Flawlessness became da Vinci's obsession. Exactness, precision, excellence. Nothing less would be accepted. There were those who died, horribly, for a tiny defect, a mark out of true that was visible only in certain lights, and viewed at certain angles, by someone with perfect vision. There was no such thing as a small error, for every scratch was a chasm.

This was the form that his obsession took.

By the time the Tower was half-built the population had already begun to leave the city. Long lines of refugees trekked across the wasteland, to set up camps in the hanging valleys beyond, where there was at least a shallow surface soil for growing meagre crops, though the mountains cast cold shadows over their fields, and high-altitude winds brought early frosts.

Or people made their way to the sea and settled on a coastal strip that could barely support the fishermen who had lived there before the multitudes arrived. Many of them died on the march, some travelled by river and drowned when the overcrowded rafts were thrown by the rapids; others perished of starvation when they arrived at the camps; thousands went down with the plague and never raised their heads above the dust again.

And still the Tower grew.

'What do you think of da Vinci?' asked Romola on the third night they were together.

'He's a genius,' said Niccolò without hesitation. 'He is the greatest architect and builder the world has ever known.'

'Does his genius come from God?'

She peered at him through the firelight.

'What do you mean?' he asked.

'I mean does God give him instruction?'

'That sounds close to blasphemy,' he said, staring hard. 'You're suggesting that God, not the High Priest, should take credit for the Tower. It is da Vinci's work, not the Lord's.'

He drew away from her then, away from the fire, despite his fear of the night snakes amongst the darkness of the rocks.

She continued to talk.

'I used to be one of the Holy Guardians – until I was thrown out on my ear . . .'

He looked at her, then behind him at the Tower, then back to her again.

'Ah,' he said, 'you didn't come from the refugee camp? You came from the Tower itself?'

'I . . . I didn't know what else to do, when we were told to leave, I thought about looking for my parents' former home, thinking it was a long way from the Tower and something of it might have survived.'

'Why were you asked to leave?'

'New guards were recruited, from distant places. The old Holy Guardians have been disbanded. We are no longer permitted to remain near the Tower. Most of my friends have gone down to the sea, to try to get work on the ships, guarding against pirates. Fighting is all we know. I intend to ask the High Priest if some of his – his closer Companions at Arms can return to our former posts. We were his Chosen, after all.'

Niccolò smiled. 'You mean he doesn't call you to his bed any more?'

She lifted her head and shook it.

'No, that's a privilege reserved for the Holy Guardians.'

'I see. So the fact that you, and most of your companions, had reached the age of thirty or thereabouts, had nothing to do with you being asked to leave? The new men and women, they're not young, handsome or pretty of course?'

She stared at Niccolò.

'He recruited a new army for very logical reasons. They now consist of many small groups of men and women from different regions, different tribes.'

'Now why did da Vinci do that?' asked Niccolò, softly.

'It's said that he's afraid of plots being formed against him, even amongst his trusted Holy Guardians. The separate new groups do not speak each other's language, they use many different tongues. If they can't communicate, they can't conspire against the High Priest, can they?' she said. 'Since he has control over a small group of interpreters, he has complete control over the whole army.'

Despite himself, Niccolò was impressed. It certainly was clever strategy on da Vinci's part. There was much to admire about da Vinci, no matter how much he was hated. The Tower was a product of a brilliant mind. The architecture, the engineering, was decades ahead of its time. Where an old support might have proved to have been too weak, da Vinci had designed a new one. He was responsible for inventing the transverse arch, the buttress, the blind arcade, and many other architectural wonders. The absolute beauty of the work – the colonnades, the windows, the ceilings – was indeed worthy of a god.

Such a pity a million people had been sacrificed to feed his egoism.

On the third Sunday Niccolò confronted her, waking her from a deep sleep.

'You've been meddling,' he said, angrily. 'You've been sticking your nose in amongst my goods.'

She shook the sleep from her head, staring up at him. Comprehension came to her gradually. He could see it appearing in her eyes.

'I was just curious,' she said. 'I didn't mean any harm.'

Niccolò pointed to one of the packs that had fallen from a camel. Its contents had spilled out, over the desert floor: marble statuettes, of angels, of cherubim, of seraphim.

She stared where he was pointing.

He said, 'When you retied the knot, you used a knot that slipped – there's the result.'

'I'm sorry. I just wanted to . . .'

'To spy,' said Niccolò.

He could see he was right by the expression on her face and he grabbed her and pulled her to her feet. She immediately struck him a sharp blow with the heel of her hand behind her ear, then as his head snapped to the side, she kicked him in the groin. He went down in the dust, excruciating pains shooting through his neck, a numbness in his genitals which quickly turned to an unbearable aching.

She had been, after all, a soldier.

'Don't you dare try that again,' she cried. 'My mother was an assassin. She taught me the martial arts. I could kill you now . . .'

In his agony he didn't need to be told.

By the time he had recovered, she had gathered his statuettes, carefully wrapped them in their protective rags, and tied them inside the pack. He hobbled over to it and inspected the knots, satisfying himself that this time they were correct and tight. Then he swung into his saddle, winced to himself, and then gestured for her to follow on with the camels.

'Those figurines,' she said, obviously trying to make friends with him again. 'They're very beautiful. Where do they come from?'

'I carved them myself,' he said, 'from the finest block of marble the eastern quarries have ever disgorged.'

She seemed impressed, though she was obviously no

judge of art, nor could she know the work that went into just one of the 333 statuettes. There was admiration in her tone.

'They're very beautiful,' she repeated.

'They're flawless,' he remarked as casually as he could. 'It took many years to carve them all, and I have only just completed them. They are a gift, for da Vinci. He can no longer carve minutely, the way one needs to be able to carve if one is to produce a piece just six inches tall – objects that need a younger steadier hand – especially since he developed arthritis.'

She was silent after this.

The Tower grew in size and height, as they drew nearer to its base, until it filled the horizon. Its immensity and resplendence overawed Niccolò so much that he almost turned around, forgot his mission, and went back to the mountains. It would now take him a day to ride, not to the end, but to the edge of the Tower's shadow. The Tower was like a carved mountain, a white pinnacle of rock that soared upwards to pierce the light blues of the upper skies. Its peak was rarely visible, being wrapped about with clouds for much of the time. The high night winds blew through its holes and hollows, so that it was like a giant flute playing eerie melodies to the moon.

By this time they had begun to eat one of the camels, and two others had been set free, their fodder having been consumed and their usefulness over. The water was almost gone.

Romola showed him how to produce water, by using the stretched membrane of the dead camel's stomach. She dug a conical pit in the sand, placed a tin cup at its bottom, and shaped the membrane so that it sagged in the centre. Water condensed on its underside and dripped into the cup.

'I'm an artist,' he stated, piqued by her superior survival knowledge, 'I don't know about these things.'

'So, an artist, but not a survivor?'

'I make out.'

They reached the Tower, footsore, weary, but alive. The Holy Guardians immediately took into custody. Romola protested, saying she was a former soldier, but she could not get them to understand what she was saying. All around the Tower was a babble of voices, men and women talking to each other in a dozen different tongues. Romola's pleas were ignored and she was thrown into the dungeons.

Niccolò found a Holy Guardian who spoke one of the three languages he knew and explained that he had brought some gifts for the High Priest and that da Vinci would be greatly angered if Niccolò were not permitted an audience with the one on high.

'I am the High Priest's son,' said Niccolò, 'and I wish to pay homage to my father.'

Messages were sent, answers received, and eventually Niccolò found himself being hoisted in silver cages up the various stages of the Tower: pulled rapidly aloft by winches through which ran golden chains with counterweights. An invention of his father.

With him went his bundles of statuettes.

He reached the summit of the Tower and was ushered into a huge room on his knees, before the powerful presence of the High Priest, da Vinci. The room was decorated to the quintessence of perfection, its ceilings painted by great artists, its walls carved with wonderful bas-relief friezes, and on the cloud-patterned marble floor stood statues sculpted by the genius da Vinci himself.

A thin middle-aged man stared at Niccolò with hard eyes, from a safe distance. He rubbed his arthritic hands together, massaging the pain, while the guards stood poised with heavy swords, ready to decapitate Niccolò if their master so gestured.

'You claim to be my son,' he said, 'but I have many sons, many daughters – bastards all of them.'

Niccolò replied, 'It's true, I'm illegitimate, but how could it be otherwise? You've never married.'

The old man laughed softly. 'That's true. I loved only one woman – and she failed me.'

Niccolò assumed a puzzled expression. 'How did she fail you, my lord?'

'She scarred herself, making her loveliness ugly to my sight. She was a vision of beauty, that became horrible to my eyes . . .' The memory was obviously painful to da Vinci, for he paused for a moment in deep thought, a frown upon his face, then his mood changed, and he said, 'What? What is it? Why did you request, no *demand* to see me?'

'I bring you a gift, my lord,' said Niccolò. 'A present for my father. Three hundred and thirty-three statuettes, all carved with great skill by a talented artist – a genius – everyone of them a masterpiece.'

'Who is this artist? Raphael? Michelangelo?'

Niccolò raised his head and smiled. 'I am the artist, my lord.'

This time da Vinci roared with laughter. 'Let me see the gift.'

The guards unwrapped the rags and the statuettes began to appear, were placed carefully upon the marble floor, until they covered a huge area of the great room. Eventually, they were all on view, and the High Priest motioned for the guard to bring one to where he stood. He studied it, first while it rested in the guard's hands, then taking it in his own and turning it over and over, cautiously, but also admiringly.

'This is indeed a beautiful work of art,' said da Vinci, holding up the figurine so that the soft light caught the patterns on its buffed and polished surface. 'How many of them did you say are in the set?'

'Three hundred and thirty-three.'

Da Vinci smiled. 'You know the value of numbers. Three – the Perfect Harmony.'

'Or union of unity and diversity . . .'

'Both. And here we have the perfect number – three threes.'

'Angels, cherubim, seraphim,' said Niccolò. He began to arrange them in a large circle on the marble floor. 'As you see,' he continued as he worked, concentrating, not looking up at da Vinci, 'they are also an interlocking puzzle. Each angel fits into another, but only one other. You will notice that the pattern of the marble flows through the figures, like an ocean current, following the holy circle. I defy you to find where the pattern begins and where it ceases, for it is one continuous flowing band.'

'Marvellous . . .' Niccolò heard the High Priest breathe.

There were angels of every kind, some nude, some clothed in flowing robes, some wielding swords of justice. There were seraphim brandishing spears of truth, and cherubim with little wings, drawing on cupid bows with tiny arrows.

'But look closely, my lord, at the features . . .'

The High Priest did as he was bid.

'. . . every one of them,' continued Niccolò, 'has your face, when you were a young and beautiful youth.'

There was silence in the room for a long time.

Finally, da Vinci walked past his prisoner, looked down on the multitude of marble figures at his feet, all bearing his features from a time when he was at his most handsome.

'Superb,' he whispered, stroking the one in his hand lovingly. 'Wonderful –' but then he cried out, as if in pain, as he plucked a cherub from the holy ring.

'There's one with a broken wing,' he cried.

A guard near to Niccolò moved uncertainly, as if he believed he was expected to do something about his master's anguish, but da Vinci held up a withered arthritic hand.

Niccolò spoke quickly. 'An accident, Father. I shall carve another to replace it. I brought enough of the marble with me to carve three more statuettes, should it be necessary.'

'But the patterns . . . ?'

'I can match them. As a sculptor of figurines I have no equal, save yourself in the days when your joints were supple. I am you, when you were younger, without your arthritis.'

Once more the middle-aged man studied the statuette, minutely, weighing it in his hands. Then he picked up another and did the same.

'This is truly a great work of art,' he said when he had finished, 'but I shall have them inspected closely before I allow them into my chambers. After all, you may have hidden a spring-loaded trap amongst them? One of those cherubs perhaps, lets loose its arrow as I hold it up to my eye? Or some devious device to administer poison? Perhaps if I pricked my finger on one of those spearpoints? I have lived so long, because I am without trust.'

'It is part of your genius.'

'Which has rubbed off on you, it seems.'

'Am I not my father's son?'

Da Vinci placed a hand on Niccolò's head.

'You are indeed. You took a great risk coming here, to give me these. I almost had you beheaded before I saw you. There are many plots against me. Many. But there was something very audacious in the manner in which you *expected* an audience. I was curious to see you before you died.'

'Am I to die, my lord, for being your loyal son?'

Da Vinci snorted. 'Don't put too much faith in flesh and blood. You can't prove I'm your father, and it means nothing to me anyway. There are a thousand like you, by women whose faces I hardly looked at.'

He paused and strolled across the room. 'However, you have, as you say, great talent – no doubt inherited from me. I am an artist too. A genius. I have decided to let you live, at least until you carve the last figure. What use is three hundred and thirty-two? A broken circle? It must be three hundred and thirty-three – all with *my* face. Go down from the Tower, find your marble, and do the work. Once you have completed your task, we shall see if you are to live.'

'I understand, my lord.'

The High Priest then said to his guards, 'When you take him down, send me up a stone mason. I want to construct a raised circular platform, to display these pieces.'

They then led Niccolò away.

They released Romola, and she found Niccolò. He was pleased to see her. She had holes in her hands and feet, where they had tortured her, trying to extract some kind of confession. She knew the ways, knew the limits, having been one of them herself. She professed a profound hatred for her old master, wishing he would rot in hell for his treatment of her.

'I sent him a message, telling him I was in the dungeon, and he ignored it for the first few hours, knowing they would torture me.'

She went with Niccolò and watched him, as he spent the next week carving the final figure to complete the circle. As he worked, he told her what had passed between his father and himself, high in that room above the world. They were staying at an inn, on the far side of the river. Accommodation for those not directly connected with guarding the Tower, was on the north bank, while the Tower itself stood on the south bank. It was another safety measure, to protect the High Priest. All river traffic ceased at sundown, and anyone found on the south bank, after dusk, was immediately put to death.

'When we were out in the desert,' she told him, 'I often wondered . . . well, why didn't you bring the statuettes by river, on a barge? Why risk that terrible journey over the wasteland?'

Niccolò had left the carving of the facial features until last, and this he had completed within the last five hours of close work. He held the statuette up to the light coming through the dusty window, inspecting it. The piece, as always, was pristine, immaculate. It would fit, patterns matching exactly, into its place in the holy ring of angels. It was the sibling of the other 332 figurines – with one exception.

Instead of da Vinci's youthful countenance, it had the face of a monkey. Worse still, a monkey whose features resembled those of the High Priest. A cruel caricature.

He wrapped the statuette in a piece of cloth, before she could inspect his final work, and answered her question.

'The river is crowded, full of his agents and spies. I know how fanatical they are. I knew I could convince him, once I was here, but they would never have allowed me to reach this far. Besides, one is only permitted to carry agricultural goods by river craft, unless one bears the authority of the High Priest. I had no such authority. They would have killed me simply on suspicion, before I reached the Tower.

'The river is a deadly place, as you know. Then there are the pirates . . . I stood far more chance of being murdered on the water, than I did from dying of hunger or thirst out on the sands.'

'That's true, and it's also true that you could cross the desert relatively undetected, until you came within sight of the Tower, of course. Yet . . . you took me along with you, knowing the risk. I might have been one of his spies.'

He stared at her.

'Yes, you might. I think you were – and still are. It is fascinating, and horrifying to me, that people like you are prepared to go through torture for the sake of discovering his enemies. It's an enigma I don't think I shall ever solve

. . . but I am glad for my father's sake that he has his devoted servants.'

'You wrong me,' she said, looking into his eyes.

'No,' replied Niccolò, 'I don't think so. You are still besotted with the mystique of the man, and you think that if you can uncover some plot against him, he will reinstate you, and you'll return to his favour. You have been blinded, Romola, but I shall restore your sight.'

Niccolò dispatched the statuette to da Vinci by courier. Then he asked Romola to walk down to the river with him, so that they might cross, and gain audience with the High Priest, once that man had had time to gaze upon the final figurine.

On their way down to the river, Niccolò said to her, 'You have been asked to guard me, haven't you?'

She stared at him, then nodded.

'Yes. That's why they let me out of prison.'

'I thought so. Da Vinci would never let me run around loose, of that I was sure. So it had to be you.'

They reached the jetties, and waited for a boat to come which would carry them across.

A short while afterwards a barge came down the river with a giant man at the tiller. He had a gentle face, a good face, and he was wearing a knitted waistcoat that looked new. When his boat reached the jetty he clambered ashore. The Holy Guardians swarmed over his craft, inspecting every spar, every beam, before allowing the dockers to unload his cargo. The only goods permitted to be carried by river barge, were food and drink, and if you were found with any other freight you were executed on the spot, no excuses accepted. The big man nodded to the two people who watched him amble past them.

When the big man returned, his barge had been unloaded, and his craft stood high in the water.

'Will you take us across?' asked Niccolò.

'Two sesterces,' growled the giant.

'Agreed.'

The three of them boarded the barge, and the giant raised the lateen sail, and the craft caught the current. They headed downriver, towards the sea.

Romola looked puzzled, stared at the far shore, then into Niccolò's face. 'Where are we going?'

'Away from here,' answered Niccolò.

'Out to sea?'

'Yes. We shall be island-hopping for as long as necessary, staying one jump ahead of da Vinci's people, I hope.'

She nodded towards the giant at the tiller, with his knitted waistcoat and benign expression. Romola became angry, clenching her hands, making them into fists. Niccolò stepped away from her, warily.

'The two of you are together – conspirators?' she said.

'We came to help da Vinci destroy himself, and now we are making our escape. Now, I realize you're an ex-soldier, and I still have the lumps to prove it, but my friend Domo here . . .' he indicated the giant, 'is not an effete artist. He could snap you in two, like a twig, so no violence please.'

She stared at Domo, who smiled broadly. He did indeed appear to be a man of enormous strength, and while all three of them knew Romola would put up a spirited fight, the outcome could not be in doubt. Especially since Domo had a wicked-looking baling hook in his free hand.

Niccolò said, 'We don't want to kill you, Romola – at least, I don't, though gathering from the looks Domo has been giving me, he thinks I am a fool, and jeopardizing our mission. I'm afraid you got under my skin, out there in the desert, and I've fallen in love with you. However, if you try anything, anything at all, Domo will kill you where you stand, and throw you to the fish. Is that understood? I shall be unable to prevent him, or help you.'

She stood a long while, as if weighing up the situation, and then turned her head.

*　　*　　*

The craft eventually reached the ocean, and Domo set a course for the outer islands, behind which the sun was settling for the night. Niccolò stood in the bows, watching the prow cut through the water as the wind carried them westwards, into the red glow of the evening. When it was almost dark, Romola came and stood beside him.

'How did you do it? The assassination?' she asked.

'Oh, he's not dead yet, but he will be.'

'How? Did you poison the statuettes?'

Niccolò shook his head.

'No, I gave him a gift – an imperfect gift. Perfection is an obsession with him. Now he is caught in a cycle of madness. He will not destroy the gift, for the angels have his face and it would be like destroying himself. Yet one of the figures mocks him – resembles him in a crude way, but actually has the face of a monkey. Without this figure the ring of angels is incomplete, an obscenity – three hundred and thirty-two statuettes. The pattern on the marble is broken, the circle unfinished, yet with it, the art is marred, twisted into a joke of which he is the brunt.

'He will go mad, it will destroy him.'

Her eyes were round. 'You're sure of that?'

'I'm certain of it. He loved my mother very much – my friend the sage Cicaro was there at the time – but he had her executed after my birth, because . . . because her beauty was marred.'

'In what way?'

'Stretch marks,' said Niccolò. 'In giving birth to me, she was left with stretch marks on her abdomen. He destroyed her because she was imperfect, blemished by a natural act of which he himself was the author. He killed someone he loved because of his madness for perfection. Now he will destroy himself – he's caught in the web of his own vanity. He *has* to have the circle of angels, for they immortalize his youth and beauty, yet he cannot have them, because one of them is a mockery. He will rage, he will consume himself with frustration and fury. He will destroy himself . . .'

'You are a genius,' she said.

'I am . . . subtle.'

They stood, watching the water sliding beneath the craft, as darkness fell. When it became cooler, once the sun had finally gone, she put her arm around him.

THE ALLURE

Richard Calder

It was the year when dermaplastic became the *dernier cri* in fashion, and when Ungaro's latest muse, Babette Bonheur, modelled the *apache* collection in Paris. To the music of *Slaughter on Tenth Avenue*, Babette idled down the cat-walk, her outfit – a living culture of collagen and elastin fibres – clinging like grafted flesh. She was stunning: a beauty from the slums of Kinshasa, black as an African night. I raised my camera, the motordrive machine-gunning each pose, inflection of hip, each studied insolence.

The *apache* look was the apotheosis of Ungaro's bordello chic. Vertiginous hemlines, Breton jerseys, spidersilk nets – all the props of the French vaudeville dance – were key-notes of his show. Babette saw me; smiled. Then a male model appeared, a black pimp who, after distracting her with a feinted slap to her cheek, dragged her the length of the catwalk and into the *cabine*. Before they disappeared, focusing for a close-up, the motordrive zinging like an insect choir, I had thought: Yes, that man – why does the mantle of the thug hold, for him, so little irony? Applause, applause, and beneath the lights, a fantastic litter of roses.

After the show, backstage, in the tented courtyard of the Louvre, I looked for Babette amid a huddle of buyers, celebrities and mannequins. Prevailing upon the *directrice*, I was ushered to where Babette held court, her long, austere Giacometti-like head emerging above a knot of admirers.

'Hello, Didi.'

'How's life, Babette? Blonde on blonde?'

'O, it is very *apache*, Didi.'

'My poor martyr.' I kissed her cheek.

Babette had changed into a dermatoid bodysuit, matching thighboots (trimmed with chain), skull-cap and *faux* jewels. Customized melanocytes gave her ensemble a desertblonde pigmentation, so she seemed an embalmed princess, unearthed from crueller, more civilized times. The man who had partnered Babette on the catwalk turned his back on us, retreating into the sanctuary of his own second skin.

'Who *is* he?' I asked, as he pimp-rolled into the crowd.

'You don't know? The new Belmondo, they say. A black Belmondo.' Babette was flustered. 'His name is Saint Loup. But let's not talk about . . .' The *directrice* had taken her arm.

'Sorry, Didi. I must throw Baba to the lions.'

And she was gone, as swift as a year in the history of fashion.

I couldn't sleep. Pirouetting in whorls of darkness, Babette and her surly blackamoor acted out their mime of 'gangster and his girl' incessantly behind my eyes. About four or five o'clock I left my hotel in the Beaux Quartiers and drifted through a Paris of shopsigns and headlights, white on black, black on white; a Paris doused in rain. Babette looked down from a thousand rain-drenched hoardings. As Ungaro's muse she had launched his new perfume, *Virgin Martyr*. Colour-drained as the city, black on white, white on black, Babette writhed naked on her cross. Beneath her, a party of dinner-jacketed men rolled dice for the scent bottle at her feet. The titulus read *La Reine des Parfums*. I remembered how difficult the composition had been; how the ensuing controversy, the Papal bulls, the firebombings, had brought Babette and me fame. Now the campaign was over; the posters, peeling. And above Paris the gods of notoriety wept.

As if startled from a dream, I found myself in the Rue

de Faubourg-St-Honoré. I was soaked through, shivering, cold and adrift in the void. *Ungaro* beckoned. My nose pressed to the window, I warmed myself on embers of autumn yellow and ochre, russet, auburn and Venetian red. The boutique acknowledged my presence. Gowns and frocks rippled on their hangers, hemlines curling flirtatiously. How often had I celebrated this carnival of trivia, these fripperies that consoled a frost-bitten heart? How often, at dinner parties, I had said: 'If we want to enjoy fashions, we must not look upon them as dead things: they must be pictured as full of the life and vitality of the beautiful women who wear them?' And what were they, now, these living dresses and gowns? What were they without Babette? Flesh for dead souls; gaudy shrouds for guests at a latter-day Trimalchio's feast. A masquerade of the void.

O Babette – New York, London, Paris, Milan – why could I never say 'I love you'?

Something moved. A shadow lengthened, foreshortened, dissolved. Two shadows. And the racks of exquisitely cut tissue culture – somatic textiles patterned with exotic dermatoglyphics – divested themselves, as if obeying the invisible hands of a black theatre's puppeteers. A headlight scythed across the showroom, and a face, dark, beautiful and frightened, was briefly illuminated.

Babette? Before I could think about what I was doing, I had smiled and rapped my knuckles against the glass. But it was the 'black Belmondo' who returned my salute, stepping centrestage and transfixing me with the dark phallic eye of a handgun.

Time and the world imploded. Far, far away, at the ends of the earth, and slowly, very slowly, Babette stepped forward, her mouth a rictus; the alarm bell that had begun to ring obscured her cry; and slowly, very slowly, its clamour introduced another protagonist. A Pinkerton guard – a telerobot run, perhaps, from a surveillance office several kilometres away – had awoken. It trained its camcorder eyes on the intruders, ghosting the movements of its human operative and radioing a warning.

Saint Loup turned, casually loosing a shell into the sentinel's armoured head; the machine took a step backwards; another shot; its mouth opened and a forked tongue quivered between steel-blue lips. Grabbing Babette, Saint Loup pulled her towards the window, lifting his gun as if to smash some egress. The tongue flicked across the room, imbedding itself in Babette's bodysuit, electric venom knocking her to the floor. The gun cracked impotently against the plate-glass.

'Babette!' I cried, and ran across the street to a shopfront half-stripped of scaffolding. Picking up my weapon, I charged *Ungaro* like a battle-maddened lancer, my spear aimed at the hairline fault that threatened the window's inviolacy. The glass exploded; I went through, stumbled, collapsed. Looking up through a veil of blood, I saw the Pinkerton – three metres of scaffolding skewering it through its mouth – lying in a soft fleshy bed of couture. And I too – after disengaging the taser from Babette's clothes, and witnessing, with outraged disgust, the perfidious rent in my thigh disclose my body's wine-dark secrets – I too heard oblivion call my name. It cooed temptingly into my ear. And I lay back and thought: Mmm, why not?

'It is the allure, Didi. We are slaves to the allure.'

'Shit – what's he know about the allure?'

'Didi is an artist.'

'Nails some chick to a cross. Takes her photo. An artist!'

'Saint Loup, you are a beast! He's hurt.'

'So why bring him along? We got your *artist* bleeding all over my car.'

'Don't move, Didi.'

'Périphérique. No police. On our way.'

'Didi, I'm so sorry. But the allure. The allure!'

'Forget it, bitch-cake. He can't hear you.'

White room. Light room. Rain-washed pastel of a pavement artist who, after achieving this perfection, died. Here I had become, almost, a dream of my own dreaming. Almost, at rest.

Sometimes the voices would return. But when I opened my eyes there were only the plain white-washed walls, the meagre furniture and *djellabas*, the window beyond which lay a cloudless sky of deepest, purest blue.

And then one day there was Babette.

She was all surface and plane, like the photograph I had taken of her for *Nakayoshi Deluxe*, introducing Ungaro's 'dandy look' to Japan. She was an apparitional macaroni, a transsexual mannequin in snug-fitting breeches, riding boots, cut-away hunting coat and a cravat so elaborately knotted that it made it impossible for her to turn or lower her head. She was Mlle Brummell.

'Your fever's broken, Didi. Eat –' And she brought a spoonful of thick meaty broth to my lips. 'You haven't touched anything for days.' The broth seared my throat; a euphoria stoked my brain. Congolese music rose through the floorboards.

'Goutte d'Or?'

'We're further north. But never mind about that. You must get strong.' Beneath the sheets I ran my hand along my thigh and discovered a ribbed column of stitches.

'Babette, what sort of trouble are you in? Are *we* in?'

'I'm so sorry, Didi. About all this. But I can't stop now. The clothes . . . they have stolen my heart. Feel!' And she took hold of my hand and placed it on her plum-coloured waistcoat. The material was dermatoid. It palpitated beneath my touch, its sensory fibres relaying a voluptuous message through a peripheral nervous system that was hard-wired to Babette's own. She sighed. 'The allure, Didi . . .'

71

'Shit – I told you he don't *know* about the allure.' Saint Loup had entered, a sardonic welcome-to-the-criminal-world sort of grin cracking his face.

'No,' I said, 'I suppose I don't.'

He ran his hands down his silken lapels. 'Me and my clothes. Let me tell you. We're brothers. Symbionts. We can't live without each other. Man, I *am* my clothes.' He wrapped his arms about his chest. 'Their receptor cells give you something, man. Perfect style. You walk tall. Shit – some of these new threads even got a fucking *cortex*.' He turned to Babette, his face suddenly crushed beneath a weight of ennui. 'Bitch-cake, why am I explaining this to our convalescent? We don't need him.'

'He saved us from the Pinkerton?'

'Shit – that *man-machine*?' He went to the window and lit a cigarette.

'Don't take any notice of Saint Loup, Didi.'

'But why steal?' I asked. 'You don't need to. Both of you have money.'

'A man-machine. You think I can't handle a fucking *man-machine*?'

'It's not for ourselves, Didi. It's for the King. The King of *la Sape*!'

'That's enough!' Saint Loup ground his cigarette into the boards.

'The King is going to save the world. And then all will be allure. Allure and ambiences!' Saint Loup was stamping his feet and remonstrating; but the sound track had broken; the frames stuttered. Before I passed out, Babette's voice cut in: 'He will make a wardrobe of the world!' And I remember thinking O my, these two icons of style: derma-toid junkies, both. Then the room, dissolving and reforming, cool and opalescent, ushered me into a world of sweet, sweet exhaustion where my thoughts were as nothing. Nothing at all.

*   *   *

As my strength returned so the little white-washed cell no longer instilled in me its dreamy complaisance; and the memory of my early morning walk, *Ungaro*, the telerobot, my charge into looking-glass land, came to disturb my rest. Night-times, listening to a far-away police siren that seemed like the melancholy cry of a country to which I would never return, I knew my life as a glittering child of the *aube de millénium* was over. I had few regrets. Babette shared my exile. And though she was not mine (what hold did Saint Loup have over her?) I began to construct expansive, romantic scenarios of our life together 'on the run'.

After feeding me, Babette would sit by my bedside. We would talk clothes. 'Flesh of my flesh,' she would say, addressing her dermatoid apparel, sometimes retro New Look or A-Line, sometimes Space Baby or Buffalo. 'Superlycras, polyurethanes – they're out, out. Dermaplastic is the apocalypse of fashion.'

For a long time she deflected all questions pertaining to her co-conspirator and the mysterious 'King of *la Sape*.' Then, one day, after an angry exchange downstairs, she burst into my room and said: 'We have been summoned.' I looked at her questioningly. 'To the land of sapeurdom,' she added. 'To the court of the sapeur King.' I did not interrupt. I could tell she was about to unburden herself.

'It was Saint Loup who introduced us. Saint Loup would take me to clubs like *Mambo* and *La Plantation*. Saint Loup was a big man. His film *La Puissance* had just been released. His friends were all boys from Zaire and the Congo. Musicians, mostly. Poor boys trying to strike it rich in Paris. After a few drinks they would talk of *la Sape*. It was like a religion to them. The latest clothes, the latest walk, the latest talk. The latest ambiences. Saint Loup was their hero. But Saint Loup spoke of one who was greater than he. A King of Style. A man who bestowed the miracle of *couture* upon the poor. It was only when I met the King that I knew . . .' She bowed her head and fiddled with the crucifix between her breasts. 'How empty my life was. He saved me, Didi. He can save us all. He teaches us that you are what you wear. That you can be what you want to be by dressing the part. That you can *become* your clothes.'

So this was Babette's gambit against the void: some fashion guru – and Paris now was lousy with them – a celebrant of surface and plane, had become, for her, a means of denying the emptiness of her life. For how many years had I been equally served by a camera and a roll of film? We each had our drugs.

'And now,' said Babette, 'it is time to go.'

A gun muzzle in my back (unnecessary; I would have followed Babette anywhere), I was half-carried by Saint Loup down three flights of stairs and into the awaiting Citroën. The car's leopard-skin upholstery was mottled with blood. 'Should charge you for that, man,' muttered Saint Loup.

We were all dressed *apache*. The fibres of my ensemble had begun to insinuate themselves into my pores as soon as I had dressed, my ascending nerve tract channelling their supersensual impulses to my brain. Clothes and flesh merged; neurons fired; and the night-streets, white on black, black on white, assaulted me with dreams. A sheep's head in the window of a Halal butcher whispered verses from the *Rubáiyát*; a lost African tribe danced before the juke-box of a nearby café; and a ravaged poster for *Virgin Martyr* – torn from the pages of a medieval manuscript – solicited the world's tears. We pulled away, the fleapit hotel that had been our bolthole now a Moorish palace and shimmering like a nocturnal mirage.

Babette drove. I sat next to her, Saint Loup's gun occasionally icing my neck. On the dashboard was a still of Eddie Constantine from *Alphaville*. Life was vision and texture, music and scent.

'Do you understand now?' said Babette. 'It gives us everything. And we are its faithful.' Her legs, encased in spidersilk nets, momentarily brushed against my own, couture coupling with couture. In sartorial oneness I saw, heard, felt as Babette. I knew her loneliness, how she clove to the bright-spinning, effervescent world of her amplified senses so desperately.

We drove south into the immigrant ghetto of the Goutte d'Or and parked in the Rue de Suez.

We sat at a long table of African mahogany. The ball gown that was serving drinks – a parlourmaid of sorts – fluttered about my chair. As it bent over to offer me a liqueur I peeped inside the décolletage to seek the mechanics of its animation. There was nothing but satin finery. 'It's a beautiful dress,' I said at last, breaking the silence that had lasted throughout the meal.

General Kitendi smiled. 'She was a beautiful woman. Once. Now she is her more beautiful clothes. She has become her clothes . . .'

Kitendi – 'The King of *la Sape*' – had fled Kinshasa after a failed coup attempt last year. ('I am flattered you recognize me, monsieur,' he'd said as I'd entered the loft conversion. If he had been possible to forget, his clothes, remembered from a dozen newspaper clips, would still have identified him. They were spectacular, their gorgeousness thrown into relief by the squalor of his rooms.)

'Louise,' said Kitendi, addressing the sentient ball gown, 'would you please serve the *crêpes suzettes*?' The thing made something like a genuflection and floated through the door. 'I can hardly believe it,' he continued. 'Didier Dessinée at my table. The notorious blasphemer! Hate-boy of feminists!' He turned to Babette, who sat between us, opposite Saint Loup. 'My poor girl. Was working for him as uncomfortable as it looked?'

'She thinks he's an artist,' said Saint Loup, dryly.

'And so he is,' said the General. 'But Monsieur Dessinée celebrates human flesh; I, the flesh of spirits.' The ball gown re-entered, aflame with *crêpes*. I salivated. Though without appetite, my artificially enhanced sense of taste and smell had had me drooling over each course.

'And who's your cook?' I asked. 'Another fashion victim?'

'Victim? In this world one either dresses as a victim or victor. And it is the latter style that *we* choose, monsieur.'

'It is for the revolution,' interrupted Babette. 'That is why we had to steal the clothes. We need hundreds, thousands.'

'An army,' said Saint Loup. 'An army of *sapeurs*.'

'Peace,' said Kitendi, 'before the *crêpes* grow cold.' We all picked up our forks. 'The revolution!' he continued, while indulging his mouth. 'That is only partly why they follow me. These days, monsieur, a cause is not enough. People need persuasion. A persuasion beyond politics. My boys and girls leave Kinshasa with nothing in their pockets and with stars in their eyes. When they arrive in Paris I give them clothes. Dermatoid clothes. Clothes they could never afford in a thousand years. Soon they crave more. "The allure," they moan, "O, the allure!" The neurons in dermaplastic are designed to decay. Did you know that, monsieur? Designers programme the fibres to decay even as they grow them in their tanks. So that the world, the privileged world, will cry out for more. But to my boys and girls I say, no, you cannot have more. I give them, monsieur, a little cold turkey. But I also teach them how to survive. Your clothes give you dreams, I say; now you must return the gift. You must *become* your clothes. The couture must bear the print of your consciousness. And then you and the allure can be as one.'

'We're fucking *headhunters*!' Saint Loup spat out the words with glee. Kitendi looked at him crossly.

'In my village,' said Kitendi, '(please excuse my crude lieutenant) there was a man who could put his spirit into a rock, a tree, a clod of earth. He lived to a great age. But my *sapeurs*, of course . . .'

'The body dies,' said Babette, 'but the spirit lives on in the couture.'

'Together they become,' said Kitendi, 'a juju. A fetish.'

'That old black magic,' said Saint Loup.

'And a little of the new,' said Kitendi. 'I employ some very good doctors. All good Congolese men. One of them patched up your leg. Satisfactorily, I hope?' He looked about the room, frowning. 'Louise? Ah, there you are. Go to Monsieur Dessinée. Yes, that's right, monsieur, touch her. See what she has become.'

Tentatively, I ran my fingers through the rippling rucks and folds of artificial flesh. The gown was a revival of early eighteenth-century style: an arrangement of bodice and skirt (the bodice, decorated in bows and stiffened with whalebone; the skirt opened, in front, to reveal a lavishly embroidered petticoat). It seemed as if it had stepped from a canvas by Watteau.

'Move your hand,' said Kitendi, 'to the small of the back.' My hand closed on bone. 'Only Ungaro and Gaultier have ever incorporated a cortex into their fashions. Something smaller, I am told, than the hind brain of certain dinosaurs. Gives an extra *frisson*. They always look for something new, no, monsieur? First it was to synthesize a polymer that could compete with biological materials such as leather, catgut, silk: molecularly-knitted plastic made of ring-molecules interlinked like quantum chain-mail. Dermaplastic! Then to make it live, monsieur! To give it nerve endings that would interact with the somatic system of the human body. Nerve endings programmed to give, not pain, but pleasure. Such psychotropic pleasure! Electro-muscles, next. And then – O exquisite – a cortex to fine-tune those delights!'

'No fashion brain, there,' said Saint Loup, pointing to my hand. 'That's the real thing. Nature's finest.'

'We found,' said Kitendi, 'that the lobes of the human cortex could be grafted onto those of a dress, a suit, whatever – the temporal, parietal, occipital lobes, wholly successfully. But the frontal lobe, the *thinking* part of the cortex . . . Well, monsieur, there were, as you would expect, some difficulties.'

The ball gown floated away, the fibres of its hemline – like microscopic pseudopodia – carrying it gracefully across the floor.

'Chicks don't need to think,' said Saint Loup. 'Soldiers *shouldn't* think.'

'Babette,' I said, 'what have you done, what have you done.'

'The revolution,' she said, with a child-like earnestness that approached panic, 'tell Didi about the revolution.'

Kitendi leaned back in his chair, his redbreasted smoking jacket swelling.

'Soon I shall return to my village,' he said.

'A whole army,' said Saint Loup, 'in packing cases. Every day we fly more *sapeurs* to Zaire to be pawed over and worn by the rich, the corrupt. When we give the order –' He drew a finger across his throat.

'My excitable lieutenant,' said Kitendi.

'Zaire will be the home of the allure,' said Babette. 'And all will be allure and ambiences!'

'And mine,' Kitendi added, an expression of pity for Babette's ingenuousness a flicker in the dark continent of his face.

'So many poor people,' said Babette, who was becoming increasingly distraught. 'The allure can help them, Didi. I know it can!'

Kitendi set down his fork and pushed his plate aside. 'One is either victim or victor, monsieur. And you . . .' He gestured to Saint Loup and said something in Swahili.

'Shit – I haven't finished my *crêpe*!'

'You are a complication, monsieur,' said Kitendi.

Saint Loup was reaching inside his jacket.

'Skin,' said Kitendi, 'is everything. Above this abyss

78

which is our life is stretched the only reality we know: this skin of sensation. It is the skin I care about, monsieur. It is skin I fight for. The black skin of my fathers.'

'And *monsieur*,' said Saint Loup, pausing in a parody of fastidiousness, 'is *white*.'

The glint of gun metal.

'Saint Loup tells me you want Babette,' said Kitendi. 'Saint Loup can be very perspicacious.'

'I've seen them together,' said Saint Loup, pointing his phallic toy into my face. 'The white boy and his piece of chocolate.'

'I –'

'Shh!' said Kitendi, putting a finger to his lips. 'Babette has been very useful. How else could I have acquired so many Ungaro designs? She is an excellent thief. And now, monsieur, you propose to take her from me. Feelings, monsieur. They have betrayed you. I must say I am surprised. Like me, you have long served the surface of this world. You are a photographer. An observer. Your kind should consign their feelings to the abyss, to the nothingness that lies below. The skin of clothes, the skin of humans: it is all the same to me, monsieur. But I cannot have *whiteness* in my wardrobe. It simply *clashes* with my plans.'

Babette had bowed her head. She fiddled with a napkin.

'When you broke into *Ungaro* – such gallantry – you punctured the skin of the world. *My* world. You would, I think, monsieur, betray us all to the depths . . .'

'My King – he *saved* us. You promised . . .' Babette was crying.

'You see what you have done?' said Kitendi. 'But my beautiful Baba shall soon also be subsumed by her clothes. She shall be the most beautiful collection in my wardrobe! Purest, blackest skin!'

'And the allure shall wipe away her tears,' said Saint Loup, grinning.

'Don't worry, monsieur,' said Kitendi, 'there is still time to finish your *crêpe*.'

But 'Louise' was already bringing our hats and coats.

My execution, I was informed, would take place at the river. The TV in the back of the car was playing a video: *Alphaville*. 'Love this film,' said Saint Loup. 'If they ever do a re-make my agent . . .'

'Quiet,' said Kitendi, who drove. 'Keep your eyes on our guest.'

Tied and gagged, I watched Eddie Constantine stride through the corridors of Alpha 60. Outside, Sacré Coeur looked down. God will not hear you now, Didi Dessinée, 'famous blasphemer,' I thought. So ends your glittering career. So end your romantic dreams.

My clothes, like my flesh, began to crawl. Withdrawal. The world was becoming quotidian. Commonplace. Wretched. Allure, do not desert me now, I prayed. Give this crazy life a little colour, sheen, before I depart. The money, the women, the cars, the fame. I give you all these. But let me share you, unholy spirit of fashion, just once more, with Babette.

Rue de Clichy. Gare St Lazare. Boulevard Haussmann. Opéra. 'Going swimming, man,' mumbled Saint Loup. Alpha 60 was choking on its own heartlessness.

Rue de Faubourg-St-Honoré. *Pierre Cardin. Chloé. Lanvin. Saint-Laurent.*

'Stop!' cried Babette.

'What is it?' said Kitendi, slowing.

'Stop the car! Here! Quickly!' We pulled into the kerb opposite the darkened window of *Ungaro*.

'Let him go,' said Babette. 'Please – the allure – it is angry – I can tell!'

Kitendi tapped his fingers on the wheel. 'Have you finished?' he said.

'White boy wants his swim,' said Saint Loup.

Babette turned to face me. 'We were poor,' she said, 'very poor, Didi. Like so many people in Kinshasa. When I was little I always dreamed about clothes. The clothes movie stars would wear, the clothes in old fashion magazines cut up and stuck to my bedroom walls. I always dreamed of Paris, Didi. I always dreamed of escape. So many people are still there, dreaming. Forgive me, Didi. I couldn't stand it: so many hopeless dreams. I wanted to give them beautiful things, beautiful lives. I wanted to give them the allure . . .'

Kitendi revved the engine; engaged first gear.

'Stop!' said Babette. 'Don't make me –'

'Don't make you *what*?' said Kitendi.

As the car began to pull away Babette opened the door and threw herself onto the pavement. The car jerked to a halt. Kitendi cursed.

'Get back in here,' he shouted.

'I shall call to them, Kitendi – I shall! Let Didi go. Now!' Kitendi got out of the car.

'Give me the gun,' he said. Saint Loup wound down the window and passed out the handgun. Kitendi walked towards Babette.

'Don't come any closer,' she said. 'I believed in you – but you don't know about the allure. I don't think you ever have. Not really! Not what it is – not what it can do!' Kitendi took aim. '*Ungaro*!' she called. 'My children! My own!'

A colossal explosion and a splintering of glass. And onto the street came dresses and gowns, suits, skirts, jackets and accessories: a whole autumn collection in yellow and ochre, russet, auburn and Venetian red. Kitendi fired; a wedding dress doubled over, bleeding dye; and then the King of Sapeurdom was enveloped by the suffocating attentions of that army of *haute couture*.

Through the open window of the car a black stocking wriggled, bewitching my rival like a sorcerous viper, rooting him, wide-eyed, to his seat. 'Bitch-cake!' he yelled, as the hosiery found purchase about his throat. I shrank away; and when, seconds later, I looked again, it was to see Saint Loup being dragged across the street to be left suspended from the perverse gallows of a lamppost.

Cars were stopping; passersby screamed.

Babette ran back to the car, tearing off her clothes, so that by the time she had taken the wheel and begun to accelerate, she was as naked and as beautiful as a great jungle cat.

'Forgive me, Didi.'

'Those clothes, those *things* . . .'

'I taught them, Didi. Taught them with love. The allure, Didi. The allure is love.'

Alphaville was drawing to its end. Eddie Constantine and Anna Karina were driving away from the city of night.

'*You're looking at me very strangely,*' said Anna Karina.

'*Yes.*'

'*You're waiting for me to say something to you.*'

'*Yes.*'

'*I don't know what to say. They're words I don't know. I wasn't taught them. Help me.*'

'*Impossible, princess. Help yourself. Then you'll be saved. If you don't, you're as lost as the dead of Alphaville.*'

I lay back. The streets, black on white, white on black, slipped by. I knew one day, perhaps one day soon, from my lips or hers, the words would come. I could wait.

O Babette – New York, London, Paris, Milan . . .

We left Paris by the Boulevard Périphérique. Out there, the void, chill and dark; but we were travelling beyond the skin of the world, beyond all the monochrome cities of the night, speeding to that place Kitendi feared, speeding through the immense spaces of nothingness, to – where?

It was a rumoured place, a haven that we, with our atrophied, fashion-dead hearts, could only guess at.

'*A night drive across intersidereal space, and we'd be home.*'

SONG OF BULLFROGS, CRY OF GEESE

Nicola Griffith

I sat by the side of the road in the afternoon sun and watched the cranefly struggle. A breeze, hot and heavy as a tired dog's breath, coated the web and fly with dust. I shaded my eyes and squinted down the road. Empty. As usual. It was almost two years since I'd seen anything but Jud's truck on Peachtree.

Like last month, and the month before that, and the third day of every month since I'd been out here alone, I quashed the fear that maybe this time he wouldn't come. But he always did come, rolling up in the cloud of dust he'd collected on the twenty mile drive from Atlanta.

I turned my attention back to the fly. It kept right on struggling. I wondered how it felt, fighting something that didn't resist but just drained the life from it. It would take a long time to die. Like humankind.

The fly had stopped fighting by the time I heard Jud's truck. I didn't get up and brush myself off, he'd be a few minutes yet; sound travels a long way when there's nothing filling the air but bird song.

He had someone with him. I sighed. Usually, Jud would give me a ride back down to the apartment. Looked like I'd have to walk this time: the truck was only a two-seater. It pulled up and Jud and another man, about 28 I'd guess, maybe a couple of years younger than me, swung open their doors.

'How are you, Molly?' He climbed down, economical as always with his movements.

'Same as usual, Jud. Glad to see you.' I nodded at the supplies and the huge gasoline drums in the back of the truck. 'A day later and the generator would've been sucking air.'

He grinned. 'You're welcome.' His partner walked around the front of the truck. Jud gestured. 'This is Henry.' Henry nodded. Like Jud, like me, he wore shorts, sneakers and t-shirt.

Jud didn't say why Henry was along for the ride but I could guess: a relapse could hit anybody, anytime, leave you too exhausted even to keep the gas pedal down. I hoped Henry was just Jud's insurance, and not another piece in the chess game he and I played from time to time.

'Step up if you want a ride,' Jud said.

I looked questioningly at Henry.

'I can climb up into the back,' he said. I watched him haul himself over the tailgate and hunker down by a case of tuna. Showing off. He'd pay for the exertion later. I shrugged, his problem, and climbed up into the hot vinyl seat.

Jud handled the truck gently, turning into the apartment complex as carefully as though 500 people still lived here. The engine noise startled the nuthatches nesting in the postal centre into a flurry of feathers; they perched on the roof and watched us pull up ten yards in, at what had been the clubhouse. I remember when the brass Westwater Terraces sign had been shined up every week: only three years ago. Six months after I'd first moved in people had begun to slow down and die off, and the management had added a few things, like the ramps and generator, to try and keep those who were left. It felt like a lifetime ago. I was the only one still here.

'Tiger lilies are looking good,' Jud said. They were, straggling big and busy and orange all around the clubhouse; a feast for birds and bees.

The gasoline drums were lashed down, to stop them

moving around the flatbed during the drive to Duluth. Henry untied the first and trundled it forward on its casters until it rested by the tailgate.

Inside the clubhouse the dark was hot and moist; a roach whirred when I uncoiled the hose. Back out in the sun I blew through it to clear any other insects, and spat into the dust. I put one end in the first drum.

I always hated the first suck but this time I was lucky and avoided a mouthful of gas. We didn't speak while the drums drained. It was an unseasonable May: over 90 degrees and humid as hell. Just standing was tiring.

'I don't mind walking the rest,' I said to Henry.

'No need.' He pulled himself back up into the flatbed. More slowly this time. I didn't bother wasting my energy telling him not to use up his trying to impress a woman who was not in the least bit interested.

Jud started up the truck then let it coast the twenty yards down the slope to the apartment building I was using. When he cut the engine, we just sat there, listening to it tick, unwilling to step down and start the hauling around of cases that would leave us aching and tired for a week. Jud and I had worked out a routine long ago: I would go and get the trolley; he would unbolt the tailgate and slide out the ramp; he'd lift cases onto the trolley; I'd trundle them into the apartment. About halfway through we'd stop for iced tea, then swap chores and finish up.

This time, when I went to get the trolley, it was Henry who rattled the bolts on the tailgate and man-handled the ramp down from the flatbed in a squeal of metal. I did my third of the lifting and carrying, but it felt all wrong.

When we were done, and the cans of tuna and tomato and cat food, the sacks of flour and beans, the packets and cases and bottles and tins were all heaped in the middle of the living room floor and we'd bolted the tailgate back up, I invited them both into the cool apartment for iced tea.

We sat. Henry wiped his face with a bandanna and sipped.

'That's good on a dusty throat, Ms O'Connell.'

'Molly.'

He nodded acknowledgement. I felt Jud watching, and waited for the inevitable. 'Nice place you have here, Molly. Jud tells me you've stayed here on your own for almost three years.' It was closer to two since Helen died, but I let that pass. 'You ever had any accidents?'

'One or two, nothing I couldn't handle.'

'Bet they gave you a scare. Imagine if you broke your leg or something: no phone, nobody for twenty miles around to help. A person could die out here.' His tanned face looked earnest, concerned, and his eyes were very blue. I looked at Jud, who shrugged: he hadn't put him up to this.

'I'm safe enough,' I said to Henry.

He caught my tone and didn't say anything more right away. He looked around again, searching for a neutral subject, nodded at the computer. 'You use that a lot?'

'Yes.'

Jud decided to take pity on him. 'Molly's writing a book. About how all this happened, and what we know about the disease so far.'

'Syndrome,' I corrected.

Jud's mouth crooked in a half smile. 'See how knowledgeable she is?' He drained his glass, hauled himself off the couch and refilled it in the kitchen. Henry and I did not speak until he got back to the couch.

In the past, Jud had tried everything: teasing me about being a misanthrope; trying to make me feel guilty about how the city had to waste valuable resources sending me supplies every month; raging at my selfishness. This time he just tilted his head to one side and looked sad.

'We need you, Molly.'

I said nothing. We'd been through this before: he thought I might be able to find a way to cure the syndrome; I told him I hadn't much chance of succeeding where a decade of intense research had failed. I didn't blame him for trying – I was probably one of the last immunologists alive – it's just that I didn't think I could do anything to help: I and the world's best had already beaten our heads bloody against that particular brick wall and gotten nowhere. I'd done everything I could, and I'd had a very good reason to try and achieve the impossible.

I had tried everything I knew, followed every avenue of enquiry, ran down every lead. Working with support and good health, with international cooperation and resources, I got nowhere: my promising leads led to nothing, my time ran out, and Helen died. What did they think I could achieve now, on my own?

They'd told me, once, that they would take me into Atlanta forcibly. I said: fine, do that, see how far it gets you. Coercion might make me go through the motions, but that's all. Good research demanded commitment. Stalemate. But the way they saw it, I was their only hope, and maybe I would change my mind.

'Why do you stay?' Henry said into the silence.

I shrugged. 'I like it here.'

'No,' Jud said slowly, 'you stay because you still like to pretend that the rest of the world is getting on fine, that if you don't see that Atlanta is a ghost town you won't have to believe it, believe any of this is real.'

'Maybe you're right,' I said lightly, 'but I'm still not leaving.'

I stood, and went to rinse my glass. If the people of Atlanta wanted to bring me food and precious gasoline in an attempt to keep me alive until I changed my mind, I wasn't going to feel guilty. I wasn't going to change my mind either. Humanity might be dying, but I saw no reason why we should struggle, just for the sake of struggling, when it would do no good. I am not a cranefly.

*   *   *

I woke up briefly in the middle of the night to the soft sound of rain and eerie chorus of bullfrogs. Even after two years I still slept curled up on one side of the bed; I still woke expecting to see her silhouette.

My arms and hips ached. I ran a hot bath and soaked for a while, until I got too hot, then went back to bed where I lay on my back and did chi kung breathing. It helped. The song of bullfrogs steadied into a ratchety rhythm. I slept.

When I woke the sky was still red in the east. The bedroom window no longer opened so I padded stiffly through into the living room and slid open the door onto the deck. The air was cool enough for spring. I leaned on my elbows and looked out across the creek; the blind-eyed buildings on the other side of the gully were hidden by white swamp oaks that stretched their narrow trunks up into a sky the same powder blue as a bluebird's wing. To the right, sun gleamed on the lake. Birds sang, too many to identify. A cardinal flashed through the trees.

My world. I didn't want anything else. Jud was partially right: why should I want to live in Atlanta among people as sick as myself, listen to them groan when they woke up in the morning with stiff knees and stomach cramps, watch them walk slowly, like geriatrics, when I had all this? The birds weren't sick; the trees did not droop; every spring there were thousands of tadpoles in the pond. And none of them depended on me, none of them looked at me with hope in their eyes. Here, I was just me, just Molly, part of a world that offered no pain, no impossible challenge.

I went inside, but left the door open to the air and bird song. I moved jerkily, because my hips still hurt, and because I was angry with all those like Jud who wanted to fight and fight to their last breath. Human-kind was dying. It didn't take a rocket scientist to figure that out: if women had so little strength that they died after childbirth, then the population would inevitably dwindle. Only five or six generations before humanity reached vanishing point.

I wanted to enjoy what I could of it; I wanted to write this book so that those who were born, if they survived the guilt of their mothers' death, would at least understand their doom. We might not understand the passing of the dinosaurs, but we should understand our own.

After breakfast I put on some Bach harpsichord music and sat down at the keyboard. I pulled up chapter three, full of grim statistics, and looked it over. Not today. I exited, called up Chapter One: How It All Began. I wrote about Helen.

We'd been living here at Westwater Terraces for two months. I remember the brutal heat of the August move. We swore that next time we had to carry desks and packing cases, we'd make sure it was in March, or October. Helen loved it here. I'd get home from the lab after a twenty minute drive and she'd bring me iced tea and tell me all about how the fish in the lake – she called it the pond, too small for a lake, she said – were growing, or about the turtle she saw on her lunchtime walk and the way a squirrel had filled its mouth with nuts, and she'd ease away all the heat and snarl of a hard day's work and the Mad Max commute. The pond was her inspiration – all those wonderful studies of light and shadow that hang on people's walls – her comfort when a show went badly or a gallery refused to exhibit. I rarely bothered to walk by the pond myself, content to see it through her eyes.

Then she won the competition, and we flew to Bali – for the green and the sealight, she said – on the proceeds. I was grateful for those precious weeks we had in Bali.

When we got home, she was tired. The tiredness got worse. Then she began to hurt, her arms, her knees, her elbows. We assumed it was some kind of flu, and I pampered her for a while. But instead of getting better, she got worse: headaches, nausea, rashes on her face and arms. Moving too fast made her lower body go numb. When I realized she hadn't been around the pond for nine days, I knew she was very sick.

We went to the doctor who had diagnosed my gastro-enteritis last year. She suggested Helen had Chronic Fatigue Syndrome. We did some reading. The diagnosis was a blow, and a relief. The Syndrome had many names – Myalgic Encephalomyelitis, Chronic Fatigue Syndrome, Chronic Epstein-Barr, Post Viral Fatigue Syndrome, Chronic Immune Dysfunction, Yuppie Flu – but no clear pattern, no cure. Doctors scratched their heads over it, but then said not to worry: it was self-limiting, and there had been no known deaths.

We saw four different doctors, who prescribed every-thing from amino-acid supplements to antibiotics to breathing and meditation. The uncertain leading the ignor-ant. Most agreed that she would be well again, somehow, in two or three years.

There were weeks when Helen could not get out of bed, or even feed herself. Then there were weeks when we argued, taking turns to alternately complain that she did too much, or not enough. In one three-month period, we did not make love once. Then Helen found out about a support group, and for a while we felt positive, on top of things.

Then people with CFS began to die.

No one knew why. They just got worse over a period of weeks until they were too weak to breathe. Then others became infected with a variation of the syndrome: the course of the disease was identical, but the process acceler-ated. Death usually occurred a month or so after the first symptom.

Helen died here, the day the Canada geese came. She was lying on the couch, one hand in mine, the other curled loosely around Jessica, who was purring by her hip. It was

Jessica who heard the geese first. She stopped purring and lifted her head, ears pricked. Then I heard them too, honking to each other as if they owned the world. They arrowed past, necks straining, wings going like the north wind and white cheeks orangy yellow in the evening sun. Helen tried to sit up to look.

They circled the lake a couple of times before skimming in to land. Their wake was still slapping up against the bridge posts when Helen died. I sat there a long time, holding her hand, glad that she'd heard the geese.

They woke me at dawn the next day, honking and crying to each other through the trees on their way to wherever. I lay and listened to the silence they left behind, realized it would always be silent now: I would never hear Helen breathe beside me again. Jessica mewed and jumped up onto the bed; I stroked her, grateful for her mindless warmth and affection.

I came home tired from the funeral, with that bone-deep weariness that only comes from grief. Or so I thought. It took me almost a week to realize I was sick too.

The disease spread. No one knew the vector, because still no one was sure what the agent was: viral, bacterial, environmental, genetic? The spread was slow. There was plenty of time for planning by local and national bodies. It was around this time that we got the generator at the complex: the management were still thinking in terms of weathering the crisis, persuading occupants that it was safe for them to stay, that even if the city power failed, and the water systems, they'd be fine here.

There's something about the human race: as it slowly died, those that were left became more needy of each other. It seemed that we all became a little kinder, too. Everyone pulled inward, to the big cities where there was food, and power, and sewage systems. I stayed where I was. I figured I'd die soon, anyway, and I had this irrational urge to get to know the pond.

So I stayed, but I didn't die. And gradually it became clear that not everyone did. The latest count indicated that almost five percent of the world's population has survived. The deaths have been slow and inevitable enough that those of us who are still here have been able to train ourselves to do whatever it takes to stay alive. It wasn't so hard to keep things going: when the population is so small, it's surprising how many occupations become redundant. Insurance clerks now work in the power stations; company executives check sewage lines; police officers drive threshing machines. No one works more than four hours a day; we don't have the strength. None of us shows any signs of recovering. None but the most foolish still believe we will.

Westwater Terraces is built around a small lake and creek. Behind the water, to the west, are deciduous woods; other trees on the complex are a mix of conifers and hardwoods: white pine and oak, birch and yellow poplar. The apartment buildings are connected by gravel paths; three white-painted bridges span a rivulet, the creek, and the western end of the lake.

I stood on the bridge over the rivulet, the one Helen and I had always called the Billy Goats' Gruff bridge, and called for Jessica. Weeds and sycamore saplings pushed through the gravel path to my left; a dead oak straddled the path further up. Strong sun made the cat food in the dish by my feet smell unpleasantly.

The paint on the bridge was peeling. While I waited, I picked at it and wondered idly why paint always weathered in a pattern resembling a cross-section of epithelial cells, and why the wood always turned silvery grey.

Today I missed Jessica fiercely, missed the warmth of her on my lap and her fur tickling my nose when I tried to read. I hadn't seen her for over a week; sometimes the cat food I put out was eaten, sometimes it wasn't. A warbler landed on the bridge and cocked its head, close enough for me to see the gleam of its bright eye and the fine wrinkles on the joints of its feet.

I waited longer than usual, but she didn't come. I scrunched over the gravel feeling annoyed with myself for needing to hold another warm living creature.

Late morning was edging towards noon and the sun was hot on my shoulders. I was thirsty, too, but didn't want to go back to the beige walls of my apartment just yet.

The lake used to have three fountains. One still works, which I regard as a minor miracle. A breeze pulled cool moist air off the surface of the water and through my hair. A frog plopped out of sight, warned of my approach by the vibration of my footsteps. The ripple of its passing disturbed the duckweed and the water lilies. They were open to the light: white, pink, yellow. A bee hummed over the rich yellow anthers and I wondered if any ever got trapped when the lilies closed in the afternoon.

The bridge spanning the thinner, western end of the lake was roofed, a kind of watery gazebo reigned over by spiders. I crossed carefully, watchful of their webs. Helen used to call it running the gauntlet; some of the webs stretched five feet in diameter, and very few were empty.

For me, the bridge was a divide between two worlds. The lake lay on the left, the east, a wide open expanse reflecting the blue sky, rippling with fountain water, surrounded by white pine and yellow iris. The right, the western end, was the pond: green and secret, shrouded by frogbit and lily pads. Stickleback and carp hung in the shadow of cattails and reeds, finning cool water over their scales.

There are almost a dozen ducks here, mallards mostly. And their ducklings. Careful of webs, I leaned on the rail to watch. The one with the right wing sticking up at a painful angle was paddling slowly toward a weeping willow on the left bank. Two of her three ducklings hurried after her. I wondered where the other one was.

It was getting too hot to be out.

Walking around the other side of the lake to get back to the roadway was hard work. The ground sloped steeply and the heat was getting fierce. Storms brought heavy rains in the summer and they were gradually washing away the dirt path, making it unsafe in places. The lake was 25, maybe 30, feet below me now and to my left, partially screened by the trees and undergrowth on the sloping bank. I heard a peeping noise from the water, just behind a clump of arrowhead. Maybe it was the missing duckling. I stepped near to the edge to get a closer look.

I felt the bucket-size clump of dirt give and slide from under my left foot but my leg muscles, already tired from the heat and the climb, couldn't adapt to the sudden shift. My body weight dropped to one side with nothing to hold it but bone and ligament. I felt the ligament tear and pop and bones grind together. Then I fell, rolling and sliding down the slope, pain like a hot rock in my stomach.

I crashed into the knobbed bark of an oak; it took the skin off my back and shoulder. I saw the mossy rock clearly just before I hit it.

I woke to heat thick enough to stand on. My mouth was very dry and my cheek hurt. My face was pressed against a tree root. I blinked and tried to sit up. The world swooped sickeningly. This time my face fell on grass. It felt better at first, not so hard.

I was hurt. Concussion at least. Something crawled down my cheek and into my ear. It took me a moment to realize it was a tear; it felt as though someone else was crying, not me. I closed my eyes and began my testing with the left leg, moving it just an inch or so. More tears squeezed out from under my eyelids: the ankle and knee felt as if they were being cut into with a rusty ripsaw. I moved my right leg. That was fine. My left arm seemed all in one piece, but moving the right hurt my ribs. I remembered hitting the tree. Probably just bruising.

I opened my eyes. The tree root my face had been resting on belonged to a smooth-barked birch. If I was sitting up I might be able to think.

I pulled my right leg under me and hauled myself forward with my left elbow. My moan startled a lizard sunning itself behind a leafy clump of purple loose-strife; its belly flashed blue as it skittered through the undergrowth and disappeared into a rotting tree stump. Sweat wormed over my scraped ribs, stinging. I dragged myself forward again.

I had to lift my head, bring my right elbow down to hip level and twist to roll over onto my back. The pain and the dizziness pulled thick, stringy nausea up over my skin. I thought I was going to pass out. After a moment, I sat up, shuffled back a couple of feet, and leaned against the tree.

The sun shone almost directly into my eyes. The floating sunlotus were open now, damselflies flashing metallic blues and greens against the rich yellow cups: must be about three o'clock in the afternoon. The air was still and quiet; the frogs silent and the birds sleepy. Fountain water pattered and splashed. I was very thirsty, and the air felt too hot and big in my lungs.

The slope stretched more than twenty feet upward to the path. I could do it if I moved in a zig-zag and used every tree for support, and if I started soon: I was dehydrated and every moment I spent out here in the sun made it worse. The water was about ten feet away, downslope, almost hidden by the tangle of ivy, undergrowth and dead wood.

I edged myself around the bole of the birch and shuffled backwards. The next closest tree was a white pine, about five feet away to the right. I had to stop four times before I got to within touching distance of the pine. I rested against its trunk, panting. The bark was rough and smelled of sun-warmed resin.

It was taking too long: at this rate, the sun would have leached away all my strength before I got even halfway up the slope. I had to risk moving faster. That meant standing up.

I wrapped my arms around the trunk and got myself onto my right knee. The soil was cool and damp on my bare skin. I hauled myself up. The ridged trunk glided in and out of focus.

The next tree was close, only two feet directly upslope. Trying not to think how easy this would be if both legs worked, I took a deep breath and hopped.

The world came crashing down around my head.

I opened my eyes. The pool was slicked with sunset, hot and dark and mysterious. Whirligigs and waterboatmen dimpled the surface. My hand hung in the water. I pulled my face forward a few inches and lapped. Some went up my nose and dribbled down my chin, but enough went into my mouth to swallow a couple of times.

I drank again. It tasted odd, thin and green, but I could feel the good it was doing me. My cheeks felt hot and tight: sunburn. I dipped one side of my face in the water, then the other, then rested my forehead on my arm. Cicadas filled the evening with their chitinous song.

It looked as though I'd been out four hours or more. No point beating myself over the head with my stupidity. The best thing I could do for myself right now was rest, wait for the coolth of night, rehydrate. Then think.

Swallows dipped and skimmed over the centre of the lake, drinking in flight, snipping up unwary insects with wing-flicking grace. A cotton mouse nosed her way out from under a pile of leaves and scampered from the shelter of a log to a tree root. She sat up and gnawed on a seed.

I tried not to think about the green peppers ripening on

the slope behind my apartment, of the fish in the freezer and fruit in the refrigerator.

About two feet away, a big spider sat on a lily pad, perfectly still but for one of its back legs that hung in the water, twitching. I thought maybe the leg was trapped by something, some hidden weed, but the rhythm was too deliberate; the spider was using the surface of the water as a drum. A mosquito fish came to investigate. It was tiny, no longer than a fingernail. The spider shot out its front legs and hauled the fish onto the lily pad, into its mouth.

The sunset had turned to purple and I could see stars. Tonight I couldn't recognize any of them; they looked cold and alien. It was cooling rapidly now, but I made no attempt to sit up.

My concussion and exhaustion had prompted a poor decision earlier: heading upslope was not the only way. If I could see a route along the lake shore that was relatively clear of undergrowth, I could walk or crawl around it until I reached the eastern end where the bank was only four or five feet high. That route would also bring me closer to the roadway that led to the apartment.

I blinked. I'd been asleep: the moon was up. This time, I could dip my hand into the water and bring it to my mouth to drink. I felt less like a wounded animal, more like a thinking, reasoning human being.

All around the pond, bullfrogs were singing. The moon was bright enough to reflect the flutter of trapped wings four feet from where I lay: perfectly still, a frog sat half hidden by cattails, a caddisfly in its mouth. The fly stopped struggling; they only lived a few hours anyway. Born without mouths, they reproduced then died. The frog's eyes glittered cold in the moonlight, watching me. Bullfrogs lived fifteen years.

They sang louder, following each other's lead, altering duration, pitch and rhythm until the water boomed and echoed with their song. Tree frogs buzzed in the higher registers. I felt surrounded and menaced by sound.

Leaves rustled; a shadow eased through the undergrowth behind me. I turned my head slowly, faced two green eyes like headlights. Jessica. A friendly face.

'Jess. Here, baby.' She sniffed at my hip. I patted my chest, an invitation for her to snuggle. She froze. 'Come on, Jess. Come here, baby.' She sniffed my hand, and purred. I laughed. 'Yes, you wild thing. It's me.' Your friend.

She licked my hand. I lifted it to stroke her. She hissed. 'It's me, Jess. Me.' She regarded me with cold emerald eyes; in the moonlight, her teeth looked like old ivory.

A small creature, maybe the cotton mouse, scuttled somewhere close to the water. Jessica crouched, bellied forward.

I remembered how she had looked as a seven-week old kitten, the way she had comforted me when Helen died.

Now I saw her as she had always been: a hunter, a wildcat who only licked my hand for the salt. I was not part of her world. I was not any part of anything's world. What I saw when I looked into the eyes of a frog or a mouse was nothing: not fear, not affection, not even contempt.

But I stayed. For Helen. To be part of the world Helen had loved. But staying here did not make me part of Helen's world: Helen was dead. Gone. She'd gone and left me with nothing. No one. It wasn't fair. I didn't want to be alone.

I beat on the dirt with my fist. Why had she died and left me alone? Why? Why Helen?

'Tell me why!'

My scream was raw, too hot, too human for this place. Tears rolled down my cheeks, big tears, big enough to reflect the world a new way. Helen was gone, and the geese were gone; I could stay here forever and she would never come back. I shouldn't be here.

The realization made me feel remote, very calm.

I sat up, ignoring the pain. Getting my t-shirt off was difficult; stretching for the branch two feet away, even worse. The t-shirt was already ripped; it made it easier for me to tear it into strips. I had to try several times before I could tie secure knots around the makeshift splint. Whenever the pain got too much, I rested.

An owl hooted, hunting.

I levered myself up onto knee and elbows, left leg stuck out behind me, stiff in its splint. Pain was just pain.

I dragged myself forward through a monochrome world: water sleek and black; trumpet honeysuckle leached lithium grey; moonlight lying like pools of mercury on leaves the colour of graphite. Nature, thinking there was no one there to observe, let slide the greens and purples, the honey yellows, and showed her other face: flat, indifferent, anonymous.

I imagined making my pain as impersonal as nature's night face, putting it in a pouch at the small of my back, zipping the pouch shut. Out of sight, out of mind. Somewhere, I knew, there was a place where all the colours and scents of the day waited for morning, and then I would smell iris and pine resin, rich red dirt and green pond scum. And feel the hot orange jags of pain. In the morning.

Right elbow, right knee, left elbow, drag. I focused on the tree 40 yards away on the eastern bank, the tree I would use to haul myself upright and up onto the road. Right elbow, right knee, left elbow, drag.

Behind me, I heard the squeak of a small animal. The cotton mouse. Right elbow, right knee, left elbow, drag. The night stretched on.

The tree bark was rough on hands and arms already red raw. No pain until morning. I pulled myself up the incline. The road felt marvellously smooth. I laid my cheek on the asphalt and breathed in the smell of dust and artificial things. Below, the pond glimmered, obsidian. The bullfrogs sang.

* * *

My ankle was not broken. I suspected that several ligaments were torn, in my ankle and knee, but distalgesics and support bandages kept me able to manage until, eight days later, I could get around using a heavy branch as a cane. It was hard to hold the cane: the bandages wrapped around my hands and forearms were thick and clumsy.

I limped out to the deck and lowered myself into the hammock: the sky was thick with churning clouds. Usually, I loved watching the sheer power of a storm, the way it could boom and slash and drive over a hot and parched world, cooling and soaking. This time it was different. This time, when the wind tore through the stand of swamp white oak, it seemed to me that it was killing things, flattening them, exposing them: turning the oak leaves silvery side up, ripping off branches, bending the trees almost to breaking point, pressing the grasses flat to the earth and snapping the heads off the marsh marigold. It was brutal.

I swung myself off the hammock. The show could go on without me. Inside, I made myself hot tea, put on Vivaldi – human music to drown the sound of the storm – and retired to the couch with a book, facing away from the glass doors. Let it do what it wanted. I refused to watch the rain swell the creek until it rose high enough to fill the burrows of voles and mice and drown their young.

My ankle and knee improved and I could walk slowly without the cane. I took the bandages off my arms. I did not go near the pond, and walked only on the black artificial surfaces of the road.

Tonight was soft and warm; there was a quarter moon. I walked over the Billy Goats' Gruff bridge and listened to the frogs singing around the pond. I turned and walked up to the clubhouse. It took me a while to find the red switch handle. I threw it; the floodlight still worked.

I stood on the road overlooking the pond. Sodium light heaved greasily on the water next to the silver ripple of the moon. The water looked mysterious, unknowable, like an ancient harbour lit by naphtha flaming in a great bronze bowl.

I looked at it a long time. Helen was not here, she was in my heart. The pond belonged to the past.

I waited by the side of the road for Jud. There were more flowers, and it was just as hot and dusty, but this time there was no spider web, no cranefly. Just the birds singing, and me sitting on my suitcase. Three of Helen's paintings, wrapped in our sheets, leaned against the gate.

Jud was on his own. He coasted the truck to a stop and climbed down. I stood. He saw the suitcase.

'This mean what I think it means?'

'Yes.'

And that's all we said. He always did know when to speak and when to keep quiet. He helped me push the case and the paintings up into the back, in among all the cans and bottles and sacks I wouldn't be needing.

'You want to drive?' he asked. I shook my head. We climbed up. I put the seatbelt on; my life had suddenly become more precious. Jud noticed, but said nothing. He made a U-turn and we set off back along the road to Atlanta.

I leaned my head against the window and watched the dog violets nodding at the side of the road. I had nearly died out here, believing struggling was for fools and craneflies. Perhaps those who struggled were fools, but they were fools with hope. They were human. Helen was dead. I was not. I was sick, yes, but I still had intelligence, direction, purpose. And time. Something craneflies did not have. If I personally could not finish the research I intended, then those who came after me would. I could teach them what I learned; they would build on it. If I struggled and failed, that was not the end. I am not a cranefly.

PIGS, MOSTLY

Ian Lee

Heavy-breasted, amid the corn, Margery Muttock stood serene, cradling a pink infant on her ample hip. She squeezed an ear of wheat between a firm fleshy thumb and forefinger and offered the damp milky residue to the bundle in her arms. A rosy tongue collected the ambrosial gift and tiny labial flutterings suggested further consideration. Questioning innocent small brown eyes looked up into Margery's face, evoking for a moment a scene of almost religious reverence. An earthmother and infant in a fertile landscape. One might have sighed at the idyll of it all. But perhaps it was not quite so . . . so iconographic. When you knew the whole story.

And the breeze blew across the wheat field, which shimmered like a golden sea. Mice stopped in mid-nibble, skylarks clung to imaginary aerial spires and the bees . . . the bees buzzed and searched and searched again, matching, coupling, mingling with the seeds in the wind. You could feel the life beginning to ripen all around. What seemed to be a smile broke over the weanling's visage, like sun from behind a cloud. Margery puckered and blew sweet breath across the tiny brow.

Turning at the distant sound of wheels rattling the cattle grid at the entrance to the farm, Margery hitched up the bundle on her hip and tucked the infant's impish little ears inside the swaddling shawl. As one does when expecting visitors, she smoothed her blue, fashionless polyester dress around her well-cushioned form. She moved to the edge of the field and onto the grass beside the track. Across the flat fields to the west, at a distance of almost a mile, across ditches, scrappy hedges, past a derelict haybarn, standing out against the dark green backcloth of Badgers Wood, Margery could see a small white car begin to make its way towards her.

She did not know it at that moment but it was a car bringing her son back from voyages in the wide world. She sighed, unwrapped her small pink armful and put it to the ground. The piglet shook itself, making its curly tail quiver with delight or irritation – it was of course impossible to tell – and then ran off with a squeal towards the farmhouse, as if being pursued by a big bad wolf.

Perverse, polymathic, poetical, Graham Muttock turned his mind from idle fictional speculation about the cosmos and eased his white Sunbeam off the metalled lane and onto the pebblestrewn, rutted track. Dust billowed up, obscuring his line of retreat. His fingers tightened on the leathergloved steering-wheel and he peered ahead for the smoothest route across the potholes. It was a journey he had both dreamed about and dreaded for what seemed like years. Now that he was approaching the object of his quest, he found his foot begin to freeze on the accelerator. Partially dead trees hovered on the skyline, too far away to intervene. Graham caught them in the corner of his eye and heard the phrase 'sticks and stones' formulate from nowhere in the uncontrollable recesses of his . . . of his mind. He knew it was part of some larger saying but for the moment he couldn't think what. As a journalist, that bothered him. You had to know references if you wanted to be a successful journalist. You had to know what was important and what was not. His brain was speeding up as the car had slowed. He looked in the mirror and saw only the billowing pale cloud of dust. Up ahead in the distance he spotted a substantial figure moving towards the farmhouse. It appeared to be carrying something in its arms, then bending to put that something down.

As far as Graham could remember the track was about three-quarters of a mile long. It should take five minutes at the very most and he would be there. The sign at the entrance to the track had said it and its significance had not been lost on him: 'Home Farm.' The other sign, however, had been noticed only unconsciously, which was not the same thing at all – far less distracting in the short term but in the long run potentially far more significant. Over a period of time the unconscious impressions would work their way to the surface and by the time they got there they would have distracted . . . or destroyed . . . everything worth worrying about. Graham was capable of poring over such thoughts for hours late at night when he was finding it difficult to sleep. The other sign – the unnoticed one – had said: 'No Trespasses.' Without the r. Down a few layers, some Biblical connections may have rustled in a corner. Graham didn't notice that either, as you wouldn't notice a dormouse waking from winter sleep in the far corner of the field you were in. Graham was in a state of tension and expectation. He could tell he was not quite functioning as normal but he couldn't really help himself. It wasn't every day you went to call on . . . biological . . . on ancestors . . . on parents.

Graham had always been a little strange. Now expectation was making his mind restless like a tossed . . . salad . . . or like straw, yes, tossed like straw.

There were boulders . . . large stones, anyway, lining the track at intervals, painted white for night visibility. They, and the smaller stones and pebbles strewn over the track, were deeply unconscious of the passing vehicle. More unconscious than Graham was of the sign that said 'No Trespasses.' Or the sign was of him. More unconscious than Margery of the reason for Graham's return. The stones were trying hard, but consciousness of anything beyond the immediate hard stony substance of their lives was yet far beyond them. One day perhaps they would crack and some inner force would break them down until they were earth, chemical traces of iron, calcium, magnesium oxide and so on. Then they might be drawn into the stem of a plant and live again as trace elements in that plant's sap. An ear of wheat, for example. Once eaten, they might be absorbed into the blood of an animal – a pig, perhaps – and in the iron that is necessary to the blood that runs through the brain of that animal, they might then pass on and it might be that one day these stones would ... rule the world. Napoleon, thought Graham, was also a pig.

Less unconscious were the grasses, wild and cultivated, which swayed in honour of the car's passage. They could be moved by the car, or by Graham. They could have their osmotic and photosynthetic processes disturbed by the unwanted deposition of tars and lead, not to mention the momentary asphyxiation caused by the passing of the carbon monoxide cloud. The cultivated grasses, the rye, the barley, the wheat, were already weakened by the years of inbreeding and the incessant dousing of fertilizers, pesticides and acid rain. Unable to express themselves openly, they cowered away from the field edges, which remained sparse and barren like the desperate remnant-haired dome of a prematurely balding pate. Further up the evolutionary chain, hundreds of small insects became only too painfully impressed by the presence of the Sunbeam as they were buffeted by its pearly white bonnet or sucked into its discreet air intakes. Their tiny cries were too small to register on Graham's attention screen, which was focused principally on a distant figure which appeared to be leaving a field, trailing the remnants of what had been a bundle and walking towards the farmhouse.

There were birds too. They recognized the existence of the vehicle and expressed degrees of alarm about its presence. Crows and pigeons departed the trees as the droning engine and crunching tyres approached. They knew the car wasn't interested in them but something deep down, something instinctual, made them respond to certain sounds by taking flight. Whether the car reminded them of the hum of wind through the primary flight feathers of a peregrine or whether they had simply learned that the farm Land Rover sometimes gave birth to men with shotguns, the ornipsychologists had not yet revealed. They just took to the wing. They knew that in a few minutes they would have circled on the breeze to no purpose and have returned to whatever cosy intersection of branch and bough had been supporting them. Or they might find themselves drawn to the ground by a glimpse of some potential titbit overturned by a fleeing vole. Later, other sights and sounds would cause other predictable reactions. By and large, they had consciousness but they did not have will.

A lot of this mental activity was invisible to Margery, even though she was watching closely as the car made its progress up the track. It was invisible also to a nearby hovering kestrel, even though its eyes were sharper than diamonds. And yet there was a perceptible psychic shimmer in the air around the car, a disturbance akin to the dust tail that curled around behind it. What that shimmer was, it was at this stage impossible to tell.

Margery had almost reached the end of the track by the farmyard gate. She was thinking that it must be Mr and Mrs Jones's car because it was going so slowly: those who made the journey regularly lost their fear of the potholes. Mr and Mrs Jones were the only people expected, but she had not remembered them having a white car. But then they might well have changed it. Margery peered into the distance, trying to make out who was in the car. It seemed like a small car, even a sports car perhaps and not the sort of thing to carry a young family in. As the car turned a bend in the track, aligning itself directly with her angle of vision, the frame of the windscreen appeared to Margery to contain a lone driver. Surely Mr and Mrs Jones would come together? Margery's concern deepened and she turned, breaking into a heavyish trot, hoping to find her husband in the farmyard.

Margery's husband was a large man who wore check shirts with the sleeves rolled up. His jeans were very baggy at the knees and his boots were crusted with mud and other fibrous vestiges of field and yard. He wore a cloth cap – even in the height of summer – and spoke with a broad country accent. He knew 25 dialect words for rain and as many again to describe the act of mating, most of which were monosyllabic and had four letters incorporating a flat u. Margery's husband was called Joe. He came to her call.

They met at the gate into the farmyard. It marked the end of the track and the beginning of their private domain. It was the limit at which the dogs would bark and the security lighting would come on. At this point the slightly desultory 'No Trespasses' became 'Private Propety – Keep Out' on a board attached to the gate. On the side wall of the house, next to the gate, was a bell-pull and another old sign: 'Ring for Attention.' Margery and Joe stood one on each side of the gate as Margery pointed out to Joe the billowing cloud and the Sunbeam. Trundling closer, it had covered about half the distance to where they were.

'It's not the Joneses,' she said. 'I've a feeling it's . . .' She trailed off.

Whatever feeling it was, it had suddenly been supplanted by a new one. A look came into her eyes, a faraway look, as though she were trying to discern speech from muffled mumblings in an adjoining room. Finally the message came through.

'I think it's Graham,' she said.

'How do you know? We haven't seen him for . . . for years.'

'Mother's intuition,' said Margery. 'I just know.'

'He's a journalist now, isn't he?' said Joe with a slight but unmistakable note of apprehension in his voice.

Margery had been thinking along similar lines already.

'An *investigative* journalist,' she said, laying heavy emphasis on the specialism. 'With *What Farm?* magazine. You know what that means, don't you?'

'He could be just on holiday,' offered Joe, unconvincingly. 'Looking for Bed and Breakfast.'

'You don't believe that,' said Margery scornfully. 'He's been on voyages in the wide world and we've heard nothing from him for six years. You know what a strange one he is. I've always known he'd find out one day. I'd hoped to be dead first.'

'Well, slow him up a bit then,' suggested Joe. 'We'd better get things straight and start thinking up a good story.'

Margery's right hand delved sub-apronically and as it did, almost in the same instant, the Sunbeam started to pull to the left, influenced by the sudden exhalation of air from a punctured front tyre. A row of stiletto-sharp spikes retracted silently and imperceptibly into the surface of the track.

Margery turned as soon as she had ascertained that the car was stopped and, nodding at the gate catch, waited while Joe unhitched it to let her in. Beside her, unnoticed, the small pink piglet stood uncertainly on its four meatless legs and turned round rapidly in a confused circle, as though trying to catch its own curly sprig of a tail. It rolled over a couple of times onto Margery's foot.

'Let's get you back to Mum, then,' said Margery, like any nanny who was returning her charge from a morning stroll in the park. She swept the sturdy tender infant into her arms and made off through one of the shed doors that opened onto the farmyard. Inside this shed it was dark and smelly. Crumbling wooden partitions lined old straw-floored sties; chipped enamel and plastic bowls were propped in feeding troughs positioned head high to a porker and appeared to contain dregs of uneaten swill. Dung and mud had been pounded underfoot into an uninviting paste, ready for daubing on medieval cottage walls, a couple of thousand years too late.

At the far end of this shed, partially obscured by a couple of bales of straw and a casually leaning antique pitchfork, a padlocked door waited unobtrusively, expecting to be ignored by the casual visitor. Margery went to this door and opened it with a key that had appeared in her hand. The door opened remarkably easily and without creaking. The pitchfork seemed to be attached to it and opened also. Somehow the bales of straw were not in the way and Margery was able to pass unimpeded into an inner sanctum pigshed run on quite different lines. Here was fluorescent light. Here were terrazzo-lined walls and floors and stainless steel troughs and gutters. Here were taps and coloured chutes and pipes on the walls, discreet extractor vents purring in appreciation of the comfort and cleanliness. Here were thermostats and constant temperature and sprinklers and automatic floor scrubbers. There were recognizable pens along one side of the shed, separated behind a waist-high wall. And in these pens, lying on what appeared to be soft mattresses were some very svelte and contented looking pigs.

Margery went up to one of the pens and lowered the piglet she was carrying over the wall. It tottered slightly then ran over to a large Large White sow that was reclining in the corner and began immediately and with disconcerting vigour to attack one of the row of teats that hung like a fringe from the sow's underside. Margery watched the sow's expression and, satisfied that the prodigal was being accepted without murmur, turned her attention to the next pen. Here, raised above floor level in the corner of the pen was what could only be described as a crib. It was in green plastic and had an incubator dome folded back, but inside there were blue cot sheets and blankets tucked around, unmistakably, a small baby. A human baby. Its ears were slightly pointed and its nose was perhaps a little puckish – or that might have been imagination. It could not have been more than a few weeks old: it still had the closed-up tiny remoteness of the new-born, the far-away semi-smile in sleep that suggests a clinging memory of amniotic fluid, cocoons, safety, warmth and deep unconsciousness of light, air and space. In the other corner of the pen a squealing riot of piglets was tumbling over another large sow's belly like maggots over a dead dog.

Margery reached down and pressed a large green button on the outside wall of the pen. It set off a sound like a buzzsaw ripping through wood and its effect on the raucous jostling mob of piglets was instantaneous; they stopped suckling and fighting to suckle and dashed for a small opening at the back of the pen that seemed to lead through into a further quarter of some sort. As soon as they were all gone, Margery stooped down again, gingerly resting one hand on a slightly arthritic knee, and pressed the green button for a second time. A stainless steel shutter came down over the opening through which the piglet rabble had departed and their squeals were silenced. Margery proceeded to open the door of the pen and step inside. The large Large White sow watched her but did not move. Bending down over the crib, Margery reached in and carefully pulled back the covers from the infant.

'There, there,' she said in her most comforting tones, as she had spoken to the piglet earlier when crushing the ear of wheat in the field. 'Let's see if you're a little bit hungry now.'

She lifted the baby up – it was dressed in a short white

gown: it was a boy – and clutching it to her chest moved over to the sow and kneeled on the edge of the mattress. The sow continued to look supremely unconcerned, even as Margery lowered the child onto one of the recently vacated dugs and held it firmly but gently as it latched on and began to suck for all it was worth. The sow turned her head to look, then lay down flat and closed her eyes. It was the odd one of the litter, she thought, the one with different legs and face, the one that the human sow kept separate for some reason. It was the gentle one, the one that sucked slowly without fighting and had to be helped away again.

Graham soon realized that he had a puncture. He got out and surveyed the damage. One flat tyre, squashed by the weight of the car. He looked up the track towards the farmhouse and then looked back at the car. He felt undecided for a moment about whether he should be trying to mend the tyre now or come back later when things would be clearer. His brain circled the problem a few times but could find no way in. He decided to simply walk away from it. Here he was, virtually on the doorstep of his quest for his biological origin. It was really a case of going on regardless. He went to the boot of the car and took out a small suitcase. As he closed the boot he looked wistfully towards the farmhouse and saw the figure who had been standing in the field go through a gate into the farmyard. It was clearly Margery. A man was holding the gate for her. It was Joe. Even at this distance you could see that he had large brawny forearms. As indeed did Margery.

He hadn't dared to tell them he was coming. He felt too guilty about the years of voyaging, the lack of postcards, the underlying sense of fear and strangeness that arose in his mind when his memory confronted early childhood recollections. He had read that it was quite common for children who grew up on farms to suffer traumas occasioned by the close proximity of large animals. He hadn't been sure, but eventually had found it hard to resist the suggestion that he was repressing or running away from some ... some problem in his past. Something that gave rise to the difficulties he was having in hanging on to ... on to his ... his personality.

As he knelt down, looking wistfully towards the farmhouse, Graham was struck by a feeling of *déjà vu* so strong he became dizzy. He listened for a moment to the far off sounds of traffic, the coo-cooing of wood pigeons, the hum of bees, the passing of the breeze, the distant squeals of pigs and it seemed to him that he had been here before. Not just this place, but this moment. That tree, that farmhouse, those hedges, this track, the very air and smells, all seemed to be matching with some imprint of memory he was carrying, had carried, inside him since before the age of reason. They were calling to him, calling him home. He felt a strange desire to fall to the ground and roll over and over; he visualized himself doing it for several moments before restoring his ... his equilibrium. When he looked again, the two figures by the farmyard gate had disappeared.

As you get older you begin to resemble your own past. The imprinting is strong but latent; you overlay it with new experience and believe that you are forging new pathways. Then you discover that you have been selecting the experience so that it enables you to recreate yourself in the image of your own ancestry. It is like a voyage westwards through the wide world which takes you further and further from home but returns eventually from the east and tumbles over the point from which it started.

Margery knelt down and removed the baby from the dugs. She winded him gently and then lay him against her shoulder. He began to cry for a moment but had stopped by the time Margery had reached the door. Outside again, in the farmyard, she called to Joe, who was standing with a hosepipe sluicing mud off his boots before going into the house.

'Better check there's no loose papers in the office,' said Margery. 'I'll bring the baby things from the special unit and put the little one into the nursery.'

Margery was a good mother. It was a shame it was illegal. There really was no harm in it, she was sure. Satisfied customers by the dozen provided testimonials which formed the backbone of her clandestine and sparingly distributed promotional literature.

Dear Mrs Muttock, I can honestly say that the treatment I received from your husband and you was the most considerate and humane it could possibly have been. I don't mind saying that my husband and I went through a pretty sticky patch when we found out I couldn't conceive my own but finding you really saved our bacon. – Mrs B., Rotherham, South Yorkshire.

Dear Mr and Mrs Muttock, Thank you once again for all you have done for my husband and me. From the sensitive way you took my husband's 'contribution' to the sturdy little girl you passed over last month, your kindness and self-sacrifice have been worth every penny. Best wishes, Mr and Mrs T., Falkirk.

It didn't take long to ensure that there was nothing incriminating in view. Margery and Joe, despite the defensive systems on the track, were careful to keep the special operations tightly controlled. When potential clients called they were shown the farmhouse nursery, of course, but it had to look new each time; it wouldn't do to give the impression of a production line. The nursery was Graham's old bedroom at the front of the house, overlooking the ornamental garden. It had been redecorated with wallpaper depicting the tale of the three little pigs. Joe had thought it was amusing. There was a mobile too, hanging above the bed, which consisted of a set of little pink plastic piglets hanging from nylon filaments. One had 'For Market' written on its back and was wearing a chef's hat, another was wearing slippers and a cardigan, a third was sitting upright with a knife and fork in its trotters, licking its lips at a joint of meat set before it on a small plastic tray. A fourth piglet was unencumbered and a fifth was apparently rubbing tears from its eyes, while a cleverly moulded extrusion attached to its foot carried a signpost pointing to 'Home.'

Margery returned to the kitchen from tidying up the special unit. She had the sleeping baby in her arms. Joe said the office was OK and they both looked around and then at each other, wondering whether they had forgotten anything. Margery went upstairs to lay the baby down in its own cot. As she came out of the room, she smoothed her apron, thinking to herself how unfair life was. But no time for that. She would have to think of an explanation for the baby that would satisfy Graham.

Downstairs again, Joe said, 'I think we're clear on the ground. What are we going to say about the baby?'

'We tell him the truth.'

'How much truth can he take?'

'I don't know. Let's see how he reacts. I think he knows anyway. I feel it.'

'What about the Joneses?'

'They won't take long.'

The Joneses were the latest in an increasingly long list of clients who had discovered the Muttock Surrogacy Service and signed up for Margery to do their childbearing for them. She was after all a strapping country farmer's wife, with broad hips and a constitution like oak. For over four years, a succession of unfortunate or unscrupulous childless couples had found their way to the remote farmhouse to discover how parenthood could be purchased with few questions asked. Margery believed in the service she was offering. She thought of it as little more than an extension of wet-nursing and there were plenty of mythological and Biblical precedents, after all, after a fashion. She would have defended long and hard the rights of those mothers who were medically incapacitated from bearing their own offspring. She was less sympathetic to those whose inability appeared to stem from a reluctance to jeopardize or interrupt their careers or their social lives. They wanted a baby simply because their lifestyle seemed to lack something without one. It was a form of keeping up with the ... the Joneses. Some of these had even returned to collect their babies with a nanny already in attendance. One memorable couple had left with the nanny in the back seat of their car, supervising the baby in a carrycot, while they bickered in the front about who was going to drive.

In such situations Margery was sorely tempted to reveal that she was not doing the actual uterine development phase personally. But for the sake of the genuine hardship cases as much as because even simple human surrogacy was still seriously illegal, she kept the true nature of the service to herself. The Muttock Variation of surrogacy was so far beyond illegal that it was probably still considered unthinkable, if not impossible. Having adapted well established AI techniques (artificial insemination, that is, not artificial intelligence), Margery and Joe had secretly branched out into second generation surrogacy with the help of a very carefully selected squad of pigs. Margery's own infertility had been the catalyst: but they had stumbled over the precise technique by a combination of chance, Joe's natural ingenuity and detailed study of the lifestyle of several parasites, including cuckoos. Having made the discovery and kept the secret, they had decided to capitalize upon it. Conventional farming was extremely hard work, after all.

*   *   *

As Joe was asking his question about the Joneses, they were turning off the lane, over the cattle grid and onto the track. They were very excited at the prospect of their baby's delivery. Mrs Jones, a woman of 35 with blocked Fallopian tubes, held a small handkerchief in her tightly clenched fist and struggled silently towards an outward air of calm control. She tried to moderate her breathing patterns and visualize something reassuring. Mr Jones was concentrating on avoiding potholes. When he was on a clear stretch he gave her hand a little squeeze. He saw a small white car stopped in the middle of the track some way ahead but thought nothing of it and pressed on. There was sufficient verge to get past.

As Graham walked towards the farmhouse, he was unaware of the car behind him. His attention was focused forwards and it required some effort of will to keep going. He remembered the bricks, the angle of the chimney pots, the missing spar from the garden gate, the detailed topography of the ruts and cobbles in the track as it approached the farmyard. Looking forwards, he saw himself as a . . . as a toddler, playing with buckets at the rainwater trough, picking clover, trying to climb the apple trees. Further forwards, even younger, he saw himself in the farmhouse kitchen, enveloped in the warm smell of compost and fresh washing. He was tottering from his highchair to the table leg to the hem of Margery's skirt as she stood at the sink peeling potatoes. He saw himself going to the slops bucket, attracted by its sicklysweet aroma, and start pulling out potato peelings and other mixed scrapings. He put some of them to his mouth and was considering their savoury appeal when Margery spotted him and swept him up into her arms, saying, 'No, no, little boy. That's the pig's bucket, that is . . . You're in here with us now.'

Then she put him down again quickly and turned back to the sink. Graham replayed the scene in his mind. That was it. That scene had been there in his memory all this time but he had never until now been conscious of it. Those had been her words: 'You're in here with us . . . now.'

'. . . But words can never hurt me.' That was it too. Things were falling into place. Graham remembered the complete saying. 'Sticks and stones may break my bones . . .' It wasn't true, of course. Sayings so rarely were.

She had put him down and turned away just ever so slightly too quickly. Just ever so slightly like someone who has said something they ought not to have said and who wishes Time to speed up so that whatever it was can more quickly be forgotten. At the time Graham had been perhaps thirteen or fourteen months old.

Approaching the farmhouse, Graham realized he did not have the strength to confront his . . . to confront Margery and Joe directly. He decided suddenly to go round to the back gate of the farmyard and have a look in the pigsheds before he went in. Some chickens scattered as he cut through behind the shed where the old combine harvester rested but there was greater peace here on the flanks. Too predictable to stay on the track: that's what all the cars and people did. He pressed on behind the old haybarn, the redtiled roof of which was gaping pitiably as though bomb-damaged. The back door to the pigshed was rarely used. Graham had to lift it in its hinges to overcome the tussocky grass outside. He could hear muffled squealing from within and a sound that could have been the low hum of a motor or could have been the wind. It was dark inside and his eyes needed a few minutes to adjust. It seemed stuffy too, oppressive, airless, thick with warm smells he remembered too well. Graham took his jacket off and threw it on a trestle. The straw underfoot felt nice: he scuffled it with his feet. More squealing from the other side of an old wooden partition. Graham felt his heart begin to thump like a dog's tail on a drum. He loosened his shirt and kicked off his shoes.

* * *

Margery and Joe stiffened as the bell rang for attention. They knew Graham wouldn't ring. Where had he gone? Margery said, 'I'll go' and went outside to the gate.

'Sorry about the notice,' she said, greeting Mr and Mrs Jones like paying guests on a return visit, a relationship that was warm, hospitable and yet underneath still commercial. 'You wouldn't believe the crime we get in the country.'

Margery led the nervous couple round to the farmhouse door. Mrs Jones still had her handkerchief in her hand; she was glad to be moving at last. Later, Mr and Mrs Jones would have extreme difficulty recollecting the precise details of the baby's arrival. Their arrival, that is. Margery had ushered them straight upstairs to the nursery. She had gone first with Mrs Jones; Joe and Mr Jones had followed behind. As they came up the stairs, Mr Jones, just to make conversation, had asked, 'What sort of farming do you do, Mr Muttock?' Joe noticed Margery ahead of him hesitate slightly in her tread. But he knew the best reply. 'Pigs, mostly,' he said.

In the nursery, the new parents looked into the cot and saw at first nothing but a powder blue bump in the cot-sheets. Mr Jones leaned over, brushing the piglet mobile with his head as he did so, setting off the built-in musical box. It played Rock-a-bye-baby as he peered in and announced, 'Look, I can see its head!'

'His head,' corrected Mrs Jones, grasping her husband by the elbow, as if she and he were both about to tumble headlong into the cot. 'Oh, isn't he adorable!'

Oblivious as they were to what was going on around them, Mr and Mrs Jones were easy meat to be steered back downstairs and into the yard. Margery had mumbled something about it being best for the new mother to take over as quickly as possible, that it was best for she and Joe to remain shadowy figures in their past. Joe had his arms folded across his chest and was looking friendly but saying nothing. It was close as he could come to being like a shadow.

Unfortunately, as they emerged into the yard, Graham also appeared from the direction of the pigshed. He had nothing on his feet and his shirt was open to the waist. His hair had strands of straw matted in it and he seemed to have streaks of something that could have been Marmite but probably wasn't across his cheeks. Despite all this he was smiling broadly. Under his right arm, he held a small pink piglet. Mrs Jones stopped, overcome with a mixture of fear and politeness. She held her powder-blue bundle closer to her but smiled in return. Mr Jones smiled too and said, 'Er, hello.'

Then Mr and Mrs Jones both looked at Margery, who for a moment was simply agape. Composing herself, she managed, 'This is my . . . my son Graham.' A pause. 'He's a journalist.'

There was another long pause, while all those present grappled with the incongruous symmetry of the scene. Margery began to have doubts about the significance of Graham's broad smile. Joe began to wonder what had been happening in the pigshed. Eventually, Mrs Jones, felt it incumbent on her to attempt a polite enquiry.

'Er . . . and what is it you write about, Mr Muttock?'

It seemed to Margery that Graham gave an inordinately long look directly at the blue-wrapped infant before he responded. But he knew the right reply.

'Pigs, mostly,' he said.

THE TOURIST

Paul Park

whole classical era barely exists anymore. First-century Palestine is like a cultural ground zero: nothing but taxi cabs and soft-drink stands, and confused and frightened people. Thousands attend the Crucifixion every day, and the garden at Gethsemane is a mad-house at all hours. My ex-inlaws were there and they sent me a photograph, taken with a flash. It shows a panicked, harried, sad young man. (Yes, he's blond and blue-eyed, as it turns out, raising questions as to whether the past can actually be altered in retrospect by the force of popular misconception.) But at least he's out in the open. Pontius Pilate, Caiphas, and the entire family of Herod the Great are in hiding, yet still hardly a week goes by that Interpol doesn't manage to deport some new revisionist. It's amazing how difficult people find it to accept the scientific fact – that nothing they do will ever make a difference, that cause and effect, as explicative principles, are as dead as Malcolm X.

Naturally they are confused by their ability to cause short-term mayhem, and just as naturally they are seeking an outlet for their own frustrations: Adolf Hitler, for example, has survived attempts on his life every fifteen minutes between 1933 and 1945, and people are still lining up to take potshots even since the Nazis closed the border to everyone but a small group of Libyan consultants – now stormtroopers are racing back in time, hoping to provide 24-hour security to all the Fuehrer's distant ancestors. Who wants to explain to that crowd how history works? Joseph Stalin – it's the same. Recently some Lithuanian fanatic managed to break through UN security to confront him at his desk. 'Please,' he says, 'don't kill me.' (They all speak a little English now.) 'I am a democrat,' he says – 'I change my mind.' These days it requires diplomatic pressure just to get people to do what they're supposed to. It is only by promising the Confederate government $10,000,000 in new loans that the World Bank can persuade Lee to attack at Gettysburg at all – 'I have a real bad feeling about this,' he says over and over. 'I love my boys,' he says. 'Please don't make me do it.' Who can blame him? He has a book of Matthew Brady's photographs on his desk.

And in fact, why should he be persuaded? What difference does it make? People hold onto these arbitrary rules, these arbitrary patterns, out of fear. Not even all historians are able to concede the latest proofs – confirmations of everything they feared and half-suspected when they were in graduate school – that events in the past have no discernible effect upon the present. That time is not after all a continuum. That the past is like a booster rocket, constantly dropping away. Afterward, it's disposable. Except for the most recent meeting of the AHA (Vienna, 1815 – Prince Metternich the keynote speaker, and a drunken lecher, by all reports), American historians now rarely go abroad except as tourists. They are both depressed and liberated to find that their work has no practical application.

That's not completely true. It certainly changed things, for example, when people found out that the entire known opus of Rembrandt van Rijn consisted of forgeries. But that's a matter of money; it's business contacts that people want anyway, not understanding. So everywhere you go back then are phalanxes of oilmen, diplomats, arms dealers, art collectors, and teachers of English as a second language. Citibank recently pre-empted slave gangs working on the pyramid of Cheops, to help complete their Giza offices. The World Wildlife Fund has projects (Save the

Trilobites, etc.) into the Precambrian era – projects doomed to failure by their very nature.

Of course the news is not all bad: world profiles for literacy and public health have been transformed. In 1349 the International Red Cross has 700 volunteers in Northern Italy alone. And the Peace Corps, my God, they're everywhere. But nevertheless I thought I could discern a trend, that all the world and all of history would one day share the same dismal denominator. Alone in my house on Washon Island, which I'd kept after Suzanne and I broke up, I saw every reason to stay put. I am a cautious person by nature.

But that summer I was too much by myself. And so I took advantage of a special offer; there had been some terrorist attacks on Americans in Tenochtitlan, and fares were down as a result. I bought a ticket for Palaeolithic Spain. Far enough away for me to think that things might be different there. I thought there might be out-of-the-way places still. Places pure and untouched and malleable, where I could make things different. Where my imagination might still correspond in some sense to reality – I might have known. My ex-inlaws had sent me postcards. They had recently been on a mastodon safari not far from Jaca, where they had visited Suzanne. 'The food is great,' they wrote me – never a good sign.

I might have known I was making a mistake. There is something about the past which makes what we've done to it even more poignant. All the brochures and the guidebooks say it and it's true. It really is more beautiful back then. The senses come alive. Colours are brighter. Chairs are more comfortable. Things smell better, taste better. People are friendlier, or at least they were. Safe in the future, you can still feel so much potential. Yet the town I landed in – my God, it was such a sad place. San Juan de la Cruz. We came in over the Pyrenees, turned low over a lush forest, and then settled down in an enormous empty field of tarmac. The hangar space was as big as Heathrow's, but there was only one other commercial jetliner – a KLM. Everything else was US military aircraft and not even much of that, just five beige transports in a line, and a single helicopter gunship.

We taxied in toward His Excellency the Honourable Dr Wynstan Mog (PhD) International Airport, still only half built and already crumbling, from the look of it. For no perceptible reason the pilot offloaded us about 200 yards from the terminal, and then we had to stand around on the melting asphalt while the stewardesses argued with some men in uniform. I didn't mind. The sky was cobalt blue. It was hot, but there were astonishing smells blown out of the forest toward us, smells which I couldn't identify, and which mixed with the tar and the gasoline and my own sweat and the noise of the engines into a sensation that seemed to nudge at the edges of my memory, as if it almost meant something, just in itself. But what? I had been born in Bellingham; this was nothing I recognized. It was nothing from my past. I put my head back and closed my eyes, dangerously patient, while all around me my nineteen fellow passengers buzzed and twittered. And I thought, this is nothing. This feeling is nothing. Everybody feels this way.

The men in uniform collected our passports and then they marched us toward the terminal. They were not native to the time and place; they were big, fat men. I knew Dr Mog had hired mercenaries from all over – these ones looked Lebanese or Israeli. They wore sunglasses and carried machine pistols. They hustled us through the doors and into the VIP lounge, an enormous air-conditioned room with plastic furniture and a single plate-glass window that took up one whole wall. It appeared to lead directly onto the street in front of the terminal. Certainly there was a crowd out there, perhaps 150 people of all races and nationalities, and they were staring in at us, their faces pressed against the glass.

One of the uniformed men moved to a corner of the window. A cord hung from the ceiling; he pulled down on it, and a dirty brown curtain inched from left to right across the glass wall. It made no difference to the people outside, and even when the curtain was closed I was still aware of their presence, their sad stares. If anything I was more aware. I sat down in one of the moulded chairs with my back to the curtain, and watched some customs officials explain two separate hoaxes, both fairly straightforward.

There was a desk at the back of the room and they had spread our passports onto it. They were waiting for our luggage, and in the meantime they checked our visas and especially our certificates of health. I was prepared for this. The region is suffering from a high rate of AIDS infection – almost 25% of the population in San Juan de la Cruz has tested HIV positive. The government seems unconcerned, but they have required that all tourists be inoculated with the so-called AIDS vaccine, a figment in the imagination of some medical conmen in Zaire, and unavailable in the US. Nevertheless it is now mandatory for travel in large parts of the third world, as a way of extorting hard currency. I work in a hospital research lab and I had the stamp; so, apparently, had someone else in our group, a thin man my own age, deeply tanned. His name was Paul. Together we watched the others gather around the desk, and watched them as they came to understand their choice – to pay a fine of $150 per person, or to be inoculated right there on the premises with the filthiest syringe I'd ever seen. It was a good piece of theatre; one of the officials left to 'wash his hands,' and came back in a white smock with blood on it – you had to smile. At the same time one of the others was handing out bank booklets and explaining how to change money: all tourists were required to exchange $50 a week at the State Bank, for which they received a supposedly equivalent amount of the national currency – three eoliths, a bone needle, six arrowheads and two chunks of rock salt. An intrinsic value of about 40 cents, total – this in a country where in any case dollars and Deutschmarks are the only money that anyone accepts.

Paul and I lined up to buy our currency packs, which came in a convenient leather pouch. 'It's ridiculous,' he said. 'Before time travel they didn't even have domesticated animals. They lived in caves. What were they going to buy?'

He had been working in the country for about five years, and was knowledgeable about it. At first I liked him because he still seemed fresh in some ways, his moral outrage tempered with humour and a begrudging admiration for Dr Mog. 'He's not a fool,' he said. 'His PhD is a real one: political economy from the University of Colombo – the correspondence branch, of course, but his dissertation was published. An amazing accomplishment when you consider his background. And he's just about the only one of these dictators who's not a foreign puppet or an adventurer – he's a genuine Cro-Magnon, native to the area, and he's managed to stay in power despite some horrendous CIA intrigues, and get very rich in the process.'

Someone wheeled in a trolley with our luggage on it. The customs men spread out the suitcases on a long table. Paul and I were done early; we both had packed light, and were carrying no modern gadgets. The others, most of whom were with a tour group going to Altamira, stood around in abject silence while the officials went through everything, arbitrarily confiscating cameras, hairdryers, CD players on a variety of pretexts. 'This is a waste of our electrical resources,' admonished one, holding up a Norelco.

But by that time Paul and I had been given permission to leave. We had to wait in line outside the lounge to get our visas stamped, and then we made our way through the chaotic lobby. I allowed Paul to guide me, ignoring as he did the many people who accosted us and tugged upon our arms. He seemed familiar with the place, happy or at least amused to be there. Outside in the heat, he stopped to give a quarter to a beggar he appeared to recognize, and conversed with him while I looked around. I was going to get a taxi and find a hotel and stay there for a night or so before going on into the interior. I haven't travelled very much, and I was worried about choosing a taxi man from the horde that surrounded us, worried about being over-charged, taken advantage of. I put on my sunglasses, waiting for Paul, and I was relieved to find when he was finished that he expected me to follow him. 'I'll take you to the Aladeph,' he said. 'We'll get some breakfast there.'

He was scanning the crowd for someone specific, and soon a little man broke through, Chinese or Korean or Japanese – 'Mr Paul,' he said. 'This way, Mr Paul.' Then he was tugging at our bags and I, untrusting, wasn't letting go until I saw Paul surrender his own daypack. We walked over to a battered green Toyota. Rock and roll was blaring from the crummy speakers. The sun was powerful. 'We've got to get you a hat,' said Paul.

A long straight road led into town, flanked on both sides by lines of identical one-storey concrete buildings: commercial establishments selling hubcaps and used tyres, as well as piles of more anonymous metal junk. Men sat in the sandy forecourts, smoking cigarettes and talking; there were a lot of people, a lot of people in the streets as we passed an enormous statue of Dr Mog, the Father of the Nation with his arms outstretched – a gift from the Chinese government. We drove through Martyr's Gate into a neighbourhood of concrete hovels, separated from the narrow streets by drainage ditches full of sewage. People everywhere, but not one of them looked native to the time – the men wore ragged polyester shirts and pants, the women faded housedresses. Most were barefoot, some wore plastic shoes.

We passed the Catholic Cathedral, as well as numerous smaller churches of various denominations: Mormon, Seventh Day Adventist and Jehovah's Witness. We passed the headquarters of several international relief organizations, and then I must have dozed off momentarily, for when I opened my eyes we were in a different kind of neighbourhood entirely, a neighbourhood of sleek high-rises and villas covered with flowering vines.

The cab pulled up in front of a Belgian restaurant called Pepe le Moko, and we got out. Paul paid the driver before I could get my money, and then waved away the bills I offered him; he had said nothing during the ride, but had sat staring out the window with an expression half rueful and half amused. Now he smiled more broadly and motioned me inside the restaurant – it was an expensive place, full of white people in short-sleeved shirts and ties.

'I thought we'd get some breakfast,' he said.

We ordered French toast and coffee, which came almost immediately. I spooned some artificial creamer into mine and offered the jar to him, but he wrinkled his nose. 'I'm sure it's all right,' he said.

'What do you mean?'

He shrugged. 'You know the United States government pays for its projects here by shipping them some of our agricultural surplus. It's a terrible idea, because it makes the population dependent on staples that can't be grown locally; at any rate, Dr Mog sells it, and then uses the money, supposedly, to finance USAID, and famine relief, whatever. Well, my first year there was a shipment of a thousand tons of wheat, which they packed in the same container as a load of PCVs, which was being sent to some plastics factory. When it got here, the customs people claimed the wheat was contaminated and couldn't be sold.

They sequestered it in warehouses while the US sent a scientist who said it was okay. But as they argued back and forth, the wheat was sold anyway. And then the raw PCVs began to show up also here in San Juan, in some of the poorer restaurants. It's a white powder, it's soluble in water, and it's got a kind of chalky, milky taste, apparently.'

'Thanks for telling me,' I said.

'That's okay. It was a shambles. The Minister of Health was fired, before he came back last year as the Minister for Armaments. Somebody got rich. So what's a blip in the leukaemia statistics?'

He smiled. 'That's horrible,' I said.

'Yeah, well, it's not all bad. And what do you expect? It's got to be like that. People don't understand – they think it's every country's right to be modern and industrialized. Mog's been to college; he knows what's what. You and I might say, well, they're better off living in caves, chipping flint and hitting each other with bones, but who the fuck are we? Mog, he wants an army. He wants telephones. He wants roads, cars, electricity. Who can blame him? But if you can't make that stuff yourself, you've got to get it from the white man. And the thing about the white man, he doesn't offer you that shit for free.'

Paul was looking pretty white himself. 'What do you do?' I asked.

'I work for Continental Grain. We've got a project in the bush. Near Jaca.'

I looked down into my coffee cup. 'Do you know Suzanne Denier?' I asked.

'Yeah, sure. She works for an astronomy project in my area. Near the reservation there.'

I closed my eyes and opened them. I asked myself: Had she been to this restaurant? Where did she sit? Did she know the story about the powdered milk?

'She's with the Cro-Magnon,' I said. 'Is that the only

place they live? On reservations? I haven't seen a single one since we've been here.'

'You'll see one. In San Juan they're all registered. It's one of Mog's new laws. You can't kick them out of business establishments, and all the restaurants have to give them food and liquor. So they're around here begging all the time. You'll see.'

In fact, shortly after that, one did come in. She stood in the doorway and watched us as we ate our toast. She was almost six feet tall, with delicate bones, a beautiful face, and long, graceful hands. She had no hair on her head. She had green eyes and black skin. At ten o'clock in the morning she was very drunk.

After breakfast I spent most of the day with Paul. We had lunch at the Intercontinental and then went swimming at the Portuguese Club. Soon I began to find him patronizing.

In those days I was sensitive and easily annoyed. Nevertheless I stayed with him, my resentment rising all the time. I allowed him to get me a room, as he had mentioned, at the Aladeph – a guesthouse reserved for people on official business. I think it amused him to demonstrate that he could place me there, that he could manipulate the bureaucracy, which was formidable. I was grateful, in a way. Jet-lagged, I went to bed early, but I couldn't sleep until a few hours before dawn.

'Suzanne,' I said when I woke up. I said it out loud. I lay in bed with my throat dry, my skin wet. At six o'clock in the morning it was already hot. White gauze curtains moved in the hot breeze.

I lay in bed thinking about Suzanne. I thought of how when she was leaving I had not even asked her to stay.

It's not as if our marriage wasn't difficult, wasn't unsatisfying, and I remember my cold anger as I listened to her reasons why she should take a job so far from home. Later she had written and told me that even then, if I had just said something, anything, she would have stayed with me. Lying in bed at the Aladeph, I remembered her walking back and forth next to the dark long living-room window of the island house while I sat in the chair, half watching her, half reading. I remembered how her face changed as she made up her mind. I saw it happen, and I did nothing.

Lying in bed, remembering, I made myself get up and take her by the shoulders. I made myself apologize and made her listen. 'Don't go,' I said. 'I love you,' I said, and with just those three words I saw myself creating a new future for us both.

But of course we know nothing about the future, though we must push into it every day. We are frightened to look at it, and so we spend our lives looking backward, remoulding over and over again what we should leave alone, breaking it, changing it, dragging it forward through time.

Lying in bed, I thought: these things are past. They don't have anything to do with you now. I knew it, but I didn't believe it. Why else was I there? Because I imagined we could go back together to some pure and unadulterated time. I thought maybe if I could just get back about 30,000 years before I made all those mistakes . . .

That day I went down to the Mercado de Ladrones, and I took a ride on a truck out toward Pamplona.

Every year the United States donates large sums for road development in that part of the world, and every year the money is stolen by Dr Mog and his associates, though the streets around the US embassy in San Juan are obsessively repaved every few months. But in the interior the roads are horrible even in the dry season, which this mercifully was – rutted tracks of red mud through the jungle, and it took ten hours to go 200 miles. But before we even got out of the city we passed sixteen army checkpoints where soldiers extorted money from passing motorists; I found out later that none of them had been paid for over a year.

They took pleasure in intimidating me – fat, dark, sweating men with automatic rifles, and they made insulting comments in Spanish and Arabic as they searched the back of the truck where I was sitting on some lumpy burlap sacks. A green Mercedes-Benz had overturned into a garbage ditch, and the traffic was backed up for half a mile along a street of corrugated iron shacks. A stack of tyres burned in a vacant lot, and the smoke from it hurt my eyes and mixed with the exhaust fumes and the polluted air into a hot blend of gases that was scarcely breathable.

A little boy ran in and out between the trucks, and he sold me two pineapples and a piece of sugar cane. He was smiling and chattering in a language I didn't recognize; he charged me a dime, and he flicked the coin into the air and caught it behind his back. It was a hopeful gesture, and soon the truck started to move again, and soon we passed beyond the ring road into a clear-cut waste of shantytowns and landfills, and then into the jungle. I gnawed on my sugar cane and licked the pineapple juice off my fingers, and I was rehearsing all the things that I was going to tell Suzanne, rehearsing her replies – it was like trying to memorize the chess openings in a book. And because my opponent was a strong one, my only advantage, I thought, lay in preparation and surprise.

I went over conversations in my mind until the words started to lose their significance, and then the sun came out. When I looked up, the air was fresh and clean. Yellow birds hung in the trees beside the road, making nests of plaited straw. Occasionally an animal would blunder out the bushes as the truck went past. I sat looking backward, and saw a couple of wild pigs and a big rodent.

We stopped at some villages, and three people joined me in the bed of the truck: two men with jerry-cans and a gap-toothed woman, who smiled and held up her own length of sugar cane. Her yellow hair was tied back with a piece of string.

We were coming up out of the plain into the mountains, and toward sunset we passed the gates to the Krieger-Richardson Observatory. I got out, and the truck barrelled away. The air was cooler, drier here, and the vegetation had changed. The trees were lower, and they no longer presented an impermeable wall. I walked through them over the dry grass. A one-lane asphalt road came down out of the hills, and I walked up it with my bag, meeting no one, seeing no one. Suzanne had described the place in one of her letters, and it was interesting to see it now myself for the first and last time – the road climbed sharply for a mile or so until the trees gave out, and I came up over the crest and stood overlooking a wide volcanic bowl. Antennae rose out of it: this was the radio telescope, and beyond it on the summit of Madre de la Nacion rose the dome of the observatory.

Then the road sank down a bit until the telescope was out of sight. There were pine trees here, and a parking lot full of identical white cars, and beyond that a low dormitory among the rhododendron bushes. Light came from the windows, a comforting glow, for I was tired and hungry.

I came up the concrete steps and knocked on the door. It was locked, but after a minute or so somebody opened it, a teenage girl in a Chicago Bulls sweatshirt. 'Excuse me,' I said. 'I'm looking for Dr Suzanne Denier. Does she live here?'

She stared at me for a while, and then shrugged, and then peered past me at the sky. 'She's at work tonight. It's supposed to be clear after nine o'clock.'

'But she lives here?'

'She came back from Soria on Wednesday. We've had terrible weather for the past two weeks.'

She opened the door and stood aside, and I came into a corridor with brown carpeting. 'Who are you?' she said.

'Her husband.'

She stood staring at me, measuring me up, and I tried to decipher her expression. Lukewarm. Interested, so perhaps she had heard something. 'Do you have a name?' A wise-ass – she was half my age.

'Christopher,' I said.

'I'm Joan. Does she know you're coming? We don't get too many personal visitors, so I thought . . .'

'It's a surprise.'

She stared at me for a little bit with her head cocked to one side. Finally: 'Well, come in. We're just finishing dinner. Have you eaten?'

'Please,' I said, 'could I see Suzanne? Where is she?'

I waited in the corridor while Joan went back to check. I looked at the travel posters on the wall: the Taj Mahal. Malibu beach. Krieger-Richardson with a flock of birds passing over the dome. Some health statistics and some graphs. Then another, older, woman came back whom I recognized from a group photograph Suzanne had sent me. 'You're Christopher,' she said.

Her name was Anise Wilcox. She drove me out to the observatory, a twenty-minute ride up along the ridge of the mountain. We spoke little. 'The phones are down,' she said, and I didn't know whether she was giving me the chance to say that I had tried to call and failed, or whether she was telling me that she had not been able to inform Suzanne that I was here.

'Wait,' she said. We stopped in the parking lot in front of the observatory, and she slipped out of the driver's seat and ran up to the door. I sat alone in the twilight listening to the engine cool; I rolled down my window and looked out at the unlit bulk of the dome against the sky. An insect settled on my arm, a tiny delicate moth unlike any I had ever seen.

Then Dr Wilcox was there again, standing by the car. 'Come in,' she said, and I got out and followed her. She opened the metal door for me. There was a dim light inside next to an elevator, and I turned back and saw her face. She seemed nervous; she wouldn't look me in the eyes. She closed the door and locked it, and then she moved past me to the elevator. It was not until we stood next to each other inside the elevator car that she glanced up and gave me a worried smile.

'Good luck,' she said when we reached the third floor.

Inside the observatory all the rooms were cramped and small until I pushed through those final doors and stood under the dome. The air was cold. And it was dark underneath the enormous y-shaped column of the telescope; I stood looking up at it, until I heard a movement behind me, off to my right. Suzanne was there at the top of a wide shallow flight of stairs, maybe five steps high. She looked professional in a black turtleneck sweater and black denim overalls, with two pens in her breast pocket. She was carrying a mechanical notebook under one arm.

'Chris,' she said, and she came forward to the edge of the top step. Light came from the windows of the observation room. Computer screens glowed there.

I could feel her anger just in that one word. It radiated out from her small body. But I was prepared for it. I have my own way of protecting myself. I had not seen her in ten months, and as I looked at her I thought first of all how plain she was with her pinched face, her scowl, her stubborn jaw. Her skin was sallow in that light, her black hair was unbrushed. A small-boned woman with bad posture, that's what I told myself, and I thought, what am I doing here? Oh, I deserve more than this.

Because she started in immediately: 'I can't believe you're here,' she said. 'I asked you not to come. No, I told you not to. I can't believe you could be so insensitive to my wishes after everything you've done.'

'Please,' I said, and she stopped, and I found I didn't have anything to say. Much as I had rehearsed this scene,

I had not anticipated that she would speak first, that I, not she, would have to react.

'Please,' I said. 'Just listen to me for a few minutes. I came a long way . . .'

She interrupted me. 'Do you think I'm supposed to be impressed by that? What am I supposed to do, fall into your arms now that you're here?'

'No, I certainly didn't expect . . .'

'Then what? Christopher, is it too much to ask that you leave me alone? I have a lot of things to sort out, and I want to do it by myself. I can't believe you're not sensitive to that. I can't believe you think you have the right to barge in here and disrupt my life and my work whenever you feel like it. Don't you have any respect for me at all?'

'Please,' I said. 'I knew you'd be like this, and I still risked it just to come. Is there any way that you could take a smaller risk and talk to me, instead of just yelling at me and closing me out?'

'Yelling? I'm not yelling. I'm telling you how I feel.' But then she was quiet, and I realized she was giving me a chance to speak.

'Suzanne,' I said, and I really tried to sound sincere, even though half of me was whispering to the other half that I couldn't win, that I had never won and never could, and that my best tactic was to run away. 'You sounded so distant in your letters and I couldn't stand it. I couldn't stand to feel you pull away from me and not do something. I love you. I'm more sorry than I can tell you about what happened, about what I did. I want to make it up to you. I want . . .'

It sounded weak even to me. She jumped on it: 'But what about what I want, Chris? Did you think about that at all? Did you think about that for one minute? Things are different now. How can I trust you when you can't even respect my wishes enough to leave me alone here to think about what I want? What's best for me. I needed time. I told you that.'

'It's been ten months. Ten months and thirty thousand years,' I said – a line that I'd prepared. She didn't think much of it. I saw her eyebrows come together, her eyes roll upward in an expression of irritation that I'd always hated. 'Suzanne,' I said, 'I know you. I know you could just seal yourself up here for the rest of your life. We had something precious, and it made us both happy for a long time. I can't just give it up.'

'But you did give it up. Sometimes I think you forget how this all started. You're right – we were very happy. So how could you do it, Chris? She was my friend.'

'No, she wasn't.'

'Oh, so it's her fault. I can't believe you. I still can't believe you. How could you hurt me like that? How could you humiliate me so publicly?'

'It wouldn't have been so public if you hadn't told everybody.'

'Oh, and I was supposed to just smile and take it? You hurt me, Chris. You have no idea.'

'Yes,' I said, 'I do. I'm sorry.'

She turned away for a moment, and stared into the glass of the observation window. I could see the reflection of her face there, and beyond it the flash of the computer screens. 'And that's supposed to make it all right. You don't understand. I've got some thinking to do. Chris, I don't want to be the kind of woman who just takes something like this. Who tolerates it. Who just hangs on year after year, hoping her man will change.'

You could never be that kind of woman, I thought. But I said nothing. 'You don't understand,' she said. 'I trusted you. I really trusted you. Chris, I'd given you my soul to keep, and you dropped it, and things changed. I changed. I know I'll never trust anyone like that again. What I don't know is, whether we can go on from here.'

You never trusted me, I thought. I stared at her, my mind a blank.

'Well,' she said finally. 'I've got to get to work. I'll tell Anise you can spend the night in my room. I'll be back a little after sunrise, and I'd appreciate it if you were gone. I'll tell Carlos to give you a ride back to San Juan.'

I looked up at the big telescope and shook my head. 'Aren't you going to give me a tour? You said in your letter you were close to something new.'

'Yes.' She came down the steps. And then things changed for a little while. Because we knew each other so well, even then we could slip down effortlessly and immediately into another way of being, a connection that seemed so intimate and strong that I had to keep reminding myself during the next hour that it was all gone, all ruined. She showed me her work, and I took such pleasure in seeing her face light up as she explained it.

She took me all over the observatory, up into the dome, into the camera room. Then back down again into her office, where we sat drinking coffee in the dim light, and she smoked cigarettes and showed me photographs of stars. 'We knew the galaxies were moving, because of the red shift. And we assumed that they were spreading apart, because it fit the theory. But of course we didn't know, because we could observe from one point only. But now of course we have two points thirty thousand years apart, and we thought that we could see it.'

She sucked the cigarette down to the filter and then ground it out. I sat looking at her face, reminded of how she used to come over to my apartment in the early morning, when she was working on her dissertation. She would wake me up to talk to me, and she would grind her cigarettes out in a teacup that I had, and I would force myself awake, just for the pleasure of looking at the concentration in her face, as she described some theory or some project.

'So?'

'What do you think? Our results have been extraordinary. The opposite of what everyone predicted.'

'So?'

She smiled. 'I don't know if I should tell you. I don't know if you deserve to know.'

'It sounds like it's important.'

'Sure. But I don't know. Anise would kill me if I told you.'

I looked up at the ceiling. Someone had pasted up a cluster of phosphorescent stars. 'Okay,' she said, 'so here it is. We think some galaxies are farther apart now than they are in the 20th century.'

For me at least, time had gone backward in that little room. Not because of what she said – I didn't care about it. I sat watching her face.

But I was afraid that she'd stop talking and I'd have to go. She'd bring us back up to the surface again. I said: 'And what's your explanation for that?'

She gave a shrug. 'It's complicated. Either our observations are mistaken, and we're about to make fools of ourselves. Or else maybe the universe is contracting. Or part of it is. Or else it fluctuates. I have my own theory.'

I said nothing, but sat watching her, and the moment stretched on until I smiled and she laughed. 'I'll tell you anyway. I think time goes the other direction from the way we imagine. I think that's why the past doesn't affect the present like we thought.'

Not like we thought. But it does have some effect. I looked at Suzanne, her beautiful and well-loved face. 'So why not forgive me?' I said.

She glanced up at me, a quick, sly look.

'We can make the past into the future,' I said.

She smiled, and then frowned, and then: 'Sure, that's what I'm afraid of. It's just a way of talking. It's not like when we're born we actually die.'

She ground out her cigarette butt. 'Seriously,' she said. 'But maybe time flows in two directions. One of them is the direction of our ordinary experience. Our personal sense of time. But maybe cosmological time flows back the other way. Maybe the conception of the universe happens in the future from our point of view.'

I thought about it. 'Why do you think we don't meet anybody from beyond our own time?' she said. 'From our own future? Certainly the technology would still exist.'

It took me a little while to understand her. Then I said: 'Perhaps they lost interest.'

'Forever? I don't buy it. No – maybe we're talking about two big bangs. One at the end of one kind of time, one at the beginning of the other. One manmade and one not.'

I considered this. Falling in love is one. And then breaking apart. I said: 'So you're telling me that there's no future and the past is all we have.'

Soon after, Dr Wilcox drove me back to the dormitory and gave me something to eat. She heated up some spaghetti Bolognese in the microwave. She didn't say much, except for one thing which proved to be prophetic: 'You must know she won't forgive you. She can't.'

She showed me back to Suzanne's room and left me there. It was a small bare cubicle with a window overlooking the parking lot. She had put some curtains up and that was all. There was nothing on the walls. I didn't take off my clothes. I lay down on her narrow, white bed; I lay on my back with my hands clasped under my neck, staring at the ceiling. From time to time I got up and turned on the light, I opened her bureau, and the smell from her shirts made me unhappy. She had a picture of me tucked into a corner of her mirror. I was smiling. Underneath, on the bureau top, stood a framed photograph of her parents, taken at their 40th anniversary. They were smiling too.

There was a package of my letters in a corner of the drawer, maybe 75 or 100 of them, wrapped in a rubber band.

I had spoken to Carlos and had plotted an itinerary for the rest of my vacation. He told me there were some beautiful beaches on the Mediterranean, which I could reach on a rail link from San Juan. I set the alarm clock for five-thirty and lay down on the bed and listened to it ticking on the bedside table. I imagined time passing over me, forward into an uncertain future, backward into a contented past. Perhaps the ebb and flow of it lulled me, because toward three o'clock I slid beneath the surface of a dream.

I dreamt that I woke up to find Suzanne sitting beside me. 'I wanted to show you something before you left,' she said. 'You know we're close to one of the big reservations here?'

'You told me in your letter.'

'Yes. Well, there's a big family of Cro-Magnon that's moved in close by. I wanted to show you.'

I dreamt she took me out into the fresh dawn air, and we walked down a path through the woods behind the dormitory. Soon we were in a deciduous forest of aspen trees and mountain laurel, and the breeze pressed through the leaves and made them flicker back and forth. Once out of sight of the buildings, all traces of modernity were lost. We climbed downhill. 'Wait till you see them,' said Suzanne. 'They're so great. They never fight. They're so sweet to each other. It's because they can't feel love. They don't know what it feels like.'

A bird flickered through the underbrush, one of the yellow birds I'd seen that morning in the real world. 'So you're saying maybe evolution runs the other way.'

She frowned. 'Maybe we're the ones who are like animals. You know what I mean.'

We were standing in an open glade, and the light filtered through the leaves, and the little path ran backward, forward through the brush. Then I bent down and I kissed her, and even in the dream she smelled like cigarettes.

GEORGE AND THE COMET

Stephen Baxter

There was no jolt, no sharp transition from what I had been to what I have become. I didn't wake up to find I had changed. Awareness faded in, like a slow dissolve.

I was lying on my back. I felt odd. I am – was – a big man; I played a lot of rugby when I was younger . . . But now, lying there, I felt small and light, as if I might blow away.

I stared up at a sky that was very strange indeed. Half of it was covered by a diseased sun – vast, red, bloated, its surface crawling with blisters of fire and dark pits. And, directly over me, there burned a moon (I thought at first), a sphere emitting shining gases which streamed away from the sun.

That was no moon, I realized suddenly. It was a comet. What the hell was going on?

A face drifted into view: a monkey's face, a mask of fur surrounding startling blue eyes. The monkey said, 'Can you hear me? Do you remember who you are?'

I closed my eyes. So. Obviously I was at home in my Islington flat, having a bad night following a bad day.

I was 32, a middle manager in a software house. After a day of being chased from above and below I often found it difficult to switch off; I would spend hours without sleep, finally falling into that uneasy state between sleep and wakefulness, adrift amid lurid dreams.

So I knew what was happening . . . But I couldn't remember what I had done yesterday. I couldn't even work out what day of the week it had been.

Meanwhile there was a distraction, a sharp pain in my cheek.

Reluctantly I opened my eyes. The ailing sun, the comet were still there, and I became aware that the branches of some huge tree hung over me. My monkey friend hung from a branch by one hand and foot. Its body was delicate – quite graceful-looking – except that its skin looked about three sizes too large; it was looped like a furry cloak around the shoulders and legs.

The monkey's breath smelt sweet, like young wood. And it was pinching my cheek.

I lifted an arm to brush its hand away, and I was struck again by a feeling of insubstantiality. My hand blurred across my vision, pawlike and covered in a pale fur. I tried not to worry about it.

'I know what you're thinking,' the monkey said, its voice tinny. 'But it isn't a dream. It's real, all of it. I spent a week trying to wake up out of it; you may as well accept –'

'Piss off,' I squeaked.

Squeaked . . . ? My God, I sounded like Donald Duck. I rubbed my jaw and found a face that was small and round and covered in a wiry fur.

'Have it your own way,' the monkey said. It reached out its four limbs and all that loose skin stretched out in sheets, so that the creature looked like a cute, furry kite. Like a gymnast it spun around its branch once, twice, and then let go and went gliding out of my view.

I'd seen something like that at a zoo, years ago. A flying lemur with an exotic name. Colugo?

Why dream about a talking lemur?

Then again, why not?

I jammed my eyes shut.

But the world wouldn't go away. And meanwhile I was getting uncomfortable; whatever I was lying on was scratchy, like straw, and the backs of my legs prickled.

With a sigh I opened my eyes. The great sun was still there, a dome of fiery pools and pits of darkness, like some industrial landscape. The pits mottling the surface looked like photos I remembered of real sunspots.

I spread my hands below me – I found twigs and leaves – and sat up. I moved easily enough, although I felt as if I were wearing some heavy coat which snagged in the twigs.

I held my right hand in front of my face.

The hand was small and narrow, with two fingers and a thumb; hard, flat nails tipped the fingers and, although the palm was bright pink, the back of the hand was coated with mud-brown fur. There was webbing between the fingers – I could see light through the veined membranes – and more webbing, or skin, fell away from my forearm in great untidy folds. The webbing was covered with a fine fur which lay in neat, smooth streamlines, like a cat's. I lifted my arms and saw how the sheets of skin stretched down to my splayed, spindly legs; I wasn't surprised to find another pane of flesh connecting my legs too.

When I dug my nail into the webby stuff I felt a sharp pain. So this shabby cloak was part of me.

I was a monkey too. The king of the swingers, the jungle VIP. I laughed – but stopped at the squeaky scratch which emerged from my throat.

I was sitting in the topmost branches of a tree. The tree filled the world; I peered down through the branches towards a ground lost in a translucent green gloom.

There was a rustle of leaves; delicate as a sparrow my monkey friend landed before me. Its sail flaps collapsed in folds. Its face was small and delicate, with a long snout, flaring nostrils and a tiny mouth. 'My God,' it said. 'I've just realized.'

'What?'

'You speak English! My God, my God.'

'So?'

'But, don't you see – It might have been ancient

Etruscan.' It sniffled and wiped away a tear with one furry hand. 'Then again, perhaps it was all planned this way.'

I considered closing my eyes again. 'I wish I knew what you were talking about.'

'I'm sorry.' It looked at me with moist, human eyes. 'My name is George; George Newbould. I was in London. I think I remember 1985. AD,' it added helpfully.

I opened my mouth – and closed it again. 'My name's Phil Beard. But the date –' 1985? 'I don't understand. What date is it?'

It – he, I conceded – he absently scratched at one pointed ear. 'So you agree this isn't a dream?'

'I don't agree any such –' I shook my head, frustrated. 'Just tell me. Have I been in some kind of accident?'

He grinned, showing rows of flat teeth. 'You could say that. Look, Mr Beard, I don't know any more than you do. But I've been, ah, awake, a few days longer, and I've made some guesses. I used to be a teacher, you see – General Science at a middle school – so I know a little about a lot, and –'

'Perhaps we could go over your CV later.'

'All right. I'm sorry. I think we've been reconstructed.'

I pulled at a flap of skin. 'Reconstructed how? Anyway, I didn't need reconstructing. I wasn't ill, or dead . . .'

'You ask how . . . I'd guess from some fragment of DNA; a fingernail clipping, or a tooth in some fossil layer, perhaps. Like a clone.'

Fossil layer? I looked up at the swollen sun, shivering.

'That's why we don't have clear memories of what we did before, you see. The real Phil Beard threw away that nail clipping and carried on his life. The new Beard is a clone with a vague Beard-ness but without specific memories. As to who did this, I can't even guess.' He tilted his face up to the sky; comet light picked out the bones around his eyes. 'After all this time, there might not be humans any more. Maybe the ants took over the world. Or maybe life as we know it – I mean, life based on our sort of DNA – is extinct altogether; maybe a whole new order, silicon-based, has arisen to replace us, and –'

'George –' I tried to keep my voice level. 'How did I get to be a fossil? Where are we? What year is it?'

He jerked his thumb at the sky. 'I think that's the sun. Our sun, I mean. It's gone red giant. You want a date? Five billion years, AD. Give or take,' he added.

I rubbed my furry chin. 'So it's five billion years after 1985. The sun has turned into a red giant, the human race is long since extinct, and future super-creatures have reconstructed me as a small, furry edition of Batman.'

He looked at me out of the side of his face. 'That's about the size of it. You don't believe it, do you?'

'Not a word,' I said.

He shrugged and stretched out his sails. 'Suit yourself.'

'Hey. Wait for me,' I said. I tried to stand up, but my balance was funny and I toppled forward into the leaves. 'What do you do, flap?'

'No, you glide. You control the angle of the sail stuff with your thumbs. See?'

And so, by the light of the ancient sun, George and I sailed through the branches of our tree.

The tree bore fruit. I mooched through the upper branches of the tree, nibbling experimentally. The best was a bittersweet red berry. I tried the fist-sized leaves; they were bland and tasteless, but the younger specimens bulged with water; I crushed them into my mouth and felt cool liquid trickle down my throat. George said that it had rained once, and that he had managed to catch fresh water in a cup of leaves.

Some of the greener twigs were thinner than bamboo and quite flexible, and George had woven a box-shaped cocoon for himself. By shoving leaves into the gaps between the twigs he had made the walls fairly opaque. At first

I laughed at this shanty. 'George, you don't need any protection.' I flapped my sail sheets dramatically. 'It's warm and there's never more than a soft breeze. And there's no one else here . . . Is there?'

'That's not the point. Mr Beard, I'm a schoolteacher from West London. I'm not used to the lifestyle of a flying lemur. I feel safer with walls and a roof.'

I scoffed.

. . . But, when I started feeling sleepy, I made automatically for George's crude shelter. As I entered he glanced up from his task – he was making a bow from a branchlet and a liana-like trailer, patiently goading his clumsy hands through the intricate work – and then looked away, without speaking.

I made for the darkest corner of the hut and wrapped my sails around me.

When I awoke George had finished his bow. He had wrapped its string around a short length of stick; now he was experimentally rolling the stick back and forth with the bow string. Silhouetted against the dim, green light his movements were graceful, almost sensual. I felt a strange itch deep beneath the skin of my groin.

It occurred to me that I ought to be terrified. Can you fall asleep inside a dream?

But fear still hadn't hit me. And in the meantime that tickle in my groin had turned into another kind of ache; man or lemur, there's no mistaking the feeling of a full bladder. I pushed my way out of my corner, rubbing sleep from my eyes, and climbed out of the hut.

Then my problems started.

The penis of a flying lemur is nothing to show off in the changing room. Even when erect. I spent five minutes just trying to find the damn thing. Then I could barely hold it; I hosed into space, feeling hot liquid course over my hands.

As for the rest – well, I had a fur-covered backside and leaves for lavatory paper. And no running water.

But lemurs have their moments . . .

When I'd done I launched through the leaves of our world-tree, feeling the wind cup in my skin-sails; if I could catch a breeze I could hang in the air like a seagull, surrounded by comet light and the scent of growing wood.

The sun hung in the sky, vast and ill. There were no days, no nights here.

George had a theory about that too. 'I don't think we're on Earth. I think they –'

'Who?'

'The Builders, the people who reconstructed us . . . I think they built this place for us.'

'Then why didn't they give us a day and a night?'

He poked one finger into a wide nostril. 'I don't think it occurred to them. You see, eventually – long after our day – solar tides slowed the Earth; at last the sun stopped crossing the sky. No more day or night.'

'But the Builders must have known we're from a time when the Earth still turned.'

'But it was long ago to them. Mr Beard, a lot of people of our time thought that, let's say, Alexander the Great was contemporary with Julius Caesar. In fact centuries separated them . . .'

'It was that long ago?' I shivered, and the furs over my arms stood on edge. I brushed them down absently. George stared at the way my small biceps worked; then he caught himself and looked away, embarrassed.

'Why couldn't they just land us back on Earth?' I asked. 'Maybe after all this time Earth isn't habitable, do you think? The greenhouse effect, the ozone layer –'

George laughed and flapped his sails. 'Mr Beard, I fear the ozone layer, or the lack of it, is one with Nineveh and Tyre.'

'With what?'

'Never mind. The sun has exhausted its hydrogen fuel

and has swollen into that great, swimming globe above us. When the outer layers grazed the Earth's orbit the planet – or whatever blasted ruin was left – spiralled towards the core. Soon it flashed into a mist of iron, along with Mercury, Venus, Mars . . . All gone.'

I stared up at the sun. 'Makes you think, doesn't it, George?'

'Yes. We're a long way from home.'

Hour succeeded changeless hour.

I clambered through the branches into the depths of our tree. As I entered green twilight the fur on my back prickled; but the tangle of branches seemed empty. No birds, no insects even. I wondered how this tree sustained itself. Was a single-organism ecology possible?

I reached the bottom level of the branches; about 50 feet above a featureless earth I clung upside down from a ceiling of wood. Fat branches led like an inverted road network to a single, massive trunk some hundred yards away.

I scampered along the branches towards the trunk.

The trunk was about six feet across. (George and I appeared to be about a foot long – not that it was easy to tell). The bark was thick, riven by crevices wide enough for my little hands, and I clambered down easily. When I reached the roots I got to my hind legs, clinging to the trunk timidly; then, like a simian Neil Armstrong, I pushed one foot away from the roots and into the mulch. Brown, curling leaves as large as my wingspan crackled under my feet. Under the top layer the mulch was soft, decaying and even warm, as if the ground were some vast compost heap.

I took a few experimental steps – and, with a squeak, fell flat on my face. I got up and fell again, backwards this time. To my infuriation my lithe little body just wouldn't walk upright. I had to scamper on all fours, like the beast I had become.

I raged around the clearing, sail flaps billowing; I tore

at dead leaves and hurled them into the air, screeching my frustration.

At last I lay with my back to the trunk, panting, bits of ripped leaf clinging to my fur.

There was a rushing sound, somewhere far above: rain, I guessed, pattering against the upper branches. After a few minutes fat droplets seeped through the woven ceiling and splashed over my upturned face. The water tasted fresh and leafy.

There were no signs of other tree trunks, animal tracks, plants – nothing but a plain of leaves fading in the dimness under a branch canopy. I brushed away leaf fragments, picked a direction and set off, hopping and hovering stoically.

After about a hundred yards I could barely see the tree trunk. I felt small, helpless and lost.

I hurried back to the trunk and clung to its skirts of wood.

At length I tried again. This time I stopped every ten yards to make a marker, a heap of leaves and mulch taller than I was. After some minutes of this my line of cairns led off, quite straight, into the arboreal gloom.

The trunk was out of sight again.

Panic hit me. But I didn't go back; I buried myself in the compost and folded my sails around my head, and when I felt surer I clambered out and pressed on, deeper into the shadows.

I was glad nobody was watching.

There was no way of measuring time down there, of course, but some hours must have passed before I found the second trunk. It hove out of the gloom twenty or thirty yards to the right of my line of cairns. I hurried to it, thinking at first that I had circled and come back to my starting point; but there were no markers here, no sign that the forest surface had been disturbed.

Timidly I clambered up to the branch world.

The bloated sun was hidden by the tree world, as was the core of the comet; but comet streamers, twisting faster than before, filled the sky with a glow like exploded moonlight.

So I had walked over the horizon. But the branches were empty. No lemur-people; no super-aliens . . .

No answers.

I descended, swiping at the leaves with frustration.

On the ground I set off again, extending my trail of cairns. Some hours later another trunk appeared, this time some distance to the left of my trail. I hurried to it.

A line of leaf cairns, flattened by rain, led away into the darkness. I had returned to my starting point; I had walked around the world.

I spent much of the next few days repeating this exercise; soon cairns trailed pointlessly around the world.

I was marooned on a globe no more than half a mile across. The world bore a single tree, with twin trunks set opposite each other like poles. And, supported by the trunks, a shell of branches encased the world.

George was intrigued by all this. He wondered how gravity was maintained. Black holes at the core of the planet . . . ?

I wasn't interested. I went for long, searing glides through the branches, trying to work off my tension.

I had found the bounds of my prison. It contained only George and myself. And there was no way out, no one even to tell me why I was here.

I dug my nails into tree bark and screamed.

I spat berry seeds and chewed stems. 'Admit it, George. Your theory that we were cloned from fingernails is a crock.'

He sighed; he was hunched over his latest device, a slab of wood into which he was drilling a pit with a sharpened stick. 'Maybe it is. What do I know?'

'If I was a clone I'd be a physical copy but a separate individual. I'd be a man with no memories of the Phil Beard of 1991. But in fact I'm still Phil Beard, trapped in the body of a damn monkey.' I shook my sails. 'See?'

'Maybe the Builders used techniques we can't even guess at,' George whispered. 'Maybe souls leave fossils too, in some invisible sediment layer.'

I frowned. 'So they reconstructed minds and bodies – separately – and put them together? Is that what you're saying?'

'I suppose so.'

I jumped up, waving my tiny fists at him. 'But why us, George? Why me?' He dropped his head to his chest, not even trying to answer as I capered before him. 'And why make monkeys, George? Why not give us human bodies; why not reconstruct London instead of some damn jungle?'

He rubbed at his snout, leaving a glistening streak on his palm. 'Actually I've a theory about that.'

'I bet you do.'

He lifted his head. 'Distance in time, Mr Beard . . . You see, only a few per cent difference in DNA coding separates humans from the rest of the primates: chimps, gorillas. And I would guess that only a few per cent distinguishes humans from even the earliest primates.'

'Since when were flying lemurs the first primates?'

'Not lemurs, but an animal similar in structure and ecology. That's the theory, at any rate. You see, the "lemurs" developed hands and visual coordination to help with their gliding. Later they used their grasping fingers to build tools.'

I shook my head. 'Let me get this straight. The Builders, seeking to house our – soul fossils – tried to reconstruct human DNA. But they got it wrong.'

'Over ninety per cent right, actually. It was a good job. We are very remote in time.'

I screamed and jumped about the tree top, rattling my

arms. 'But you're still guessing, aren't you, George? I've been all around this damn little world; there's nobody here except you and me, and you don't know anything, do you, George?' I hurled leaves and twigs into his face. 'You don't know! You don't know!'

He wrapped his arms over his face and rocked backwards and forwards.

Suddenly my anger imploded, leaving a shell of self-disgust. 'George, George.' I squatted in front of him and pulled at his arms. 'Come on out.'

He lifted his arms so that they framed his tearful face. 'I'm sorry.'

'It's me who's sorry, George.'

'I miss my wife.'

I felt my jaw drop. 'I never knew you were married.'

He shrugged and buried his face again.

'Kids?'

He shook his head.

Hesitantly I stroked at his arms. The skin was warm and soft, and the lay of the fur seemed to guide my palms.

I felt that itch in my groin again.

I snatched my hand away. 'My God, George. You're a female, aren't you?'

He nodded miserably. 'Just another little slip by the Builders. As if I didn't have enough troubles.'

I edged away from him. 'George, this changes the whole basis of our relationship.'

He unwrapped his arms and picked up his crude tools. 'I don't want to talk about it,' he said, and he resumed his patient drilling.

I flung myself through the branches of the world tree, willing away the ache beneath my belly.

George filled the pit in his piece of wood with bits of dry leaf from the forest floor. Then he wrapped the string of his bow around a thin stick, stood the stick in the leaves, and moved the bow back and forth, patiently, making the stick spin in the leaves.

I watched, sleepily. 'Just think,' I said. 'It's all gone.'

'What?'

'Beethoven. Mozart. There's nobody but us to remember.'

He wiped at his brow and peered up at the shining comet. 'But we do remember. I think that's why we've been brought here. I think we're at a unique moment in the history of the solar system; and we've been brought back. As witnesses.'

'. . . And what about all the music we never heard, all the books we never read . . . Gone, as if they never existed.' I felt brittle; my words were a kind of shell around a cold loneliness. 'And all the other stuff, the junk that filled our heads from day to day. The Church of the Latter Day Saints. The Inland Revenue. All gone. My God, George, nobody else in all creation remembers "Born Too Late" by The Ponytails.'

'Even I don't remember it,' he said, still spinning his stick.

'Let the Builders try reconstructing The Ponytails.' My snout twitched. 'At least I know I'm not insane. Nobody could possibly dream up The Ponytails. George, I can smell the damnedest –'

A thread of smoke rose from the pit of leaves. 'I've done it,' George breathed.

For a long, frozen moment we both stared. Then George threw his sails around the smouldering heap and blew; smoke billowed around his face. Frantically I fed dead leaves into the embryonic fire, cursing as my nubs of fingers crushed the stuff.

A single flame licked at a leaf.

We howled and danced.

Then it started to rain.

I stared up in disbelief. A squat, malevolent cloud had

154

drifted across the sun's red face, and the first drops were thumping against the leaves. For a few seconds the burning leaves hissed; then our little hearth was smothered, and only scraps of soggy foliage were left.

George just folded up.

I turned my streaming face up to the sky. 'Why are you doing this? We were long dead. Why didn't you leave us be?'

Of course there was no answer; and at that moment I knew that this was real, that I was here forever, that there would never be an answer.

What happened next is . . . vague.

I tore through my world in a mist of rage. I kicked apart George's fire, smashed holes in our hut. I bit, scratched and tore at the world-tree, hurting it in a hundred tiny, futile ways. I dropped to the forest floor and shoved over my longitudinal trails. I rolled in the mulch, howling and tearing my flesh.

Then, bloody, trailing mulch, I hauled myself back to the treetop. I flipped around a branch – the dying sun, the hated world-tree, the comet, all whirled about me – and I let go and flew high into the air. For a few seconds, at the top of my arc, I hung with mouth wide and limbs outstretched, suspended between leaf-ball world and sun; the comet filled my eyes, shining more brightly than ever.

I pulled my sails close around me.

The wind of my fall plucked at my fur, and I wished beyond hope to be dashed against the ground.

Once more I lay on my back, staring up at a swollen sun. George's face hovered over me, anxious and concerned.

I tried to smile at him. Something caked around my mouth – blood? – crackled. 'It didn't work out, did it, George?'

He shrugged, seeming embarrassed. 'You're too light,

Mr Beard. I'm sorry. Your terminal velocity wasn't nearly high enough. Although you made enough noise when you came crashing through the foliage.'

I struggled to sit up; George bent over me and slipped his arms under my shoulders. 'I'm sorry to cause you such trouble, George.'

'I'm glad you're awake again.' He squatted beside me and tilted up his head; his face looked like a coin in the red and silver light. 'I think it's about to happen; I didn't want you to miss it.'

'What's about to happen?'

'What we were brought here to see. For days that comet has been getting brighter. I think we're approaching a critical point . . .'

He brought me berries, and we sat side by side in the leaves and branches, staring up at a comet which billowed like a flag in a breeze.

It came quite suddenly.

The comet head swelled – and then exploded; silver fire poured around our tree world. We cried out and threw ourselves into the leaves, peeking from under our sails at a sky gone mad.

Within minutes the blaze faded, leaving only wisps glowing pink in the light of the sun. Where the comet's head had been a handful of glowing rocks drifted. And already the glorious tail, shorn of the nucleus which had fuelled it, was dispersing.

George and I crept closer together, shivering. I said, 'What the hell was that?'

'The death of a comet,' George whispered. 'The sun has already destroyed the planets; now it is pouring out enough heat to flash the comets to steam. Soon a shell of water molecules will collect around the sun. Water lines were seen in the spectra of red giants by astronomers in our time . . .' He pulled his cloak-sail tight around him. 'It's the last death of the solar system, you see, Mr Beard. That's what the Builders brought us to witness: to mark in our own way.'

Now only muddy sunlight obscured the stars – but here and there I could see objects bigger than stars, patches of red and green like distant toys. I pointed them out to George. 'What do you suppose they are? More observers?'

George shrugged. I stared at the enigmatic forms, wondering what strange, baffled creatures, clumsily reconstructed as we had been, were cowering beneath the violent sky.

'Anyway,' George said, 'what do we do now?'

I shrugged and picked at a leaf. 'How long before the sun swallows us too?'

He frowned. 'I don't think that will be a problem. We must be shielded somehow. Otherwise the sunlight that boiled that comet would have scorched this little world dry. So perhaps we've got years. Centuries, even. I don't suppose the Builders will care what we do.'

I sniffed; it seemed colder without the comet glow. 'I guess the first thing is to fix the house.'

'We can do a lot with fire, you know,' George mused. 'We can harden wood for a start. Make better tools. And perhaps we can go down to the surface, try to clear through the mulch to the bedrock. There might be metal ores.'

'Yes ... And we ought to think about finding some substitute for paper. Bark, or chewed wood. We'll write down what we know before it dies with us.' I pointed at the discs in the sky. 'One day our kids will travel out there and meet the Builders' other victims. Maybe they will confront the Builders themselves. And they have to be able to tell our story.'

George scratched his ear. 'What kids?'

'I think we have something to discuss, George.'

*   *   *

It wasn't easy. All those sails kept getting in the way. And the first time it was more like relieving an itch.

And, my God, it was embarrassing.

But it got better. And I couldn't believe how fast the kids grew.

WARMTH

Geoff Ryman

I don't remember the first time I saw BETsi. She was like the air I breathed. She was probably there when I was born.

BETsi looked like a vacuum cleaner, bless her. She had long carpeted arms, and a carpeted top with loops of wool like hair. She was huggable, vaguely.

I don't remember hugging her much. I do remember working into that wool all kinds of unsuitable substances – spit, ice cream, dirt from the pots of basil.

My mother talked to BETsi about my behaviour. Mostly I remember my mother as a freckled and orange blur, always desperate to be moving, but sometimes she stayed still long enough for me to look at her.

'This is Booker, BETsi,' my mother said at dictation speed. 'You must stay clean, BETsi.' She thought BETsi was stupid. She was the one who sounded like a robot. 'Please repeat.'

'I must stay clean,' BETsi replied. BETsi sounded bright, alert, smooth-talking, with a built-in smile in the voice.

'This is what I mean, BETsi: You must not *let* Clancy get you dirty. Why do you let Clancy get you dirty?'

I pretended to do sums on a pretend calculator.

While BETsi said, 'Because he is a boy. From the earliest age, most boys move in a very different, more aggressive way than girls. His form of play will be rougher and can be indulged in to a certain extent.'

Booker had programmed BETsi to talk about my development in front of me. That was so I would know what

159

was going on. It was honest in a way; she did not want me to be deceived. On the other hand, I felt like some kind of long-running project in child psychology. Booker was more like a clinical consultant who popped in from time to time to see how things were progressing.

You see, I was supposed to be a genius. My mother thought she was a genius, and had selected my father out of a sperm bank for geniuses. His only flaw, she told me, was his tendency towards baldness. BETsi could have told her: baldness is inherited from the maternal line.

She showed me a picture of herself in an old *Cosmopolitan* article. It caused a stir at the time. '*The New Motherhood*,' it was called. *Business women choose a new way*.

There is a photograph of Booker looking young and almost pretty, beautifully lit and cradling her swollen tummy. Her whole face, looking down on herself, is illuminated with love.

In the article, she says: I know my son will be a genius. She says, I know he'll have the right genes, and I will make sure he has the right upbringing. *Cosmopolitan* made no comment. They were making a laughing stock out of her.

Look, my mother was Booker McCall, chief editor of a rival magazine company with a £100 million-a-year turnover and only fifteen permanent employees of which she was second in command. Nobody had a corporate job in those days, and if they did, it was wall-to-wall politics and performance. Booker McCall had stakeholders to suck up to, editors to commission, articles to read and tear to pieces. She had layouts to throw at designers' heads. She had style to maintain, she had hair to keep up, shoes to repair, menus to plan. And then she had to score whatever she was on at the time. She was a very unhappy woman, with every reason to be.

She was also very smart, and BETsi was a good idea.

I used to look out of the window of the flat and the outside world looked blue, grey, harsh. Sunlight always caught the grime on the glass and bleached everything out, and I thought that adults moved out into a hot world in which everybody shouted all the time. I never wanted to go out.

BETsi was my whole world. She had a screen, and she would show me paintings, one after another. Velasquez, Goya. She had a library of picture books – about monkeys, or fishing villages or ghosts. She would allow me one movie a week, but always the right movie. *Jurassic Park, Beauty and the Beast, Tarzan on Mars*. We'd talk about them.

'The dinosaurs are made of light,' she told me. 'The computer tells the video what light to make and what colours the light should be so that it looks like a dinosaur.'

'But dinosaurs really lived!' I remember getting very upset, I wailed at her. 'They were really really real.'

'Yes, but not those, those are just like paintings of dinosaurs.'

'I want to see a real dinosaur!' I remember being heart-broken. I think I loved their size, their bulk, the idea of their huge hot breath. In my daydreams, I had a dinosaur for a friend and it would protect me in the world outside.

'Clancy,' BETsi warned me. 'You know what is happening now.'

'Yes!' I shouted, 'but knowing doesn't stop it happening!'

BETsi had told me that I was shy. Did you know that shyness has a clinical definition?

I'd been tested for it. Once, BETsi showed me the test. First she showed me what she called the bench-mark. On her screen, through a haze of fingerprints and jam, was one fat, calm, happy baby. Not me. 'In the test,' BETsi explained, 'a brightly coloured mobile is shown to the child. An infant who will grow up to be an outgoing and confident adult will tend to look at the mobile with calm curiosity for a time, get bored, and then look away.'

The fat happy baby smiled a little bit, reached up for the spinning red ducks and bright yellow bunnies, then sighed and looked around for something new.

'A shy baby will get very excited. This is you, when we gave you the same test.'

And there I was, looking solemn, 200 years old at six months, my infant face crossed with some kind of philosophical puzzlement. Then, they show me the mobile. My face lights up, I start to bounce, I gurgle with pleasure, delight, spit shoots out of my mouth. I get over-excited, the mobile is slightly beyond my grasp. My face crumples up, I jerk with the first little cries. Moments later I am screaming myself purple, and trying to escape the mobile, which has begun to terrify me.

'That behaviour is hardwired,' BETsi explained. 'You will always find yourself getting too happy and then fearful and withdrawn. You must learn to control the excitement. Then you will be less fearful.'

It's like with VR. When they first started making that, they discovered they did not know enough about how we see and hear to duplicate the experience. They had to research people first. Same here. Before they could mimic personality, they first had to find out a lot more about what personality was.

BETsi had me doing Transcendental Meditation and yoga at three years old. She had me doing what I now recognize was the Alexander Technique. I didn't just nap, I had my knees up and my head on a raised wooden pillow. This was to elongate my back – I was already curling inward from tension.

After she got me calm, BETsi would get me treats. She had Booker's credit-card number and authorization to spend. BETsi could giggle. When the ice cream was delivered, or the new CD full of clip art, or my new S&M

Toddler black leather gear, or my Barbie Sex-Change doll, BETsi would giggle.

I know. She was programmed to giggle so that I would learn it was all right to be happy. But it sounded as though there was something who was happy just because I was. For some reason, that meant I would remember all by myself to stay calm.

'I'll open it later,' I would say, feeling very adult.

'It's ice cream, you fool,' BETsi would say. 'It'll melt.'

'It will spread all over the carpet!' I whispered in delight.

'Booker will get ma-had,' BETsi said in a sing-song voice. BETsi knew that I always called Booker by her name.

BETsi could learn. She would have had to be trained to recognize and respond to my voice and Booker's. She was programmed to learn who I was and what I needed. I needed conspiracy. I needed a confidant.

'Look. You melt the ice cream and I will clean it up,' she said.

'It's ice cream, you fool,' I giggled back. 'If it melts, I won't be able to eat it!' We both laughed.

BETsi's screen could turn into a mirror. I'd see my own face and inspect it carefully for signs of being like Tarzan. Sometimes, as a game, she would have my own face talk back to me in my own voice. Or I would give myself a beard and a deeper voice to see what I would look like as a grown up. To have revenge on Booker, I would make myself bald.

I was fascinated by men. They were mythical beasts, huge and loping like dinosaurs, only hairy. The highlight of my week was when the window cleaner arrived. I would trail after him, too shy to speak, trying to puff myself up to the same size as he was. I thought he was a hero, who cleaned windows and then saved people from evil.

'You'll have to bear with Clancy,' BETsi would say to him. 'He doesn't see many men.'

'Don't you get out, little fella?' he would say. His name was Tom.

'It's not safe,' I managed to answer.

Tom tutted. 'Oh, that's true enough. What a world, eh? You have to keep the kiddies locked in all day. S'like a prison.' I thought that all men had South London accents.

He talked to BETsi as if she was a person. I don't think Tom could have been very bright, but I do think he was a kindly soul. I think BETsi bought him things to give to me.

'Here's an articulated,' he said once, and gave me a beautifully painted Matchbox lorry.

I took it in silence. I hated myself for being so tongue-tied. I wanted to swagger around the flat with him like Nick Nolte or Wesley Snipes.

'Do men drive in these?' I managed to ask.

'Some of them, yeah.'

'Are there many men?'

He looked blank. I answered for him. 'There's no jobs for men.'

Tom hooted with laughter. 'Who's been filling your head?' he asked.

'Clancy has a very high symbol-recognition speed,' BETsi told him. 'Not genius, you understand. But very high. It will be useful for him in interpretative trades. However, he has almost no spatial reasoning. He will only ever dream of being a lorry driver.'

'I'm a klutz,' I translated.

Booker was an American – probably the most famous American in London at the time. BETsi was programmed to modulate her speech to match her owners. To this day, I can't tell English and American accents apart unless I listen carefully. And I can imitate neither. I talk like BETsi.

I remember Tom's face, like a suet pudding, pale, blotchy, uneasy. 'Poor little fella,' he said. 'I'd rather not know all that about myself.'

'So would Clancy,' said BETsi. 'But I am programmed to hide nothing from him.'

Tom sighed. 'Get him with other kids,' he told her.

'Oh, that is all part of the plan,' said BETsi.

I was sent to Social Skills class. I failed. I discovered that I was terrified without BETsi, that I did not know what to do or say to people when she wasn't there. I went off into a corner with a computer screen, but it seemed cold, almost angry with me. If I didn't do exactly the right thing it wouldn't work, and it never said anything nice to me. The other children were like ghosts. They flittered around the outside of my perceptions. In my mind, I muted the noise they made. They sounded as if they were shouting from the other side of the window, from the harsh blue-grey world.

The consultants wrote on my first report: Clancy is socially backward, even for his age.

Booker was furious. She showed up one Wednesday and argued about it.

'Do you realize that a thing like that could get in my son's record!'

'It happens to be true, Miss McCall.' The consultant was appalled and laughed from disbelief.

'This crèche leaves children unattended and blames them when their development is stunted.' Booker was yelling and pointing at the woman. 'I want that report changed. Or I will report on you!'

'Are you threatening to write us up in your magazines?' the consultant asked in a quiet voice.

'I'm telling you not to victimize my son for your own failings. If he isn't talking to the other children, it's your job to help him.'

Talking to other kids was my job. I stared at my shoes, mortified. I didn't want Booker to help me, but I half-wanted her to take me out of the class, and I knew that I would hate it if she did.

I went to BETsi for coaching.

'What you may not know,' she told me. 'Is that you have a natural warmth that attracts people.'

'I do?' I said.

'Yes. And all most people want from other people is that they be interested in them. Shall we practice?'

On her screen, she invented a series of children. I would try to talk to them. BETsi didn't make it easy.

'Do you like reading?' I'd ask a little girl on the screen.

'What?' she replied with a curling lip.

'Books,' I persisted, as brave as I could be. 'Do you read books?'

She blinked – bemused, bored, confident.

'Do . . . do you like *Jurassic Park*?'

'It's old! And it doesn't have any story.'

'Do you like new movies?' I was getting desperate.

'I play games. *Bloodlust Demon*.' The little girl's eyes went narrow and fierce. That was it. I gave up.

'BETsi,' I complained. 'This isn't fair.' Booker would not allow me to play computer games.

BETsi chuckled and used her own voice. 'That's what it's going to be like, kiddo.'

'Then show me some games.'

'Can't,' she said.

'Not in the program,' I murmured angrily.

'If I tried to show you one, I'd crash,' she explained.

So I went back to Social Skills class determined to talk and it was every bit as awful as BETsi had said, but at least I was ready.

I told them all, straight out: I can't play games, I'm a klutz, all I can do is draw. So, I said, tell me about the games.

And that was the right thing to do. At five I gave up being Tarzan and started to listen, because the kids could at least tell me about video games. They could get puffed up and important, and I would seep envy, which must have been very satisfying for them. But. In a funny kind of way they sort of liked me.

There was a bully called Ian Aston, and suddenly one day the kids told him: 'Clancy can't fight, so don't pick on him.' He couldn't stand up to all of them.

'See if your Mum will let you visit,' they said, 'and we'll show you some games.'

Booker said no. 'It's very nice you're progressing socially, Clancy. But I'm not having you mix just yet. I know what sort of things are in the homes of parents like that, and I'm not having you exposed.'

'Your Mum's a posh git,' the children said.

'And a half,' I replied.

She was also a drug addict. One evening she didn't collect me from Social Class. The consultant tried to reach her PDA, and couldn't.

'You have a Home Help, don't you?' the consultant asked.

She rang BETsi. BETsi said she had no record in her diary of where Miss McCall might be if not collecting me. BETsi sent round a taxi.

Booker was out for two weeks. She just disappeared.

She'd collapsed on the street, and everything was taken – her hand bag, her shoes, her PDA, even her contact lenses. She woke up blind and raving from barbiturate withdrawal in an NHS ward, which would have mortified her. She claimed to be Booker McCall and several other people as well. I suppose it was also a kind of breakdown. Nobody knew who she was, nobody told us what had happened.

BETsi and I just sat alone in the apartment, eating ice cream and Kellogg's Crunchy Nut Cornflakes.

'Do you suppose Booker will ever come back?' I asked her.

'I do not know where Booker is, kiddo. I'm afraid something bad must have happened to her.'

I felt guilty because I didn't care. I didn't care if Booker never came back. But I was scared.

'What happens if you have a disc fault?' I asked BETsi.

'I've just renewed the service contract,' she replied. She whirred closer to me, and put a carpeted arm around me.

'But how would they know that something was wrong?'

She gave me a little rousing shake. 'I'm monitored, all day so that if there is a problem when your mother isn't here, they come round and repair me.'

'But what if you're broken for a real long time? Hours and hours. Days?'

'They'll have a replacement.'

'I don't want a replacement.'

'In a few hours, she'll be trained to recognize your voice.'

'What if it doesn't work? What if the contractors don't hear? What do I do then?'

She printed out a number to call, and a password to enter.

'It probably won't happen,' she said. 'So I'm going to ask you to do your exercises.'

She meant calm me down, as if my fears weren't real, as if it couldn't happen that a machine would break down.

'I don't want to do my exercises. Exercises won't help.'

'Do you want to see *Jurassic Park*?' she asked.

'It's old,' I said, and thought of my friends at Social Class and of their mothers who were with them.

There was a whirring sound. A panel came up on the screen, like what happened during a service when the engineers came and checked her programming and reloaded the operational system. CONFIGURATION OVERRIDE the panels said.

When that was over BETsi asked, 'Would you like to learn how to play *Bloodlust Demon*?'

'Oh!' I said and nothing else. 'Oh! Oh! BETsi! Oh!'

And she giggled.

I remember the light on the beige carpet making a

highway towards the screen. I remember the sound of traffic outside, peeping, hooting, the sound of nightfall and loneliness, the time I usually hated the most. But now I was playing *Bloodlust Demon*.

I played it very badly. I kept getting blown up.

'Just keep trying,' she said.

'I have no spatial reasoning,' I replied. I was learning that I did not like computer games. But for the time being, I had forgotten everything else.

After two weeks, I assumed that Booker had gotten bored and had gone away and would never be back. Then one morning, when the hot world seemed to be pouring in through the grimy windows, someone kicked down the front door.

BETsi made a cage around me with her arms.

'I am programmed for both laser and bullet defence. Take what you want, but do not harm the child. I cannot take your photograph or video you. You will not be recognized. There is no need to damage me.'

They broke the glass tables, they threw drawers onto the floor. They dropped their trousers and shat in the kitchen. They took silver dresses, Booker's black box, her jewellery. One of the thieves took hold of my Matchbox lorry and I knew the meaning of loss. I was going to lose my truck. Then the thief walked back across the carpet towards me. BETsi's arms closed more tightly around me. The thief chuckled under his ski mask and left the truck nearby on the sofa.

'There you go, little fella,' he said. I never told anyone. It was Tom. Like I said, he wasn't very bright. BETsi was programmed not to recognize him.

So. I knew then what men were; they could go bad. There was part of them that was only ever caged up. I was frightened of men after that.

The men left the door open, and the flat was a ruin,

smashed and broken, and BETsi's cage of arms was lifted up, and I began to cry, and then I began to scream over and over and over, and finally some neighbours came, and finally the search was on for Booker McCall.

How could an editor-in-chief disappear for two weeks? 'We thought she'd gone off with a new boyfriend,' her colleagues said, in the press, to damage her. Politics, wall to wall. It was on TV, the Uncaring Society they called it. No father, no grandparents, neighbours who were oblivious – the deserted child was only found because of a traumatic break in.

Booker was gone a very long time. Barbiturates are the worst withdrawal of all. I visited her, with one of the consultants from my Class. It got her picture in the papers, and a caption that made it sound as though the consultants were the only people who cared.

Booker looked awful. Bright yellow with blue circles under her eyes. She smelled of thin stale sweat.

'Hello, Clancy,' she whispered. 'I've been in withdrawal.'

So what? Tell me something I didn't know. I was hard-hearted. I had been deserted, she had no call on my respect.

'Did you miss me?' She looked like a cut flower that had been left in a vase too long, with smelly water.

I didn't want to hurt her, so all I said was: 'I was scared.'

'Poor baby,' she whispered. She meant it, but the wave of sympathy exhausted her and she lay back on the pillow. She held out her hand.

I took it and I looked at it.

'Did BETsi take good care of you?' she asked, with her eyes closed.

'Yes,' I replied, and began to think, still looking at her fingers. She really can't help all of this, all of this is hard-wired. I bet she'd like to be like BETsi, but can't. Anyway, barbiturates don't work on metal and plastic.

Suddenly she was crying, and she'd pushed my hand

onto her moist cheek. It was sticky and I wanted to get away, and she said, 'Tell me a story. Tell me some beautiful stories.'

So I sat and told her the story of *Jurassic Park*. She lay still, my hand on her cheek. At times I thought she was asleep, other times I found I hoped she loved the story as much as I did, raptors and brachiosaurs and T Rex.

When I was finished, she murmured, 'At least somebody's happy.' She meant me. That was what she wanted to think, that I was all right, that she would not have to worry about me. And that too, I realized, would never change.

She came home. She stayed in bed all day for two more weeks, driving me nuts. 'My life is such a mess!' she said, itchy and anxious. She promised me she would spend more time with me, God forbid. She raged against the bastards at BPC. We'd be moving as soon as she was up, she promised me, filling my heart with terror. She succeeded in disrupting my books, my movies, my painting. Finally she threw off the sheets a month early and went back to work. I gathered she still went in for treatment every fortnight. I gathered that booze now took the place of barbies. The smell of the flat changed. And now that I hated men, there were a lot of them, loose after work.

'This is my boy,' she would say, with a kind of wobbly pride and introduce me to yet another middle-aged man with a ponytail. 'Mr d'Angelo is a designer,' she would say, as if she went out with their professions. She started to wear wobbly red lipstick. It got everywhere, on pillows, sheets, walls, and worst of all on my Nutella tumblers.

The flat had been my real world, against the outside, and now all that had changed. I went to school. I had to say goodbye to BETsi, every morning, and goodbye to Booker, who left wobbly red lipstick on my collar. I went to school in a taxi.

'You see,' said BETsi, after my first day. 'It wasn't bad was it? It works, doesn't it?'

'Yes, BETsi,' I remember saying. 'It does.' The 'it' was me. We both meant my precious self. She had done her job.

Through my later school days, BETsi would sit unused in my room – most of the time. Sometimes at night, under the covers, I would reboot her, and the screen would open up to all the old things, still there. My childhood was already another world – dinosaurs and space cats and puzzles. BETsi would pick up where we had left off, with no sense of neglect, no sense of time or self.

'You're older,' she would say. 'About twelve. Let me look at you.' She would mirror my face, and whir to herself. 'Are you drawing?'

'Lots,' I would say.

'Want to mess around with the clip art, kiddo?' she would ask.

And long into the night, when I should have been learning algebra, we would make collages on her screen. I showed surfers on waves that rose up amid galaxies blue and white in space, and through space there poured streams of roses. A row of identical dancing Buddhas was an audience.

'Tell me about your friends, and what you do,' she asked, as I cut and pasted. And I'd tell her about my friend John and his big black dog, Toro, and how we were caught in his neighbours' garden. I ran and escaped, but John was caught. John lived outside town in the countryside. And I'd tell her about John's grandfather's farm, full of daffodils in rows. People use them to signal spring, to spell the end of winter. Symbol recognition.

'I've got some daffodils,' BETsi said. 'In my memory.'

And I would put them into the montage for her, though it was not spring any longer.

172

I failed at algebra. Like everything else in Booker's life, I was something that did not quite pan out as planned. She was good about it. She never upbraided me for not being a genius. There was something in the way she ground out her cigarette that said it all.

'Well, there's always art school,' she said, and forced out a blast of blue-white smoke.

It was BETsi I showed my projects to – the A-level exercises in sketching elephants in pencil.

'From a photo,' BETsi said. 'You can always tell. So. You can draw as well as a photograph. Now what?'

'That's what I think,' I said. 'I need a style of my own.'

'You need to do that for yourself,' she said.

'I know,' I said, casually.

'You won't always have me to help,' she said.

The one thing I will never forgive Booker for is selling BETsi without telling me. I came back from first term at college to find the machine gone. I remember that I shouted, probably for the first time ever, 'You did what?'

I remember Booker's eyes widening, blinking. 'It's just a machine, Clancy. I mean, it wasn't as if she was a member of the family or anything.'

'How could you do it! Where is she?'

'I don't know. I didn't think you'd be so upset. You're being awfully babyish about this.'

'What did you do with her?'

'I sold her back to the contract people, that's all.' Booker was genuinely bemused. 'Look. You are hardly ever here, it isn't as though you use her for anything. She's a child-development tool, for Chrissakes. Are you still a child?'

I'd thought Booker had been smart. I'd thought that she had recognized she would not have time to be a mother, and so had bought in BETsi. I thought that meant she understood what BETsi was. She didn't and that meant she had not understood, not even been smart.

'You,' I said, 'have sold the only real mother I have ever had.' I was no longer shouting. I said it at dictation speed. I'm not sure Booker has ever forgiven me.

Serial numbers, I thought. They have serial numbers, maybe I could trace her through those. I rang up the contractors. The kid on the phone sighed.

'You want to trace your BETsi,' he said before I'd finished, sounding bored.

'Yes,' I said. 'I do.'

He grunted and I heard a flicker of fingertips on a keyboard.

'She's been placed with another family. Still operational. But,' he said, 'I can't tell you where she is.'

'Why not?'

'Well, Mr McCall. Another family is paying for the service, and the developer is now working with another child. Look. You are not unusual, OK? In fact this happens about half the time, and we cannot have customers disturbed by previous charges looking up their machines.'

'Why not?'

'Well,' he chortled; it was so obvious to him. 'You might try imagining it from the child's point of view. They have a new developer of their own, and then this other person, a stranger, tries to muscle in.'

'Just. Please. Tell me where she is.'

'Her memory has been wiped,' he said, abruptly.

It took a little while. I remember hearing the hiss on the line.

'She won't recognize your voice. She won't remember anything about you. She is just a service vehicle. Try to remember that.'

I wanted to strangle the receiver. I sputtered down the line like a car cold-starting. 'Don't . . . couldn't you keep a copy! You know this happens, you bastard. Couldn't you warn people, offer them the disc? Something?'

'I'm sorry sir, but we do, and you turned the offer down.'

'I'm sorry?' I was dazed.

'That's what your entry says.'

Booker, I thought. Booker, Booker, Booker. And I realized; she couldn't understand, she's just too old. She's just from another world.

'I'm sorry, sir, but I have other calls on the line.'

'I understand,' I replied.

All my books, all my collages, my own face in the mirror. It had been like a library I could visit whenever I wanted to see something from the past. It was as if my own life had been wiped.

Then for some reason, I remembered Tom.

He was fat and 40 and defeated, a bloke. I asked him to break in to the contractor's office and read the files and find who had her.

'So,' he said. 'You knew then.'

'Yup.'

He blew out hard through his lips and looked at me askance.

'Thanks for the lorry,' I said, by way of explanation.

'I always liked you, you know. You were a nice little kid.' His fingers were tobacco-stained. 'I can see why you want her back. She was all you had.'

He found her all right. I sent him a cheque. Sometimes even now I send him a cheque.

Booker would have been dismayed – BETsi had ended in a resold council flat. I remember, the lift was broken and the stairs smelled of pee. The door itself was painted fire-engine red and had a non-breakable plaque on the doorway. The Andersons, it said amid ceramic pansies. I knocked.

BETsi answered the door. Boom. There she was, arms extended defensively to prevent entry. She'd been cleaned up but there was still rice pudding in her hair. Beyond her, I saw a slumped three-piece suite and beige carpet littered with toys. There was a smell of baby food and damp flannel.

'BETsi?' I asked, and knelt down in front of her. She scanned me, clicking. I could almost see the wheels turning, and for some reason, I found it funny. 'It's OK,' I said, 'you won't know me, dear.'

'Who is it, Betty?' A little girl came running. To breathe the air that flows in through an open door, to see someone new, to see anyone at all.

'A caller, Bumps,' replied BETsi. Her voice was different, a harsher, East End lilt. 'And I think he's just about to be on his way.'

I found that funny too; I still forgave her. It wasn't her fault. Doughty old BETsi still doing her job, with this doubtful man she didn't know trying to gain entry.

There might be, though, one thing she could do.

I talked to her slowly, I tried to imitate an English accent. 'You do not take orders from someone with my voice. But I mean no harm, and you may be able to do this. Can you show me my face on your screen?'

She whirred. Her screen flipped out of sleep. There I was.

'I am an old charge of yours,' I said – both of us, me and my image, his voice echoing mine. 'My name is Clancy. All I ask you to do is remember me. Can you do that?'

'I understand what you mean,' she said. 'I don't have a security reason not to.'

'Thank you,' I said. 'And. See if you can program the following further instructions.'

'I cannot take instruction from you.'

'I know. But check if this violates security. Set aside part of your memory. Put Bumps into it. Put me and Bumps in the same place, so that even when they wipe you again. You'll remember us.'

She whirred. I began to get excited; I talked like myself.

'Because they're going to wipe you BETsi, whenever they resell you. They'll wipe you clean. It might be nice

176

for Bumps if you remember her. Because we'll always remember you.'

The little girl's eyes were on me, dark and serious, 200 years old. 'Do what he says, Betty,' the child said.

Files opened and closed like mouths. 'I can put information in an iced file,' said BETsi. 'It will not link with any other files, so it will not be usable to gain entry to my systems.' Robots and people: these days we all know too much about our inner workings.

I said thank you and goodbye, and said it silently looking into the eyes of the little girl, and she spun away on her heel as if to say: I did that.

I still felt happy, running all the way back to the tube station. I just felt joy.

So that's the story.

It took me a long time to make friends in school, but they were good ones. I still know them, though they are now middle-aged men, clothiers in Toronto, or hearty freelancers in New York who talk about their men and their cats. Make a long story short. I grew up to be one of the people my mother used to hire and abuse.

I am a commercial artist, though more for book and CD covers than magazines. I'm about to be a Dad. One of my clients, a very nice woman. We used to see each other and get drunk at shows. In the hotel bedrooms I'd see myself in the mirror – not quite middle-aged, but with a pony tail. Her name is some kind of mistake. Bertha.

Bertha is very calm and cool and reliable. She called me and said coolly, I'm having a baby and you're the father, but don't worry. I don't want anything from you.

I wanted her to want something from me. I wanted her to say marry me, you bastard. Or at least: could you take care of it on weekends? Not only didn't she want me to worry – it was clear that she didn't want me at all. It was also clear I could expect no more commissions from her.

I knew then what I wanted to do. I went to Hamleys.

There they were, the Next Degradation. Now they call them things like Best Friend or Home Companions, and they've tried to make them look human. They have latex skins and wigs and stiff little smiles. They look like burn victims after plastic surgery, and they recognize absolutely everybody. Some of them are modelled after *Little Women*. You can buy Beth or Amy or Jo. Some poor little rich girls start dressing them up in high fashion – the bills are said to be staggering. You can also buy male models – a lively Huckleberry, or big Jim. I wonder if those might not be more for the Mums, particularly if all parts are in working order.

'Do you . . . do you have any older models?' I ask at the counter.

The assistant is a sweet woman, apple cheeked, young, pretty, and she sees straight through me. 'We have BETsis,' she says archly.

'They still make them?' I say, softly.

'Oh, they're very popular,' she says, and pauses, and decides to drop the patter. 'People want their children to have them. They loved them.'

History repeats like indigestion.

I turn up at conventions like this one. I can't afford a stand but my livelihood depends on getting noticed anyway.

And if I get carried away and believe a keynote speaker trying to be a visionary, if he talks about, say, Virtual Government or Loose Working Practices, then I get overexcited. I think I see God, or the future or something and I get all jittery. And I go into the exhibition hall and there is a wall of faces I don't know and I think: I've got to talk to them, I've got to sell to them. I freeze, and I go back to my room.

And I know what to do. I think of BETsi, and I stretch

out on the floor and take hold of my shoulders and my breathing and I get off the emotional roller-coaster. I can go back downstairs, and back into the hall. And I remember that something once said: you have a natural warmth that attracts people, and I go in, and even though I'm a bit diffident, by the end of the convention, we're laughing and shaking hands, and I have their business card. Or maybe we've stayed up drinking till four in the morning, playing *Bloodlust Demon*. They always win. They like that, and we laugh.

It is necessary to be loved. I'm not sentimental: I don't think a computer loved me. But I was hugged, I was noticed, I was cared for. I was made to feel that I was important, special, at least to something. I fear for all the people who do not have that. Like everything else, it is now something that can be bought. It is therefore something that can be denied. It is possible that without BETsi, I might have to stay upstairs in that hotel room, panicked. It is possible that I would end up on barbiturates. It is possible that I could have ended up one of those sweet sad people sitting in the rain in shop doorways saying the same thing in London or New York, in exactly the same accent: any spare change please?

But I didn't. I put a proposition to you.

If there were a God who saw and cared for us and was merciful, then when I died and went to Heaven, I would find among all the other things, a copy of that wiped disc.

THE FAMILY FOOTBALL

Ian R. MacLeod

Dad came home as a centaur that day. He rapped his hooves impatiently on the front door for someone to let him in. My sister Anne and I were playing rats on the kitchen floor, running around the table legs and tickling Mum's legs with our whiskers as she fixed tea.

'Go see to your Dad,' Mum snapped at me, 'and you should be past these silly games. You know how much I hate those long pink tails.'

I wandered grumpily down the hall, climbing back into human form as I did so. Dad's horse-and-man shape loomed through the frosted glass. He humphed at me when I opened the door as though I'd been a long time coming, then pushed past and trotted into the lounge. He tried to sit down on the sofa, gave up, and clumsily bent his four legs to lower himself down on the carpet.

'You should be doing your homework,' he said as I stood watching from the doorway.

'I'll do it all straight after tea.'

'Well just don't expect . . .' he winced. The long joints of his equine legs were hurting in the position he was sitting. As he changed into the shape of a large labrador, I stood waiting for the end of a sentence I knew by heart. '. . . don't expect to play football afterwards.'

I nodded. If I hadn't already known what he was saying, his dog's vocal chords would have given me few clues. Dad was a physically clumsy man. He often changed shapes on the way home on the train when he'd had a bad day at work to try to get it out of his system. But no matter what shape he took, he was never able to make himself either well understood or comfortable.

At tea, we all came as ourselves. Only babies did otherwise, squirming from half-formed shape to shape as I could still (and with some disgust) remember Anne doing in her high chair.

Mum said, 'I went to see Doctor Shaw today.'

'Oh,' Dad said, not looking, chasing a few stray peas around the plate with his fork.

'He says they'll need to do more tests to see what the problem is.'

'You can get the time off at the shop?'

'They have to give it, don't they? It's the law.'

'I told you when you started there, it's a mistake to work anywhere where there's no union.'

'Well, I'm going to go anyway, day after tomorrow. I'm sick of . . . sick of this thing.'

Mum was gazing down at her plate. She'd only given herself baked beans on a slice of toast instead of the gammon and egg the rest of us had. It had been the same now for two or three months, since her problem had started. She really couldn't face up to meat, and would have been happier – if she could have faced the indignity – climbing trees and nibbling at bits of green stuff out in the garden. Anne and I had caught her doing just that on a couple of occasions when we were home all day at half term. Hanging upside down from the almond tree with her apron flapping over her face. She'd shooed us all the way out of the house, her face flushing between anger and embarrassment.

'You've got rights,' Dad said. 'Just you tell me if they cause you any trouble.'

Mum said nothing. She dropped her fork onto the tablecloth with her good left hand, leaving a streak of tomato. I knew even then that she was going through a bad time, what with her right hand. At the moment, she had it hidden beneath the table, not so much because she didn't want us to see it – she'd given up after the first few weeks wearing gloves and bandages except when she went out of the house – but because she hated having to look at it herself. Her right hand was hairy, hairy with hairs that only petered out around her elbow. And it had the three long hooked claws of *brandypus griesus*, the three-toed sloth or ai. It had been a mystery to us all how she'd even come up with that shape in the first place, as Mum wasn't a great changer and was never very imaginative about it when she did. But it had happened in the night when she was asleep, which was always more difficult because you didn't have the normal control. She put it down to the cheese she'd had before she'd gone to bed, and some wildlife programme she'd been watching – which was odd, because all the rest of us could remember seeing that night was a quiz programme, some football and the news.

'Well anyway,' she said. 'Tomorrow's another day.'

'That's right,' said Dad. 'And I'm due some overtime from all the supplementary bills we've had to send out. How about we get a baby sitter for these two here and go out for a few drinks.'

Anne piped in, 'Please, not Mrs Bossom again.'

But Mum shook her head anyway. 'I'm sorry dear. I've promised to take the kids over for tea to see Grandma. Of course, I'll leave something nice for you to microwave.'

Dad nodded and chewed his food, glaring across at the microwave.

I finished homework at about eight, and ran out to play football on the balding patch of grass in front of our houses. Anne came too, and the rest of our gang were there, apart from Harry Blaines, whose parents were having marital difficulties and were always taking him off with them to see some counsellor as though the whole thing was his fault.

There was a problem; the last time we'd played, Charlie Miller had lobbed our plastic ball over the high fence into the Halls' back garden. The Halls were a mad and angry couple, and spent most of the time at home rowing and flying around the place as birds, pecking at each other, and at anyone who dared to ring the doorbell.

We all stood around arguing in the twilight. But then I remembered something – there was an old leather football in our garage. Cracked and deflated, it had been there for as long as I could remember, tucked out of sight and reach behind the old paint tins. On the off-chance that it might be of use, I went in, found the steps and pulled it down in a shower of rust and cobwebs. The odd thing was this; when I managed to fit in the nozzle of my bicycle pump, it began to wheeze and expand even before I started to inflate it.

I played in the side attacking the goal towards the brick wall by the row of garages. We all sprouted tentacles on our heads to distinguish us from the other side. As usual, I was centre forward. So were the rest of the team – Charlie, Bob, Peter, the two Ford sisters – apart from Anne, who was the smallest and ended up in goal between the piles of trainer tops and pullovers. For some reason, she decided she could do the job better as a baby stegosaurus. I had to go over and have a quiet word with her after we had let in five quick and quite unnecessary goals.

'Saw your Mama in that shop today,' John Williams came over and said to me as I stood rubbing a bruised feeler and catching my breath. 'The shirt department. That's where she works, isn't it?'

'What if she does?' I said.

'You should have seen her. There was this man wanted his shirt taken out of the wrapper. You know, all the bits of card and the pins. Jesus H. Christ, your poor Mum was all over the bloody counter. Hasn't got two proper hands these days has she?'

'At least she is my Mum,' I said, which – as John Williams had a family who were all step-this-or-that – was a good below-the-belt swipe. I followed it up with a good below-the-belt kick.

When we'd finally finished fighting, we both felt better, and pleased with ourselves for being tough. I'd turned into a grizzly bear by then, and John was a tiger. But as always when you were fighting, you could never really manage the shape well enough to do any damage. That was probably a good thing, as I didn't really hate him anyway. He was just a loud-mouthed prat.

We got back to the game. The final score was Side The Tentacles, fourteen: Side Without, seventeen. In my view, at least five of the latter goals would have been disallowed if there had been a referee. An argument started over whether we should settle the thing on penalties.

That was when Mum came out. She was in her old blue dressing gown and I could tell that something was the matter from the way she didn't try to hide her hand. Without saying a word to anyone, she walked out beneath the widening pools of streetlight and bent down to pick up the football. She said something to it, and held it close to her. Everyone just stood staring as she walked back inside.

Anne and I followed her back into the house a few minutes after. It was getting dark by then, and penalties were out of the question anyway.

Next day at school was pretty ordinary. Steven Halier got into trouble in Maths for changing into a porcupine, and was hauled out to the front. We all laughed when Mister Craig pulled off Steven's shoe before he'd had time to properly change back into it and plonked it there on the desk, bits of shoe-leather, flesh and spines all mangled up together. As punishment, he made Steven leave class without the opportunity to get the thing back on, and he had to hobble around the playground all through the lunch break with only half a foot.

I always kept well away from Anne at school. She was four years below me, and beneath my height of third-form dignity. The girls in her year were all crazy about horses, and took turns to change into one so that the others could take rides. The whole thing looked incredibly stupid from where I was standing by the goalposts on the playing fields, talking about the mysteries of the universe and whether Jane Jolly in the year above us had really got glandular fever or had actually been missing all term so she could have an abortion. Still, I recognized my little sis as she lumbered past me along the touchline, hoofed and on all fours. It was generally easy enough to tell someone you knew well no matter what shape they were in. She was stumbling with a cheap-looking plastic bridle, having trouble with the weight of the fat girl classmate on her back.

After lunch, just as history was starting, Anne and I were both called to the headmaster's office. The headmaster was sitting behind his desk in the form of a big teddy bear. We both let out a sigh of relief to see him that way – Mister Anderson often assumed that shape, but only when he was in a good mood and wasn't after your blood. It wasn't a terribly attractive teddy bear – the eyes really did look like glass buttons – but he entertained the idea that it made him appear friendly and approachable.

'I've had a phone call from your father at work,' he said. 'He's had to go off to the hospital now. It's your mother, I'm afraid. She's been taken ill. Your grandmother's coming round here to the school to pick you up.'

Gran arrived a few minutes later in her little Austin and drove us back to the bungalow that she and Grandad had moved into after he retired from the fire service. Grandad didn't come, of course; Grandad didn't go anywhere now, except for walks. It had been a big family story about what had happened to him when he retired, one of those things which had gone past the stage of being sad – or even a joke – and was now simply accepted. After the first few job-free weeks of gardening and sitting around in the pub drinking more than he could afford, Grandad had started to get depressed. He said it was a dog's life, doing nothing every day. Why, he'd had ten men under him when he was working, with people's lives at stake. The Christmas when I was about six, Grandad had changed into a black and white mongrel with a jaunty eye patch, and he had never changed back since.

Gran now accepted Grandad that way, taking him for walks, buying tins of good-quality dog food at the supermarket, sending him to kennels and going off on holidays on her own. And so did we, the whole family. Not that Grandad was a particularly fun sort of dog to have around, the kind that you could throw sticks for and get into scrapes with. He was past 60 after all, crotchety half the time with rheumatism, his muzzle going grey. Still, he came up to me and Anne in the hall of their bungalow with his tail wagging. I patted his head and let him lick my hand for a while before Gran took us into the lounge.

Gran made us both sit down. She still hadn't said anything about Mum. Grandad scratched his ear and curled up in front of the gas fire, which, as always – and even now in the middle of summer – was on, and muttering to itself.

'My dears, you both look worried,' she said – which I suppose we probably did. It hadn't really occurred to us that Mama might be seriously ill, but once before when Mum had gone into hospital to have something done, we'd had to spend a whole week with them in the bungalow whilst Dad went to work and tried to cook himself spam fritters at home for tea. Grandad and Grandma were fine in small doses, but not to stay with.

'Your Mum's really not that *bad*,' Grandma added. 'But you know she's been having trouble with that hand of hers. Now,' Gran leaned forward, as though she was sharing a secret, 'it's started to spread. And she can't do a thing about it.'

We went to see Mum in hospital that evening. The three-toed sloth business with her hand hadn't so much spread as taken over. She wasn't in any of the usual wards, but in a new place at the back of the maternity wing that had bare concrete floors and smelled like a zoo. Mama was behind bars, hanging upside down from an old branch, with big brown eyes staring out. The doctor warned us not to try to put our hands through the bars, because Mum had really lost all control, and although sloths were herbivores, they could give you a nasty bite. Anne began to cry. She thought a herbivore was like cancer. I was older, and I guessed the truth – that Mama becoming a sloth wasn't that different to what had happened to Grandad, and that even though she hadn't done it deliberately, it was probably a kind of mental thing.

Mama just hung there, looking at us, her flattened muzzle gently twitching. She had a long shaggy coat that hung down around her, and the doctor explained that in the wild – and if Mum really had been a three-toed sloth – it would have been green with a special kind of algae. It was pretty boring really, and the chocolates and the stack of old women's magazines Gran had made us bring were obviously a waste of time. So as Gran wittered on uselessly through the bars about the WI fête, Anne and I opened up the chocolates and started munching them and squabbling over the centres, wandering along the cages to see who else was here.

They were an odd-looking bunch. You can usually spot a shape-changed human from the real thing a mile off, but most of these were different. If it hadn't been for the medical charts with the names and graphs hanging by the padlocked doors, you'd never have guessed that most of them weren't what they pretended to be. Even Grandad, who'd been a mongrel for nearly five years now, wasn't anything like this convincing.

There was a llama, a coyote, a huge insect with mandibles like a lawnmower, and a creature-from-the-black-lagoon thing that seemed to be rotting at the fins and smelled like an old canal. There were bubbling tanks filled with fishes. One of them was recognizably a catfish, but was scooting around the bottom of the tank on wheels. At the far end, there was a plastic chair behind a rope that we thought was just a chair until it moved when Anne climbed over and tried to sit on it.

'What's that supposed to be?' Anne asked, pointing to a patch of turf in a glass case. I looked at the medical chart clipped to the side. It said: *Lumbricus terrestris.* I'd just done that in science and was able to tell Anne that it meant an earthworm.

Dad arrived soon afterwards. He'd picked up a big bouquet of roses from the caravan that sold flowers in the hospital carpark, and pushed them towards Mum through a flap in the bars. Mum reached out a long, lugubrious hand and took them. One by one, she ate the lot, thorns and all. Between wincing, Anne and I could hardly stop ourselves from laughing.

We didn't have to stay with Gran and Grandad that night. Dad had taken time off from work. That was a relief – we didn't even mind the soggy spam fritters too much, although at the same time it was a little worrying. I mean, I thought as the three of us sat in the lounge watching TV afterwards, this in-the-head business must be a lot worse than the secret-down-below business that had got Mum into hospital before. By chance, the people in the soap opera we were watching were sitting around in someone's kitchen talking about another of the characters who had supposedly become ill a couple of episodes before but was probably leaving the series. They were all in the shape of armadillos – which Dad said was the only way these people could act – and there were subtitles in case you had any difficulty understanding what they were saying. It seemed that the ill character had had a nervous breakdown, and that, like Mama, he was in a special wing of the local hospital. A nervous breakdown, was, I decided, exactly what Mama was having.

Dad was grumpy. He shooed us off to bed as if we didn't have any right to our usual books and baths. He didn't even ask if we'd done our homework, which any other time would have been reassuring.

Anne and I both climbed out of bed and squatted out of sight in the shadows at the top of the stairs as Dad rang up various relatives to explain what had happened. Mostly, it was an extended version of the stuff he'd told us, with the business about the hand and how Mum had been tired lately. But the last phone call he made to Mum's sister Joan was slightly different.

'Yeah,' he said, sitting back on the creaky chair by the phone. 'I guess it's all made it come back to her.'

Dad nodded vigorously as Aunt Joan said something to him.

'Funny thing is,' he said. 'I thought she'd got over this thing years ago. I mean, you were there then, and I wasn't.'

Eventually, he put down the phone and went back into the lounge, closing the door, turning up the TV loud as though he was trying to hide his thoughts. What *thing*, I wondered, lying awake in bed long after the house had gone silent. I was in one of those sweaty, tossy states when you're not sure whether you're awake or dreaming. I woke up fully with the figures of my alarm clock showing past two, and found that I had three long black claws on each hand, and that I was covered with hair. Although I changed back with no difficulty, the incident scared me. I knew now that what Mama had was a head-thing, but did that mean it couldn't be hereditary?

Next morning, Anne and I went to school as though it was any other day. The only difference was that Dad dropped us off in the car on his way to visit Mum at the hospital. Word had got around. All the teachers were nice to us that day, and even the other kids. Everyone seemed to know about Mum. I glared at John Williams when he came up to me during break, silently daring him to say the kind of thing that had got us into the fight when we were playing football. But one look at his face told me that it had gone beyond all that – that he actually felt sorry for me. More than anything, I think it was that that made me realize that Mum really was ill.

Gran and Grandad were there with Dad when we went to see Mum at hospital that evening. And Grandad was human. Anne didn't even recognize him. He looked pretty neat, the way you want your Grandad to look when you're a kid, not old and stooped and smelly, but with silver hair brushed back and long, in a white colonial suit with a dark blue waistcoat and paisley cravat bulging out at the collar. The only thing he hadn't changed was the jaunty black patch over one eye. It was probably a kind of birthmark.

Dad was very edgy. He'd come as a snake and kept climbing up over the bars as though he wanted to get into the cage with Mum, although at the same time he obviously didn't want to.

There was a doctor there too. A different doctor from the one we'd seen the night before. He was in a suit, and from the way he talked, I guessed he was a head-doctor, the type that you see in films. I thought, Oh no, we're going to end up like Harry Blaines, going to family therapy, but he turned out to be young and quite nice, and kept saying that he really thought Mum was doing well. She was eating plenty of leaves and fruit, and hanging there by her long arms the way sloths were apparently supposed to.

Back at home, Dad made us stay at the table in the kitchen after we'd eaten, which was the last thing we really wanted, what with the taste of his cooking and the room still filled with smoke from the blackened frying pan. But he said it was time we had a talk, and we knew from the look on his face (he'd turned back from a snake to drive the car home) that he really meant it.

'Your Mum,' he said, 'she didn't have a happy childhood. Well, she was a woman by then really, the time I'm talking about.'

'But it was before she met you,' I said, and Dad gave me a look as though he guessed that we'd been listening to him on the phone to Aunt Joan last evening. For some reason, the thought of being a sneak made me turn into an elephant. It was embarrassing – but for a while, I just couldn't help it.

Ignoring me – not even making his usual warning about the strength of the furniture – Dad went on: 'Your Mum had a – a difficult time when she was in her late teens.'

I nodded, my trunk swinging slightly and knocking over the bottle of brown sauce before I had a chance to pull it back in. If Mum was late teens at the time, I guessed that it probably had to do with sex and babies. From my experience, there was not much else that kids of that age got up to, apart from maybe doing drugs and stealing cars, and I couldn't see Mum ever being like that.

'She wasn't very happy,' I suggested, 'and now she's not feeling happy again.'

Dad nodded, and then he shook his head. 'That's exactly it . . .'

I thought he was going to say something more. From the way Dad had his mouth half-open, he obviously thought so too. But, looking at us, he changed his mind.

*   *   *

Afterwards, Anne and I decided we might as well go out and play. Dad was shut in the lounge watching TV, one of those wrestling matches where they put Godzilla against King Kong and you can tell it's just people really and nothing like as good as the special effects you get in films. I looked around for the football, but it had gone from the garage. Dad had obviously hidden it, but I had a pretty good idea where to look – he and Mum were never very imaginative about hiding things. The football was tucked away with the dust under Mum and Dad's bed.

It was a good game that evening. And close. For once, Anne played out of goal – and she wasn't bad either, scoring twice, and with only one own goal. We forgot about the time. Dad came out in his vest when it was almost dark and we were just having fun. He went mad when he saw the ball we were using. He put his hand up to hit me, and only just managed to stop himself.

Dad took the ball inside and dumped it in the sink in the kitchen, wrapped up in a towel as though he could hardly bear to touch it.

He found me staring at it when I came down after my bath to get a drink of orange.

'Son, I'm sorry about what happened on the green,' he said, patting my shoulder with a shaky hand. 'But under no circumstances are you ever to touch that football. Not you or even Annie. Not ever again.'

I didn't say anything, and I didn't sleep much. In the morning, Dad took the football along with him when he dropped us off on the way to the hospital. He had it on the front passenger seat, still wrapped up in the towel. To stop it rolling, he had put the seatbelt around it.

Grandad picked us up from school that evening. He was still a human, but I wasn't too keen on the idea of him driving Gran's Austin: normally, he travelled around in it with his head out of the back window, barking at pedestrians.

'Is Mum any better?' I asked, sitting on the front passenger seat beside him, thinking how odd it was to be talking to this smart grey-haired gent.

'I think she is,' he said, smiling.

Grandad was keeping his eye firmly on the road. The skin around the dark patch on his left eye was crinkled. I could tell he was working up to saying something more.

'What has your Dad told you?' he asked.

From the back, picking the white dog hairs off her school blazer, Anne chirped, 'He told us that Mum wasn't very happy once.'

'Not very happy.' Grandad shifted into gear as the lights changed. The car gave a jerk and nearly stalled. Grandad was okay at driving, but not *that* good. 'I suppose that's right. You're, ah, both very young for the thing I'm going to have to tell you now. But we've spoken to the doctors at the hospital, and we reckon it's the best way. If you want your Mum to get better . . . you do want that, don't you?'

We both said yes. We were driving along the high street past the shops now. A couple of salamanders were lounging in the sun outside the new DIY superstore. I recognized them as tough older kids from school.

'Your Mum had a baby when she was . . . when she was far too young. Before she even met your Dad. You understand what that means?'

We both nodded. I decided it wasn't worth the bother of letting Grandad know that I'd worked that much out already.

'So we thought we could have the baby adopted. You know, given to some people who couldn't have a baby, but wanted one. It was a kind of . . . family secret.'

'That the baby was adopted?' I asked.

'No.' Grandad grated the gears. 'That it wasn't. Even your Dad didn't know that when he and your Mum were courting. We hid it. I guess now we're all to blame, I suppose . . . apart from you kids of course. Your Mum couldn't part with the baby, and I don't think anyone else would have had him anyway. The poor little thing wasn't – isn't – right in the head. He can't change shapes like the rest of us. For a while, we didn't think he could change at all. He was always just asleep, not really growing or living. Then one day, I put him down in the corner of my study, by this old football. When I looked . . .'

We'd reached the hospital. Grandad parked the car at the far end, but we didn't get out.

I asked, 'Did Dad know about this?'

Slowly, still gripping the wheel tight, Grandad nodded. 'Just before they got married, yes. But he always found it hard to take. He couldn't stand to have Tom around, reminding him. That was why he ended up in the garage. There for years. As a football.'

'And he's called Tom,' I said eventually.

Grandad nodded. He reached and took both of our hands to help us out of the car.

'Come on,' he said, 'let's see how your Mum is. She's got Tom with her now.'

We went and saw Mum. She was still a sloth, but she'd changed her face enough to smile, and it was obvious that she was a little better. She had Tom, our old family football, cradled in her arms. Dad was Dad. I could tell he was fidgeting to change into a snake or something, but tonight he stayed himself.

We all stood around with the head-doctor, smiling and talking in big shaky voices. Eventually, Anne started to cry. I was glad when she blurted out the thing that had been worrying me too. I mean, we'd been kicking Tom around the night before. I could still hear that leathery slap he made when he hit the back wall of the garages. But the head-doctor was reassuring. Tom wasn't really like us. He *was* a football. He probably even liked being played. It was better, after all, than the years he'd spent hidden behind the paint tins in our garage.

Anne stopped crying, and I took hold of her hand. Now that everything was out in the open, I felt relieved. But Dad was just standing there, gazing down at the concrete. Apart from Mum herself, I suppose this whole thing was most difficult for him out of all of us. It took a week of visits to the hospital before he could bring himself to reach through the bars and take Tom from Mum's incredibly long arms. A few moments later, he had to give him back, but next day, he kept hold. Gran and Grandad were there too, and I suppose we were wondering what Dad was going to do next. But he surprised us all by lobbing Tom gently into the air, then kicking him on the volley towards me. He came over at head height, and I nodded him down towards Anne, and she caught him. It was perfect, one of those miraculous moments that hardly ever happen. And we all started to laugh and pat each other's back and in the excitement Grandad forgot he was human and started to bark.

That was the real beginning of Mum getting better. Next day, her head had changed back into the person we knew. And the day after that – after we'd borrowed Tom for a big game down at the park against the lot from the next estate – we came late with Gran back to the hospital to tell Mum about it, and found her sitting up on a log in her old house coat. She was complaining about the noise and the smell in her ward, but she was smiling.

They soon moved her to a proper ward. And not long after that, she came home for good. Even her right hand was back to normal. The head-doctor said it had all been a kind of hysterical paralysis. The hand had been a warning sign, but what probably tipped the balance was seeing me and Anne playing football with Tom out on the grass in front of our houses.

When Grandma and Grandad came around for tea on

the Sunday after Mum got out, Grandad had gone back to being a dog again. We all felt a little sad to lose him that way – he had been such a nice old man. But at least he'd changed from a mongrel into a red setter, and although he was still old – and he still had the black patch – he was more fun to be with from then on. We used to go around to Gran's to bring him along with us when we took Tom to play in the park.

Tom stayed a football. I suppose he always will, never changing, never getting old. Sometimes I talk to him, but I don't think he hears, or understands if he does. One evening that summer when we were playing with him on the green, the inevitable happened and he flew over the fence into the Halls' back garden. Knowing we couldn't just leave him there the way we had with all the other footballs, Anne and I went up and rang their front door. Mrs Hall answered. She was shaped as an octopus actually, not a bird at all. And she simply let us in to collect up all the balls and everything else that had landed in their garden over the years.

With all the other balls back, we still always played with Tom. Of course, the other kids knew about him, and were a little edgy at first, passing gently, using side-foots towards goal. But I realized that Tom was finally accepted when John Williams missed a penalty and ran over to the fence to yell down at him as though it was his fault. We all fell about laughing at that, and when I happened to look up at the top windows of our house, I saw that Mum was standing in the bedroom with the net curtains pulled back. She was smiling.

We were well into the summer holidays by then. Dad had had a couple of good pay cheques, and we agreed that all of us would go on holiday together, and abroad for a change. Dad, Mum, me, Anne, Gran, and Tom. Even Grandad agreed to change back into a human for the fortnight to save any problems with quarantine.

I can still remember packing my case for that holiday on the night before we took the plane. Filling it up with books and shorts and tee shirts and cream for mosquito bites and clean pairs of pants. I could already picture that white beach, the white hotels, the cool old-fashioned streets at the back, the warm sea beckoning in the sunshine. First day, we'd all run out straight after breakfast and kick Tom across the smooth hot sand towards the breakers, changing into porpoises as we did so. Diving down into the stream of the ocean, bobbing Tom on our noses, dancing in the dappled light.

Which, as things turned out, is exactly what we did.

AHEAD!

Ian Watson

1: THE HEAD RACE

There's an old saying: it'll cost you an arm and a leg.

For me the cost amounted to two arms, two legs, and a torso. Everything below the neck, in fact. Thus my head and my brain would survive until posterity. How I pitied people of the past who were dead forever. How I pitied my contemporaries who were too blind to seize the chance of cryogenic preservation.

Here we were on the threshold of potential immortality. How could I not avail myself of the Jones legislation? The opportunity might not be available in our own country for longer than a couple of years. The population might drop to a sustainable level. A change of administration might bring a change of heart. There could be rancour at the cost of maintaining increasing numbers of frozen and unproductive heads.

Until then, though, we were in the Head Race with China and Japan and India and other overpopulated nations. The previous deterrent to freezing had been guillotined away. Now no one was compelled to wait for natural death by cancer or car crash – and thus risk their brain degenerating during vital lost minutes.

Farewell, likewise, to the fear of senile dementia or Alzheimer's! The head would be surgically removed swiftly in prime condition and frozen immediately. This knowledge was immensely comforting to me. It was also a little scary. I was among the earliest to register. Yet I must wait almost a month till my appointment with the blade. A whole month! What if I were murderously mugged before I could be decapitated? What if my head was mashed to pulp?

Fortunately, I was part of a nationwide support group of like minds linked by our PCs. To a fair extent our lobbying had finally resulted in the Jones Law. Yes, *ours*; along with lobbying by ecologists concerned with the welfare of the planet – and also, I have to admit, pressure from certain powerful right wing groups (but it's the outcome which counts).

So whilst awaiting decapitation (now a proud word!) there was quite a sense of emotional and intellectual solidarity.

As regards storage or tagging of our heads, would a distinction be made between idealists such as ourselves – and those who were incurably ill or who had despaired of their current lives – and so-called Obligatories?

Initially, the Obligatories would be processed separately by the Justice or Medical systems. Would storage be mixed or segregated? This remained unclear. We had no wish to stir any suspicion of discrimination! Yet surely there was a significant distinction between idealists and non-idealists. The permission/identification form we all signed upon registering contained a box reserved for our motive.

Reportedly, the majority of idealists would be withdrawing from the world for altruistic, ecological reasons. Too many people on the planet for the health of the world! These volunteers would forgo their lives.

Enthusiasts such as myself nursed more personal motives, although I would never call those motives selfish. *Immortality* is not a selfish concept but is a watchword of faith in the survival and advancement of the human race. Immortality treasures what we have been, what we are, and what we shall become in the huge aeons ahead of us.

In a state of considerable excitement, we of the Immortalist Network confided the motives which we had inserted in our box.

To share in the Future.

To know what will be.

To reach the Stars. (That was mine.)

To strive, to seek, to find.

Manifest destiny of Homo Sap!

$p = fpncflfifc$. (Which is the famous Drake Equation for the number of extraterrestrial civilizations out in space.)

Even: *To go boldly.*

And, wittily: *I want to keep ahead.* (To Keep A Head. Ho!)

In the future world, would our heads be provided with new bodies? New bottles for the old wine, as it were? The Forethought Institute assured us that nanotechnology was just around the corner. Another 30 or 40 years, judging by state of the art and according to Delphi Polls. Eighty years at the most. Working in vats of raw materials, millions of molecule-size programmed assemblers would speedily construct, if not living bodies, then at least excellent artificial prosthetic bodies. These might be preferable to living bodies, being more resilient and versatile.

Even failing this, surely our minds could be mapped into electronic storage with the processing capacity to simulate entire virtual-reality worlds, as well as interfacing with the real world. Those who had despaired would be fulfilled. Idealists would reap their reward.

Ought criminal Obligatories to receive resilient versatile new bodies? Should their electronic versions be allowed full access to a virtual-reality domain? That was for the future to decide – a future where the roots of mischief were better understood, and could be pruned or edited.

With what hopes and longings I approach the decapitation clinic on this my last day. My healthy organs will be harvested for transplants. My heart and kidneys and

retinas will disperse. My blood will be bottled for trans-
fusions. I imagine the anaesthetic as sweet, even though
it will be delivered by injection. I imagine the farewell
kiss of the blade, even though the anaesthetic will rob me
of sensation. Farewell, Old Regime. Welcome, the Revolution.

2: THE HEAD WAR

Smell, first of all, as the primitive reptilian brain-root re-
awakens: an overpowering odour of hair-gel, though without any actual sensation of breathing. No lungs to breathe
with?

Taste: slick and sour-sweet.

Sound: high-speed warbling.

Tactile: soft pressure all around my head. Otherwise:
nothing at all, sheer absence.

Vision! Slightly wobbly, as if through liquid. There's a
pyramid! It's composed of decomposing *heads*. Squinting
sidelong, I spy another pyramid – of whitened skulls.

And another, beyond it.

I must be hallucinating.

Or else information is being presented to me sym-
bolically.

My viewpoint is rising up, disclosing yet more pyramids
upon a flat white plain, perhaps a salt-flat. Ovoids are
airborne. Eggs hover and dart to and fro. One of these
floats close to me. The rounded bottom is opaque. The
transparent ellipsoid of the upper two-thirds contains a
hairless head, surely female. I believe that a clear gel wraps
and cushions the head. I must look likewise. Twin antennae
protrude from the top of the egg. She's a mobile disembodied head. I mouth at her, making my lips form mute
words. (*Hullo. What's happening? Where are we?*)

She mouths at me but I can't read her lips. No thoughts

transmit from those antennae to what I presume must be my own corresponding overhead antennae. Her egg-vehicle begins to swing away. I urge mine to follow but it continues onward lazily under its own impetus.

Can this white vista, with its menacing pyramids and its hovering heads, be actual? How can this be? Surely my head is being used. What seems to be happening is not what is really happening. It is a by-product.

Of a sudden two head-vehicles rush directly at one another. They collide and burst open. Briefly two faces kiss bruisingly while spilling gel hangs down elastically. Moments later both vehicles plummet down to the salt-flat. There they shatter entirely. Both heads roll out, surely oblivious by now.

From under the surface, two mobile crab-like devices emerge. In their claws they seize the heads. They scuttle towards a fledgling pyramid. Clambering, they nudge the heads into position, upright, where I suppose they will rot.

The female egg hasn't gone away, after all. It – or rather she – is swinging back towards me. At least I think that it is the selfsame egg. Now it's picking up speed. It's rushing at me. Will we shatter, and kiss hideously, and fall? I'm terrified.

At the very last moment, my vehicle tilts. I'm staring upward at blue sky and high wispy clouds. A fierce blow strikes my base. Such a stunning shock vibrates through me. Nevertheless I'm intact. I haven't ruptured. I think I am sinking down slowly towards the salt. Slowly, slowly.

Of her, there's no sight. She must have broken against my base and tumbled rapidly. Overhead, a dozen heads cruise by. What grim aerial game is this?

Or is this the only way in which I can experience a selection procedure whereby worthwhile heads are chosen for survival? Whereby hundreds of thousands are discarded?

Have I been selected or rejected?

Again I hear that high-speed warbling, as of bird-song

speeded up a hundredfold. With a slight bump I have come to rest. Sky and salt-flat and flying eggs and a nearby pyramid are fading – until I'm seeing only ... invisibility. There's nothing to see, nothing to taste, nothing to hear. Is this worse than being a disembodied head used as a game-piece by unknown forces?

Amidst this deprivation, for the first time in many years, I find myself praying to a force I scarcely believed in. *Dear God, help me*. Will an angel appear to me, coagulating out of nothingness?

All that can fill this void is a million memories of childhood. Of schooldays. Of my parents (forever dead, gone utterly!). Of first sex, first drug trip, first sight of the steaming teeming canyons of New York through which by night the roaming wailing vehicles suggested to my mind lugubrious monsters prowling for prey ...

Presently my memories attain a vivid visionary actuality against the all-pervading nothingness.

I realize that my identity is being reinforced and stabilized – and perhaps scrutinized. The episode of the flying eggheads was akin to a pre-uterine experience. All of those heads in the sky were equivalent to so many sperms surging for existence, all of them failing except for one, myself, being fertilized in that shocking collision and sinking down to become attached to the ground. Surely that was the significance. Maybe most frozen brains fail to reintegrate.

Now, like cells multiplying, my memories multiply until –

3: EMBODIED

– *I am embodied.*

I'm aware of *limbs*. Of arms and legs and hands and feet! They're so real to me, as I lie face downward with my eyes tight shut. How intensely I treasure this moment.

I cause my limbs to move just a little at first, like a beached swimmer. My fingers wiggle, and my toes.

I feel ampler than I used to be. I'm larger, superior, more muscular.

Arms and legs and – *wings* . . .

Wings? Yes, great furled wings are socketed into my shoulders! Already I'm sensing which new muscles to flex so as to use my amazing wings. These wings are why I am lying face downward and not upon my back; otherwise I would crush my wings uncomfortably.

Wings? Wings? A body with wings? Now I do open my eyes in wonder.

A veil of tiny flies fills the air, flitting around me like a myriad airborne workers around some vast construction project, which is myself. I have arisen. My new body is golden, ambery, its fabric not of flesh but of some flexible responsive robust plastic – inorganic yet endowed with organic performance.

This is a substance for which there is no word, since it never existed previously. Perhaps *protoplast* is a suitable term. Undoubtedly energy cells, charged by sunlight, are woven throughout my new skin, powering inner engines which can defy the thrall of gravity – else how, when I unfurl my wings, do I rise and hover like some colossal deity of this cloud of flies? The wings must be of some ingenious anti-gravitic bio-technology, to uplift my weight.

My head is still enclosed in a protective helmet. My new golden winged body is an ingenious prosthetic device sustaining and serving my natural head, in perfect harmony with my head.

Those flies are beginning to disperse, as if wafted away by my slow wingbeats. The veil is thinning – except over to my right. There, a dense cloud of flies begins to vibrate audibly. Vibrations become a voice, announcing my task . . .

There has been a nanocatastrophe.

The Forethought Institute were correct in their promise of rampant nanotechnology transforming the world. (How, otherwise, could I possess this angelic body, golden and winged and of miracle substance? How else would this body interface with my head of flesh and bone and blood and brain-cells, sustaining and obeying and augmenting me?) Alas, the whole world is as smooth as a billiard ball. Farewell to mountains and valleys. Farewell to forests and seas. Farewell, likewise, to all the species of fish, flesh, and fowl which once inhabited sea or land. Farewell to all plants and fungi and bacteria.

Due to the nanocatastrophe nothing remained of life except for these sealed frozen heads of ours, preserved perfectly – as if the human race had intuited the need for such a global insurance policy in the event of a nano-plague.

When I say that the planet is smooth and perfectly spherical I am omitting to mention the 100 equidistant colossi which rise from the surface. Seen from space, under modest magnification, the colossi might seem like so many individual whiskers upon a huge chin, or like so many stiff short freak hairs upon an otherwise gleaming bald head – few and far between, and exactly spaced.

Seen from the ground – or whilst hovering with our wings – each colossus towers vastly and baroquely up through the clouds. Some are still under construction by the untold trillions of mobile microscopic nano-assemblers, or by larger macro-machines forever being assembled and disassembled. Other colossi are almost complete, soaring to their designed height of ten kilometres.

Rooted by deep thermal spikes which exploit the inner

heat of the planet, these colossi are *ships*. When the construction is completed, their matrix-engines will all activate in unison. This will generate a global matrix-field. As the world implodes towards a vanishing point, all of the 1,000 great ornate darts will be translated outward simultaneously through the cosmic matrix – not to mere stars in our own galaxy, but each to the vicinity of some planet roughly similar to Earth yet in a different galaxy millions or tens of millions of light years away.

This is the Project for which the world was smoothed flat, erasing all life in the process, except for our preserved heads. Expansion throughout the universe!

5: BUT . . .

But even at speeds far slower than that of light, surely nanos in tiny vessels could reach the furthest part of our own galaxy within, say, twenty million years at most. They could arrive in other galaxies within 100 million years. The universe is due to endure for 50 times longer than that. At least!

Why the urgency? Why convert the entire Earth into a catapult which will destroy itself?

The pace of activity of microscopic nanos must be far faster than that of creatures such as Man (and Woman) – yet why could the nanos not become dormant en route to the stars, like spores, simply switching themselves off?

The reason for their hurry provides an answer to the *Von Neuman Enigma* – as I discover in conversation with another golden Angel nine kilometres up the ship to which we are both assigned.

The Von Neuman Enigma: If life already arose anywhere in the universe and sent out self-replicating probes, why is the universe not already full of probes? In the whole of the cosmos did adventurous, intelligent life only ever arise on one single planet, Earth?

My companion and I soar on thermals, ascending alongside the ship. We arrive at a platform in the stratosphere. With our robust bodies of protoplast we are to assist macro-machines to construct a spire which will support yet another tier of the colossus.

My companion is Hispanic. With bald tan head enshrined in transparent holder fixed upon golden body – and his wings folded dorsally from shoulders down to knees now that we had arrived high above the clouds – he is magnificent. Daunting.

After some labour we rest . . . not that our new bodies ever became fatigued. We do not sleep, though we might daydream while we absorb nutrition through valves in our ankles. Nanos in our heads repair any physical degener-ation. A device in our throats permits us to speak aloud.

'What year do you think this is?' I ask my colleague.

'The Year Zero,' he replies. His comment makes sense. All human history has vanished except for what we each remember. The time of the nanocatastrophe constitutes an absolute gulf between *before* and *now*.

I broach the matter of the Von Neuman Enigma, which bothered me even in the old days.

'The answer,' he declares, 'is that the Hayflick Limit applies to all social entities as well as to individual organ-isms.' Such is the profound conversation of angels.

But of course, but of course . . . !

The bugbear of the damned *Hayflick Limit* used to tor-ment me. Body cells only replace themselves a finite number of times before the process fails. For human beings this limit is 70 times or thereabouts. Then comes decay and death.

'The Hayflick Limit also applies,' says this Hispanic angel, 'to the Congregation of Nanos. Social entities such as civilizations obey the same limiting constraint as the cells in bodies – a law as binding as entropy. No matter how well the nanos stabilize their collective activity, over a period of millions of years this would lose all coherence.'

'Collectively they would suffer entropy . . .'

'Exactly so!' he tells me. 'With our slower thoughts, we serve as an anchor – as the *root* from which they arose. Their source and origin. We are their touchstone and criterion. Their pacemaker, their talisman. Furthermore, in an important sense we provide purpose. People uniquely possess a sense of far-reaching purpose – because that is our nature. This is true even if only one person remains in existence, provided that he never yields to despair.'

In the terms of a ship (for the Colossi are certainly ships) we are, quite literally, to be –

6: FIGUREHEADS

– figureheads, no less!

At the very summit of each colossus, protected by a cone of energy, right there at the tip of the ship, one of us will ride head-first.

On a thousand colossal ships a thousand proud heads (attached to protoplast bodies) will each gaze upon a new galaxy, and a new world similar to Earth.

Translation through the matrix will ensure comparability – similarity as regards mass and diameter and distance from a star which will closely resemble Earth's own sun. The planet in question *might* be barren, or be at boiling point due to greenhouse gases, or be an ice-desert. Yet surely hundreds may be habitats of some kind of life, or potential for life; for cosmic companionship.

This, mine eyes shall behold . . .

A thousand ships, a thousand heads! What if more than a thousand heads still survive?

At this moment the Hispanic angel launches himself at me.

How we wrestle. How well-matched we are.

Our struggle ranges to and fro across this uppermost platform. Will he try to butt my helmet with his own, to crack it open if he can? When I realize that he has no intention of risking this, I am less cautious in my grips and clutches.

Pulling free and half-turning, he unfurls his wings to buffet and batter me. I punch with all the force of my golden fist at the base of one wing . . . which sags, which droops. I have fractured the attachment.

We are at the edge of the platform, where a thin breeze streams by. Gathering myself – and against all former human instinct – I hurtle against him, carrying him over the side along with myself.

For a moment, as we fall, he can't free an arm to grasp me. In that moment I deploy my own wings and release him.

Down, down he drops, crippled, spinning single-winged, accelerating willy-nilly. Nine kilometres he will fall to the billiard-ball ground. I'm alone upon the ship except for machines and invisible nanos.

7: TRIUMPH

The Project is complete at last.

I stand erect, the very pinnacle of the galaxy-ship. No thunderous surge of acceleration will raise this colossus upon a column of fire. When the matrix-field activates world-wide – when the smooth ball of the world begins to implode – translation will occur instantaneously.

Even so, like a swimmer upon the highest diving board I raise my golden arms above my bottled head, palms pressed together steeple-style as if to leap and cleave the heavens.

Do my 999 brothers and sisters likewise signal their imminent departure?

A humming vibration commences.

8: FULFILMENT

Lakes of brilliant stars! A ball of blinding yellow light which is the local sun! Its radiance illuminates a full hemisphere of another nearby ball – a world white with clouds and blue with ocean, mottled with land-masses.

Earthlike. Similar . . .

Maybe the oceans and the land are sterile. Maybe not. To stare from space at this spectacle is to be Columbus and Cortez and Captain Cook all in one. I may be ten million light years away from my birth-place. Or 100 million. This, in itself, is an ultimate achievement.

All because I dared to be decapitated!

Within a day or so, my colossus will be in orbit – like some titanic statue equipped with a tiny living head. I assume that the nanos will reshape the ship into hundreds of gliding wings which will descend. I presume that provision will be made for me.

Or what purpose could there be?

BAD TIMING

Molly Brown

'Time travel is an inexact science. And its study is fraught with paradoxes.' Samuel Colson, b. 2301 d. 2197.

Alan rushed through the archway without even glancing at the inscription across the top. It was Monday morning and he was late again. He often thought about the idea that time was a point in space, and he didn't like it. That meant that at this particular point in space it was always Monday morning and he was always late for a job he hated. And it always had been. And it always would be. Unless somebody tampered with it, which was strictly forbidden.

'Oh my Holy Matrix,' Joe Twofingers exclaimed as Alan raced past him to register his palmprint before losing an extra 30 minutes' pay. 'You wouldn't believe what I found in the fiction section!'

Alan slapped down his hand. The recorder's metallic voice responded with, 'Employee number 057, Archives Department, Alan Strong. Thirty minutes and seven point two seconds late. One hour's credit deducted.'

Alan shrugged and turned back towards Joe. 'Since I'm not getting paid, I guess I'll put my feet up and have a cup of liquid caffeine. So tell me what you found.'

'Well, I was tidying up the files – fiction section is a mess as you know – and I came across this magazine. And I thought, "what's *this* doing here?" It's something from the twentieth century called *Woman's Secrets*, and it's all knitting patterns, recipes, and gooey little romance stories: "He grabbed her roughly, bruising her soft pale skin, and pulled her to his rock hard chest" and so on. I figured it was in there by mistake and nearly threw it out. But then I saw this story called "The Love That Conquered Time" and I realized that must be what they're keeping it for. So I had a look at it, and it was . . .' He made a face and stuck a finger down his throat. 'But I really think you ought to read it.'

'Why?'

'Because you're in it.'

'You're a funny guy, Joe. You almost had me going for a minute.'

'I'm serious! Have a look at the drebbing thing. It's by some woman called Cecily Walker, it's in that funny old vernacular they used to use, and it's positively dire. But the guy in the story is definitely you.'

Alan didn't believe him for a minute. Joe was a joker, and always had been. Alan would never forget the time Joe had laced his drink with a combination aphrodisiac-hallucinogen at a party and he'd made a total fool of himself with the section leader's overcoat. He closed his eyes and shuddered as Joe handed him the magazine.

Like all the early relics made of paper, the magazine had been dipped in preservative and the individual pages coated with a clear protective covering which gave them a horrible chemical smell and a tendency to stick together. After a little difficulty, Alan found the page he wanted. He rolled his eyes at the painted illustration of a couple locked in a passionate but chaste embrace, and dutifully began to read.

It was all about a beautiful but lonely and unfulfilled woman who still lives in the house where she was born. One day there is a knock at the door, and she opens it to a mysterious stranger: tall, handsome, and extremely charismatic.

Alan chuckled to himself.

A few paragraphs later, over a candle-lit dinner, the man tells the woman that he comes from the future, where time travel has become a reality, and he works at the Colson Time Studies Institute in the Department of Archives.

Alan stopped laughing.

The man tells her that only certain people are allowed to time travel, and they are not allowed to interfere in any way, only observe. He confesses that he is not a qualified traveller – he broke into the lab one night and stole a machine. The woman asks him why and he tells her, 'You're the only reason, Claudia. I did it for you. I read a story that you wrote and I knew it was about me and that it was about you. I searched in the Archives and I found your picture and then I knew that I loved you and that I had always loved you and that I always would.'

'But I never wrote a story, Alan.'

'You will, Claudia. You will.'

The Alan in the story goes on to describe the Project, and the Archives, in detail. The woman asks him how people live in the twenty-fourth century, and he tells her about the gadgets in his apartment.

The hairs at the back of Alan's neck rose at the mention of his Neuro-Pleasatron. He'd never told *anybody* that he'd bought one, not even Joe.

After that, there's a lot of grabbing and pulling to his rock hard chest, melting sighs and kisses, and finally a wedding and a 'happily ever after' existing at one point in space where it always has and always will.

Alan turned the magazine over and looked at the date on the cover. March 14, 1973.

He wiped the sweat off his forehead and shook himself. He looked up and saw that Joe was standing over him.

'You wouldn't really do that, would you,' Joe said. 'Because you know I'd have to stop you.'

Cecily Walker stood in front of her bedroom mirror and turned from right to left. She rolled the waistband over one more time, making sure both sides were even. Great;

the skirt looked like a real mini. Now all she had to do was get out of the house without her mother seeing her.

She was in the record shop wondering if she really should spend her whole allowance on the new Monkees album, but she really liked Peter Tork, he was so cute, when Tommy Johnson walked in with Roger Hanley. 'Hey, Cesspit! Whaddya do, lose the bottom half of your dress?'

The boys at her school were just so creepy. She left the shop and turned down the main road, heading toward her friend Candy's house. She never noticed the tall blonde man who stood across the street, or heard him call her name.

When Joe went on his lunch break, Alan turned to the wall above his desk and said, 'File required: Authors, fiction, twentieth century, initial "W".'

'Checking,' the wall said. 'File located.'

'Biography required: Walker, Cecily.'

'Checking. Biography located. Display? Yes or no.'

'Yes.'

A section of wall the size of a small television screen lit up at eye-level, directly in front of Alan. He leaned forward and read: Walker, Cecily. b. Danville, Illinois, USA. 1948 d. 2037. Published works: 'The Love That Conquered Time,' March, 1973. Accuracy rating: fair.

'Any other published works?'

'Checking. None found.'

Alan looked down at the magazine in his lap.

'I don't understand,' Claudia said, looking pleadingly into his deep blue eyes. Eyes the colour of the sea on a cloudless morning, and eyes that contained an ocean's depth of feeling for her, and her alone. 'How is it possible to travel through time?'

'I'll try to make this simple,' he told her, pulling her close. She took a deep breath, inhaling his manly aroma, and rested her head on his shoulder with a sigh. 'Imagine

214

that the universe is like a string. And every point on that string is a moment in space and time. But instead of stretching out in a straight line, it's all coiled and tangled and it overlaps in layers. Then all you have to do is move from point to point.'

Alan wrinkled his forehead in consternation. 'File?'

'Yes. Waiting.'

'Information required: further data on Walker, Cecily. Education, family background.'

'Checking. Found. Display? Yes or –'

'Yes!'

Walker, Cecily. Education: Graduate Lincoln High, Danville, 1967. Family background: Father Walker, Matthew. Mechanic, automobile. d. 1969. Mother no data.

Alan shook his head. Minimal education, no scientific background. How could she know so much? 'Information required: photographic likeness of subject. If available, display.'

He blinked and there she was, smiling at him across his desk. She was oddly dressed, in a multi-coloured tee-shirt that ended above her waist and dark blue trousers that were cut so low they exposed her navel and seemed to balloon out below her knees into giant flaps of loose-hanging material. But she had long dark hair that fell across her shoulders and down to her waist, crimson lips and the most incredible eyes he had ever seen – huge and green. She was beautiful. He looked at the caption: Walker, Cecily. Author: Fiction related to time-travel theory. Photographic likeness circa 1970.

'File,' he said. 'Further data required: personal details, ie. marriage. Display.'

Walker, Cecily m. Strong, Alan.

'Date?'

No data.

'Biographical details of husband, Strong, Alan?'

None found.

'Redisplay photographic likeness. Enlarge.' He stared at the wall for several minutes. 'Print,' he said.

Only half a block to go, the woman thought, struggling with two bags of groceries. The sun was high in the sky and the smell of Mrs Henderson's roses, three doors down, filled the air with a lovely perfume. But she wasn't in the mood to appreciate it. All the sun made her feel was hot, and all the smell of flowers made her feel was ill. It had been a difficult pregnancy, but thank goodness it was nearly over now.

She wondered who the man was, standing on her front porch. He might be the new mechanic at her husband's garage, judging by his orange coveralls. Nice-looking, she thought, wishing that she didn't look as if there was a bowling ball underneath her dress.

'Excuse me,' the man said, reaching out to help her with her bags. 'I'm looking for Cecily Walker.'

'My name's Walker,' the woman told him. 'But I don't know any Cecily.'

'Cecily,' she repeated when the man had gone. What a pretty name.

Alan decided to work late that night. Joe left at the usual time and told him he'd see him tomorrow.

'Yeah, tomorrow,' Alan said.

He waited until Joe was gone, and then he took the printed photo of Cecily Walker out of his desk drawer and sat for a long time, staring at it. What did he know about this woman? Only that she'd written one published story, badly, and that she was the most gorgeous creature he had ever seen. Of course, what he was feeling was ridiculous. She'd been dead more than 300 years.

But there were ways of getting around that.

Alan couldn't believe what he was actually considering. It was lunacy. He'd be caught, and he'd lose his job. But then he realized that he could never have read about it if he hadn't already done it and got away with it. He decided to have another look at the story.

It wasn't there. Under Fiction: Paper Relics: 20th Century, sub-section Magazines, American, there was shelf after shelf full of *Amazing Stories, Astounding, Analog, Weird Tales* and *Isaac Asimov's Science Fiction Magazine*, but not one single copy of *Woman's Secrets*.

Well, he thought, if the magazine isn't there, I guess I never made it after all. Maybe it's better that way. Then he thought, but if I never made it, how can I be looking for the story? I shouldn't even know about it. And then he had another thought.

'File,' he said. 'Information required: magazines on loan.'

'Display?'

'No, just tell me.'

'*Woman's Secrets*, date 1973. *Astounding*, date . . .'

'Skip the rest. Who's got *Woman's Secrets*?'

'Checking. Signed out to Project Control through Joe Twofingers.'

Project Control was on to him! If he didn't act quickly, it would be too late.

It was amazingly easy to get into the lab. He just walked in. The machines were all lined up against one wall, and there was no one around to stop him. He sat down on the nearest machine. The earliest model developed by Samuel Colson had looked like an English telephone box (he'd been a big *Doctor Who* fan), but it was hardly inconspicuous and extremely heavy, so refinements were made until the latest models were lightweight, collapsible, and made to look exactly like (and double up as) a folding bicycle. The control board was hidden from general view, inside a wicker basket.

None of the instruments was labelled. Alan tentatively pushed one button. Nothing happened. He pushed another. Still nothing.

He jumped off and looked for an instruction book. There had to be one somewhere. He was ransacking a desk when the door opened.

'I thought I'd find you here, Alan.'

'Joe! I . . . uh . . . was just . . .'

'I know what you're doing, and I can't let you go through with it. It's against every rule of the Institute and you know it. If you interfere with the past, who knows what harm you might do?'

'But Joe, you know me. I wouldn't do any harm. I won't do anything to affect history, I swear it. I just want to see her, that's all. Besides, it's already happened, or you couldn't have read that magazine. And that's another thing! You're the one who showed it to me! I never would have known about her if it hadn't been for you. So if I'm going now, it's down to you.'

'Alan, I'm sorry, but my job is on the line here, too, you know. So don't give me any trouble and come along quietly.'

Joe moved towards him, holding a pair of handcuffs. Attempted theft of Institute property was a felony punishable by five years' imprisonment without pay. Alan picked up the nearest bike and brought it down over the top of Joe's head. The machine lay in pieces and Joe lay unconscious. Alan bent down and felt his pulse. He would be okay. 'Sorry, Joe. I had to do it. File!'

'Yes.'

'Information required: instruction manual for usage of . . .' he checked the number on the handlebars, 'Colson Model 44B Time Traveller.'

'Checking. Found. Display?'

'No. Just print. And fast.'

The printer was only on page five when Alan heard running footsteps. Five pages would have to do.

* - * * *

Dear Cher,

My name is Cecily Walker and all my friends tell me I look just like you. Well, a little bit. Anyway, the reason that I'm writing to you is this: I'm starting my senior year in high school, and I've never had a steady boyfriend. I've gone out with a couple of boys, but they only want one thing, and I guess you know what that is. I keep thinking there's gotta be somebody out there who's the right one for me, but I just haven't met him. Was it love at first sight for you and Sonny?

Alan sat on a London park bench with his printout and tried to figure out what he'd done wrong. Under Location: Setting, it just said 'See page 29.' Great, he thought. And he had no idea what year it was. Every time he tried to ask someone, they'd give him a funny look and walk away in a hurry. He folded up the bike and took a walk. It wasn't long before he found a news-stand and saw the date: July 19, 1998. At least he had the right century.

Back in the park, he sat astride the machine with the printout in one hand, frowning and wondering what might happen if he twisted a particular dial from right to left.

'Can't get your bike to start, mate?' someone shouted from nearby. 'Just click your heels three times and think of home.'

'Thanks, I'll try that,' Alan shouted back. Then he vanished.

'I am a pirate from yonder ship,' the man with the eye patch told her, 'and well used to treasure. But I tell thee, lass, I've never seen the like of you.'

Cecily groaned and ripped the page in half. She bit her lip and started again.

'I have travelled many galaxies, Madeleine,' the alien bleeped. 'But you are a life-form beyond compare.'

'No, don't. Please don't,' Madeleine pleaded as the alien reached out to pull her towards its rock-hard chest.

Her mother appeared in the doorway. 'Whatcha doin', hon?'

She dropped the pen and flipped the writing pad face down. 'My homework.'

The next thing Alan knew he was in the middle of a cornfield. He hitched a lift with a truck driver who asked a lot of questions, ranging from 'You work in a gas station, do you?' to 'What are you, foreign or something?' and 'What do you call that thing?' On being told 'that thing' was a folding bicycle, the man muttered something about whatever would they think of next, and now his kid would be wanting one.

There were several Walkers listed in the Danville phone book. When he finally found the right house, Cecily was in the middle of her third birthday party.

He pedalled around a corner, checked his printout, and set the controls on 'Fast Forward.' He folded the machine and hid it behind a bush before walking back to the house. It was big and painted green, just as in the story. There was an apple tree in the garden, just as in the story. The porch swing moved ever so slightly, rocked by an early summer breeze. He could hear crickets chirping and birds singing. Everything was just the way it had been in the story, so he walked up the path, nervously clearing his throat and pushing back a stray lock of hair, just the way Cecily Walker had described him in *Woman's Secrets*, before finally taking a deep breath and knocking on the door. There was movement inside the house. The clack of high-heeled shoes across a wooden floor, the rustle of a cotton dress.

'Yes?'

Alan stared at her, open-mouthed. 'You've cut your hair,' he told her.

'What?'

'Your hair. It used to hang down to your waist, now it's up to your shoulders.'

'Do I know you?'

'You will,' he told her. He'd said that in the story.

She was supposed to take one look at him and realize with a fluttering heart that this was the man she'd dreamed of all her life. Instead, she looked at his orange jumpsuit and slapped her hand to her forehead in enlightenment. 'You're from the garage! Of course, Mack said he'd be sending the new guy.' She looked past him into the street. 'So where's your tow truck?'

'My what?' There was nothing in 'The Love That Conquered Time' about a tow truck. The woman stared at him, looking confused. Alan stared back, equally confused. He started to wonder if he'd made a mistake. But then he saw those eyes, bigger and greener than he'd ever thought possible. 'Matrix,' he said out loud.

'What?'

'I'm sorry. It's just that meeting you is so bullasic.'

'Mister, I don't understand one word you're saying.' Cecily knew she should tell the man to go away. He was obviously deranged; she should call the police. But something held her back, a flicker of recognition, the dim stirrings of a memory. Where had she seen this man before?

'I'm sorry,' Alan said again. 'My American isn't very good. I come from English-speaking Europe, you see.'

'English-speaking Europe?' Cecily repeated. 'You mean England?'

'Not exactly. Can I come inside? I'll explain everything.'

She let him come in after warning him that her neighbours would come running in with shotguns if they heard her scream, and that she had a black belt in Kung Fu. Alan nodded and followed her inside, wondering where Kung Fu was, and why she'd left her belt there.

He was ushered into the living room and told to have a

seat. He sat down on the red velveteen-upholstered sofa and stared in awe at such historical artefacts as a black-and-white television with rabbit-ear antennae, floral-printed wallpaper, a phone you had to dial, and shelf after shelf of unpreserved books. She picked up a wooden chair and carried it to the far side of the room before sitting down. 'Okay,' she said. 'Talk.'

Alan felt it would have been better to talk over a candle-lit dinner in a restaurant, as they did in the story, but he went ahead and told her everything, quoting parts of the story verbatim, such as the passage where she described him as the perfect lover she'd been longing for all her life.

When he was finished, she managed a frozen smile. 'So you've come all the way from the future just to visit little ole me. Isn't that nice.'

Oh Matrix, Alan thought. She's humouring me. She's convinced I'm insane and probably dangerous as well. 'I know this must sound crazy to you,' he said.

'Not at all,' she told him, gripping the arms of her chair. He could see the blood draining out of her fingers.

'Please don't be afraid. I'd never harm you.' He sighed and put a hand to his forehead. 'It was all so different in the story.'

'But I never wrote any story. Well, I started one once, but I never got beyond the second page.'

'But you will. You see, it doesn't get published until 1973.'

'You do know this is 1979, don't you?'

'WHAT?'

'Looks like your timing's off,' she said. She watched him sink his head into his hands with an exaggerated groan. She rested her chin on one hand and regarded him silently. He didn't seem so frightening now. Crazy, yes, but not frightening. She might even find him quite attractive, if only things were different. He looked up at her and smiled. It was a crooked, little boy's smile that made his eyes sparkle. For a moment, she almost let herself imagine waking up to that smile . . . She pulled herself up in her chair, her back rigid.

'Look,' he said. 'So I'm a few years behind schedule. The main thing is I found you. And so what if the story comes out a bit later, it's nothing we can't handle. It's only a minor problem. A little case of bad timing.'

'Excuse me,' Cecily said. 'But I think that in this case, timing is everything. If any of this made the least bit of sense, which it doesn't, you would've turned up before now. You said yourself the story was published in 1973 – if it was based on fact, you'd need to arrive here much earlier.'

'I did get here earlier, but I was *too* early.'

Cecily's eyes widened involuntarily. 'What do you mean?'

'I mean I was here before. I met you. I spoke to you.'

'When?'

'You wouldn't remember. You were three years old, and your parents threw a party for you out in the garden. Of course I realized my mistake instantly, but I bluffed it out by telling your mother that I'd just dropped by to apologize because my kid was sick and couldn't come – it was a pretty safe bet that someone wouldn't have shown – and she said, "Oh you must be little Sammy's father" and asked me in. I was going to leave immediately, but your father handed me a beer and started talking about something called baseball. Of course I didn't have a present for you . . .'

'But you gave me a rose and told my mother to press it into a book so that I'd have it forever.'

'You remember.'

'Wait there. Don't move.' She leapt from her chair and ran upstairs. There was a lot of noise from above – paper rattling, doors opening and closing, things being thrown about. She returned clutching several books to her chest, her face flushed and streaked with dust. She flopped down on the floor and spread them out in front of her. When Alan got up to join her, she told him to stay where he was or she'd scream. He sat back down.

She opened the first book, and then Alan saw that they weren't books at all; they were photo albums. He watched in silence as she flipped through the pages and then tossed it aside. She tossed three of them away before she found what she was looking for. She stared open-mouthed at the brittle yellow page and then she looked up at Alan. 'I don't understand this,' she said, turning her eyes back to the album and a faded black and white photograph stuck to the paper with thick, flaking paste. Someone had written in ink across the top: Cecily's 3rd birthday, August 2nd, 1951. There was her father, who'd been dead for ten years, young and smiling, holding out a bottle to another young man, tall and blonde and dressed like a gas-station attendant. 'I don't understand this at all.' She pushed the album across the floor towards Alan. 'You haven't changed one bit. You're even wearing the same clothes.'

'Did you keep the rose?'

She walked over to a wooden cabinet and pulled out a slim hardback with the title, *My First Reader*. She opened it and showed him the dried, flattened flower. 'You're telling me the truth, aren't you?' she said. 'This is all true. You risked everything to find me because we were meant to be together, and nothing, not even time itself, could keep us apart.'

Alan nodded. There was a speech just like that in 'The Love That Conquered Time.'

'Bastard,' she said.

Alan jumped. He didn't remember that part. 'Pardon me?'

'Bastard,' she said again. 'You bastard!'

'I . . . I don't understand.'

She got up and started to pace the room. 'So you're the

one, huh? You're "Mister Right," Mister Happily Ever After, caring, compassionate and great in bed. And you decide to turn up now. Well, isn't that just great.'

'Is something the matter?' Alan asked her.

'Is something the matter?' she repeated. 'He asks me if something's the matter! I'll tell you what's the matter. I got married four weeks ago, you son of a bitch!'

'You're married?'

'That's what I said, isn't it?'

'But you can't be married. We were supposed to find perfect happiness together at a particular point in space that has always existed and always will. This ruins everything.'

'All those years . . . all those years. I went through hell in high school, you know. I was the only girl in my class who didn't have a date for the prom. So where were you then, huh? While I was sitting alone at home, crying my goddamn eyes out? How about all those Saturday nights I spent washing my hair? And even worse, those nights I worked at Hastings' Bar serving drinks to salesmen pretending they don't have wives. Why couldn't you have been around then, when I needed you?'

'Well, I've only got the first five pages of the manual . . .' He walked over to her and put his hands on her shoulders. She didn't move away. He gently pulled her closer to him. She didn't resist. 'Look,' he said, 'I'm sorry. I'm a real zark-head. I've made a mess of everything. You're happily married, you never wrote the story . . . I'll just go back where I came from, and none of this will have ever happened.'

'Who said I was happy?'

'But you just got married.'

She pushed him away. 'I got married because I'm thirty years old and figured I'd never have another chance. People do that, you know. They reach a certain age and they figure it's now or never . . . Damn you! If only you'd come when you were supposed to!'

'You're thirty? Matrix, in half an hour you've gone from a toddler to someone older than me.' He saw the expression on her face, and mumbled an apology.

'Look,' she said. 'You're gonna have to go. My husband'll be back any minute.'

'I know I have to leave. But the trouble is, that drebbing story was true! I took one look at your photo, and I knew that I loved you and I always had. Always. That's the way time works, you see. And even if this whole thing vanishes as the result of some paradox, I swear to you I won't forget. Somewhere there's a point in space that belongs to us. I know it.' He turned to go. 'Good-bye, Cecily.'

'Alan, wait! That point in space – I want to go there. Isn't there anything we can do? I mean, you've got a time machine, after all.'

What an idiot, he thought. The solution's been staring me in the face and I've been too blind to see it. 'The machine!' He ran down the front porch steps and turned around to see her standing in the doorway. 'I'll see you later,' he told her. He knew it was a ridiculous thing to say the minute he'd said it. What he meant was, 'I'll see you earlier.'

Five men sat together inside a tent made of animal hide. The land of their fathers was under threat, and they met in council to discuss the problem. The one called Swiftly Running Stream advocated war, but Foot Of The Crow was more cautious. 'The paleface is too great in number, and his weapons give him an unfair advantage.' Flying Bird suggested that they smoke before speaking further.

Black Elk took the pipe into his mouth. He closed his eyes for a moment and declared that the Great Spirit would give them a sign if they were meant to go to war. As soon as he said the word, 'war,' a paleface materialized among them. They all saw him. The white man's body was covered in a strange bright garment such as they had never seen, and he rode a fleshless horse with silver bones. The vision vanished as suddenly as it had appeared, leaving them with this message to ponder: *Oops*.

There was no one home, so he waited on the porch. It was a beautiful day, with a gentle breeze that carried the scent of roses: certainly better than that smoke-filled teepee.

A woman appeared in the distance. He wondered if that was her. But then he saw that it couldn't be, the woman's walk was strange and her body was misshapen. She's pregnant, he realized. It was a common thing in the days of over-population, but he couldn't remember the last time he'd seen a pregnant woman back home – it must have been years. She looked at him questioningly as she waddled up the steps balancing two paper bags. Alan thought the woman looked familiar; he knew that face. He reached out to help her.

'Excuse me,' he said. 'I'm looking for Cecily Walker.'

'My name's Walker,' the woman told him. 'But I don't know any Cecily.'

Matrix, what a moron, Alan thought, wanting to kick himself. Of course he knew the woman; it was Cecily's mother, and if she was pregnant, it had to be 1948. 'My mistake,' he told her. 'It's been a long day.'

The smell of roses had vanished, along with the leaves on the trees. There was snow on the ground and a strong northeasterly wind. Alan set the thermostat on his jumpsuit accordingly and jumped off the bike.

'So it's you again,' Cecily said ironically. 'Another case of perfect timing.' She was twenty pounds heavier and there were lines around her mouth and her eyes. She wore a heavy wool cardigan sweater over an oversized tee-shirt, jeans, and a pair of fuzzy slippers. She looked him up and down. 'You don't age at all, do you?'

'Please can I come in? It's freezing.'

'Yeah, yeah. Come in. You like a cup of coffee?'

'You mean liquid caffeine? That'd be great.'

He followed her into the living room and his mouth dropped open. The red sofa was gone, replaced by something that looked like a giant banana. The television was four times bigger and had lost the rabbit-ears. The floral wallpaper had been replaced by plain white walls not very different from those of his apartment. 'Sit,' she told him. She left the room for a moment and returned with two mugs, one of which she slammed down in front of him, causing a miniature brown tidal wave to splash across his legs.

'Cecily, are you upset about something?'

'That's a good one! He comes back after fifteen years and asks me if I'm upset.'

'Fifteen years!' Alan sputtered.

'That's right. It's 1994, you bozo.'

'Oh darling, and you've been waiting all this time . . .'

'Like hell I have,' she interrupted. 'When I met you, back in 1979, I realized that I couldn't stay in that sham of a marriage for another minute. So I must have set some kind of a record for quickie marriage and divorce, by Danville standards, anyway. So I was a thirty-year-old divorcee whose marriage had fallen apart in less than two months, and I was back to washing my hair alone on Saturday nights. And people talked. Lord, how they talked. But I didn't care, because I'd finally met my soul-mate and everything was going to be all right. He told me he'd fix it. He'd be back. So I waited. I waited for a year. Then I waited two years. Then I waited three. After ten, I got tired of waiting. And if you think I'm going through another divorce, you're crazy.'

'You mean you're married again?'

'What else was I supposed to do? A man wants you when you're forty, you jump at it. As far as I knew, you were gone forever.'

'I've never been away, Cecily. I've been here all along, but never at the right time. It's that drebbing machine; I can't figure out the controls.'

'Maybe Arnie can have a look at it when he gets in, he's pretty good at that sort of thing – what am I saying?'

'Tell me, did you ever write the story?'

'What's to write about? Anyway, what difference does it make? *Woman's Secrets* went bankrupt years ago.'

'Matrix! If you never wrote the story, then I shouldn't even know about you. So how can I be here? Dammit, it's a paradox. And I wasn't supposed to cause any of those. Plus, I think I may have started an Indian war. Have you noticed any change in local history?'

'Huh?'

'Never mind. Look, I have an idea. When exactly did you get divorced?'

'I don't know, late '79. October, November, something like that.'

'All right, that's what I'll aim for. November, 1979. Be waiting for me.'

'How?'

'Good point. Okay, just take my word for it, you and me are going to be sitting in this room right here, right now, with one big difference: we'll have been married for fifteen years, okay?'

'But what about Arnie?'

'Arnie won't know the difference. You'll never have married him in the first place.' He kissed her on the cheek. 'I'll be back in a minute. Well, in 1979. You know what I mean.' He headed for the door.

'Hold on,' she said. 'You're like the guy who goes out for a pack of cigarettes and doesn't come back for thirty years.'

'What guy?'

'Never mind. I wanna make sure you don't turn up anywhere else. Bring the machine in here.'

'Is that it?' she said one minute later.

'That's it.'

'But it looks like a goddamn bicycle.'

'Where do you want me to put it?'

She led him upstairs. 'Here,' she said. Alan unfolded the bike next to the bed. 'I don't want you getting away from me next time,' she told him.

'I don't have to get away from you now.'

'You do. I'm married and I'm at least fifteen years older than you.'

'Your age doesn't matter to me,' Alan told her. 'When I first fell in love with you, you'd been dead three hundred years.'

'You really know how to flatter a girl, don't you? Anyway, don't aim for '79. I don't understand paradoxes, but I know I don't like them. If we're ever gonna get this thing straightened out, you must arrive before 1973, when the story is meant to be published. Try for '71 or '72. Now that I think about it, those were a strange couple of years for me. Nothing seemed real to me then. Nothing seemed worth bothering about, nothing mattered; I always felt like I was waiting for something. Day after day I waited, though I never knew what for.'

She stepped back and watched him slowly turn a dial until he vanished. Then she remembered something.

How could she have ever have forgotten such a thing? She was eleven and she was combing her hair in front of her bedroom mirror. She screamed. When both her parents burst into the room and demanded to know what was wrong, she told them she'd seen a man on a bicycle. They nearly sent her to a child psychiatrist.

Damn that Alan, she thought. He's screwed up again.

The same room, different decor, different time of day. Alan blinked several times; his eyes had difficulty adjusting to the darkness. He could barely make out the shape on the bed, but he could see all he needed to. The shape was alone, and it was adult size. He leaned close to her ear. 'Cecily,' he whispered. 'It's me.' He touched her shoulder and shook her slightly. He felt for a pulse.

He switched on the bedside lamp. He gazed down at a withered face framed by silver hair, and sighed. 'Sorry, love,' he said. He covered her head with a sheet, and sighed again.

He sat down on the bike and unfolded the printout. He'd get it right eventually.

WORLD WARS III

Paul Di Filippo

'Is history personal or statistical?'
– T. Pynchon

This happened in Hamburg on the eve of J-Day, the night
of that now legendary USO triple bill: the Beatles opening
for the Supremes and Elvis. Sort of a chorus of pop Valkyr-
ies the brass had kindly arranged for all us Jivey G. I. Joes
and Jolly Jack Tars, before booting us over the edge of the
steaming crevasse – filled with prop dry ice, or leading
straight to Hell? – into the gaping maw of the massed
Warsaw Pact troops, chivvied so recently out of West Germany, harried and weary, but far, far from beaten.

Half the North Atlantic fleet, it seemed had put in at
Kiel two days before, for refuelling and provisioning. All
hands were forbidden shore leave. Scuttlebutt had it we all
– or at least my ship, the USS *Rainbow Warrior* – would
soon be steaming for Gdansk, to participate in a humong-
ous amphibious attack, which – given the Polish defences
around their shipyards, led by the already legendary young
Major Walesa – had about as much chance of success as
the Republicans had of beating JFK and Stevenson in the
next elections, or Woody Allen had of playing the romantic
lead against Sinatra's wife Mia.

Those were our chances, that is, if the patrolling Russkie
subs didn't sink us first *en route*.

This prospect did not sit well with Pig Bodine and me.
It wasn't so much that we were scared of dying. Gee whiz,
no. Three years of battle had cured us of that childish

fear, inoculating us with the universal vaccine known as war-anomie. It was simply that we didn't want to miss the big show down Hamburg way.

'I seen the Beatles before the war,' said Pig, 'right in Hamburg, at the Star Club. Man, they could rock. I thought they were going somewhere, but I never heard any more about them. I didn't even know they were still playing together.'

Bodine was lying upside down on his bunk, head hanging floorward, trying to get a cheap – and the only available – high from the rush of blood to his head. Physiology recapitulates pharmacology. Above the bunk hung a tattered poster of James Dean and Brigitte Bardot in *From Russia With Love*. (The Prez, that lover of Fleming's novels, had an identical one, only autographed, hanging in the Oval Office.)

Pig's enormous hairy stomach was exposed below – or, more precisely, above – his dirty shirt: his navel was plugged with some disgusting smegma that resembled bearing-grease and Crisco.

Bodine's navel-jam fascinated me at the same time it repelled me. Coming from a white-bread background, illustrious Puritan forebears and all that, good school and the prospect of a slick entrance into the corporate life at Boeing, I had never met anyone quite like Bodine before. He represented some kind of earth-force to me, a troll of mythic proportions, liable at any moment to unleash a storm of belches and farts capable of toppling trees, accompanied by a downpour of sweat and jizm.

I had known Bodine for ten years now, since I had dropped out of Cornell and enlisted in the Navy in '55. Peacetime. It seems so long ago, and so short. Twenty years between the first two, and twenty more till the third. Had They been planning it all along, just biding their time until the wounds had healed and the people had forgotten, until the factories could retool to meet the new specs from the R. & D. labs? Was peace, in fact, like diplomacy, merely another means of waging war . . . ?

Bodine had been my constant companion through all that time, even when I had made it briefly into officers' territory, before being busted back. (And that's another story entirely, but one also not entirely innocent of the Presence of the Pig, Germanic totem of death, he.) We had been through a lot of craziness together. But even so, even knowing him as I did, I could not have calculated the vector of the madness we were about to embark on now, nor its fatal terminus.

'I think I heard something about them a year or two ago,' I replied, imagining Pig's mouth as occupying his forehead and his eyes his chin. It barely improved his looks. 'The guy named McCarthy –'

'McCartney,' interrupted Pig.

'Whatever. He was arrested on a morals charge. Got caught with some jailbait. And then his buddy, Lemon –'

'Lennon.'

'All right already with the teacher riff. Do you wanna hear the story or not? Lennon started shooting heroin when the war broke out, and had to spend some time in a clinic. This must be a comeback tour.'

'I could use a little cum back myself,' snorted Pig. 'Left too much in the last port! Snurg, snarf, hyuck!' This last approximating Piggy laughter. 'God, I'm going ship-crazy! I gotta see that show and get laid! Dig me – do you still have that Shore Patrol rig we swiped?'

'Yeah, why?'

'Just lissen –'

And so, several hours later, all tricked out, we prepared to breach our own force's defences.

It was dark, and Benny Yoyodyne, slowest of the slow, was on duty guarding the gangway. I was wearing the

SP armband, harness and nightstick, and had my sidearm strapped on. Pig was in cuffs.

'Halt!' said Yoyodyne, brandishing his rifle like some Annapolis frosh. 'No one's permitted to disembark.'

'It's okay, Benny. They just need Bodine on shore for his court-martial tomorrow.'

Yoyodyne lowered his gun and scratched under his cap. 'Court-martial? Gee, I'm sorry to hear that. What'd he do?'

'You know the soup we had last week? The one that tasted so grungy? He pissed in it. They discovered it when they saw the distinctive urine corrosion in the kettles. The Captain had seconds, and nearly died.'

Yoyodyne turned six shades of green. 'Good Christ! what a – a pig!'

'C'mon, Bodine, it's time to meet your fate.'

Pig started struggling. 'No, no, I won't go, don't make me, General LeMay will hang me by the balls!'

Yoyodyne prodded him with the rifle. 'Quit fighting, and take it like a man. You can do at least one noble thing in your miserable life.'

Pig straightened up. 'You've made me see the error of my ways, Benny. C'mon, Tom, I'm ready now.'

I marched Pig down the ramp to the dock. He exuded such an air of holy martyrdom that I found myself almost feeling sorry for him.

As soon as we rounded the corner of a warehouse, Pig unsnapped the shackles from his wrists and collapsed atop a barrel, racked by laughter.

'As Bugs Bunny would say,' I commented, ' "Ehhh, what a maroon!" '

'He really thought I was like all reformed in an instant. Jesus, some guys deserve the Navy. Let's hit the road, Jack Ker-oh-wack!'

It was a sweet warm July evening, we were instantly and unforgivably AWOL, and the King was playing the next night about 100 miles to the south. Uncle Sam and the rest of the western world was pausing like a punchdrunk fighter between the penultimate and final round in a senseless slugfest, a brief moment of mocking peace, to have his mouth spritzed and the blood wiped from his brow, before plunging back into the fray with the pug-ugly, cauliflower-eared Papa Nikita and his robotic Commie hordes.

I had never felt more alive, nor ever would.

Kiel was crawling with SPs and MPs (S&MPs one and all, fer shure), striding imperially among the crowds of refugees, black-marketeers, NATO-deputized civilian cops and homeless war-orphans, all Dondi-eyed in rags and viscous as lampreys as they tried to attach themselves to Pig and me as unlikely saviours. The kids were dressed in Carnaby Street rags collected by Swinging London matrons and debs. Polka-dotted caps, paisley shirts, striped trousers. Fab gear.

Pig and I had to dart from shadow to shadow, down rubble-filled alleys, into doorways that were all that remained of the buildings they had been attached to, and up stairs leading to nowhere to avoid getting orphan-mobbed or cop-trammelled. Using the moon, we worked our way south, to the outskirts of the city. On the autobahn, we were lucky enough to hook a ride with a camo-decorated canvas-backed Mustang-model truck heading Hamburg-way.

The driver was a blonde English lieutenant named Jane 'Sugarbunny' Lane. Her cuddly co-pilot was a dark-haired Romanian exile with the handle of Viorica Tokes, now also a member of the British armed forces. Ribbons from a double handful of campaigns: the Congo, Panama, Algeria, Finland, Manchuria ... Experienced, these two! Been in more theatres than Hope, Burns and Berle combined. The gals, it developed, were also illicitly on their way to the Presley show, having wrangled the assignment of delivering the truck's contents to the big DP camp outside Hamburg.

Viorica reached across my lap to crack the glove compartment and liberate a bottle of Swedish vodka, which Pig immediately and immoderately snatched away. I flipped on the truck's radio, tuning for the NATO station, which, once found, proved to be broadcasting a bland diet of anti-war tunes. Streisand singing 'A Pox on Marx (And Lenin Too).' Barry Sadler with 'The Day We Took Moscow.' Dionne Warwick doing the Bacharach tune 'Do You Know the Way to Riga Bay?' You dig, I'm sure. I snapped it off.

'So what kind of mercy mission is this?' asked Pig after a swig, squeezing Sugarbunny's thigh as she drove. To ease the crowding – the door lever was pushing my service revolver into my hip – I placed my arm around Viorica, whose accented English I found entrancing.

'Is that a billygoat club pressing my hip, or are you just being glad to see me?' the Romanian babe responded, sending Pig into gales of vodka-scented laughter. When Bodine's snorts tapered off, I repeated his question, rephrased.

'Yeah, what's in the back? Blankets, medicines, powdered eggs?'

Sugarbunny smiled. 'Something even more vital. Propaganda. Namely, comics.'

My heart nearly stopped. 'American?' I asked, not daring to hope. 'New?'

Viorica nodded. 'Americanski comics, yes. And very much recently up-to-date.'

'Stop the truck right now.' Sensing the urgency in my voice, Sugarbunny did as I asked. In less time than it takes to tell, I was back in the cab with a shrink-wrapped bundle in my lap. I couldn't believe my luck. This whole crazy misadventure was starting to remind me of an episode of *Hogan's Heroes*. The one where Hogan talks the idiotic camp commander Gerasimov into letting him and the boys borrow a truck to deliver some beets to the borscht factory and they make a sidetrip to blow up the tank factory, along the way pulling a truckload of beautiful female Young Soviet Pioneers out of a ditch.

With trembling hands I ripped the shrink-wrapping off.

The Fantastic Four had been enlisted on the Middle-Eastern front. The sight of the Human Torch zipping through Red Egyptian jets, hot metal splattering above the Sphinx, was just what I needed to remind me of the United States media machine I had left behind. The Invisible Girl fell in love with a handsome Israeli soldier, and the Thing called 'Clobberin' Time!' on a bunch of Russian generals. Meanwhile Superman was busy in the Pacific, lifting entire Commie aircraft carriers out of the sea and dashing them down off the coast of sleepy and ostensibly neutral Japan, inadvertently causing a tidal wave which he then had to outrace before it washed over the ruins of Tokyo. And there was more. The Flash picked up General Westmoreland and rushed him across China just in time to meet Chiang Kai-Shek. The Submariner in Australia, Captain America in Tibet, Green Lantern in French Indochina . . .

So engrossed had I become that I barely noticed when the truck pulled off the road, into the grounds of an abandoned farm.

'Dibs on the barn!' yelled Pig, pulling Sugarbunny by the hand toward that relatively unscathed structure full of mouldering but comfortable and soon-to-be-rolled-in hay, leaving me and Viorica to sack out in the ruins of the farmhouse. We unrolled some bedding in the angle of two standing walls and a bit of roof. The air was effervescent on our bare skins, the stars jealous of what they saw. After sex, she told me a little about herself.

'I survive conscription work in Soviet munitions factory at Timisoara, until I can take no more. I sneak across the border of my soon-to-be-ex country then journey through all of Yugoslavia to Adriatic, dodging all kinds of bad men, and swing passage on hobo ship which is sunk off Sicily. For six months I am prisoner of hill-bandits who use me like love-doll. Rescue comes in a big shoot-up with Britishers – Special Forces – who are looking for their kidnapped ambassador but find me instead. I arrive in London just in time for guess what?'

'Not Napalm Night?'

'You bet. Whole city and plenty of citizens burned up by flaming Russian Vaseline. Some kind of big mess.'

That about summed up the whole world just then, so we fell asleep.

In the morning we were awakened early by a rooster's arrogant assertion that life was worth living. We tracked him down, found his harem and rustled up some eggs. The girls produced government-issue Tang and Pop-Tarts, and we had a fine breakfast in the ruins of civilization. Pig ate enough for two – horses, that is.

Back on the road we raced over the remaining miles to Hamburg. The tanks and trucks and Jeeps and APCs we passed were all heading toward the city; no one was leaving. It seemed the entire European theatre of operations was funnelling into the old Hanseatic city for the big show, their courses bent like rays of light around the King's sun. We saw teams from all three Stateside networks and the BBC. I thought I recognized Walter Cronkite.

'Make me a star!' shouted Pig as we zipped by.

The gals dropped us off in the centre of the war-torn town well before noon. 'We've got to get these capitalist colour catechisms to the people who really need them, boys,' said Sugarbunny. 'We'll catch you at the show tonight. Thanks for the company.'

'Lady Jane,' I said, trying my best to sound like Jagger, 'may I kiss your hand?'

She extended it graciously out the driver's window. 'You coulda had more than that to kiss if you asked,' said Pig. 'Nyuck, hyuck, snurt.'

'Pig, it would insult the entire species to call you a sorry example of humanity.'

'Heads up for anti-personnel mines,' Viorica advised as Sugarbunny shifted gears. 'Ivan planted plenty before he retreat!'

Made wary by Viorica's parting words, we picked our way gingerly down the centre of the empty street, two cautious cocks come to Cuxhaven.

'What now?' I asked Pig.

'Get drunk, of course. That was half the reason for going AWOL, remember?'

We found a functioning rathskeller, The Iron Stein, occupying the roofed-over basement of a building that didn't exist any more. Inside, patchily illuminated, various locals mingled with off-duty troops from all nations. A cadre of Canadians consorted with a flock of Kiwis, while a gaggle of Gurkhas slopped swill with a passel of Portuguese. B-girls and con-men lived lower down on the foodchain. Pig and I were liberally supplied with occupation scrip, and we plunked it down on the bar for some of Herr Feldverein's best homebrew.

Pig, on my right, slurped down two boilermakers to my every one, and was soon snoring gently on the bar. I doubted he had gotten much sleep with Sugarbunny. I myself was at the stage where vision is muzzily enhanced, and thoughts flit free as dogs in a Dylan song.

The fellow on my left gradually became the focus of my attention. He was an older man, easily past 60, but in good shape. Bearded, dressed in a kind of modified safari getup popular with correspondents and other white guys slumming in foreign climes, he radiated an air of melancholy wisdom the likes of which I had never felt before. In my boozy condition, I felt it incumbent upon me to try and cheer him up.

'Mister Hemingway, I presume,' I said, lifting my glass in mock recognition.

'Sorry, son, he's got the glamour assignment with the occupying forces in Cuba.'

I could tell by his voice that he was completely sober, perhaps the only such soul in the room. 'You are a writer, though?'

'Yes. *Herald-Tribune*. And you?'

An inexplicable shiver unzipped my spine. Was I misinterpreting his question? And if not, why had he asked such a thing? My uniform was obvious as Senator Johnson's hernia scars, and I had thought none of my bruised karma was showing. I swigged my beer and said, 'No, 'fraid not. In another lifetime, maybe, if I hadn't left school . . .'

He laughed then, as bitterly as I've ever heard anyone laugh. 'Another lifetime . . . You wouldn't want one, believe me.'

'And how can you be so certain?'

He grabbed my sleeve and stared me down. 'I'll tell you a good story, son, and let you decide.'

He let me go, and then began.

'I was eighteen in 1985 –'

I had to interrupt. 'Twenty years in the future.'

'Your future. Once my present. Now, nobody's future. Anyway, shut up. I don't tell this one often, and might change my mind. I was eighteen in 1985, and a simple soldier. The world I lived in was one you probably can't imagine. You see, in my world the United States and the Soviet Union were both armed to the teeth with atomic bombs. Do you have any notion what those are?'

'Something to do with atoms, I bet,' I managed to wise-mouth.

'That's right. Explosive devices that split atoms to

unleash unimaginable destructive power. They were invented during World War Two –'

'They were?'

'In my world, yes, they were. And after the war, thousands were manufactured and mounted on rockets –'

'Rockets now,' I said. 'This is quite a story. I've always liked rockets, but I've never seen any big enough to carry a bomb. A firecracker, maybe.'

'Believe me, they can be built big enough to cross continents. Can you picture such a world? Held hostage by two insane superpowers with enough megatonnage to destroy the whole ecosphere?'

Megatonnage? I thought. Ecosphere? A madman's glossolalia . . . But the putative nutcase ran right past my speculations with his story.

'Well, in 1985 it finally happened. The Soviet premier was Yuri Andropov, a mean bastard, former KGB man. The Russians were losing in Afghanistan –'

'Afghanistan? Didn't the British have something to say about that?'

'The British Empire fell to pieces after my Second World War. They meant nothing. No, the geopolitical scene was strictly the US versus Russia. They were the only players who really mattered. Well, the Russians invaded Pakistan, our ally, where the Afghanistan rebels had their bases. We responded with conventional forces, and the conflict escalated from there. The next thing we knew, the birds were launched, and World War Three had begun.

'I was assigned as a simple guard in the command centre under the Rockies. That's how deadly those bombs were – we had to hide our asses under the weight of mountains just to survive. Well, in the first few minutes of the war – and it only lasted an hour or two – everything went like clockwork. The generals gave the launch codes to the soldiers manning the silos, read the damage reports handed to them, counted up their losses and launched a second batch of missiles in response . . . But then things began to break down. We were still getting a few visual feeds along the fibreoptics – the whole atmosphere was churning with electromagnetic pulses of course – and the sights that we saw –'

The man began to weep at the catastrophe that hadn't happened yet, and apparently never would. His face was briefly contorted with an intensity of deep emotion. I was rapidly becoming bummed out. This had gone from being a kind of half-amusing, half-draggy conversation with a lively minded liar to a Coleridge-style buttonholing by a certified maniac.

Tears in his beard, the old reporter pulled himself back together, obviously drawing on some immense reservoir of will. He caught me by the elbow, and I was frozen. His touch had communicated to me the certainty that every word he spoke was the truth as he knew it.

'The carnage was awful. It drove technicians and soldiers alike mad. Nobody had predicted this. There was mutiny, rebellion, firefights and suicides in the command centre, some pushing to continue the war, others to cease.

'I couldn't take sides. My mind was paralysed. Instead, I dropped my rifle and fled, deeper into the enormous bunker.

'When I came to myself again, I was in a lab. Everyone there was dead, suicides. I slammed the door, locking myself in.

'There was an apparatus there. It was a time machine.'

'Jesus!' I shook his hand off and looked around me for help in dealing with this madman, but everyone was busy getting drunk, except Pig, who was still blissfully snoring. I was on my own. 'Atomic bombs, rockets, okay, maybe. A time machine, though. Do you expect me –'

'I don't expect anything. Just listen. As soon as I discovered what the device was – an experimental, one-way, last-ditch project that had never even been tried – I knew what I had to do.

'I wanted to live out most of the century again, up to the year the final war had broken out, so I set the machine for seventy years in my past, 1915. I figured I could hang on till my eighties. And the second decade of the century was early enough to start changing things.

'There were spatial settings as well. I put myself in New York. Instant transition, very elegant. There I stood, dressed all wrong, eighteen years old, the tears still wet on my face. But quite certain of what I had to do.

'Very quickly, I established myself as a reporter. It's amazing the scoops you can deliver when the future is an open book. Then I began systematically killing some very important people.

'Einstein was first. He had already published some papers of course, but I staged his death so as to discredit his work as much as possible. Travelling to Switzerland, I carried with me the government-issued poison the lab technicians had offed themselves with. I had grabbed it before entering the wayback. Traceless, efficient stuff. It was no problem to slip some into the coffee Einstein and I shared. I paid a Zurich orphan boy to report to the authorities that the "Jewish pervert" had died during sex with him. Quite a remarkable scandal. No respectable scientist would touch his theories afterwards with a ten-foot pole.'

'Walesa?' I half-heartedly quipped. He ignored me.

'After such an obvious target, I began working through a list of everyone who had had a hand in developing either atomic fission or rocketry.

'Bohr, Lawrence, Fermi, Dyson, Alvarez, Feynmann, Panofsky, Teller, Oppenheimer, Goddard, Sakarhov, the Joliot-Curies, von Braun, Wigner, Ley, Dirac – I completely wiped the slate of history clean of most of 20th-century nuclear physics. It was easier than I had ever dreamed.

Those people were vital, indispensable geniuses. And so trusting. Scientists love to talk to reporters. I had easy access to almost anyone. The Army had taught me traceless ways to kill, and I used them once my stock of poison ran out. It was pathetically simple. The hardest part was keeping my name clean, staying free and unimplicated. I visited the victims at night, usually at their homes, without witnesses. I misrepresented my employers, my name, my nationality. Oh, I was cunning, a regular serial killer. Bundy and Gacy had nothing on me, and I eventually beat their score. But for the salvation of the world!'

None of the names he had mentioned meant anything to me, except Einstein's, whom I recalled as a crazy Jewish physicist who had died in disgrace in Switzerland. I had to assume that they were real people though, and had been as pivotal as he claimed. 'Why did you have to kill scientists, though? Why didn't you go the political route, try to change the political structures that led to war, or eliminate certain leaders?'

'Too much inertia. The politics had been in place for decades, centuries. The science was just being born. And it was the scientists' fault anyway. They deserved to die, the arrogant bastards, unleashing something they could barely comprehend or control like that, like children chipping away at a dam for the thrill of it. And besides, what difference would it have made if, say, I could have gotten someone different elected as president, or nominated as premier? Would Russia have gone democratic under someone other than Andropov, released its satellite nations, disengaged from Afghanistan? Bloody unlikely. But still, I didn't neglect politics. I reported favourably on the creation of the president's scientific advisory council that started under Roosevelt, and curried favour with its members. I wrote slanted stories ridiculing the notion of funding anything even remotely connected with rocketry or atomic power. Not that there were many such proposals, after the devastation I had wreaked. Of course, I kept killing off as many of the second-stringers as I could who had popped up to take the place of the missing geniuses.

'History remained pretty much as I remembered it, right up till the Second World War. Nuclear physics just didn't have much impact on life until the 'forties. But by the time Hitler invaded Poland, I was certain I had succeeded. There would be no atomic ending to the war. I had staved off the ultimate destruction of the earth.

'Naturally, my actions meant a huge loss of American lives in the invasion of Japan. Hundreds of thousands of extra deaths, all directly attributable to my intervention in history. Don't think I haven't thought about those men night after night, weighing their lives in the balance against those of the helpless civilians in Hiroshima and Nagasaki, and, later, every city on the globe. But the scale always tipped the same way. Atomic destruction was infinitely worse.'

He was talking almost to himself now, more and more frantic, trying to justify his life, and my incomprehension meant nothing. By my side, Pig had stopped snoring.

'After the war, though, events really began to diverge from what I knew. It all slithered out of my control. The permanent American presence in a devastated Japan led to stronger support of the Chinese Republicans against Mao and his guerrillas, resulting in their defeat. How could I know though that having the Americans on their Mongolian border would make the Russians so paranoid and trigger-happy? I couldn't be expected to predict everything, could I? The border incident that started your World War Three – a total freak accident! Out of my hands entirely! But what does a little global skirmish mean anyway? As long as there's no atomic bombs. And there's not, are there? You've never seen any, have you?'

I could only stare. He grabbed my shirtfront.

'I fucking saved your ass from frying,' he hissed. 'I'm bigger than Jesus! You all owe me, you suckers. I made your world –'

There was a shot, followed by screams and the sound of clattering chairs and shattering glasses. The time-traveller's hands loosened and he fell to the floor.

Pig Bodine had my service revolver in his shaky hand.

'My dad died in the invasion of Japan,' said Pig.

'Bodine,' I opined, 'I think you've just killed God.'

'This is war, man. Why should God get off free?'

We split fast from The Iron Stein before anyone could gather their wits to detail us. We found Sugarbunny and Viorica and shacked up in a safe spot till the show, which we thought it would be okay to attend under cover of darkness. After all we had been through, it would have been a shame to miss it.

The Beatles played superbly, especially Pete Best on drums. The whole crowd forgot their J-Day jitters and began to groove. During their last number – a little ditty called 'Tomorrow Never Knows' – I began to cry so hard that I missed all of the Supremes' set, and the opening notes of the King's 'Mystery Train.'

But Presley's singing made my world seem real enough again, and more important than ever before.

After the concert the four of us ambled off hand-in-hand through the nighted streets, lit only by the stars so impossibly high above, where no 'rocket' bearing 'atomic bombs' had ever trespassed, back toward the truck, now as empty of its four-colour contents as my brain was of plans.

Yet somehow I felt content.

'Where to, boys?' asked Sugarbunny.

'The future,' I said. 'Where else?'

'Nyuck, nyuck,' snuffled Pig. 'How about tripping into the past? I'd like to be in that barn again.'

'If you get the chance, please don't ever try it, Pig. Living in a world created by a moral idealist is bad enough.

One made by an amoral hedonist – I can't even begin to imagine it.'

The girls were puzzled. Pig sought to explain by goosing them simultaneously so they squealed.

'Could it be worse, Tom? Could it be? Snurg, snarf, hyuck!'

BIRD ON A TIME BRANCH

Cherry Wilder

About this time Bird was minding a small house at Lily
Beach for a friend and trying to meet a deadline. His work
habits improved, he lost weight, he mowed the grass round
his pink frame house. He found that by making what he
called 'a forced march' now and then, he could complete
a story in a week.

No one knew where he was except the friend, Ed, who
was junketing around Europe on ten dollars a day. He cut
out drinking, he was not troubled by lack of sex, he was
not even troubled by lack of love. He had no car and no
telephone. His ex-wife, Gloria, could only write long, mean
polemical letters to which he replied with saintly patience,
admitting his faults.

He accepted a female kitten from Mrs O'Hara, his neigh-
bour, and called her Missy Scarlett. She was tiger-striped,
wild, and shy, flying under the house when the trash men
came around. Mrs O'Hara laughed when she heard the
name.

'You wouldn't believe,' she said. 'but I have cousins in
Georgia, name of Butler.'

He sat on the steps in the long summer nights, smoked
a joint now and then. This is too good to be true, he
thought, something absolutely unbelievable is going to happen. A dark window will open in my brain. My body is
preparing to get cancer. That asshole D. will reject my book.

At the earliest possible opportunity Missy, the shy one,
became pregnant. She rounded out indecently. Mrs O'Hara
opined that she might have one, in fact she had two. He

stayed up all night and helped her through this difficult experience. The two kittens, one black and white, one striped, were both male. When they were six weeks old Mrs O'Hara generously took the striped one to live with its grandmother and gave it the name of Tiger. The black and white kitten had patches on its face which gave it a comical bandito look; he called it Pancho Villa.

Poor Missy disappeared. He searched and called through the warm grassy lanes all the way to the beach. There was reason to believe that she had been run over by a truck, crossing Victory Drive. The black and white kitten took to sleeping in the crook of his knees.

Every afternoon Bird walked up to the post office to clear his mail box. Some days, when he was restless, he went in the morning, but mostly he held out until afternoon. This meant that he got nothing but junk mail at the pink house and he was able to control his habit of watching for the postman. He was becoming master of his fate.

One Friday afternoon he collected a royalty cheque for $179.80 (but no letter) from his agent and a post-card of a Dali painting from Ed in Paris, France. Soft watches draped upon a bough. Ed wrote 'time keeps slipping away . . .' He took the long way home, strolling along the road above the beach.

An engine purred like a great cat and a huge spectral automobile, pale grey with window curtains of olive-green oiled silk, drew up alongside. It was a Rolls Royce Silver Ghost. A blonde girl with bobbed hair and a green uniform sat in the driver's seat. For a few seconds, before he recognized the Egyptian logo on the doors, he wondered if he might have been transferred to the twenties.

'Mr Bird?' asked the girl. 'Hector Bird?'

'Yes.'

'Jump in,' she said. 'Mr Jones wants to see you.'

He protested feebly because he felt unkempt. Osiris Jones

was his guru, one of the few people he loved, a source of hand-outs and crazy ideas. The old man was a cranky ex-producer who inhabited a crumbling hacienda in the Hollywood hills.

'Come as you are,' said the pretty chauffeuse. 'The old man is dying.'

He slipped into the cool, cavernous interior of the Silver Ghost and was whirled away. During the long drive he fortified himself with two shots of Irish whisky and a packet of Cheesi Snax from the built-in bar. He tapped on the partition, and the girl's voice said:

'Use the tube.'

The speaking tube at his side emitted a draught of cool air.

'You're new,' he said. 'What became of Dean Proudfoot, the other chauffeur?'

'He retired,' said the girl. 'His daughter took over the job. My name is Jenny Proudfoot.'

'Who's with the old man? Did any of his children show up?'

'No,' she said. 'There's just Ramona. The doctor comes around, but he can't play chess any more.'

He knew then that Osiris was really on the skids. It was dark when they reached El Paradiso. In the hall Ramona, a tiny woman, her skin patterned with wrinkles like the lace of her mantilla, embraced him and wept. She had been a famous beauty, star of the old man's films.

'Agree with him!' she begged. 'Just agree with anything he says, Heck. He has had so many disappointments.'

Osiris was propped up in a metal hospital bed, which occupied one corner of his vast bedroom. His knobbly old man's body was covered by a sheet; his long, smooth face had become angular and hard. It was no time to scoff at the comparative disappointments of a rich man. Bird knew very well that money didn't buy happiness or bring those neurotic middle-aged kids to their father's bedside. He settled himself in a chair and talked about anything that came into the old man's head. The Spanish American War, women, thought-transference, the plots of old comedy films, the Book of the Dead. Around midnight the nurse, Frank, came in and said he must give Osiris his medication.

'Fifteen minutes,' wheezed the old man. 'I have to do some business with Mr Bird.'

When they were alone again he said:

'I'm leaving you five thousand dollars. All that's left of a certain slush fund. Won't go through the books.'

He thanked the old man.

'I want you to do something for me, Heck,' said Osiris. 'You must go to the Camax Conversation. The Drum Ceremony is performed once every seven years at a certain conjunction of the moon and Venus. You go as my deputy . . . the token is in that lacquer box on the night table.'

'Right,' he said. 'I'll go. Who are these people, Osiris?'

He guessed the answer. Osiris believed that California was a fulcrum of the dark world, where occult sects were gathering for the last days of mankind. Osiris counted himself as part of this magical drift to the west coast: he worshipped the gods of ancient Egypt. The Camax circle, he assured Bird, had rediscovered the secrets of the Maya. They searched the world for rifts in the fabric of space-time. Ho-hum. He was not excited at the prospect of attending an occult ceremony, it was simply his duty to the old man. Besides, Osiris said that Jenny Proudfoot would make arrangements, and this cheered him up. He reached into the lacquer box and found a kind of golden dog-tag stamped with the representation of a bird's head. He slipped it around his neck.

Frank, the night nurse, came back, and Osiris pressed Bird's hand. The old man was hoarse from talking too much; his breath came in shuddering gasps. He knew that he would never see Osiris alive again.

* * *

It was too late for him to be driven home. He ate supper with Ramona – bean salad and cold chicken, washed down with red wine – and slept in one of the guest rooms. In the morning he put on a clean T-shirt with Osiris' trademark of a lotus and a winged sun disc. He fixed himself eggs and coffee in the kitchen; about ten o'clock Jenny Proudfoot drove him back to Lily Beach in a more modest car, a black Chevrolet.

He sat beside her and she explained how he would reach the Camax Conversation. He would be called for at six o'clock on the evening of the following day; he must wait outside the Lily Beach post office. Wait for her? No, for a man named Westbury, who drove a pale blue pick-up. She gave him its number, told him to be sure to wear his token and carry some identification. He felt depressed. Jenny Proudfoot had maintained a forbidding attitude throughout their drive. Now she said bitterly:

'You'll still get your money if you don't go along.'

Bird was shocked.

'Of course I'll go along!' he said. 'I promised the old man!'

'Okay,' she said. 'I'm sorry. We've had some trouble with freeloaders.'

She stopped the car at a gas station and drew out a zippered roll of navy-blue nylon that he didn't recognize at first.

'Sleeping bag,' she said. 'The old man wanted you to use it at the meeting. It gets cold where they are.'

He took the bag, which was a much more expensive item than the ones he remembered, but he did not have time to get on a better footing with Jenny. They came into his street, and there was a bright red sports car parked outside the pink house. He guessed what this meant and did not ask her in to see Pancho or have a coke. When the Chevy was driving away in a cloud of dust Gloria came storming out of the little house and started in.

253

'So this is where you've been hiding, you son of a bitch!' she shouted. 'Harvey! Harvey! Get the number of that car! That must be one of his women! You think I'm blind, or what? You think I don't know what you're planning? You think I don't see through this set-up?'

Harvey, Gloria's new lawyer, was a neat, toothy young man, completely under her spell. Between them they quieted Gloria down and got her into the house. Bird, sick at heart, tried to explain where he had been. Gloria let off another blast or two at Osiris and swore to take Bird for every penny of the million dollar legacy she was sure he would receive if the old faker really did kick out. Gloria knew, she just knew, that Bird was planning to go to Mexico. Bird gave her the cheque for $179.80. He told her he wasn't planning to go anywhere, he was minding the house for Ed. Another of his broken-down cronies, another lying bum, snarled Gloria. He told her he had sent in the novel, which was true, and that D. was delighted with it. He had no idea whether this was true or not.

'This time, you make a penny I'll take it out at the source!' growled Gloria. 'Hear what he says, Harvey. Hear how he goes on . . . Isn't he every bit as bad as I told you? I *know* you, Heck. I can read you like one of your own trash paperback books. You are a monster, Heck, an unfeeling, dishonest, bug-eyed monster. You want the Señoritas, don't you, Heck?'

He became more and more silent. He made tea. Finally Gloria and Harvey went away. He coaxed Pancho out from under the house and opened a can of cat food. He was sorry for Gloria, but at the same time he hated her for making ugly scenes. He realized that certain things she had said about him were true; he wondered what he had done to her to make her behave like a crazy woman. He wondered how he could give Gloria maybe $1000 from his legacy without her taking the lot. He wondered where she had gotten this crazy idea about Mexico. Thank heavens she hadn't heard the name of his kitten! He sat on the porch in the evening smoking a last joint and watching Pancho Villa dance about chasing moths.

Next day he dressed carefully for his rendezvous with the Maya. He put on his dark red shirt and leather jacket, dug out his boots because he had some idea they might be walking into the mountains. He asked Mrs O'Hara to feed Pancho in case he was late back; he wrote a note to his agent warning him that Gloria was on the war-path.

He sauntered off to the post office in plenty of time; his mail was disappointing – all his box contained was a request to give blood in a good cause. Still, this was the way of things on the day after a cheque.

The blue pick-up arrived on the dot of six; the driver lowered his shades to scrutinize Bird and his ID. Westbury was a powerfully built man of about 40 with an olive complexion, high cheek bones, black eyes and black hair, shoulder length, clubbed back with a thong. Bird could not decide if he had Indian blood or if he was simply the kind of Caucasian who got to play Indians in the movies.

They drove onto the freeway, heading due east; night came down swiftly, and the lights of the city sprang up in glittering rows. They talked in a desultory fashion, and Westbury began to drive furiously, spinning the pick-up through clover-leafs, down underpasses, leaving the freeway entirely, then scooting back on.

Bird, whose sense of direction had never been good, found that he had lost it entirely when he gave up driving a car. For a moment he felt that he had oriented himself ... they passed a motel called 'Cactus Flower' which he believed was not far from the town of Mojave. Then Westbury began twisting and turning again. Finally he slowed a fraction and said:

'Got a tail. Can't shake him.'

'You mean we're being followed?'

'Little bitty red devil,' nodded Westbury. 'Some European make. Sure as hell hope it isn't . . .'

'It isn't!' said Bird miserably.

Afterwards he wondered who Westbury hoped that it wasn't. A reporter? The finance company? A rival coven? He went on to explain that it was his ex-wife and her lawyer. Gloria had this fixed idea that he was lighting out for Mexico. He half-expected Westbury to leave him on the side of the road. The big man laughed, however, and was sympathetic. One touch of spouse trouble made the whole world kin.

'That lawyer fellow, Howard . . .'

'Harvey.'

'He sure can drive,' said Westbury. 'But man, we're *not* heading for Mexico. We're nowhere near the border!'

'That wouldn't matter to Gloria.'

They dodged about again, and Westbury seemed satisfied with the result. They drove on and on, and the pattern of the stars led Bird to believe that they had made a circle and were somewhere southeast of Mojave. They came to something like a ghost town; Westbury said no, there were half a dozen families still living there to cater for the tourists.

They drove through a canyon and into the shadow of low hills, ochre under the moon. Bird saw grey-green scrub in the headlights and imagined the bright eyes of desert creatures. A cyclone fence weaved in and out on the right-hand side of the road, among boulders. Westbury had reduced speed.

'Feel it?' he asked. 'Hear it?'

He throttled down, and Bird heard for the first time a sound like distant thunder. Drums! When he rolled down his window the night air prickled against his skin. The pick-up swerved to avoid something that was not quite mist spilling over the road. Westbury laughed at himself.

'Effect of the light, I guess,' he said. 'Makes me jumpy.

All this area near the fence is *in slippage*, you could say. Never know where you are . . . or when.'

They turned right, drove over a culvert and through an open metal gate. Bird saw points of light like tiny globules of St Elmo's fire on the gate's hinges. Westbury slid the truck up a gentle slope to a parking area, cleared of boulders. They were climbing out when the red sports car came at the gateway below them with a scream of tyres. Harvey seemed to check at some invisible barrier, then miss the angle for the turn. There was a rending crash; the red car turned over, crumpled, plunged over the far side of the road, out of sight.

'*Gloria!*'

Bird was shouting, so was Westbury who caught him by the arm.

'. . . *an accident*!' said the big man.

'Help them!' shouted Bird. 'I have to help them!'

'We got to keep going on in!' said Westbury.

'Are you crazy?' cried Bird. 'They're bleeding! They're dying! The car will *burn*!'

Westbury, incredibly, checked the two large chronometers strapped to his wrist.

'Okay,' he said. 'But remember, you can't come back. The ceremony is *out* for you, understand. We had seven minutes in hand, now it's about five. You run hard as you can down to the gate and *shut it* . . . so they got NO ALTERNATIVE TRACK . . .'

He was yelling this to Bird who was already running as hard as he could go. He felt the crazy sleeping bag slap against his back but could not wait to shuck it off. He heaved at the massive gate and it swung to, lightly; he shut a long bolt. He leaned on the cool tingling gatepost, gasping for breath, and the red sports car shot past on the road. He saw Gloria and Harvey quite distinctly, heading after that will-o'-the-wisp, Hector Bird, en route to Mexico.

When he got his breath and looked back there was no

sign of Westbury or the pick-up. He thought of disobeying orders and following the dark road into the hills. He was aching from the run and light-headed. He wondered if there had been some Mayan magic in the coffee he had taken from Westbury's thermos flask. He climbed over the gate, walked across the road and looked down: nothing, no smouldering wreck.

He started out walking back the way they had come, but he was feeble, his legs could hardly carry him. He felt exposed and vulnerable out there on the moonlit road and crossed back to the shadows. There was a weak place in the fence about half a mile from the gate. He climbed through and found his way to an inviting patch of white sand, dry and insect-free, screened from the road by a rock pile. He took off his boots, unrolled the sleeping bag, and crawled inside. He addressed Osiris in his mind, apologizing: Sorry, this was the best he could do. He fell deeply asleep, lulled by the music of a distant drum.

He woke at first light; the eastern sky was red, it was going to be another hot day. There had been some condensation, the outer surface of his sleeping bag was a little damp. An old farm truck rattled past on the road. He saw a damp scrap of paper taped to a zipper pocket on the bag: it bore his own name and the hieroglyphic signature of Osiris Jones. Inside the pocket was a manila envelope like a bulky manuscript. It contained $5000 in used bills, twenties and hundreds.

Bird was terrified. There was his legacy, more cash money than he had ever had his hands on in his life and he was alone, unprotected, in the god-damned desert. It was this circumstance, of course, which carried him all the way back to Lily Beach in a state of blessed ignorance. He took out $300 then taped the envelope with the rest of the money against his skin with sticking plaster from the first-aid pocket of the sleeping bag. He walked grimly back to the ghost town, got a lift to a larger town, rode a bus to the city and took a cab to Lily Beach. He was unusually taciturn, hugging his cash. He made no conversation, saw no papers, exchanged no pleasantries.

He had the driver let him out at the corner and strolled back to the pink house. He saw that the grass had grown up thickly around the steps. Hadn't he mowed it just last week? Now the grass was tall, there were daisies and a butterfly or two; he heard the sound of the sea. A black and white cat was sitting on the overgrown path in the sunshine.

Bird reeled against the hedge; his beard had grown to his knees, his old flintlock was covered with rust. He opened the gate warily and whispered:

'Pancho? Hey, Pancho?'

The cat rose up politely as if it knew its name. Bird's breath was tight in his chest; no, it was some drop-in, visiting cat.

'Pancho? It's me, old buddy . . .'

The cat, still a young cat surely, came forward cautiously with its head cocked, listening. Then, quite visibly Pancho remembered. He came bounding up to Bird, who sat down on the path. He rubbed himself against Bird's chest and purred outrageously. A boy went past on a bike and nearly hit the pair of them with a rolled-up copy of the *Lily Beach (Happy) Times*, an advertising throwaway. Bird learned that he had been absent from the house ten months and two days. When he staggered up to his front door, Mrs O'Hara called cheerily over the fence:

'Hey there! How was Mexico?'

He did not break down and tell her, there and then; the moment passed. He accepted the verdict of the majority with Gloria and Harvey who had spotted him in Tijuana, just missed him in Cuernavaca, discovered his alias on the border with Guatemala. He accepted the kidding of his agent, who sang 'South of the Border.' He made it his business to find out everything that had happened while he was away. Osiris was dead. Robert Kennedy was dead. Nixon was President. D. had rejected his novel but B., good man, had been delighted with it. Ed was planning to stay longer in Europe. Jenny Proudfoot had moved to New York.

Certain things worked out. Gloria settled for $1000, married Harvey and navigated for him on auto rallies. They made a great team. Bird was glad they were alive, even if it meant that he had missed out on a secret of the universe.

He settled up with Mrs O'Hara for cat food and veterinary treatment; Pancho and Tiger had both been fixed at six months. He spent some of his legacy on a Volkswagen, got a licence all over again and went to find the place where time had slipped. It was arid and uninteresting in daylight, when the moon was not in conjunction with Venus. A mining company owned the land inside the fence. In the ghost town he shopped for souvenirs and asked questions about a commune or a sect who met in the hills. No one knew anything. He saw Westbury again – the true Westbury, not some look-alike – years later, playing an old Indian construction worker on daytime television.

Eventually he went to Mexico. He and Pancho took a house for the summer in Yucatan, and he began his Mexican time-branch trilogy. He met his true love and second wife, Elaine, buying a shawl in the market. He embroidered his Mexican experience the more lovingly because it stood for something else. For the intrusion of the hidden world into everyday life.

'Mexico' was for him the land of dreams. He studied the Maya and the Aztecs. He pondered the fate of Ambrose Bierce. He recalled the story of the mad Empress, poor Carlotta, who survived the Emperor Maximilian by more than 60 years. She spent her declining years in a Belgian château, with a park, and as she was taken rowing on the lake would often say: 'Tomorrow *we are going to Mexico . . .*'

Pancho lived for seventeen years and remained the most lovable of all Bird's cats. In the course of time, Bird had a daughter, and the daughter her own pet kitten.

'Daddy,' she asked, 'will Pancho and Mimsy remember us if we go away for a whole year?'

Bird was studying a travel guide entitled *Europe on $20 a Day.*

'Take it from me, honey,' he said. 'Cats *can* remember!'

NORBERT AND THE SYSTEM

Timons Esaias

Her skirt had a stylish cut; the boots accented the shapeliness of her legs; and her social beacon, cunningly mounted above her left ear, was flashing green. Norbert, instantly taken by her graceful yet careless walk, summoned his analysis program for her personality profile and a suitable introductory line. But while he waited for the printout to flash on his lens, she stepped up onto a passing trolley-shuttle – and the moment was lost.

When the display arrived he angrily subaudibled to his Personal System, 'A fine lot of good it does me now!'

'Do you want an identity search for her address and access code?' his PS inquired.

'No, I do not. Clear.' His lens screen returned to the basic display. Still seething, he demanded, 'How long did you take to process my request?'

'Three seconds, request and display inclusive.'

It won't do, he thought. How could he ever get a girl with a time-lag like that? His shyness might be a factor, but Personal Systems are supposed to make up for that.

He needed to invest in some new equipment.

While the kitchsys made his dinner, he sprawled in the bedchair and summoned the showroom program. A list of 65 Personal Systems in his price range crawled down his left lens, while his right displayed an index of nearly 1,000 second-level options.

'Civilization can be tedious at times,' he remarked.

Judging his tone as dissatisfaction, the General System

262

brought up a salesperson. 'Good day, Shopper Kamdar! How may we assist you?'

Norbert explained his problem.

'Ah, yes. We've had a lot of replacement orders from shoppers with the 1200 series. Time marches on! Ha, ha!' The salesperson simulation paused for a change of mood. 'Frankly, an eligible bachelor like yourself shouldn't have to ask his PS to assess a young lady. A modern System would have started on it the second your cortex responded to her positive features. You should have had the output before the hormones hit.'

Letting that message sink in, the salesrepresentation got down to cases. 'How much surgical adjustment are you willing to tolerate? . . . Ah! Well, then, I would suggest the latest thing out of Gabon, the 15B Jizmet. It's powerful, but economical, and most of the hardware is rib-mounted. It takes ten ribs on a male your size, but that means three pounds *less* on the head mounting you already have with the 1200! Could I consult your mounting diagram? . . . Yes, I see you already have four ribs converted, that'll save on installation . . .'

'Gabonese?' Norbert interrupted. 'What's their track-record?'

Instantly a series of charts and tables came up on his left lens. Then his right lens scrolled a list of sports personalities currently using Gabonese Systems: heavy on defensive backs and third basemen. Quick response time.

'They're fairly new in the market, but quite reliable. They have to be to be licensed by our Administration. Do you have a particular concern?' The rep struck just the right note of reassurance and mild contempt.

'Actually, I was just wondering how you turn it off.' Norbert chuckled awkwardly. Come to think of it, how did you turn off the System he had?

The salesrep paused for some quick processing. 'Off?' it asked with a tilt of its head.

'Yeah, you know, if it malfunctioned. An over-ride command, or an off switch. Whatever.' Norbert tried to act in control, even though he knew that a sophisticated showroom program like this could detect his insecurity in a millisecond. That's why he rarely shopped. The salesreps reminded him of all his inadequacies, without even trying.

'An off switch? Frankly, I've never heard of such . . .' There was clearly a reset. 'I do see your point, Shopper Kamdar. One does not have an off switch, however, because the failure rate for PSs is vastly lower than that for people on their own, not that there are people without Systems any more!' A statistical comparison of deaths by malfunction as opposed to expected deaths without Personal Systems flashed on his lens. 'As you see, if one could shut the PS off it would put the owner at increased risk. It would be gross negligence on our part to allow that.'

'That makes sense,' Norbert admitted, getting out of his stupid question as gracefully as possible.

Norbert dropped into the hospital that Saturday to have his new PS installed. The waiting room bored him – everyone in it being loaded with anti-anxiety shots by their PSs – so he called up the latest flick. He hadn't even seen the opening titles before his message light blinked: would he please go to Room 45921?

Room 45921 was in the Counselling Section, which seemed odd. He hadn't needed counselling for the last PS. Odder still, the counsellor appeared in person, not just represented through the GS. A short, round European of some sort with an old-style half-helmet covering the back of his skull. What could a guy with an archaic set-up like that tell him about a PS?

'Shopper Kamdar, Norbert Kamdar! Sit down, sit down!' The man's jovial manner surprised Norbert. Counsellors were usually so downbeat and concerned. 'Just a few questions before we do the installation.'

'Is there a problem?' Norbert hated problems, and he already sensed his PS generating soothing currents in his shoulder muscles.

'We don't think so. We just want to make sure that you're getting the right product.'

'I don't think I can afford to go up much further,' Norbert objected, calling up his spread-sheets.

'I see that,' the counsellor agreed. He scanned something on his lens. 'Actually, I'm looking into your concern about System safety. This very original remark you made about an "off switch," to be precise.'

Norbert tried, and failed, to suppress a wince. 'The showroom explained that to me. I don't really know what made me think of that. Probably something about Africans and that dam that collapsed.'

The counsellor paused for an update. 'Ah, in Egypt. Yes. That was probably it.'

'I really want this System,' Norbert pointed out.

'Of course. Your PS doesn't report any unusual nightmares or anxiety problems. Is that correct?'

How did they get that data from the GS? It must be in the installation contract. Norbert agreed with the assessment. All he dreamed about were the beautiful, interesting women he never seemed to attract.

The counsellor went on in the careful tone of a prepared speech, 'Shopper Kamdar, as you know, your Personal System is carefully designed to protect you from health hazards both internal and external. Your heart, lungs, brain, liver and other organs are constantly monitored for any sign of trouble. Your enzymes and hormones are adjusted for maximum health and efficiency, and your caloric intake is restricted, if necessary, by the kitchsys interface to assure proper nutrition.'

'Quite. Counsellor, I . . .'

'But that's just part of it. Your PS is constantly updated with weather, traffic, fire, and hazard conditions which could threaten your safety. You've heard of crime in the history films, haven't you? Crime posed a significant threat to physical, financial and emotional well-being in former times, but our Personal Systems and the General System just don't allow it now. I'm sure you agree that this is all for the good.'

'Yes, I do.'

'Then why would you want to turn a PS off? If you were injured, it couldn't bring assistance. If people could turn their Systems off, we could have crime again! Do you want that?' The man leaned forward in an authoritative pose, which seemed too artificial. He really needed to update his software.

'No. Of course not. What I want is my new System.'

The Counsellor pointed his gnarled finger at Norbert. 'But are *you* satisfied that the System is safe? We're not going to have you bringing up this switch business after the installation, are we?'

'No, Counsellor. I'm sorry I ever mentioned it.'

'All right, then.'

The guys from work dropped by to admire his new set-up. They group-viewed the latest Victoria's Secret ads, and compared baseball statistics software. Norbert found that he entertained more cleverly with the new System, and the gang stayed more than an hour before they excused themselves. A record. And he earned a party invitation, his first in weeks.

But one guy from Engineering, Howardi, stayed behind. Howardi designed bureaucracy networks, and knew people who ran things. Talking with him always reminded Norbert of the gangsters in the oldies. He always had the inside dope on everything.

'So, Norb, I got something about you on the GS the other day. Strictly upstairs stuff, but flagged to my attention. What's this about over-riding your PS?' Howardi swirled his drink in the manner management Systems tended to suggest.

Norbert's System blocked any hesitation more smoothly than he'd ever experienced before. 'Oh, that! It was a silly question I asked the showroom. I don't follow hardware much, so a really dumb idea leaked out. My old PS just didn't catch it.' Why would Howardi have been flagged for this? What had he stumbled into?

'Yeah, I've had some funny ideas in my time,' Howardi admitted. 'I've missed a warning message a time or two, as well. Embarrassing.'

NOD SAGELY. Norbert nodded, though he couldn't remember ignoring a warning message in his whole life.

'You're probably wondering what the fuss is about, right? I think you may have proposed the heresy of our time! And you thought you were just a regular guy! But seriously, Norb, the PS is the cornerstone of our material culture. When the archaeology teams dig us up it's going to be our defining element, the "PS People" or something. So questioning the PS would be like an ancient Greek questioning pottery or amphorae or something.' He contemplated his drink before swallowing the last.

Norbert's new System flagged him: SEE PYTHAGORAS. SEE DIOGENES.

'I sure didn't mean anything by it, Howie.' Norbert said in his best subdued voice. 'They straightened me out at the hospital before it went in.'

'Well, that's good.' Howardi got up to go. 'Don't get all subversive on us, eh, Norb?'

The party wasn't bad, and he even managed to get two dates in the weeks following his new installation. The first date ended early, because she suddenly remembered that her hair needed washing.

The second girl was political. She wanted to spend the

evening sitting on the benches in a public lounge area, reading political bulletin boards together.

Norbert had never kept up with politics, and didn't read the bulletin boards much. He had only posted an opinion once in his life, back when the Colts were trying to get the franchise law changed so they could get out of Key West. An evening lounging around sharing reactions wasn't what he had had in mind, but if that's what Vodkette wanted, that's what he'd put up with.

They picked the Tribune board, very mainstream, and filled with the usual drivel. Norbert kept his remarks fairly tame, so as not to offend, but he had his PS check the background of the bulletin board contributors. The read-outs indicated that every political opinion originated in an expected financial benefit for the shopper who posted it. 'I bet almost every opinion on this board is directly linked to the financial gain of the shopper who posted it,' Norbert observed in a moment of wild abandon.

'Really!' exclaimed a startled Vodkette. Norbert suddenly remembered that she had done studies in social theory, and that he had probably put his foot in it. He quickly flashed her the background data his PS had been finding on each posting.

While she was looking it over, Norbert's System signalled a startling development: an arousal spike in the young lady, corresponding to his political observation. What had he done?

She smiled. 'What made you check that out?' she asked.

'I dunno. It's like at work, I guess. If you're on the way up, you side with management. If you're up for retraining, you hate the place. Opinions are all rather predictable.' His System red-flagged his comments: SOCIALLY RISKY.

But her arousal level spiked again, and plateaued higher than Norbert had ever encountered on a date. He ran a quick diagnostic, just to be sure.

She arched a sceptical eyebrow, which just showed above

her lenses. 'And I suppose *you* have some *un*predictable opinions?'

'Oh, I dunno. I dunno,' he stalled, desperately trying to subvocalize a search order for his wildest opinion.

His PS was way ahead of him. Before he could phrase the command, he was looking at a list of his five most original opinions, and their deviation value. Two of them were just errors of fact on his part (his old System hadn't caught them in time), and two more varied less than .45 from the norm. But at the top of the list stood an idea with a colossal deviation.

He swallowed. He took a chance. 'I've often thought that we ought to be able to switch off our PSs. I've never heard anybody say that, and some people get on my case if I mention it.'

She sat there stunned. His System told him that her System was going crazy refuting this remark. But her arousal level doubled.

Her personal distance markers dropped to zero, and her health history became available to his System for review.

Norbert never looked back.

When Norbert returned to his rooms that night he couldn't believe a number of things about the date. That she had liked him. That he had had a good time. That he had brought up the off-switch idea. That he had, against the advice of his System, allowed her to talk him into posting it for all to see.

His PS seemed insistent that he should examine the replies already coming in, and that he should prepare to deal with repercussions. It certainly was a fine new System, with much more foresight than the 1200; and it didn't rely so much on that nagging voice in the ear.

But Norbert didn't want to think about politics and opinions tonight. He wanted to think about Vodkette, about her responses, about her shape, about the delicious way her rib-mount curved into the swell of her breast. And that is what he thought about until the System put him to sleep.

He awoke to find himself a famous revolutionary.

His System was so backlogged with urgent messages that he had to cancel work for the day. Norbert had never cancelled work before, but his System revealed that he was fully within his rights to do so.

There were thousands of responses to his political posting. Thousands. 16% were completely irrelevant; 12% confused; 61% irately opposed; 2% concerned about his mental health. But 8.63% agreed. Hundreds of shoppers had taken time out to make a point of agreeing with Norbert.

The feeling it gave him was so overwhelmingly wonderful that his PS had to intervene chemically.

After breakfast and coffoid, he looked at the urgent message traffic.

The counsellor at the installation hospital wanted him to come in for an appointment. The precinct bureaucrat urgently demanded a meeting. It looked ominous, and his bloodstream soon filled with anti-anxiety formulations. There were some dozen threats from angry fellow-shoppers. He had to have his PS explain some of the epithets.

He had been in trouble with Authority before, but no one had ever bothered to send him hate messages.

The most surprising thing was the long, long list of paying messages. Like other shoppers he made a few bucks each month scanning the advertisements offered to him, but it rarely seemed worth the money to sit through more than a few. Besides, the ads were so convincing that you usually bought the product, so what good was it?

But these messages had respectable fees. A long list of lawyers, publicists, writers and interviewers clamoured for his business or co-operation. He spent most of the morning scanning their pitches, and in just three hours earned ten months' salary. Norbert had the uneasy feeling that he might soon need the cash.

After lunch, Norbert screwed up his courage and called the counsellor – the counsellor whom he had assured that the off switch would never be mentioned again. The counsellor's phone-male smiled and redirected his call to another office. A very slick managementwoman greeted him with effusive warmth.

'Shopper Kamdar! How good of you to return our message! Let me assure you that we will reimburse you for this call. Say five hundred dollars a minute?' Her pose suggested a willingness to pay more.

'Ah, sure. But I was supposed to talk to Counselling.' Norbert suspected a run-around of some kind.

'Yes, well, we're sorry about that. A lot has changed since we sent that message. You may find this hard to believe, but we've been swamped with calls from shoppers just dying to know what PS you're currently using. You've probably experienced a touch of celebrity yourself since yesterday?'

'Yes, er. Yes, I have.' What were they up to?

'Well, as a political celebrity you're entitled to realize the rewards of your position. We'd like to offer you an eight per cent commission on all the Jizmet 15s we sell in the next six months, if you'll let us release your System information to the public. We'd gladly raise that to twenty-five per cent if you could find the time to tape an endorsement.'

'Why that'd be just ... Excuse me.' His PS urgently flashed: GET AN AGENT across both lenses, as well as a prioritized list of those whose messages had been received that morning. 'Sorry, but all this is a little sudden,' he dutifully read from his optiprompter. 'I'm sure something can be worked out. My lawyer will call to work out the details.'

Just the briefest moue of disappointment was replaced by a broad smile of pleasure. She changed the subject. 'We did notice one thing about your System that needs correction, and we'll gladly return half of the installation fee to cover your trouble. Ha, ha! The boys in the showroom sadly mis-read your character profile, I'm afraid. No one knew you were such an original, forceful young man. We've been hiding our light a bit, haven't we?'

'Well, perhaps a little . . .'

'So pardon us but we need to give you a more sophisticated repartee package, and damp down some of those annoying inhibition messages that less forthright individuals require. We can do that by remote, if you'll okay it?'

'Sure. I guess.'

'Fine, then. And again our apologies.' She hesitated. 'Oh! I nearly forgot. The factory is designing that off switch you wanted as an option. We'll let you have an exclusive on that for sixty days, if you'll allow us to use you to market it afterwards. Good shopping!'

His PS-chosen lawyer was on his lens before her smile had even begun to fade out.

While his new agent worked out his contracts, Norbert entered further uncharted territory. He informed his employer that he just wouldn't be able to show up for the next two months, maybe longer. (To his surprise, they were understanding and willing to accommodate.) Then he began a careful screening of the social messages on the queue. Dozens of women had sent paying offers of their company. Only a few of them were professional escorts, the majority were single women with a taste for adventure; and adventure, in this case, meant Norbert!

His PS took a decidedly worldly approach to the situation, which told Norbert that the new software had already been transferred from the company. Norbert felt enormous gratitude to them for this new life. He would gladly endorse the Jizmet line. It was a fine product.

The interview programme would probably be Norbert's finest hour, if he didn't mess up. His PS, armed with a special celebrity-interview package, had been coaching him for days. They had practiced a dozen different gemphrases, the kind that get millions of replay requests, and all the royalties that go with it.

Their chief problem had been justifying his iconoclastic action. Norbert's vagueness on politics and philosophy kept showing through, and he wasn't pig-headed enough to carry it off on emotional insistence alone. So they ended up with a consistently ambiguous set of prepared tactical responses, and a persistent uneasiness in the pit of Norbert's soul.

The presence of a live audience threw him. Forty people had paid large sums, of which he got twelve per cent, to view the taping session in person. Norbert couldn't remember ever having been in one place with that many people in his life. His PS confirmed it; he never had.

The repetitious takes also bothered him. Most shoppers assumed that these programmes were taped in one seamless session. Actually, the interviewer asked the same questions over and over in different tones and moods, in order to elicit a variety of responses. Editing would patch them together later.

'Is it true that you get the famous off switch installed tomorrow?' – Yes . . .

'What do you intend to do with your switch once you have it?' – I should think that was obvious . . .

'How long do you intend to leave your PS off?' – I'll have to see . . .

'What about crime, Shopper? What's to assure other shoppers that you won't go on a, what did they call it, skree?' – Spree. Perhaps you should invest in a Jizmet yourself. (PAUSE FOR STUDIO LAUGHTER, IF ANY) No, the switch is being installed under the condition that the GS can over-ride if any shopper's System detects me in criminal activity. I will have the power to try to commit a crime, just not the power to succeed . . .

'Why did you want an off switch in the first place?' – It was just an excruciatingly original idea I had. (SMILE IN SELF-DEPRECATING FASHION) . . .

'Why do you think the shoppers of this world need these switches?' – I didn't say that other shoppers need them. I did say that the option should be available . . .

'But really, what purpose does an off switch serve? What good is a PS that's not in use?' – The purpose of the off switch is to turn the PS off. A shut-down PS serves no purpose but the purpose of waiting to serve. (DON'T USE THIS IF YOU THINK YOU'LL GARBLE IT) . . .

'But, Shopper Kamdar, I really don't think you've answered the question. Why put such a dangerous power in the hands of mere mortals?'

'For the tenth time . . .' Norbert caught himself, and tried to read his prompt. But the answers didn't mean anything to him, and he was angry and afraid. He ignored the prompt. 'Because I'm a human and my PS is just a tool, and it's not right . . .' and he slumped in his chair, suddenly unable to speak at all – which his PS had decided was the best thing for everybody.

The published version, which omitted the slumping at the end, soared up the charts. The commentator explained, 'And so, like Lewis Carroll's Humpty Dumpty, Norbert Kamdar insists that it all comes down to "who is to be the master," and that's all.'

In the end Norbert never spent a dime on legal fees. The Shoppers' Defence Fund gladly staved off all the challenges from the bureaucrats and Jizmet's competitors. The courts managed to tie up installation of the switch for an entire month, but the publicity kept the interview selling and the Jizmet orders pouring in. By the day the switch was installed, Norbert was set up for life.

The 'switch' could be activated by entering a code on a keypad mounted on his belt, next to the battery charging plug, followed by a subvocal command. If the PS suspected a suicide attempt, it would immobilize him instead of shutting off, and call for help. Otherwise it would wait until he hit the button again to turn back on.

Norbert carried it around for two days before he decided to give it a try. It seemed that every time he thought about it for very long his PS had to sedate him. He spent hours asleep, or in a torpor. What good is it if I can never use it, he thought. But finally, on the spur of the moment, he reached down and twisted the arming cover, flipped off the lid, tapped in the code, and then repeated the command phrase that appeared on his optiprompter. His lens went blank. After a few moments, even the cooling fan shut off.

It was astonishingly quiet without the sound-track. He hadn't realized that it was part of the PS, until now.

Both lenses began to steam up. It took him a while to understand that he wasn't going blind. But the light became otherworldly, and his room very fuzzy. He shouldn't have done this before he'd become familiar with his new rooms.

His head hurt! How can a head hurt on the inside? And he could hear his heart pounding. And his stomach felt very strange, and he began to taste something unpleasant near his throat . . . he reached down and turned the PS back on. It quickly reset and rushed to his aid.

But not in time to save the carpet.

Norbert waited a day to make sure he'd fully recovered from the experiment, and then decided to take a walk through the corridors. Almost immediately he ran into

Howardi, who shouted a hearty. 'How's shopping!'

'Always a sale. Yourself?'

'Never better. Say, Norb, the guys at work keep asking about you.'

'Really?' Norbert found that idea odd. 'Say hello for me.'

'Of course. Hey, have you had any more weird ideas I can tell 'em about?'

'No.' Norbert shook his head in self-deprecation. 'I'm in enough trouble from just the one.'

'You're a wild man, Norbert. A real stitch.'

Norbert watched Howardi continue down the hall and turn a corner. INSINCERE, said the Jizmet 15.

Her smoky lenses spoke volumes, but her mouth said, 'Have you used it?'

'Oh, yeah.'

'What's it like?'

'Like nothing I've ever done before. I don't think most people would like it, though.'

She reached across the table and stroked his arm. His twentieth date, in the twentieth restaurant, since the interview. It seemed almost routine, now.

Her smoky lenses spoke volumes, but her mouth said, 'How long do you leave it off?'

'Long enough.'

'Long enough for what?'

'Long enough to show it who's boss.'

His hundredth conquest in about 100 tries. It really was seeming rather routine, now. Norbert considered cutting back to three a day.

Her smoky lenses spoke volumes. He excused himself and went for a long walk.

* * *

His PS guided him along routes he'd never taken, but he didn't take much in. Despite the mood-levellers his System was pumping, the halls and galleries all looked the same. He thought back to Vodkette, who had helped start all this. His first conquest. What was she doing now?

SAME EMPLOYMENT. SAME SHOPPING PATTERNS. There was a note reminding him that her System was probably hopelessly incompatible with his Jizmet. She would bore him now, after all the sophisticated, upscale shoppers he'd been dating since.

That realization made him a tiny bit sad, a tiny bit lonely.

By mid-afternoon he found himself on the edge of the nature park. He decided to explore it. The trees and shrubs here were allowed to grow freely, unless they interfered with the pathways. Few shoppers came here and Norbert could see why. The confusion of shapes and densities seemed quite odd, and the dead leaves and branches accumulating on the ground was somewhat disturbing. Still, his software gave him permission to continue.

At first he stayed on the concrete walkways, which were lined with stone lanterns and other pointless artefacts. The PS offered a series of lectures on their significance, but he declined. Impulsively he stepped onto an unpaved pathway, and during his first few steps switched off his System.

Again the stunning silence in the absence of the sound-track, the pounding of his heart and the rising nausea. The grass under his feet felt very irregular, like a poorly designed pile carpet, and made walking unsteady. He stopped, and tried to control the panic that mounted in his mind. The lenses steamed up, first the right, then the left. He reached up to his face and, for the first time he could remember, unsnapped the lenspiece and flipped it up.

His eyes, unused to the raw air, filled with tears. He could barely keep them open, the impulse to blink was so strong.

The vertigo became overwhelming, and he fell to his hands and knees. The unfamiliar feel of grass and earth under his hands distracted him momentarily, and allowed him to fight off the nausea. This is how his ancestors had once lived, in the wild, under the trees, listening to the song-birds. How could they stand it, he wondered; how could they shop, feeling like this?

He heard footsteps rapidly approaching.

'Are you all right?'

Norbert reached up unsteadily and restarted his PS, then flipped down the lenspiece. He gestured unsteadily for patience, though he knew his interrogator's System would be monitoring his rapid return to normal. Then he sensed two people squatting down beside him, and his PS said, 'Park rangers.'

'Shopper? Do you need assistance?'

Norbert, his head clearing, sat back on his heels and read through the last of his tears, 'Certainly not. But thank you. I was just having a rather ... extraordinary experience.'

The PS cleared him to stand, so he did, brushing himself off, and smiling his best enigmatic-#3 said, 'Yes ... that was quite extraordinary. Good day, gentleshoppers.'

As he walked back toward the concrete he heard one exclaim, 'I tell you, it's him!'

'Imagine that. Right out here!'

Howardi had left messages, as had the bureaucrat's office. The Jizmet sales people left messages, more and more urgent as the evening wore on. Norbert realized that the General System probably told them about the incident in the park. With the new switch going on sale in a few days, they might be panic-stricken. His PS urged him to return their calls.

He was right. They wanted to know 'if he had experienced any difficulties' with the new switch.

'No,' he told them. 'But it's not for the timid.'

They liked that. They quoted him in their ads.

For a few days afterward Norbert stayed home, cancelling all his dates and postponing his investment counselling sessions. His Jizmet supported very conservative financial software, and tended to veto all the schemes that were proposed. Besides, he didn't really need more money.

He wasn't sure what he did need. He did some shopping, but the salesreps annoyed him. He took in some games, but his teams didn't inspire him the way they once had. The flicks couldn't compete with his own sex life of recent weeks.

Norbert was lonely.

He considered several new hobbies, but he knew that they weren't the answer. He tried a couple of the banter-lines, but the interesting people on them were all computer-generated; the rest were shoppers like himself, who didn't know what they were looking for. Finally, he decided to keep one of his dinner dates. Back to the sugar mines, he thought.

Artemia did not have her lenses set to 'smoky,' nor did she ask about the switch before the first course of paste was finished. She inquired about his interests and reading preferences, and seemed a bit unsure of herself when she discovered that he had none.

Norbert stuck strictly to the suggested comments, feeling utterly lost with this woman. He had dated the educated classes before, but they never seemed to stray much from their software – the conversations being carefully scripted until simple curiosity inevitably led to the same questions, the same responses, and bed.

Until now, Norbert had never quite understood how artificial those conversations had been.

He recklessly strayed from the script. 'Excuse me, could we just talk about you for a while?'

She paused. 'I suppose you want to know why I decided to ask for a date?'

'Not really. I'd just like to know what you really ... what you're like.' IF YOU DON'T MIND. 'If you don't mind?'

Artemia reviewed her likes and dislikes, hobbies and interests, for the most part reciting the pre-date resumé her System had provided to his. Growing bored, he asked for elaboration, and she responded with complicated details. The Jizmet barraged him with definitions and explanations in both earspeakers, while filling both lenses with charts and graphs. He had to be prompted to realize that she had stopped talking some time before and expected a reply.

'Pardon me?' he tried.

'I said ... well, never mind.' She frowned. 'You're not really very well educated, are you? I didn't know quite what to expect, but you're not really much like your pop-image, are you?'

A long silence fell between them, and Norbert considered the RUDENESS: OFF SCALE blinking in his left lens, and the series of pointed replies scrolling down his right.

He took a deep breath and shut off his PS. Her System must have informed her, because she immediately sat quite straight.

'No,' he said. 'No, I'm not very well educated. I'm not very smart, either. I just asked a very silly question while I was shopping one day, and all this...' He gestured vaguely, not even sure she was still there, beyond his foggy lenses. 'All this ... happened. I'm sorry.' He switched back on.

She was still there. She slowly sat back in her chair, and her mouth dropped open. His prompt signalled STRONG EMOTIONAL RESPONSE. CONFUSED.

'You shut it off,' she said. 'You answered my question without a prompter.'

He shrugged.

She leaned forward. 'I don't think I've ever been given an unprompted answer to anything.'

RESPECT INDICATED.

'Well, Shopper Kamdar,' she said, smiling in a way he would always remember, 'you might just have possibilities . . .'

EMOTIONAL COMPLICATIONS PENDING.

The switch proved quite a popular option for several years before fading into disfavour and oblivion, though not until the royalties made a fortune for the newlyweds. Norbert never used his again, except for brief moments – just long enough to whisper in Artemia's ear that he loved her. This often punctuated the lessons they took together in a most delightful, if not instructive, way.

Artemia never did buy a switch for her own System. And though their friends and acquaintances often sported the device, the question of actually trying it never seemed to come up in conversation. 'Someday we ought to ask Jizmet how often they were used,' she used to say – but it never seemed all that important.

SHARP TANG

John Meaney

Sharp was excited, almost dancing, as he walked along the wide avenue, conscious of Father's presence beside him. He stole a glance at Father: broad shouldered and square jawed, towering over most of the people thronging Mint City's thoroughfares. Very dark, with a craftsman's strong blunt fingers, an intellectual's deep amber eyes. Several wives on their way to market, robed in rich high-caste silks, looked longingly at Father's heavy black virile antlers, spreading broader than his shoulders. Sharp grew warm with mingled pride and embarrassment. He rubbed a hand across his own smooth forehead, imagining the day when he might have antlers of his own.

The market! Such a bustle of individuals, thousands of people from hundreds of castes thronging the temporary booths and tents in the square, milling around the permanent shops among the surrounding cloisters and colonnades. The scents and sights were overwhelming: there were so many people here, you could almost hear them.

People moved out of Father's way, automatically deferential. Father was wearing his best white tunic, heavy with the gold brocade of the Geometers Caste, fastened with expensive brooches. Some passing Mint City Geometers, dressed less formally, hesitated. Father politely insisted that they precede him. Sharp felt proud. Correct manners always, even at moments of urgency.

Father's pace quickened as they entered a shaded alleyway. From a previous visit, last year, Sharp remembered that this was a short-cut to the Forum. He forced himself to match Father's pace. They did not want to be late for the ceremony.

Walking through the alleyway, Sharp caught a stale scent from a doorway. Last night, one of the house daughters had entertained an illicit visit from a young warrior, probably a proctor from the City Guard. Hot with embarrassment, he looked to see if Father had noticed. There was no sign that he had.

– Dad? he queried. You're not scared, are you?

The answering scent was reassuring. – Everything will be fine, son.

They walked out into the bright Central Plaza, a vast circular paved area dotted with passers-by, as Sharp was analysing the aftertaste of Father's reply. The bitter hint of fear was unmistakable.

Sharp straightened his robe as they ascended the Forum's gleaming steps – flanked by two bannermen, their scarlet and gold standards fluttering in the breeze – and entered the shaded atrium. In dark alcoves draped with odour-absorbing ivy for privacy, lobbyists were discreetly cajoling or bribing their way through tangles of bureaucracy.

Sharp wanted to take Father's hand, but that would not be dignified. Patience. Two servants scurried past with covered pots. A hint of amusement from Father surprised Sharp, since Father never made fun of lower castes. Maybe it reminded him of yesterday morning.

Mother and Bittersweet had been with them on the family cart, drawn slowly by plodding draught beasts through the outlying settlements. In a village with open courtyards, in view of the city walls, a poor family had been eating their vegetables right out in the open, where anybody could see them feeding. Bittersweet had jumped around hilariously, until Mother's disapproval had quelled her. Poverty was not funny.

Having a younger sister was a complete pain, but Sharp

wished she were here, not back at the hostel. The Forum's atmosphere was too stuffy.

An unmistakable scent. Tang! Father was being summoned.

The Council Chamber was a hemisphere, decorated by the finest artists. Its central skylight admitted a pillar of sunlight, under which a white marble armchair shone brilliantly. In the surrounding gloom, three concentric circles of benches held only a handful of Council Elders, although in a full Council session they would be packed. Today's few attendees sat as far apart as possible. At least one of them was asleep.

Sharp watched Father walk slowly, dignified, along the blue strip of carpet leading to the chair. Sharp jumped at a touch on his shoulder. A servant was indicating a public gallery where Sharp could sit. As Sharp sat down on a low uncomfortable bench, he saw a delicate silver-furred maiden looking at him, nostrils wide. Demurely, she slipped her robe's cowl forwards to hide her face. Sharp, entranced, forgot for a moment why he was here.

The Chief Librarian, trailed by four acolytes bearing silk-wrapped instruments, was already standing beside Father's chair. The slender Librarian looked distinguished, fur touched with white, once-heavy antlers hollowed and brittle with age. His sleeveless robe revealed long arms bearing complex whorls of scars, pale against his fur.

The Librarian launched upon a common-language sermon, designed to invoke racial memories of evolution from the pre-civilized plains. Sharp yawned. Couldn't they just get on with it? He thought he sensed the maiden watching him, but when he looked her cowl was pulled lower and her attention was on Father.

Sharp had often watched Architects and Engineers copying Father's designs in clay. And Father's intricate silver sculptures, his main hobby, were often exhibited in the

Community Hall. In his sandpits, Father plotted the courses of the stars in the night-sky, analysing their movements. Among the people of their own settlement, descended from a dark northern tribe, Father was considered brilliant. Mature in his profession, Father was the first immigrant from their settlement to be invited to Share his knowledge in the city. When he was younger, Sharp used to have a fantasy of Father being uplifted to the Council Elders caste. He hadn't realized how stuffy and old the Elders would be.

Bronze glinted as the lead acolyte unwrapped the small sickle and handed it to the Chief Librarian with a bow. Father's face was impassive. This was it! The Chief Librarian's hand was raised high, then swept down swiftly, carving a slender slice from Father's shoulder. Did the Librarian wince? Then two acolytes rushed forward with goblet and platter. Father's face was tight with agony as they squeezed blood into the goblet, but not the slightest scent of pain escaped him.

Yes, Father! Sharp's chest filled with pride as the Librarian bore his offerings to the Prime Elder, ceremoniously extending the golden plate as the Elder picked up the offering between thumb and forefinger and raised it . . .

The Prime Elder spat Father's offering onto the floor, face twisted with revulsion. Numbness swept over Sharp. The red gobbet was a stark accusation, glistening on the pristine floor.

They gave Father another chance. The Secondary Elder, trembling, also tried. The taste was too bitter and nothing passed his lips.

Father rose quietly, shoulders bowed. An awful aroma of disgust arose from the Elders and the public gallery. Sharp went helplessly to his Father's side.

As they left, Sharp saw the silver-furred maiden rubbing a disgusted hand across her nose. He hated Father then, hated his own dark fur, a damning genetic indictment.

They were bitter immigrants, unable to share knowledge with the indigenous people of their new homeland.

It was evening when they reached the hostel on the outskirts of Mint City, near one of the many fragrant gardens which gave the city its name. Once inside the foyer, Sharp pretended an urgent need to go to the eating room. He didn't want to witness Father's explanations to Mother and Bittersweet.

Avoiding the hostel staff, Sharp took a flight of stairs up to the roof garden. It was almost deserted and, as night fell, the few remaining guests went down to their rooms. Sharp sat on the small lawn. drinking in the herbal border's scents. He began to shiver as the temperature dropped. In the clear night sky, stars twinkled, silver against black.

Suddenly, like an omen, a green light burst into being far away, out over distant hills. Something was falling – no, floating – down to the ground. It was like nothing he had ever seen or heard about.

Sharp scrambled to his feet, frightened. He went indoors, fumbled his way down dark stairs till he reached a corridor lit by sweet candles. Mother's and Father's room. There was no scent of conversation from inside. Asleep. He had to waken Father –

But who was Father to spread the knowledge of whatever Sharp had seen? Trembling with self-loathing, Sharp backed away. Careful not to betray any scent, he went to Bittersweet's door and looked in. His sister was sleeping, a faint trace of milk and blood staining her lips, from her evening lesson with Mother. Always a quick learner. Sharp looked at her fondly, forgiving her for being such a brat. Time to leave.

He took his warmest cloak and – trying to be practical, trying not to be embarrassed – a bag of vegetables from the discreet cupboard in his room. If necessary he could survive on vegetation growing wild in the hills. A nauseating thought.

He slipped out of the hostel. Unsure of his destination, certain only that he could not stay where he was, Sharp shrugged his cloak around his shoulders, and set off down the empty road which led out into the night.

Rekka Chandri felt sick with fear as she set up her camp. The first thing she unpacked was her set of microwards, and she set them in the ground, hands trembling, before turning her attention to the rest of the gear. The single heaviest item was the biofact, two metres long, its mass mostly in its protective casing. She tugged it onto a level patch of ground – covered in a close analogue of grass – in the centre of her campsite. Then she booted it up and invoked the build program for her beeswarm. Okay, she told herself, you can start relaxing now.

She couldn't, of course. A month ago she had been working in a warm biotech lab on the outskirts of chilly elegant Zurich, which itself was like a different world from the circumstances of her childhood. She spent her days sitting in front of a terminal, programming and testing, and loved it. But now she was alone on a new world. Some of her friends in grad school had been adrenaline junkies – a climber, two skydivers, a powerglide racer. But quiet unassuming homeloving Rekka had taken the biggest jump of all, snatching the unique opportunity when her employers won the UNSA contract and the bioanthropologist team-members had all, prosaically, contracted flu. (The anti-virus virus was as bad as leaving the flu untreated.) Management had asked, and she had accepted, shutting out her fear.

I've never even been on a camping trip, she thought. And now I'm alone for six months, on a world too new to be called anything other than 'EM36.'

A month ago, the *mu*-space ship which discovered this

place had performed one orbit, spotted probable civilization – the twelfth such world, if true – then left immediately. Civilization meant low-key research, and Rekka, little Rekka Chandri, was the first human being to set foot upon this world.

In the pale glow of a small lamp, she opened a self-heating carton of vegetable curry. She had supplies for a week, but should be able to turn the biofact over to manufacturing food in a day or two. During her three weeks training at a UNSA flight centre, the rations had seemed inedible. Now, the same food tasted heavenly.

Meal over, she unshipped bed and tent from the small carrying-pack and unfolded them both. What else to do?

I've been fussing around inside the lamplight, she realized. As though I were in a room.

Taking a deep breath, she turned out the light.

Rekka gasped.

There were no eerie sounds, no eyes glinting in the surrounding darkness. Yet she felt stripped by the cool air, shaken by the steady ground. As her eyes adapted, the stars grew bright in a black sky which had never known pollution, the Milky Way arcing straight overhead. A deep realization: she was alien here.

She sat down on the ground beside the faintly humming biofact. Time for her routine. Rekka slowly twisted her body into the intricate postures of Hatha Yoga. Wherever she was, she carried this discipline inside her. Slowly, she relaxed.

Rekka crawled into her small tent, which she kept tuned to transparency. Nagging doubts returned. The microwards would function as alarms, but their ultrasonic defences might be useless. She wanted to go home. She had a fantasy, of the ship bursting through from *mu*-space in an explosion of light, coming to pick her up. But that was six months away. The contract said so.

She picked up a flat portable screen and scrolled through

her document file, characters glowing strongly in the dark. She browsed through the Terms of Reference for her assignment. Biochemical, ecological research. Anthropological observation, from a distance. Her objectives were to produce overview reports in each of those three fields. Large expeditions had twice caused disaster on other worlds. Current procedures specified one person only, very low-key, with full project control. She lay back and wondered just what they thought one person on her own could accomplish.

Waking up was a surprise, because she had thought sleep would never come. She lay back looking at a spectacular dawn, pale lime and silver grey painting the sky. Her body tingled with anticipation. Her world!

When she sat up there was a sudden flurry of movement. Something large and dark shot into the purple undergrowth which surrounded her hillside camp. What was that? Just one impression endured: startling amber eyes, almost feline but slitted horizontally, profoundly curious. And intelligent.

Rekka began to shake.

Sharp did not retreat far. Sniffing the changing wind currents, he moved to a position that should remain downwind. Crouched within fragrant bushes for further cover, he strained to track the creature's scent. It moved strange artefacts around its campsite. Though solitary and small, it bore objects as intricate and manufactured as Father's sculptures, and its hands were as agile as a person's, though having only one thumb apiece. Was it intelligent?

Its species was unknown to Sharp's race memory, so its habitat must be distant. Was it an outcast, casteless like him?

The thought crystallized. I am casteless, he realized, without friends or code of conduct. He felt childhood drop away from him, felt the instinctive adult strength of his northern nomadic ancestors well up inside him. Strangely without fear, he stepped out of cover and walked into the creature's camp.

It rose from its haunches, its head coming no higher than Sharp's mid-torso. Its coverings were definitely clothing. His interior ear detected a faint sound, not unpleasant. He half noticed a dozen or so black insects hovering above him, curiously scentless, tracking his movements.

Sharp broadcast a greeting. The slender creature stood straighter, muscles taut. Its answering scent was strangely flat, without overtones. Less than primitive.

Sharp named himself. The creature's response was to rush over to its burnished metal box, and stare at intricate patterns of light on its surface. Patience. He sniffed at the creature, trying to guess its scent range, trying to attune to its strange bodily chemistry.

Sharp! His own name came blasting back at him from the metal box.

Hearts thumping, Sharp emitted a wild uncontrolled blast of happiness. Aided by the creature's device, they could communicate! Sharp, casteless and untouchable, would yet taste knowledge beyond the imagination of the Council Elders.

The thought made him salivate profusely.

For Rekka, the creature's presence was a brooding shadow watching her with deep amber eyes. Hunkered down on its haunches, its ursine body was huge, visibly muscular beneath the dark fur. Its short sleeveless robe, hood thrown back, was fine and light, decorative more than protective. In that seated posture, its head was level with hers. It watched patiently as she moved about the camp. She had the sense that it was keeping still so as not to alarm her. Was her fear so evident?

A light rain began to fall, softer than tears. Rekka walked slowly up to the creature, wiping back the raindrops from her forehead, feeling shaky inside and hoping that it didn't show. Stopping in front of it, she reached out and touched its cheek. Soft fur over hard bone. Its face was long, almost baboon-like, but widejawed. Rekka swallowed as it took her hand in its own great double-thumbed mitt, its thick fingers like rope. It held her hand palm up, and licked it once, its pale brown tongue rasping gently. Rekka shivered. She closed her eyes. This close, the warm smell of its damp fur reminded her of her step-parents' dog shaking himself indoors after a rainy walk.

It released her, and she opened her eyes. Backing away carefully, she returned to her biofact in the centre of the campsite.

She felt light-headed. Alternating between elation and fear, Rekka tried to concentrate on reprogramming the biofact so it could broadcast to the creature. Twice she had to repeat commands because her voice was shaky. All the time she watched the alien – no, no, *she* was the alien – watched the native who, she arbitrarily decided, was probably male. She referred to him as Whiff in the journal entries which she dictated to the two bees who hovered over her, logging every move on video.

With this top-of-the-range biofact, she was able to set up three main processes running in parallel. The highest priority task was encoding/decoding simple commands and queries in Whiff's language. The second jobstream, using the same framework modules to analyse Whiff's biochemistry, was the evolution of killer bees which would protect her should Whiff's curiosity turn to rage.

The third task was considerably more speculative. The biofact was evolving nanospectrometers which would fit her bees. If it worked, she would have a way of eavesdropping on Whiff's fellows.

By the end of the day, unbelievably, she was able to carry out a conversation with her new friend, so long as they both stayed within about ten feet of the biofact.

'Whiff? Raise right hand.' The biofact translated her voice command into odour. The first time it had succeeded in broadcasting a sentence, Whiff's nostrils had flared and his slitted amber eyes had widened to round black circles.

This time, Whiff calmly raised a powerful-looking arm. Though the rain had stopped some time ago, his fur still looked a little damp and stringy.

'Rekka? Sit.' The biofact decoded Whiff's scent and voiced it neutrally. Rekka sat down obediently. The vocabulary of posture and body parts was as far as they'd got. But that little was a great deal, childish though their communication was.

She chuckled to herself, at the thought of replaying her bees' video log in six months' time, back on Earth. Kindergarten for cuddly aliens.

Sitting down on the hard ground made her realize how tired she was. Running on adrenaline all day, she had not even eaten. Groaning, Rekka fetched two cartons of rations from the pack by her tent. Should she offer him food? She pressed the heating tag on one carton, waited 30 seconds, and opened it. Watching Whiff, she picked up a vegetable samosa with her fingers and bit into it.

Whiff turned and lurched out of the camp. A part of Rekka's mind noted that Whiff walked bipedally, though she had expected he might drop to all fours.

'Three bees – follow Whiff.'

Would Whiff come back? She remembered her sudden intuition that his exotic fragrance, suddenly broadcast when they met, had not been accidental, but a form of communication. She replayed the moment several times in her mind, savouring it. Beautiful. She had been nobody's first choice for this project – would not even have picked herself – but she had succeeded. And if this turned into a programming assignment, well, she could practically make a biofact sit up and beg.

The fragrance of her meal was suddenly enticing. She tucked in ravenously.

Later that night, going through the video logs of her beeswarm, she watched the recorded image of Whiff munching raw vegetables, solitary in the undergrowth, his massively broad shoulders rounded, almost hunched. Almost furtive, though that might be taking common body language too far. The signs of parallel evolution were startling enough already: of the other inhabited worlds, only one other even held organisms which had evolved jointed limbs and endoskeletons.

Did Whiff need to eat alone? Were his reasons biological, religious, aesthetic? She resolved not to eat whenever he was near. If he returned.

That night her dreams were haunted by dark looming shapes. Broad shouldered and strong. Sometimes warm and protective, sometimes hard and dangerous. Vishnu or Shiva, preserver or destroyer, it was impossible to tell.

Once, when she woke in the dark with tears stinging her eyes, she thought she had dreamed of her biological mother. She had been weeping in her sleep. Unseen in the night, she knew, her tiny bees were hovering outside her transparent tent, logging everything. Let them. Let them all know how scared she was.

Sharp remembered his sister Bittersweet's antics when she had seen the untouchables eating vegetables in public. Think of the strange creature as intelligent but not civilized, he told himself. Deal with it.

The next day, he forced himself to return to the frail creature's camp. Thankfully, it didn't try to eat in front of him again. He did not think he would have been able to come back another time.

Conversation progressed a little. Again, Sharp spent the night in cold misery away from the camp. On the third night, he slept inside the camp perimeter, near the almost-clear sleeping-dwelling. Its heat source kept him comfortably warm.

Over the coming days, Sharp found the slender creature capable of understanding complex statements, including different tenses. Though small, it was very intelligent. Sharp also began to watch the insects closely.

At night, he would remember how alone he was, and long for his family, his caste fellows, the thousand subtle hints that told him at any time of day what he ought to be doing, reminding him he was part of a community.

The pains of adulthood were running through his body as it changed. Triggered by the stress of running away? The child Sharp, who had been himself just days ago, seemed more and more a distant dream.

The creature's metal box, the one about the size of Father's tool chest, contained a crystal window holding blurred moving images. After the creature had examined Sharp's eyes with strange instruments, it adjusted the box so the pictures were clear. Somehow the box projected what the creature's trained insects saw!

Sharp spent time watching the images, sitting beside the creature. He had grown used to its scent, could smell some of its emotions even before it used the wonderful box to translate sound into common-language. It was fascinated, like him, by the sights in the window.

Such sights! Scenes from Mint City, and other cities he did not recognize, with their own distinctive towers and domes. Scenes of nomadic life on the plains, invoking Sharp's ancestral memories. The first time they watched a Sharing, Sharp could not look away. The creature, though, trembled violently and emptied the contents of its stomach on the ground. Sharp puzzled over the significance of this.

For a while the insects mostly spied on Sharings, and on parents – faces etched with pain – teaching their voracious young. The creature seemed fascinated. Eventually, its box became capable of transmitting crude scents picked up by the roving insects, and Sharp could get a vague idea of a lesson's content.

One day, though, the insects observed a type of meeting which Sharp had not thought about before. It was a convocation of Librarians, in a vast gathering of tents on the plains. That was not unusual, for their unique caste depended on knowledge sharing, though they transmitted little of their own knowledge to other castes. But their furs! Though similarly robed, the Librarians had a vast range of fur coloration. Some were striped or dappled! How could such a mix of races possibly share anything?

When they began to use sandpits and clay tablets, Sharp turned away in boredom and began to poke about the camp. Everyone knew vaguely about the writing of Librarians, an arcane and useless skill. The creature, though, continued watching closely.

Sharp thought. Father was unpalatable in Mint City. But Librarians of different races needed more than the scents of common-language with which to share their knowledge. Limited and linear though this writing was, maybe the creature was right to be interested. He returned to the screen; and he and the creature watched together. Watched, and learned.

For days the images of blood and pain haunted Rekka's waking moments as well as her sleep. Her first sight of a Sharing was something that would live with her always. It was not until later, when she saw parents sacrificing parts of themselves for their otherwise vegetarian young to feed on, that she guessed the ceremony's function. Such love their parents must feel for their offspring! Dangerous to anthropomorphize again, but they seemed nobler in their pain than humans. She thought of her step-parents' kindness and warmth. Yet they had never made such sacrifices.

With an increasing number of observations, she noticed

no cases where sharing took place beyond the bounds of close genetic relationships. She must be safe from Whiff. Nevertheless, she reprogrammed six of her most potent killer bees to follow closely, buzzing around her head, on guard at all times.

For exercise, as the weeks passed, they began to take long rambles around the picturesque hills, occasionally venturing close to villages and watching the inhabitants. Rekka trusted her friend to keep them downwind. She was becoming more aware of scent, and now referred to him as 'Sharp' in her journal entries.

She stayed close to him on their excursions, admiring his strong economic movements, the play of muscles beneath his dark fur. Sometimes the wind ruffled that fur, like ripples on wheatfields. Often unconsciously, she would stroke him as they walked. Small dark buds on his forehead, unnoticed when they had first met, now seemed to Rekka to be growing bigger by the day. Soon, she guessed, antlers would begin to sprout. She thought that puberty might be a very rapid process for Sharp's people.

On their return to camp, Rekka would always feel a renewed enthusiasm for the project, a spring of boundless energy within her. She worked hard on the biofact's AI interface, developing the thinkware to learn the Librarians' secret written language and teach it to Sharp. She was vaguely aware of neglecting the rest of her research, but this was of prime importance.

One afternoon, 40 days into the project, she found herself staring at Sharp's strong form and blushing. Warmth spread across her entire body. The local male and female forms were closely analogous to Earth genders, and her bees' logs had long since confirmed Sharp's maleness. Their reproductive processes were related, closely enough for some form of mutual gratification –

Whimpering, fighting her desire, Rekka retreated to her

tent, crawled inside and sealed it tight behind her. With longing eyes, she watched Sharp continue at his lessons, pretending to be unaware of her.

The creature became less tractable over the coming days, but Sharp hardly cared. He became immersed in this new form of knowledge, swimming in writing like a fish. Fish were a newly unearthed ancestral memory.

The insects spied on hundreds of texts. To read about painting, say, was not to know how painting felt, or to absorb the physical technique. Yet there was much knowledge, of a sort.

The creature created a portable crystal window. Sharp could finger-trace writing on it, or the creature's box could cause writing to etch itself onto the window. Poorly, the mechanism could translate some simple common-language.

He learned that the frail creature was female. Through scent and script, they moved on to increasingly abstract conversations.

Months later, Sharp was seated on a small carbon-fibre camp-stool while Rekka, leaning against his massive furred shoulder, rubbed soothing cream around the roots of his antlers, obsidian fractals spreading proudly from his brow. The itchiness, currently intense, would pass in a few days. There was no denying it: he was an adult, in a community of only two. No matter. He squeezed his eyes shut in pleasure.

'That feels good.' Sharp's synthesized voice came from his portable screen, lying on the ground at his feet. The system had evolved to full common-language voice translation.

'Okay. You're just about done.' Rekka's words were translated into a mixture of scent, issued from transmitters on the portable screen, and characters displayed on its surface.

She wiped her hands on a small towel, then picked up a brush to groom Sharp's fur. He held up a hand to stop her, thumbs spread wide.

'Your turn for pleasure,' he said.

'OK.'

She could imagine the laughter when sequences like this would be played back from her log, but she was past caring. She sat down on the ground in front of Sharp, and he began to give her a back and neck massage, expertly using his iron-hard fingers to dig into the knots of muscle tension. His grip was strong enough to snap her spine, if he so desired.

'The ship will be here in five days,' said Sharp.

'That's right.' Rekka closed her eyes and moaned in pleasure. She would have preferred to take her clothes off, but her bees were recording, as always. Maybe she did care what her employers would think.

'And you'll be going home. You'll see your parents.'

'Yeah. Well . . . they're not my real, biological, parents. They adopted me.'

Sharp paused in his massage. 'Your real parents died?' He knew that humans died without leaving memories in their descendants, and felt profoundly sad for them.

'My real mother tried to kill me.' Rekka leaned back against Sharp. 'I was born in an area of Earth where mothers still try to murder their daughters, being worthless burdens who cannot earn their way.'

'A waste,' said Sharp, suppressing a shudder.

Rekka shrugged. 'I went back once, to the village near the rescue mission, but I was a stranger there. There was no role for me to play.'

'Like me,' said Sharp. 'Casteless.'

'Just like you, my friend.' She leaned her head back against his heavy warm chest.

Friend. The concept of friendship included mutual tasting but, as with so much else, Sharp reminded himself that the scents were not literally true. Sharing ceremonies upset Rekka, he now understood, almost as much as Earth relationships upset him.

'Will you take me with you?' asked Sharp.

Rekka thought a long time before answering.

'Yes,' she said.

Sharp's teeth closed gently on her shoulder. A brief warm lick, and then he released her.

The night before the ship was due to arrive, to take them to a world beyond the sky's black dome, Sharp jogged slowly away from the camp. A handful of Rekka's bees followed him. Rekka had not asked why he needed to go. He did not really know why.

The bees were more than spying devices. Rekka had recently used them to take tiny portions of people's bodies, a notion Sharp had found disquieting at first. Humans stored their memories in their bodies, in their brains, yet could not transmit them. Rekka was investigating the superior way in which Sharp's people remembered things.

He jogged for a long time, until he reached the settlement. Lungs burning, trying not to transmit scents of exhaustion, he walked slowly through the wide streets, past low huts and grand villas, to his parents' two-storied house.

He walked around to the small courtyard at the back, and saw Father's silhouette against the drapes, his shadow made huge by the candlelight.

Father! Sharp felt like a child again.

Afraid to go in, unable to retreat, Sharp froze. Then a sudden movement at a ground-level window brought him back to his senses.

– Sharp?

– Bittersweet!

– You're alive! Where have you been?

His sister's lithe form slipped over the windowsill and rushed into his arms. Sharp hugged her mightily.

– Mother and Father, how are they?

Bittersweet stepped back. – Father ... has not worked much, since you ran away. We searched for ages ... Are you back for always?

– Not yet, sweet sister. Soon I'll know enough, that they can never cast us out. I promise.

Bittersweet reached up to touch his antlers, gently.

– You've grown, big brother.

Sharp started to reply but stopped, raising his head and sniffing. Strangers, not from the settlement. Maybe a dozen of them, coming down the main street in the darkness.

Bittersweet grabbed his arm.

– Proctors from the city guard. There are patrols nowadays. Rumours of lights and strange creatures up in the hills.

Over the courtyard wall, faintly against the night sky, Sharp could see the bobbing outline of the tops of the standards carried by the troop's bannermen.

– Sharp? Don't go!

Sharp disengaged himself from her grip.

– I've learned much, little sister. We can think for ourselves, without people around us at every moment. Remember that. Tell Father ... I don't hate him, though I thought so at first. Tell him, his dishonour will be forgotten. I swear it!

Then Sharp turned and slipped out through a narrow gap in the courtyard wall, into the street. An alarm scent carried on a draught. The proctors! Sharp dodged down the smallest alleyways, running hard, heading for the area where the settlement came right up to shoulder-high scrub growth, full of thorns and very fragrant.

He ran out into the thorny scrub, pushing hard, ignoring the pain, and disappeared into the night.

Rekka and Sharp stood in the centre of the campsite looking upwards, hand in hand, but not so close that their position could be mistaken for a struggle. A blaze of light, a crack of sound, and a huge *mu*-space ship was hanging over them like a great silver bird. A tiny automated shuttle slipped out of a hold and began its descent.

'There are two of us coming up,' said Rekka into her wrist comm.

'Really? That should be interesting.' The pilot's voice was dry. The wrist-comm screen remained blank, but she sounded about Rekka's age. 'I think that contravenes the spirit of the regulations, if not the letter.'

'Nevertheless . . .' began Rekka.

'Please, no arguments from me. I could give a rat's ass what the bureaucrats think. If you're coming, better get in the shuttle quickly. You have an armed raiding party heading towards you.'

'I know.' Sentimentally, Rekka had recalled most of her beeswarm and packed them away for shipment. A few, though, remained on sentry duty and would self-destruct after her departure. Some of those bees were transmitting pictures of a squad of proctors moving steadily through the undergrowth, less than two kilometres away.

Rekka and Sharp boarded the small shuttle. The biofact, which Sharp carried easily in one hand, was rapidly transmitting his physiological profile to the shuttle's medical systems. Rekka and Sharp strapped in. Though Sharp's seat attempted to adjust itself to his shape, it was still half the required size, and he shifted uncomfortably.

'Remember, we'll be asleep during the trip,' said Rekka, wincing as her chair inserted a hypodermic into her hand. 'We can't survive the transition to *mu*-space otherwise.'

'What about the pilot?' asked Sharp. His portable screen, hanging by a cord round his neck, was still communicating via the biofact's translation program.

The pilot's voice broke in from a speaker. 'We're not quite human any more. We find the real universe pretty uncomfortable, in fact.'

Sharp's reply was translated as 'Oh.'

By the time the shuttle had completed docking in its hold, its two passengers were fast asleep.

Rekka's employers were delighted with their preliminary scan of her assignment logs. Less than pleased with her presumption in bringing back Sharp, nevertheless they acknowledged that she had more than met her objectives. Maybe Sharp's presence would speed up investigation of the memory mechanism.

On her first day out of quarantine, three of her bosses took her to dinner at an exclusive restaurant overlooking the placid mirror of Lake Geneva.

Rekka, in her new evening gown, examined the other diners as though they were another species. Some of them were eating meat. She had spent her early childhood in a culture where the number of meat-eaters was growing – as half the population attempted to throw off the traditions of Hinduist-Buddhist doctrine – in contrast to the rest of the world. She steeled herself when one of her own table companions ordered steak.

When the meal arrived, however, it was the sight of people eating vegetables in public which broke her. She rushed to the ladies' room and promptly threw up.

Several months later, Rekka's divisional director, a prematurely balding man called Simon Simmonds, called her into his office. His shaky voice seemed always on the verge of a stutter.

'We have an issue with UNSA regarding EM36. They haven't authorized payment of our latest invoice.'

'Oh. Why's that?' Rekka was learning the system here. Keep things impersonal, and blame the system rather than people when things broke down . . . at least in public. In the background, back-stabbing as usual.

'It seems Sharp is – causing some problems at their Education Centre,' said Simmonds.

'He looked okay to me last Thursday.' She tried to see him once or twice a week. The people who were both studying and teaching Sharp had gelled into a very happy team.

'The trouble is, everything's been too okay. Sharp has been allowed free access to any information on the Infonet, public domain or UNSA-confidential. They've fallen over backwards to satisfy its – his – every whim.'

'Why is that our problem?'

'Because . . . Well, I'm not sure how to put this. They think that Sharp has been manipulating them with, um, pheromones.' Simmonds looked uncomfortable.

'Right.' Rekka reached into her pocket with a swiftness which made Simmonds jump. She dropped two small fibrous pellets on his desktop.

'What are those?'

'Nose filters. Very useful, if you don't want Sharp twisting you round his little finger.'

Simmonds' face went blotchy. 'You mean you knew this all the time?'

'After the first couple of weeks, when I began to feel – let's say, desires for him. I sealed myself in my tent till he was out of the way, then grew these in the biofact in about two minutes flat.'

When Simmonds said nothing, Rekka added, 'Sharp's natural behaviour is no reason not to pay our invoice, Simon. The standard terms and conditions give them full rights to the beeswarm logs and absolutely nothing else.'

'We have a relationship to maintain, Rekka. UNSA could become our biggest client. Our bio-memory research has given us a great deal of kudos.'

Rekka said nothing, giving Simmonds a chance to remember just who had performed 'our' research.

'Anyway.' Simmonds cleared his throat. 'They've set up a return mission, to return him to his native habitat.'

'And you want me to accompany him?' asked Rekka, scratching at a small spot on the back of her hand.

'No. Not at all. That's not, um, not what they . . .' His voice trailed off. There was a worried look in his eyes.

'Thank you, Simon,' she said. 'Shall we let them know now?'

She dictated a memo to UNSA on his terminal, and waited until he had confirmed and sent it.

Simmonds watched her with a bemused expression.

'I'd better get packed for good old EM36,' said Rekka. 'Poor name, really. Lacks romance. We could do with more romance, don't you think?'

'Ah –' Simmonds cleared his throat. 'Rekka? I wondered if you were, ah, free tonight –'

'Sorry,' she said gently. 'I really do have to pack. I'll see you when I get back.'

She left Simmonds' office and headed back to her lab, rubbing her hand as she walked. She felt both guilty and smug about her handling of Simmonds, and disturbed by both feelings. She rubbed her hand again. Now that the small adhesive patch was gone, the spot where her Simmonds-manipulating pheromones had been stored was itching like crazy.

As they were strapping themselves into the shuttle at Zurich, Sharp turned his large head carefully, making sure not to hit anything with his antlers. 'A man called Simmonds gave me a message for you.' The voice issued from a tiny speaker at his throat, the latest upgrade to his translation system.

'What?' Rekka stiffened.

'You are not pleased?' said Sharp. 'He said, the first human on a planet names it. UNSA standard terms and conditions.'

'Really?'

'He also said, bring back some duty-free scent.'

Rekka laughed. 'Maybe I misjudged him.'

'Humans,' said Sharp, his upgraded speech system injecting wry overtones.

'So what do you – ouch – really think of Earth?' She laid her head back against the headrest as the tranquillizing injection took hold.

Sharp's eyes grew slitted, turning almost yellow. 'Your Elders, like mine, taste the works of others for amusement, furnish their lives with artefacts they never make themselves.'

Did he mean the rich? Politicians? Was this the same goofy young male she had befriended less than a year ago?

'Do you really think – ?' Rekka closed her eyes as the cabin seemed to sway. It was a short step from there to drifting away entirely.

They were waiting in a small courtyard, with hanging plants bearing pale orange flowers, a tiny fountain tinkling in its centre. Outside, one of the great roads led to the plaza, maybe a kilometre away in the very centre of the city. Rekka was surrounded by huge muscular males in ornate robes, massive antlers sweeping the air as they looked around. She felt tiny and weak. Though they blocked her view, she could hear the shuffling footsteps of thousands of their people passing by on the road outside, the sense of their presence like a tangible weight upon her. She felt shaky with anticipation.

She turned her wrist-comm screen to her beeswarm's realtime video, flicking through the images from each bee in turn. Some images were jerking chaotically – turbulence round the great columns ringing the plaza – but the day was clear and sunny and most of her bees were transmitting perfect pictures.

* * *

The massed rows of scarlet and gold banners cracked like whips in the breeze, stretching across the vast width of Mint City's Central Plaza. Row upon row of Elders, from all the cities of the continent, sitting expectantly upon their velvet-cushioned seats, filled the plaza as though it were some gigantic stadium. There had not been such a gathering in 1,000 years.

At each of the gateways which ringed the plaza, thronging crowds were milling, eager to get in. Ten thousand of them had already flooded through the archways. Proctors of the City Guard were now letting them through in a more controlled fashion, handing a flat crystalline plate to each spectator as they entered. Inside, it was hard to think in the mind-numbing complexity of scents.

An empty seat of honour was arranged on a wide dais facing the Elders. Opposite, in the first row of Prime Elders, were three empty stools. A narrow roadway of scarlet carpet ran from one gateway directly to the plaza's centre, past the front row of the most eminent Elders and terminating at the raised seat waiting for the guest of honour.

Along the red roadway came a glinting bronze wagon, drawn by a dozen draught beasts. It halted before the Elders, and a bewildered family of three were helped down by massive broad-shouldered proctors and led to the cushioned stools in the first row. Surrounded by Prime Elders, they scarcely dared to look around, almost too scared to breathe.

The scents of the crowd became cloyed with expectancy at the first signs of the formal procession. A long column of bannermen walked through an archway, followed by Librarians and other dignitaries in ornate robes. In their midst walked Sharp and Rekka, both visibly trembling.

Though Rekka could not decipher the crowd's scents directly, she felt powerfully uplifted as she walked by Sharp's side along the passageway through the vast crowd.

It was headily unreal, a maelstrom of impressions: here a vast square-jawed wide-antlered head silhouetted against the sky, there a youngster's wide amber eyes, a blue brocaded robe, pelts of grey, of brown, of black, even something like a silver tabby. Rustling, shuffling natural sounds amplified ten-thousandfold. An uproar of scents instead of voices, keen and intoxicating, stinging her nose and clearing her head.

Suddenly Sharp turned, and looked at three individuals, plainly robed, out of place among this section of the crowd, where the rest were older males with dull grey antlers and white-tipped fur, with rich clothes covering their frail limbs. Rekka, in a moment of sudden intuition, knew she was looking at Sharp's abandoned family.

They had caught Sharp's scent as the procession drew near. Father's head was lifted proudly, amber eyes wide at his lost son's sudden preeminence. Mother and Bittersweet radiated love and welcome. Sharp felt their love flowing into him and sustaining him ... Rekka knew this, could feel it as though she were one of Sharp's people. She knew, too, how scared he was. She touched Sharp's arm gently, feeling the trembling beneath his soft fur. He was depending on her, depending on his family, to support him. For he, the outcast, was going to address this great audience and, by extension, every civilized being upon this planet.

Sharp ascended to the chair of honour, flanked by the Chief Librarians of a dozen major cities. Rekka, light-headed, climbed the dais with difficulty and stood at Sharp's side.

– I return to you from a city beyond the sky.

Awe swept the crowds. Sharp's scents were reproduced by the crystal pads they were holding, simultaneously broadcasting to all of the thousands in the plaza. A tiny earplug provided a voice translation for Rekka, a pleasant baritone talking in her right ear.

– I bring knowledge of arts unknown to our peoples, from a species who can become our friends.

There were many Librarians scattered among the onlookers. As written script began to flow across the crystal screens, the Librarians translated, supplementing with common-language scents.

– The lights in the crystals are language. With them, we can talk to humans. And to each other.

Neophyte Librarians twitched nervously as their caste's knowledge was made public, but the Chief Librarians, tall and dignified behind Sharp's chair on the dais, made no movement. They all knew Sharp's announcement in advance. Rekka gathered that the political intrigue had been complex, but she knew the vast majority supported this initiative.

Her vision stung; the image of the vast dark crowd, robed and antlered, was blurred with tears. Knowledge and civilization. Such a price Sharp's people had paid, a tithe of blood and pain, of suffering and sacrifice, for every advance. In her mind's eye she saw a tableau of grief stretching back through millions of years of evolutionary history. What a dream it was, to free them of such a burden!

Thinking this, she saw without comprehension the Chief Librarians fold back their robes and withdraw short bronze sickles. She felt Sharp's great paw take her hand, and raise it up to his mouth. His teeth closed gently round her hand.

'No!' she screamed.

Sharp released her.

'Rekka, stop!' The voice from his translation unit seemed subdued. 'This is the only way to make my people learn.'

Rekka looked into Sharp's amber eyes, full of fear, and froze.

'Please, Sharp –' She started to back off.

'Stay with me, Rekka. I'm scared.'

Tears ran freely down her cheeks.

'I'll stay,' she said.

She looked at Sharp's family. Their eyes were on their son, their bearing erect and proud.

Even before it started, she knew: this was no mere community sharing of a tiny slice. Sharp was to be honoured by an entire world. However awful the taste, his people needed this knowledge, and the Prime Elders would be forced to swallow it. There were hundreds of them here, thousands more of secondary Elders.

In her mind was one burning thought. Her beeswarm, poised above the plaza, could swoop and kill. She need only raise her wrist comm and speak a phrase, words loaded with certain death . . .

Rekka looked away. A procession of silver-furred maidens was approaching, delicate, elegant, strewing fragrant flower petals as Sharp's agony began. One of the maidens, seeing Sharp, seemed to falter, but recovered quickly. The dance-like movement continued. Curved lines of maidens, slowly crossing and recrossing in intricate choreography, scattered blossoms from seemingly bottomless baskets, masking the pain. Throughout a ceremony that seemed to last a thousand years, petals fell like swirling snow.

Some unknown length of time later, Rekka was standing alone on a hillside overlooking the newly-renamed Sharp City. Its proud architecture was a monstrous joke, like the purple-flecked slope on which she stood and the beautifully clear sky above. Some things, she thought dully, were just too large to comprehend.

There was a clap like thunder high above her head, then the whining descent of the automatic shuttle. She should have been reluctant to leave, but she found herself at the small craft's hatch while it was still rocking on its landing gear.

She climbed in and strapped herself into the nearest couch. She stared at the intricate console with unseeing eyes.

'Hello, Rekka.' It was the same pilot's voice, coming from the intercom.

'Hello,' she answered listlessly.

Acceleration pressed her into the couch as the shuttle rose.

'So what did you call her?' asked the pilot.

'Call? Who?'

'The planet. I heard your conversation on the trip out.'

There was a pinprick of pain as the tranquilliser entered her hand.

'Name . . . Vijaya.' There was a moment of clarity, when Rekka could see briefly beyond the pain. 'Means . . . Victory.'

Merciful sleep claimed her before the shuttle docked.

The great shining vessel made one complete orbit of Vijaya's blue and ochre sphere. For a moment it seemed to hang above it, like a vast gliding bird free of gravity's restraints. Then it disappeared into *mu*-space, heading home.

OFF THE TRACK

David Garnett

They drove on down the road. Stretching ahead to the horizon, it was straight and empty. An hour had passed since they'd seen another vehicle; an hour before that, they'd taken the wrong road.

Michael had realized his mistake almost at once but had said nothing. It would make little real difference.

He kept his speed down. If they went any faster, the cracks and potholes in the road shook the car too much. Not that he cared about the hired car, but there was no hurry. They were on holiday – or supposed to be.

'There's nothing,' said Angela, as she turned the radio dial. 'Nothing.'

Michael heard all kinds of different sounds fading in and out between the crackles of interference – news reports, advertising and sports commentary; a string quartet, a choir singing hymns and a swing band – but Angela switched the radio off and leaned back in her seat.

He watched from the corner of his eye as she looked down at the book in her lap and turned the page. Michael couldn't believe Angela was as bored as she pretended. She kept complaining about the heat, saying they should have hired a car with air conditioning; but he knew she wouldn't have complained about the heat if she'd been stretched out on a beach. Her window was wound down, and the hot desert wind blew her hair back.

Angela could be on the beach again in a few days when they went back, but this was his part of the holiday, something he'd always wanted to do.

He had not been disappointed. The desolate landscape and the distant rock formations were even more spectacular than he'd imagined. He liked everything about the place; he even liked the potholed road.

Driving was meant to be like this, without long queues, without being jammed solid in a city street. Back in Britain, there was nowhere he could have driven as far without having to stop. The same was true wherever he'd travelled in Europe.

They had driven through Holland and Germany, France and Spain and Portugal, but always in their own car. This was the first time Michael had driven a left-hand drive vehicle, and he was surprised how soon he got used to it. Angela had refused to drive, another demonstration of her feelings about this part of the holiday.

'Town coming up,' said Michael, as he saw the signpost at the side of the road. He glanced at the fuel gauge. It was still half full, but it was best to keep the tank filled up. 'Maybe we should get some petrol.'

Angela said nothing.

'Could do some shopping,' he added.

Angela turned her head. He couldn't see her eyes because of her dark glasses.

'Shopping?' she said. 'Shopping!'

Then she smiled and swiped at his shoulder.

'You Inglish? I make you a deal!' said Michael, and Angela laughed.

'How big's this town?' she asked. 'Two houses or three?'

'Horses, did you say, or houses?'

Angela kept looking at him. 'You're enjoying yourself, aren't you?'

He nodded. 'But you're not?'

She shrugged, then studied the silver bracelet around her wrist, lightly rubbing at the turquoise stone with her thumb.

'Some of it is all right,' she said. 'I suppose.'

Even after so long together, Michael was always amazed how much Angela could say in a few words. Almost as much as she could say with a single look.

As far as she was concerned, they could have returned an hour after crossing the border. By then she'd bought everything she wanted from the handful of tourist shops clustered on the northern side of the frontier. Michael had to admit that it all seemed good quality stuff, and of course the prices were ridiculously cheap. Tourists had only been allowed in very recently, and they'd had to buy their visas before they left Britain.

When it came to shopping, Angela was an expert; she could find what she wanted almost immediately. She had bought hand-crafted jewellery and woven rugs to take back as gifts. Michael had restricted her to the number of rugs they could fit in a large suitcase, but told her to buy as much jewellery as she wished – and not to forget herself. Angela had tried to persuade him to buy a pair of fancy leather boots, but Michael knew he would never wear them. To keep her happy, he bought a snakeskin belt. He would never wear that, either, but at least it was less bulky and a lot cheaper.

That had been yesterday morning, and they had spent the night in an approved hotel. Michael had filled the fuel tank before they crossed the border, and again where the Volkswagen had been garaged for the night.

'If nothing else,' said Angela, 'perhaps we can get some lunch. Even if they don't have petrol, they've got to eat.'

'You want to risk it?'

'It can't be worse than some of the food we've eaten abroad, and it will be a lot cheaper. We've got to try the local cuisine while we're here.'

They had enough food, a packed lunch prepared at the hotel; but maybe Angela was finally coming to terms with this trip.

'Just don't drink the water,' said Michael, as one of them

always did wherever they went. 'I wouldn't even put it in the radiator.'

Angela nodded, then glanced back at Michael. 'Air-cooled engine, right?' she said. 'I just wish this air would cool me.' She fanned her face with her book, then gazed out of the windscreen as they neared the town.

They had driven through several similar small towns, and compared to those in Europe the roads were all very wide, even the side streets, and the buildings were set far apart. None of them were very tall, many of them only single storey. There was no need to build up when it was easier to build out. If there was one thing in surplus here, it was land.

Michael wondered what possible reason there could be for a town out here in the wilderness. Why had it ever been settled? Which came first, the road or the town? Almost every building was built of wood. Nothing looked new, nothing looked old. A decade or a century, it made little difference. A swirl of dust blew across the street ahead of them, a reminder that the desert was waiting to reclaim the whole area.

It only took a minute to reach the centre of town, and the road was lined with shops on either side. At least half of them were boarded up or derelict. Michael saw two other vehicles going by in the opposite direction, one of them a pickup truck, the other a battered old saloon. The driver of the first stared, the driver of the second raised a hand in greeting. Michael started to wave back, but he was too late.

He noticed two petrol pumps on the other side of the road, and he took his foot off the accelerator.

'Is that garage open?' he asked.

'It looks deserted.'

'That might not mean anything. They won't get many customers.'

As he drove past, he saw the open door of what might have been a workshop.

'There!' said Angela. 'Someone's inside.'

'We'll give it a try.'

He checked the mirror. There was nothing behind. There had been nothing behind since the border. He did a U-turn and pulled into the forecourt. A huge black and white dog was lying in the shade on one side of the petrol pumps. It didn't move when Michael halted on the other side.

'Got any petrol?' Michael said to the dog.

It opened its eyes, then closed them again.

'Maybe it's self-service,' said Angela.

'I'm not going to risk it. Are you?'

He stretched back in his seat, trying to see into the workshop. One vehicle was up on a ramp inside. There were a number of others nearby, but all of them were on flat tyres or without wheels. In such a climate, it would take a long time for them to rust.

He heard a chatter of voices and leaned back. There were three or four children at Angela's door, their hands thrust in through the window. Two more appeared next to him, begging.

'Ignore them,' he said.

Angela opened her purse and started handing out coins.

'All right, ignore me,' muttered Michael, as the two children at his window ran around to join the others.

He straightened his tie, opened the door and stepped out of the car. Then he noticed a shadow on the ground, and he turned around quickly, taking a step back when he saw the man only two yards away from him.

'Petrol?' he said. 'Have you any petrol?'

The man was tall and lean, wearing an oily vest and stained denim trousers. He stared at Michael, then looked at the car. He touched the shiny new metal with his grimy fingers. When he drew back, there were greasy fingerprints on the wheel arch. He bent down and started to wipe the paintwork with the rag he was holding. His hand became still when he noticed Angela in the passenger seat. He stared at her for a few seconds, then finished cleaning the dirt and stood up. He walked around the car, studying it, then looked at the number plate at the front.

Michael wondered if the man had understood him.

Carefully, he repeated: 'Have you any petrol?'

'Gas,' Angela told him.

'Have you any gasoline?'

'Nice car,' said the man.

'It's hired,' Michael said quickly.

'Where you folks from?'

'England.'

The man nodded slowly, then spat on the windscreen.

Michael took a deep breath and wondered how fast he could get back into the car and drive away.

Then the man leaned towards the bucket by the pumps and picked up the wash rag. He began to clean the windscreen – and Michael slowly exhaled.

He seemed quite old; but his face was so lined and weatherbeaten, it was hard to be sure of his true age. His hair was still thick, although almost totally grey.

'Out of here!' he yelled at the children, flicking water at them.

They ran off, laughing, and Angela climbed out of the Volkswagen. The man's eyes followed as she walked over towards the dog. Michael wanted to tell her not to touch the animal, but he knew it would make no difference. She stroked the dog's head, and its tail began to beat lazily against the ground, sending up clouds of dust.

'What's his name?' she asked.

'Dunno,' said the man.

Angela glanced up at him.

'But I call him Duke,' he added, and he smiled.

'*Dook*? Oh, Duke!' She laughed and rubbed at the dog's ears. 'Are you a good boy, Duke? Are you? Aren't you handsome? Yes, you are. Yes, you are.'

Angela was crazy about dogs. Michael had married her five years ago, and her boxer had been the dowry. It had taken a long time for Michael to persuade her to leave the animal in kennels so they could go away for foreign holidays. These three weeks were the longest time she had ever been separated from her dog – and this would probably be the last time Michael and Angela would be alone together for a very long time. Their first child was due in six months.

The dog rolled over onto its back, its legs in the air. The man looked at Michael, then back at Angela.

'Yessir,' he said, as he finished washing the screen, 'I've got gas. Even got an electric pump. You got vouchers?'

Michael nodded and reached for his wallet, pulling out several petrol vouchers. They had been overprinted in red: *Tourist Issue Only Federal Penalty For Illegal Use.* He'd had to buy them at the border, paying in advance for any fuel he would use. He had tried to calculate how many gallons they might need, converting imperial gallons and estimating fuel consumption, only to discover that he had to buy a minimum number of vouchers.

The same was true of the currency; both of them had exchanged travellers cheques for the minimum of 20,000 dollars in cash. Once they returned to the frontier, they would have to surrender any dollars and fuel vouchers they had left. There were no refunds.

Michael found it strange how all American banknotes were exactly the same size and colour, whatever the denomination. Inflation was finally down to under 100 per cent a year, however, and before too long the currency must surely be revalued to reflect its relative stability.

'Okay,' said the man. 'You want it full?'

'Please.'

He unscrewed the fuel cap, unhooked the hose from one of the pumps and slid the nozzle into the filler. Setting the trigger onto automatic, he walked to the rear of the car.

'England, huh?' he said. 'I spent an hour in Scotland once. The plane was refuelling.' He opened the back of the Volkswagen. 'But I spent much longer in Germany.' He pulled out the dipstick, wiped it with a cloth, slid it back, pulled it out again, nodded.

'They make these in Mexico now,' said Michael.

'I know.'

'That's where we hired this.'

'I know.' He closed up the engine. 'They're beginning to build cars in America again, I hear.'

He turned to face Michael, looking him directly in the eye for the first time.

Michael felt he had to say something. 'Were you on holiday in Germany?' he asked.

'In the army. I was conscripted in 'fifty-eight. Korea was over, and the only war they had was the cold one. Ten years later, and I'd probably be dead.'

This time Michael could think of nothing to say.

The man shrugged. 'It's all over now, I guess. We should never have been there, should never have done what we did. But what happened to us should never have happened, either.'

The fuel nozzle switched off, and the man pulled it part way out. He gently squeezed the trigger, rounding off the figures on the pump dial, then replaced the nozzle in its slot.

'How much?' Michael asked.

'Twelve hundred bucks.'

Michael counted out twelve vouchers and handed them over. He ought to pay more, as a tip, but he felt guilty about doing so. If he added another voucher, it would be as if he were trying to make up for what had happened – as though it were his personal responsibility. He wondered if he should give the man a hundred dollars for washing the windscreen, and he opened the other part of his wallet.

The man realized what Michael was doing, and he shook his head. 'That's okay,' he said, and he turned to look at Angela. The dog was licking the back of her hand.

'Angela,' said Michael, 'we'd better leave.'

'We've got to go now, Duke,' she told the dog, and she stood up. 'Is there anywhere we can get a cup of tea?' she asked the man. 'A proper cup. Hot, with milk and sugar.'

'A cup of tea?' He smiled. 'No, ma'am, I doubt it. But I've just made some coffee, and you're welcome to a cup.'

'We'd better leave,' Michael reminded her.

'That's very kind of you,' she said. 'We'd love a cup of coffee.'

'Come on through into the house.' The man turned and walked away.

'Angela,' said Michael, waving her towards the car.

'Michael,' said Angela, and she gestured towards the service station. She began following the man.

Michael drummed his fingers on the roof of the car for a few seconds, wound up the windows and locked the doors. He quickly combed his hair, then followed Angela. They went around the back of the garage. A one storey clapboard house stood there, surrounded by even more derelict cars and trucks.

'Come on in,' said the man. 'You'll have to excuse the mess, but I'm packing up. I'll soon be gone.'

'Where are you going?' asked Angela, as she followed him through to the kitchen. A pot of coffee was simmering on the stove.

'Tennessee. Always said I'd go back there some day. Now's as good a time as any.'

'Were you born there?'

'No, born in Mississippi. My folks moved to Tennessee when I was thirteen. Here, take a seat.' He lifted a pile of magazines from a chair, and Angela sat down.

Despite his annoyance, Michael found himself fascinated by what little the man had said. Tennessee. Mississippi.

They had always seemed to be names from some ancient myth, but meeting someone who had lived there was almost like becoming part of the legend.

'Ever since I was a child,' said Michael, 'I've always wanted to visit the USA.'

'Uh-huh.'

Michael's abiding images of America had been of Westerns, the exotic landscapes of prairies and deserts, of mesas and buttes – which was exactly what he'd discovered in Arizona.

'How long have you been here?'

'About ten years. After the army, I moved to Texas to work in the oil industry.' He laughed for a moment, but there was no humour in his voice. 'When we had an oil industry.'

Texas, thought Michael, another evocative name.

'But you weren't there when . . . when . . .'

'No. I was up in Colorado on a fishing vacation with some buddies. Lucky, I guess.' He was standing by the sink, washing out tin mugs. 'You folks got any kids?'

Angela and Michael glanced at each other, both knowing what the man must have been remembering.

'Not yet,' said Angela. She licked her lips. 'You?'

'Two, a boy and a girl. Their momma and me, we split up. She took them with her to California.' He paused. 'Los Angeles.'

When there was a Los Angeles, thought Michael, but he remained silent. So did Angela. The man poured them both a cup of coffee, boiling hot and very strong.

'I'm working on my truck right now,' he said. 'Soon as everything's ready, Duke and I are gone.'

'Will you be able to carry all your belongings?' asked Angela.

'All I need. What I can't carry, I'll leave or try to sell. You interested in buying anything?'

The man was smiling, but he meant what he said.

'Thank you, but I don't think so,' said Michael.

'What have you got?' said Angela.

'All kinds of junk,' said the man.

'Authentic American souvenirs, you mean,' she told him.

'Exactly. You're welcome to take a look around.'

Angela's eyes widened. 'What's for sale?' she asked.

'Everything. Even Duke.'

She looked at him sharply.

'Except Duke,' he amended.

Michael knew he couldn't win. He sipped at his coffee – and he didn't like that, either.

Angela gazed around the kitchen, at the old crockery and the dented pots, but Michael was certain there was nothing here that she wanted. Even if there were, he would throw it out as soon as she wasn't looking. He didn't want any of this stuff in his house, and Angela certainly couldn't give any of it as presents.

'We can't take anything bulky,' he told her. 'It's only a small car, remember. And we have to think of our luggage allowance on the flight.'

'Take your time.' Somehow the man had managed to finish his scalding coffee. 'I'll be out front if there's anything you find.' He left the kitchen.

'Angela,' said Michael, 'you can't be serious. There's nothing here you can possibly want.'

'Probably not, but I want to look around. Give me your wallet.'

Michael did as he was asked. 'Hurry up,' he said.

He poured his coffee down the sink and picked up one of the magazines from the stack on the floor. It was a motoring magazine, quarter of a century old. He wondered if they were worth much. Even if they were, they were too heavy to take back to Britain.

It was too hot to remain in the room, and Michael let the magazine fall back, then left the kitchen. He turned right into the hallway. There was another door at the end, and he pushed it open.

The room was filled with junk, real junk, all kinds of obsolete household electrical equipment, most of it dusty and dismantled. There was a pile of old paperbacks on top of a doorless refrigerator. Michael picked up a few and glanced at the covers. They were all Westerns. He put them back, but the top one fell to the floor. Bending down to retrieve it, he saw something narrow wedged between a vacuum cleaner and the blade of a broken fan. He didn't recognize the object, so he pulled it free. It was only an old record, he realized, as he brushed the dust from his sleeve.

There couldn't have been anything of value in the house. House? It was more like a shack. If there were anything, the man wouldn't have left them alone in the place. Or maybe that was the whole idea. What if he claimed Michael and Angela were trying to rob him? He probably had a gun somewhere. All Americans had guns. He might have gone for it now so he could threaten them. It was time to get out of here.

'Angela!' he yelled, and turned to leave the room. 'Angela!'

The man was standing in the hallway.

'What you got there?' he asked.

'Nothing,' said Michael, then he noticed he was still holding the record.

'Is that what you want?'

'Er . . . yes.'

'What is it?'

Michael studied it for the first time. The label was visible through a circular hole in the paper cover.

'*Rock around the Clock*,' he read. '*Bill Haley and his Comets.*'

'Rock around the Clock!' laughed the man. 'Number one in the hit parade! Didn't know I still had that. Remember buying it in Memphis. Shit, must have been nearly forty years ago! Look, I even wrote my name on the sleeve.'

'You should keep it.' Michael tried to hand the record back.

The man hesitated, then shook his head. 'It's no good to me. I can't play it. But it's a real piece of American history, believe you me.'

'Is it? One of those, er, long-playing records, is it?'

'No, it's a seventy-eight.'

'Seventy-eight what?'

'Revs per minute. Forty-fives came in soon after, if I remember right.'

'Ah, yes.' When Michael was younger, a couple of his friends used to buy records.

'Rock and roll! God, what that meant to us when we were young. It was our symbol of rebellion, you know what I'm saying?'

Michael said nothing.

'No,' said the man, looking him up and down, 'maybe you don't. Our parents hated rock and roll, and radio stations banned it. But it was our music, and it was going to be our world. We felt everything would be different from then on.' He shrugged. 'But it wasn't. I guess it never is.'

He gazed at the record but his eyes were unfocused, and he was obviously remembering the past.

'How much?' asked Michael, to break the silence.

'It's priceless – and it's worthless. So take it. It's a gift.'

'No, we'll pay,' said Angela, suddenly appearing behind the man. 'And I'd like this, and this, and this, if they're for sale.'

She'd found a small lacquered box with tiny drawers, an oval mirror with a wicker frame and handle, and a crystal perfume spray.

'If you want them, ma'am, they're for sale.'

'Five thousand dollars?'

The man stared at Angela in amazement.

'Not enough?'

'No. Yes, I mean. More than enough. Too much. They ain't worth anywhere near as much.'

'They are to me.'

Angela counted the notes from Michael's wallet, handing them to the man. He tried to refuse, but Michael knew how difficult Angela was to dissuade.

'Is there anything else you want?' he asked, shaking his head in bewilderment. 'Take anything.' He looked at the money, and he smiled. 'Take everything.'

'We must be going,' Angela told him. 'Thank you for the coffee.'

'You're welcome, ma'am.'

He held out his hand, and Angela shook it. Michael backed away out of reach.

'Come on, Michael.'

They left the house and began making their way back to the Volkswagen.

'Five thousand dollars?' whispered Michael.

'You know the rate of exchange. You earn that in a day. Come on, quickly.'

'What's the rush?'

'I don't want him to find those petrol vouchers until we've gone.'

Michael halted. 'The what! How many did you leave?'

She tugged at his arm. 'We've still got plenty. We don't need them all.'

'But he won't be able to use them. They're only for tourists.'

'He'll find a way if he has to,' said Angela. She paused to stroke the dog, which was still lying in the same place. 'Give me the keys, I'll drive.'

She unlocked her door and carefully put the things she had bought on the back seat, then climbed into the car and opened the passenger door. It was roasting inside.

Michael swung his door backwards and forwards, trying to force some cooler air into the vehicle. Angela slid the key into the ignition and started the engine. Michael sat down, closed his door and opened the window.

By then, the man was standing next to the driver's door.

'Where you heading for?' he asked.

Angela glanced at Michael.

'The Grand Canyon,' he answered.

'You won't be disappointed.' The man nodded.

'It's Tennessee for you?' said Angela.

'And Mississippi. I reckon it's time I visited my brother's grave again.'

'He died when ... er ... ?' Angela's voice tailed away.

'Died at birth.'

Michael noticed his wife's right hand leave the steering wheel and touch her stomach.

'He was my twin brother.' The man wiped his forehead with the back of his arm. He seemed to study the town, but his gaze encompassed far more. 'Sometimes I think he was the lucky one.'

He and Angela looked at each other for a moment, and he said: 'Have a good vacation, you hear?'

'We will,' she said, nodding. 'Goodbye.'

The man waved as the car drove off into the street.

'This is America,' said Michael. 'They drive on the right.'

The Volkswagen swerved to the other side of the road.

Angela glanced at Michael, then she grinned.

'Are you angry?' she asked.

'At giving away five thousand dollars to a complete stranger? Why should I be?'

But his anger was already ebbing away. For the first time Angela no longer seemed to resent them being here, which was all that mattered.

They had only driven a few hundred yards when she suddenly braked and pulled the car into the side. She pointed across the road to the war memorial.

It stood in a small plot, surrounded by flowers. There was a fountain in one corner, a flagpole in another. There were still 50 stars on the American flag.

'It's like a tombstone,' said Angela, softly.

In the centre was a simple slab of white marble, with carved lettering highlighted in black.

In Memory of the One Million

When the casualty list reached that high, official figures were no longer issued. Some said the total was one and a half million American dead, others two million.

Two million dead in Vietnam, but that was nothing compared to the number who had died when the war suddenly reached the USA. There was no memorial to them, and the death toll was even more speculative. Perhaps 30 million on the day the missiles landed, perhaps twice as many in the years that followed. And there must have been at least as many fatalities in the Soviet Union.

'Why did they go when they knew they'd be killed?' asked Angela.

'Orders. It was their duty.'

'But it was all so stupid. What were they fighting for? What were they dying for? Why didn't anyone protest, try to stop the war?'

Michael didn't really know what she meant.

'They did try to stop the war,' he said. 'They dropped nuclear bombs on Hanoi.'

'And look what happened! They were warned not to, but they went ahead. The whole world could have been destroyed. A lot of it was. And for what? For what?'

She turned towards Michael, and there were tears in her eyes.

'Let's get out of here,' he told her. 'Are you all right to drive?'

'Yes.' Angela nodded. 'It's just . . . just . . .'

She glanced at the memorial again, shook her head, then drove off.

'What are you going to do with that stuff?' he asked, hoping to change the subject. 'Give it to someone you don't like?'

'What?'

'The stuff you got from Jesse G. Presley.'

'How do you know his name?'

Michael was still holding the record, and he showed Angela the name written on the cover.

'I'm going to keep it all,' Angela said. 'But what are you going to do with that?'

'Nothing. What can we do with it? Do we know anyone with a gramophone?' He glanced at the title again. '*Rock around the Clock*.'

'What does that mean?'

'Who knows? Who cares?'

Michael turned and threw the record onto the back seat, watching the town recede in the distance. He wished they had stayed on the right road, wished they hadn't stopped. Everything had been fine until then; but now it was almost as if there was something missing, and he had no idea what it could have been.

In silence, they drove on down the road.

THE EYE-OPENER

Brian Aldiss

On the first day, the Head was visible only to armies. Many armies of many kinds ceased to advance or retreat. Men crawling on their bellies stood to view. Boy soldiers eased their bandoliers and looked up.

It created a far greater disturbance than war. As it happened, I was up on the moor as usual. I saw the Head first by moonlight on a cloudless night, when it most resembled a giant cactus.

Of course its effect was fearsome. For a start, it was enormous. It seemed at first to fill the whole quarter of the western skies, as later it came to fill our lives. What we have never experienced always stands in our path like a land mine. Like the first time you have an enemy in your gun-sights. However, I speak for many when I say that apprehension was accompanied by a sense of relief. Without consulting others, I knew that here was a different mode of life for everyone, a spot of adventure just when you were growing a bit long in the tooth . . .

Between the stark alternatives of Life and Death, a third force was interposed – if that doesn't sound too grand.

It is not too much to say that I just stood there, transfixed. Couldn't keep my eyes off the thing. Extraordinary. Bizarre. There were no words for it.

What I didn't realize was that all round the world everything was grinding to a halt. Pretty well the entire human race was staring upwards. Not a posture you usually hold for long.

In the first hours of its manifestation, no one had any

conception of time as it related to the Head: was it a transitory phenomenon, or was permanence one of its unknown characteristics? The appearance of the Head was in itself so enigmatic, like a private dream, that other considerations took a while to dawn. Although I had been used to trouble all round the world, this was something entirely new.

My resolve was to stay observing the Head until moonset and daybreak. As the light changed and the moon in its third quarter sloped towards the west, the face of the Head became less well defined, while the bulbous nature of the skull became more pronounced. In saying this I do not express what my inner feelings were at the time. So novel was this grotesque thing, so far beyond nature, that I remained for some while uncertain as to whether we had received a visitation from a Head or a vegetable growth roughly resembling a Head. It occurred to me that this might be a new psychological weapon, launched by some unknown enemy.

In which case, it might come in handy for some astronomical target practice!

Despite the mixture of elation and misgiving which filled me, I fell asleep on the moor. When I woke, a new day had barely begun; Earth's dewy shadow still lay over the moor. The Head was still there, immense in the pallid sky, bathed in sunlight.

I should explain that my worldly fortunes had varied greatly. I had joined the army at an early age. My family connections entitled me to early promotion. During the war with Groznia, I was made general, when my courage and grasp of strategy were instrumental in winning a swift victory. After the war, I entered politics on a tide of popularity. In two years I was made a junior minister and in five appointed Minister of Defence. Unfortunately, my so-called 'illegal dealing in arms,' undertaken purely for the good of my country, was brought to light and misinterpreted; this, coupled with my brief affair with the Kirghis princesses, brought about my downfall.

Disillusioned, I purchased a few hundred acres of this moor, to become a farmer of sorts, a calling some of my mother's ancestors had followed. At least it kept me outdoors. There I reared the black-faced horned sheep common in this part of the country. I had the odd stag to pot at now and again, to relieve the boredom. Of course I retained my connections with the highest in the land. And with other lands.

After a swig from my hip flask, I rose to my feet and stared into the sky. Nearby, the sheep rooted about between heather and bracken, eyes to the ground, in the manner of all grazing animals. I looked up, in the manner of carnivores. All that interested my animals was what passed between their black lips.

The Head was turned full face in my direction. With all else that was strange, this did not strike me at the time as particularly strange.

Wispy cloud partly obscured the immense Head. I saw brutish lips, a large squashed nose, and eyelids heavy like unbaked pastry covering the closed eyes. The expression, it seemed at first, was one of an unutterable contempt. Yet at a later moment, as the vapours drifted, I perceived – or thought I perceived – an expression of calm resignation to sorrow. What sorrow I knew not. I'm not an imaginative man, I'm happy to say.

Such nobility as the face might possess was negated by a nest of stiff 'hair' (so I must call it) surrounding it. The chin sank into a neck much resembling the trunk of a sequoia. A suggestion of shoulders was obscured by the mists of the horizon.

I stared up at this apparition. I was alone on the moor, without even my dog for company. A sudden emotion seized me. Awe of an unprecedented nature, I suppose, but something more; *a dark sense of the artificiality of human life* . . .

As if I had been living on half-rations all my natural.

What in hell had we all been up to, all these thousands of years?

Just supposing those eyes opened and it saw me . . .

Somehow, just to look up at that thing made you feel mighty small.

So I ran, ran towards the nearby lane where my all-terrain stood. Kicking it into gear, I drove furiously back to my house in the valley.

Once there, I dashed inside and snatched up my binoculars.

The binoculars gave me a better view of the immense thing in the sky: better, yes, but more enigmatic. It scarcely appeared to have a face: the features I thought I had seen proved almost as imaginary under higher magnification as the canals on Mars. The mouth was but a vast furrow, the nose and closed eyes were mere protuberances on a wrinkled surface. That surface seemed to be constituted of a material like dried mud, impenetrably surrounded by what resembled a forest destroyed by fire, of which only blackened stumps remained. The thing was some kind of vast vegetable growth, only to my anthropomorphic imagination resembling a human being.

Yet lowering the glasses brought back that face of gloom and resignation.

It is typical of my limited thinking that I try to puzzle out these minor details while the major puzzle remains. How did this monstrous thing arrive? What order of monstrous thing was it?

Was it meant to be a caricature of someone living? I knew a Major Trapido once in Belize who looked somewhat similar. Couldn't help wondering what Cynthia (just temporary) would say about the thing.

Re-entering the house, I switched on my computer.

Already the Internet was buzzing. Reports of sightings were coming in from all over the world. At least the Head was no solitary creation of my own imagination, as I had almost been tempted to believe! It was clear no one knew more than I did.

I fed in a private number and spoke to well-placed friends in other parts of the world. Disquieting facts emerged.

Most estimates placed the Head in the upper ionosphere, where the ionosphere fades into the exosphere. Which is to say, about 250 miles above the earth's surface. This figure was arrived at by observing the times at which the Head entered and quitted earth's shadow. To an observer, the Head filled an angle of 22.5 degrees. By triangulation, it was established therefore that it measured all but 100 miles across. So much for mensuration.

But numbers and figures, for long mankind's consolation, were soon to provide no comfort. My contact in Vladivostok, Vladimir Mironets, reported that he saw the Head full-face. Colin Steele from Canberra gave the same report. From Leslie Howle in Seattle came the same answer: the Head was seen full-face. Always full-face, from any vantage point on Earth.

Perhaps you will understand the mixture of bewilderment and despair which overcame my psyche at this point. Perhaps you remember feeling the same yourself. No stolid Victorian preacher, confronted with the truths of Darwinism and facing the knowledge that he was descended from apes and mistier creatures back in time could have suffered a greater sense of betrayal. The Head by its very presence set all scientific knowledge at nought.

I reached the conclusion that this could not possibly be an enemy psychological weapon. No nation had technology advanced enough to project such a thing into Earth's skies.

There were others who did not despair. More disconcerting news revealed that the Head could not be photographed. As Count Dracula showed no reflection in a mirror, so the Head did not register on any kind of film.

Whilst I was sitting in a limbo of thought, Cynthia Goodwin-Jones came downstairs, wearing her white satin wrap, her hair entangled in towelling.

'You've seen it?' I asked.

'The product of a hangover. I need orange juice, aspirin, black coffee, sympathy. Not necessarily in that order.' She disappeared in the direction of the kitchen. I made some phone calls.

As I was getting myself a drink, Cynthia returned, coffee mug in hand, and sprawled on my chaise longue.

'The bloody thing's about a hundred miles across – from ear to ear, as it were. The size of one of Jupiter's moons.'

She said, 'You were on the phone. Not calling any of Claude's friends, I hope?'

Goodwin-Jones was a cabinet minister, currently indulging in an affair with a female American rock singer half his age, name of Babbles. How he kept these affairs out of the tabloids I shall never know.

'Why are you always paranoid as soon as you get up? You should take more exercise.'

She hugged her coffee cup. 'Why go on about Jupiter's moons? That object up there is not an astronomical object. Surely you can understand that? It's just an image of some sort.'

'Image?'

'It expresses religious anxiety, guilt – all the things people wallow in at present, me included. Not to mention sexual dilemma.'

'You mean, like someone giving you head?'

She ignored my wit. 'UFOs having had their day, along comes this new image. Who knows what? End of human egotism? Some hopes!' A tiresome woman in some ways, but with a good bone structure. Goodwin-Jones had never appreciated Cynth enough. After a silence, she said, 'The dawning of the age of philosophical life? Is that what it means? Or maybe it will come down here and eat us all . . .'

'I got on to Purvis in Washington. Remember him? They're going to send a shuttle up.'

She gave her high pitched laugh. 'Claim this bloody cranium in the name of the UN? Trust the Yanks! How crazy can you get?'

'You have to do something. You can't just sit around, can you?'

Her expression said, Don't bore me with your male platitudes.

Later, we went out and observed the Head together. The cloud had cleared as the morning advanced. The Head took on an appearance of pewtery lambency, as if lightly powdered with aluminium.

'In my opinion, for what it's worth, you could land a shuttle on it,' I said.

I had to go to London on business in the week. Cynthia stayed in sole possession of the house. I managed to get a half-hour's conversation with Claude Goodwin-Jones in his Whitehall office. He sat at his desk, turning a pen over and over in his paper-thin hands. He said the government was consulting with other EC leaders and with the Americans. There was much to be optimistic about. For example, the Head had advanced no nearer Earth, as had been feared it might. It had caused no meteorological upsets, as might have been anticipated. And astronomers reported absolutely no gravitational disturbance to Earth's orbit. The Head had no detectable substance.

'Meaning in fact it doesn't exist.'

'Wouldn't say that, old chum.' He spun his chair round to stare gloomily out of the window. 'That might frighten the populace. Bit too much for them. The populace can see, or thinks it can see, that the bloody thing exists, whatever instrumentation says to the contrary. Personally, I can tell you the PM regards the Head with a pinch of affection – takes everyone's minds off the financial crisis. Let's just say that whatever it is – well, you've seen the line we are putting out for general consumption – it exists in a different dimension of space-time from the rest of the universe.'

Trying to put him in his place, I said, 'It probably spells the end of human egotism.'

Claude gave me a penumbral glance. 'Where would that leave you, old chum?'

As I rose to leave, he treated his pen to another twiddle and asked after Cynthia.

'I do feel bad about her, you know.'

Handing in my pass, leaving the building, I thought to myself, So you damned well should, old chum.

'The Ghost from Outer Space' . . . Was it first a headline in the Miami *Sun-Sentinel*? Wherever the phrase came from, it caught on.

Thus the unfamiliar, the outré, the monstrous, became familiarized – a kind of a joke, a child's bogeyman, a cultural reference. 'Ordinary life' is an obsessive habit: something which must continue, even in the midst of war or catastrophe. Women in cities devastated by earthquake, their houses in ruin, still peg out their washing to dry in the sun. I've seen them at it.

'Political life' also continued. Pronouncements were issued on all sides of the spectrum. The pronouncements always sounded like distortions of the truth, rather in the way that the most innocent person feels he or she is lying when talking to a policeman. Religious leaders, as was inevitable, called upon sinners to repent. They handle any kind of crisis that way. I suppose it must work for a day or two.

I liked a quotation from Thoreau, which a friend in Alma Ata sent me via the net: 'Men can be wise only with the wisdom of their age; they also share its ignorance. Even the greatest minds must yield in some degree to the suppositions of their age.' (I translate roughly from the Turkic.) True, I thought, though happily it did not apply to me.

Then there was Bishop Archer, with his pronouncements. A pompous fellow. I had bumped into him several times in my more palmy days. It was said of him he had slept with his mother. More than once, I mean. There were other evil rumours too, of which I took no notice. 'The Head is a manifestation of all mankind's unlived days . . .' And so on. Enough to make you sick. 'Those who don't know how to use their lives . . .'

I continued to manage my farm. The Head loomed high above the moor. I studied it often. This is purely subjective, but it seemed to me that the face was undergoing subtle alterations as the season unfolded. The eyes remained closed, the mouth held its contemptuous pout. But a slow refinement crept over the features; even the 'hair' seemed less barbaric. It may have been that I was growing accustomed to the Head, so that now I could see in it almost a kind of beauty. The way people used to talk about seeing the Man in the Moon.

When I said as much to Cynthia, I added – I thought modestly – that possibly I was alone in perceiving this beauty.

'You always were a conceited old thing,' she said. 'What makes you think you're unique? From the start, commentators have pointed out a delicate resemblance between that enigmatic face and certain races in the South Seas. It's a beauty to which we are going to grow accustomed if it remains there for long . . . You miss a great deal, reading those boring old military journals of yours.'

With admirable patience, for the woman was still in a nervous state, I asked what I should be reading. *Home Chat*, for instance?

Cynthia tapped the magazine she was carrying. She liked to make out she was a bit of a thinker.

'This chap Brady has an interesting lead article in this month's *Art and Illusion*. He points out that every transitional age produces a major disturbance – wars, revolutions, or just deep psychological changes. We may be undergoing such a transitional period now. Faith in technological progress has reached its nadir. We are now, Brady suggests, leaving the Technological Age. What is coming cannot be foretold, but he claims that the Head may be produced by a kind of mass-myth-wish, as he calls it. The Head poses no threat beyond its mystery. Indeed, the threat of something coming from outer space has been one of the psychoses haunting the Technological Age.'

'So what does this chap believe this thing is? What could it be, if not a threat?'

She gave me one of her tiresome you-dummy smiles. 'Try and hear what I am saying. Brady believes that the Head is connected with our moral life, which could be re-awakening.'

'Then moral life is fast asleep!' I laughed. 'I like that!'

'For those who can receive it, the Head speaks a secret language, the language of meditation. Some see human features on the face, others merely natural features. In short, the Head is there, quite separate from our physical world, as an object of contemplation. It is by its nature necessarily and testingly obscure: not an answer but a question.'

'Whose question, for heaven's sake?'

'*Our* question, of course. "Une grande port ouverte sur le mystère éternal . . ."'

'Ha ha! When in doubt, lapse into French . . .'

'Brady has his reasons. He likens the Head to a French symbolist painter called Odilon Redon. Redon painted isolated Heads, male and female, according to an inscrutable private code, intended to convey to those who might understand, "les esprits de silence", and –'

'Oh, turn it off, Cynthia. This is all high-flown tosh, and

you must know it. Besides, the Head's male, not female.'

She arched her fine brows and regarded me with a hard gaze. '*I* certainly see it as female.'

I said, 'Anyhow, enough of all this. The Americans are sending up a shuttle next Thursday.'

It was so vexing. I wanted to end the argument. Instead, another one blazed up. This time, it was about the feasibility of launching the US exploratory shuttle. Supposing, she said, the vehicle burst the illusion and the Head disappeared? Excellent, I said. Rubbish, she said. She said she liked it. Really, there are times when I can see how old Claude chucked her over.

Thursday approached. And on the Tuesday, President Yeltsin – never the most reliable of men – sent up three SS-20s from his vast stash of nuclear missiles.

Two of the missiles spiralled off into space, as you might expect. The third detonated somewhere near the bridge of the thing's nose.

Nothing happened. Absolutely nothing. The Head was unscathed.

Yeltsin quit the following Monday. Now lives in Oklahoma City, tending the Alienated People's Penitential Church.

I was out late that night, rescuing a ewe stuck in a ditch. Cynthia was having another of her fits of whatever it was, and I had phoned her sister, Judith, to come down to stay, thinking that the two of them looking after each other would make life a bit easier. Cynthia and I drove down to the railway station to collect her.

The all-terrain was bumping back to the house when the moon rose, freeing itself from cloud.

Cynthia made us stop to look at the Head. Judith was keen.

There it was, immense as ever. I was growing pretty fond of it, to tell the truth. The resemblance to Major Trapido in Belize was always pretty remote. And a change was overtaking it. Even I could see that.

It was becoming a female Head. Altering in outline, becoming female. Or was that it? Perhaps the thing was disintegrating.

Of course I said nothing of the sort to the women, but in my heart I felt a deep sorrow to think it might be about to disappear. After all – ever since the war, really – the world had become pretty flat. Prosaic.

There had been something missing, an extra dimension it used to possess.

A vacuum not exactly filled by black-faced sheep.

We stood there by the vehicle, the three of us, watching. Luckily, we had a flask of coffee with us, plus my hip flask. Judith has not got half her sister's style. Smells pretty good, though.

The transformation taking place was uncertain. In the darkness, details were elusive, but it appeared that the hair was no longer hedgehoglike but smooth and flowing, outlining a more graceful shape of head. A woman? A man of a somewhat hippie type? Hard to tell. The sisters discussed it while I kept pretty mum, butting in only when Cynthia became too pretentious.

She was telling Judith of this fellow Brady's criticism in her magazine. Judith agreed most of the time. I took a swig of whisky.

'We aren't meant to understand,' Judith said. 'I have to say I have become quite a different person under its influence, less worldly. I used to be a Capricorn, too. To my mind, the Head represents something different to everyone who looks at it. To me, it's just a big conundrum, like – oh, like family problems – like the conundrum of human existence. I don't really feel I'm up to modern life.'

People say things like that when they get on the moors by moonlight.

* * *

Long before dawn visited our part of the world, sunlight lit upon the Head. We saw now a more classical countenance. Long straight nose, small mouth, large eyes, closed as ever and shielded by pale oval lids. Hard to tell whether it was male or female. Neither, maybe. The ladies went on about Christ and the Buddha.

'Do you think she looks a bit like Mother?' Judith asked, anxiously. 'Something about the mouth . . .'

I could see a suspicion of a bare shoulder. The immense torso rose from a mist, pale and yellowish, much like thin cream, but with a hint of motion as if troubled. It was something newly born, awesome yet full of pathos. Unblemished, I'd say.

Now the new light softly illuminated the left side of the face. The temple, the cheekbone, the corner of the lips, that side of the chin, making the right side obscure. Something in that expression with the closed eyes made a picture of endurance and meditation and – well, I found myself so moved I had to turn away for another swig of the Glenfiddich. It would have been too ridiculous to have shed a tear. And for what, exactly?

The women were weeping, heads on each other's shoulders.

The first birds began to twitter about us. The bracken remained dark. The sheep were grazing as ever, looking down all the while, munch, munch, munch. Silly things, sheep.

'You see, she's rising out of the seas of the unconscious,' said Cynthia. 'Oh, it's so sexy! She's – oh, I always hoped – I mean, to be redeemed – no, it's impossible, but –'

She stopped in mid-sentence. Without thinking, we seized each other and stood huddled, the three of us close, staring upwards in hope and fear at the great change taking place in the sky.

The thing's eyes were opening.

Then it spoke to us about those unlived days.

THE WELFARE MAN

Chris Beckett

On Sunday his daughter and the boys came over and they all went to the Zoo.

Zoos were different now, all smilodons and woolly rhinos – creatures that in Cyril's childhood had existed only in picture books – but of course the boys took it in their stride. Alex, Jan's eleven-year-old, was a great authority on genetic archaeology; he explained incessantly and in great detail the many clever ways in which the scientists had recovered fragments of DNA from frozen corpses and desiccated skins, and how these tiny fragments were painstakingly reassembled along chromosomes extracted from modern mammals, and . . .

Jan saw that Cyril was getting tired.

'Wow, look at that, Dad!' she said, taking his arm and giving it a squeeze. 'Mammoths!'

An awesome sight! Six of the huge Ice Age animals were being led past by their keepers.

'Did you know, Mum,' said Alex, 'that these Bristol mammoths are the most authentic mammoths in the whole *world*? They are actually more than ninety-five per cent real mammoth's genes. The Japanese ones are only seventy per cent. The Russian ones – well – they're really just Indian elephants with long hair . . .'

Ben was afraid – he was only four – and wanted the comfort of his mother's arms. Alex had an almost equally powerful need to pour out to her all the interesting facts about mammoths that he carried in his brain. As nobody had any attention left for Cyril, he left them to it, wandering ahead by himself, following the six great Pleistocene beasts as they were led back to their enclosure.

Much though he loved his daughter and grandsons, there was a gulf between him and them. With her brisk, bustling, successful life, Jan could not really comprehend the sheer emptiness of his solitary widower's existence. Still less could she understand the world he inhabited at work, so many lightyears away from the world in which she lived, and from the jolly, affluent, interested world of this zoo.

Magnificently indifferent to the chitter-chatter all around them, the mammoths passed through the crowds of little human creatures.

'Where the Japanese scientists went wrong, Mum, was this . . .' Cyril heard Alex saying.

He snorted. These creatures were nobody's creation. Scientists just happened to be the agents that had awoken them. But if you waited long enough, everything would return.

From the far side of the zoo a smilodon screamed.

One day this whole city would be buried again beneath the ice: all these roads, all these signs, all these excited jabbering words . . . And then the mammoths, in their vast herds, would roam the earth once more.

Strangely comforted, Cyril smiled.

'Grandad! Grandad! We're going to look at the baby megatherium!'

Next morning he woke up alone in his widower's bedroom. Jan and the boys had gone home. He had only their photo on the shelf, next to the photo of Sarah. He dressed, drank a coffee and picked up his briefcase. The house was clean but lifeless, having lost its animating spirit.

He shut the door behind him and got into his car, immediately switching on the news.

'Serbia and the EC: Time to come in out of the cold?. America: New laws outlaw Einstein and Darwin . . .'

He backed out of his drive.

'South Asia: Another day of ethnic conflict in the former India and Pakistan . . . But first: Compassion or Oppression? The Democratic Party speaks out on the Social Compromise . . .'

Cyril flinched. His first impulse was to switch off immediately, but he made himself listen as he headed down to the main road-track, and set the controls for the ten-kilometre journey via the Portway, Ashton Gate and Bedminster to his place of work.

'The Social Compromise is degrading and a violation of human dignity,' said a Democrat politician.

'But what is so wrong about it?' said the minister. 'A bank is entitled to attach conditions when it makes a loan, a Receiver is entitled to impose restrictions on a bankrupt company. So why is society not entitled to impose some restrictions on those of its citizens who ask it to provide for them financially?'

Outside: the leafy streets, the famous Gorge . . .

'You see,' said the minister, in that confiding voice which politicians use, 'however much we might like it, you just can't mix a free market economy with a universal safety net. One always undermines the other. That was where we went wrong in the last century. If you want both a market and the safety net, you have to ensure there is a clear boundary between the two – a "formal frontier" – so that everyone knows when they move from one to another, and knows that different rules apply . . .'

They put the Democrat back on again then, but Cyril switched off. He was a *deskie*, a welfare man; the Social Compromise was his life – and he could not afford to lose what little faith remained.

And, in any case, he had reached the Line.

There was a checkpoint manned by an officer of the DeSCA constabulary and his robot minder (the robot was ferociously armed). Cyril pulled up and leant out of the window. He smiled, though he didn't feel like smiling. His stomach always clenched as he entered the Estate.

'Quiet night, Dave?'

'Yep, not bad,' said the policeman. 'Dan Wheeler and a couple of his mates tried to shift some dodgy dreamer units over the Line *again*, but we spotted the labels had been tampered with. So we nicked them!'

Cyril laughed. The enormous Wheeler/Pendant/Delaney clan were well known on the Estate. 'What I'll never understand is why he *keeps* trying! I mean, holding down a steady job would be child's play by comparison!'

The policeman shrugged. 'Well, that's dreggies for you.'

Sensitized by the criticisms of the Democrat politician, Cyril winced.

Electronic readers in the road checked out the registration, chassis and engine numbers of his car as he passed over the Line into the West Country's largest Special Category estate.

Special Category. Anyone in Europe would have instantly recognized what kind of place this was: the concrete buildings, the trampled parks, the graffiti, the ubiquitous Dreamer Shops renting out software with names like 'WARM GORE,' 'SEX HEAVEN,' 'BARBARIAN RAIDER' ... It was a *dreg* estate and the people who inhabited it were *dreggies*. Their ID cards were different to other people's, they were subject to different laws, they spoke differently, smelled differently, they wore tattoos and shaved bald patches on their heads for the ingestion of electronic dreams ...

Cyril drove down a road called Axis One. (The side roads, where people lived in concrete semis and lowrise flats, had flower names: Asphodel Way, Buttercup Crescent, Catmint Drive, Daisy Close, Edelweiss Grove ...)

With a bewildered, guilty affection he peered out at the people passing by.

Many of them he knew. (He had worked in this Estate since it was built.) Here was old Janie Pendant, who lived in a third-floor flat piled high with twenty years'-worth of tabloid papers, and insisted on cooking over a candle; there was crazy Alien Watson, already ranting at the top of his voice on the corner of Magnolia Street about Sin and Filth and the End of the World, but pausing to give Cyril a thumbs-up and a mischievous smile. Here was fat, sweaty Tracey Parkin, who Cyril himself had taken into care from her chaotic, drug-abusing mother when he was a social worker all those years ago and placed with a foster-family in Clifton. Now she was pushing her own baby along in a buggy, with her mother – as ever – beside her.

'Why did we bother?' thought Cyril. 'What did we think we were trying to do?'

He had got up to Yucca Walk and Zinnia Avenue – and Axis One opened into Knowle South's Central Square.

Here were a chippie, two dreamer places, a grocery, a sweetshop. There were four boys mixing glue and home-grown tobacco on the steps of the long-defunct fountain. There were shaven-headed young mums pushing buggies. There was a block of offices with bars over the windows and a three-metre-high wire fence. The office had a large blue sign with a logo that depicted one hand reaching down protectively to another. DEPARTMENT OF SPECIAL CATEGORY ADMINISTRATION, it said, or would have done, if someone had not painted a thick blue line through 'SPECIAL CATEGORY ADMINISTRATION' and written 'NIGGER-LOVERS.'

Last night someone else had drawn a *red* line through this and written 'RACIST APRESSERS.'

Cyril made some comment about the new inscription to the policeman on duty at the gate. The officer grinned: 'If we can be accused of being racists *and* nigger lovers, maybe that means we are getting the balance about right!'

And he laughed uproariously, his huge minder looking down from behind like some kind of mutant praying mantis.

'Fort Apache' the Knowle South DeSCA office was called by the staff who worked within its walls.

Another car entered the compound as Cyril was getting out of his.

'Mr Burkett!' called out its driver. 'I believe I'm coming to the same meeting as you.'

Cyril stared blankly. He was getting old. He found it increasingly hard to remember faces. Or perhaps it was just that he didn't try.

'Oh ... yes ... Dr Rajman, isn't it?'

The young Asian nodded. He was a Sponsored GP, maintaining a quota of non-fee-paying Special Category patients on his list, for which he was paid a retainer by the Department's Health & Hygiene Service – a sort of vestigial remnant of the old NHS.

'Of course the meeting isn't for another twenty minutes,' said Cyril.

'I know, but I've got a bone to pick with the H&H people and I thought I might as well sort it out while I'm here. They've sent me the wrong cheque three times in a row.'

Cyril smiled, a little sourly. Most young doctors did Sponsored work for a few years until they built up their own lists of private patients. Complaining about the DeSCA bureaucracy was all part of the drill. It gave them a principled reason for dropping their sponsored work later, when the private work had got going. ('I'm a doctor, damn it, not a filler-in of forms!')

He placed his forefinger on the Print Reader outside the steel door and spoke into the Voice Check: 'Cyril Burkett.

346

My companion is Dr Rajman, who is attending the 9.20 registration conference.'

The steel door slid open. Inside was a small reception area, where Cyril and the doctor were scrutinized for a few seconds by wall-mounted video cameras before a second door opened.

'Security has tightened up a bit since I was last here,' Rajman observed.

'It's because of Oxford, I'm afraid,' said Cyril as they went through.

'Blackbird Leys,' he added, when Rajman still looked blank.

But the GP seemed not to have heard of the latest lynchings. Perhaps that was understandable. It was only deskies that were killed, after all.

Up in Cyril's fifth-floor office, his colleague Alice had his coffee ready.

'Alice, you're a gem.'

He settled gratefully into a swivel chair and accepted the warm cup. Since Sarah's death, his relationship with Alice had come to mean a great deal to him. She looked after him. Her husband was paraplegic and had a drink problem. She looked after him too.

'Are you all right, Cyril? You look troubled.'

'Just tired really. Oh, and there was this damned Democrat politician on the radio this morning, going on about the Compromise . . .'

Alice laughed, misunderstanding the source of his unease. 'Well, there's not much chance of the Democrats doing anything about it, is there?'

She was right of course. The two wings of the old Tory party – *Britain First* and *Forward with Europe* – had passed the roles of government and opposition to and fro between themselves for more than twenty years.

'It's not that,' Cyril said, 'it's the fact that they may be *right*. I mean, I agree with them on most other things. I *vote* Democrat in fact. Maybe they're right about the Compromise too. Maybe we *are* just agents of oppression.'

'Oh, surely not,' said Alice, gathering together her papers for a nine o'clock meeting.

She was a generous person, a wise person in many ways, but she was politically blind. She could work for a firm producing nerve gas – and she would still feel quite happy and satisfied that she was *helping*, just so long as she was allowed to remember the birthdays of the other staff, and bring them little thoughtful presents when they were down.

'See you later, Cyril,' said Alice, giving him a concerned pat on the arm as she went out.

Cyril got up and went to the big north-facing window. You could see straight down Axis One to the Line and to the Fringe estates beyond (where the working-class inhabitants clung precariously to their jobs and their non-Special status). And beyond that, across the Cumberland Basin, the *real* Bristol stood, prosperous and sparkling, on her seven hills: a city where vandalism and disorder were rarely seen, a city where children played in parks that were clean and full of flowers, a city where the price of a glass of white wine at the Westbury Arms had remained constant at thirty Units for the past *eight* years. (While Asia fractured herself into a hundred bleeding pieces, while Africa burned, while America languished under the TV-religious tyranny of President Elisha Jones and his Committee for the Reception of Jesus . . . Who could really tell? Maybe the Compromise *was* a price worth paying?)

His phone rang. Inwardly cursing, he picked it up.

'Hello! Cyril Burkett here . . .'

From the deepest pit of hell a faint voice whispered: 'Burkett. You deskie swine. You piece of shit. I'll get you, I'll get you, I'll get you . . .'

'Who are you? Who . . .'

But the line went dead. He stood alone in his office, a dry leaf shrivelling in a flame.

'Well, colleagues. It's 9.25, so perhaps we had better make a start. For those of you that don't know me, my name is Cyril Burkett and I am the Assistant Regional Registration Officer. This is a Contested Initial Registration Conference within the meaning of the 2003 Act, concerning Stacey Blows of 34 Lilac Flats. Miss Blows herself has been invited to attend at ten o'clock. Let's start with a round of introductions . . .'

Jovial Charlie Blossom, with his sports jacket and his Scout tie, explained he was the Registration Liaison Officer from the Housing Section.

'Joy Frost, Headmistress, Virginia Bottomley Memorial School,' barked out the dapper woman to Charlie's left. 'Stacey Blows' daughter, Ulrike, is our pupil.'

Cyril smiled. Joy was a tough old boot. You had to be to teach in a Special Category School – and face the abuse not only of the children but of the rest of your profession. Teachers in the last remnant of the state sector were seen as no-hopers unable to cope with the fiercely competitive world that was education outside the Estates.

Dr Rajman introduced himself irritably. (Why should he attend meetings at the DeSCA if they couldn't pay his fees?)

A very young and pretty WPC called Fran Stimbling explained that she was on temporary secondment to the DeSCA Constabulary from Avon & Somerset Police and that she had come in the absence of Sergeant Walker and had no personal knowledge of Stacey Blows.

'Welcome, Fran,' said Cyril.

Then a small, thin, frightened woman introduced herself as Christine Wothersmere, a Welfare Investigator in the Community Hygiene Team (as the Child Protection Unit had been renamed since accepting sponsorship from the manufacturers of TCP). She was, in other words, a kind of social worker, a member of Cyril's own former profession – though it was very different nowadays, an almost entirely clerical function, feeding statistics into data-processing systems, reporting to computers and lawyers for instructions.

And a very elegant, large person beside her explained that she was Harriet Vere-Richards and was a voluntary Lay Representative appointed by Bristol City Council.

There were letters of apology from the Probation Service and from the Benefits Section.

'Good,' said Cyril, 'welcome, everybody. Stacey Blows, who was born on 6th September 1995, holds *de facto* Special Category citizenship as a result of having grown up in this Estate and having a Special Category parent. Now that she is approaching twenty-one, it is our task to determine whether she ought to be registered as a Special Category citizen in her own right.'

'I don't think there's much doubt about it in dear old Stacey's case,' said Charlie with his friendly laugh, 'half the neighbourhood knows her as the Two-Ecu Bang.'

Cyril ignored this. 'Stacey, as is her legal right, has indicated that she would oppose registration, and she will be here to put her views to us in person after we have had a preliminary discussion among ourselves. A transcript of the meeting will be made available to her and she will be entitled to take the matter to court under section eight of the Act if she does not agree with our decision.'

He tapped the keyboard of the speech processor, which proceeded to read out the background report.

'Stacey Blows' mother is Jennifer Pendant, White British, of 65 Corner . . .'

(Here Charlie and Joy chuckled knowingly, as old Knowle South hands generally did whenever a member of the Wheeler/Pendant/Delaney tribe was mentioned.)

'Her father is Roger Blows, Mixed Race British, of 105 John Major Way, Hartcliffe North. She attended South

Knowle Secondary School and left without any formal qualifications, though she possesses basic literacy and numeracy skills up to Age Ten Standard. She has never worked and now lives on National Basic Benefit. From the ages of fourteen to sixteen she was accommodated under the 2005 Children Act at one of the Child Protection Service's Group Homes. She then moved into a flat at 58c Japonica Gardens where her first child, Ulrike, was born on May 1st, 2011. Stacey Blows indicates that she is not sure who Ulrike's father is and has named two different possible men when asked.'

Joy Frost sighed. The computer went on: 'Her second child, Wolfgang, was born in 2012. His father was allegedly one Archduke Wayne Delphonse Delaney, now serving a prison sentence for armed robbery and Line offences. Following the birth of Wolfgang, she moved to her present address where Kazuo was born in 2014.'

The conference – or those members of it who were listening – smiled at the German and Japanese names. It was a fashion that had swept the British Estates because of the dominance of the Dreamer market by the two superpowers. (In the case of the Germans, who increasingly did not bother to dub their Dreamware in English, not only the names but the language itself was starting to penetrate the Dreamer-fed *argot* of the Estates.)

'Kazuo's father was allegedly one Benjamin Tonsil, whose present whereabouts Stacey does not know. Stacey has several offences for shoplifting and two minor Line violations. The Community Hygiene Team have also been involved in investigating various allegations of child neglect, which Mrs Wothersmere will fill us in on.'

Christine Wothersmere gave a little gasp and rummaged through her papers . . .

'We'll come to that in a minute,' said Cyril. 'Are there any questions at this stage? Mrs Vere-Richards? Is everything clear to you so far?'

'Yes, yes, *thank you*!' gushed the Lay Representative. 'I can only say how struck I am by the sheer complexity of the problems you . . .'

But whatever else she said was drowned out by a police helicopter passing low overhead.

Since a mob had burned down that DeSCA sub-office in Blackbird Leys, and eight of its staff had died, the Department had nearly doubled its helicopter force across the country. Helicopters had always patrolled the Lines but now they monitored 'People flow' within the Estates themselves, looking out for unusual confluences, for worrying aggregation patterns . . .

Cyril suddenly thought, '*Yes*, of *course*!'

He remembered a young man at a meeting just like this one: a human face almost totally obliterated under a lurid tattoo of a bloody skull, muscles taut, eyes icy with hatred . . . '*I'll get you*,' mouthed the lips of the skull face, unseen by anyone else but him, '*I'll get you, you deskie swine* . . .'

'How many people?' he thought, 'how many people out there would kill me if they only got the chance?'

Everyone was watching him. The room was silent except for the frantic rustling of Mrs Wothersmere, who had brought the wrong notes.

Cyril cleared his throat. 'Yes . . . Now . . . Before going any further, I need to remind the conference of the criteria for registration laid down under section 5 of the Act. If you remember we have firstly to be able to agree that Stacey demonstrates what is called in the legal jargon "*substantial fecklessness*" in two or more of the "*core areas*": Financial Affairs, Family Relationships, Basic Citizenship, Health and Hygiene. Secondly, as this is a contested case, we have to demonstrate that non-registration would be, in the words of the Act "*contrary to the public interest*." Now, if we can start with the first core area, which is Financial Affairs. Any comments here?'

Charlie Blossom immediately launched into the long and (to him) hilarious story of Stacey Blows' repeatedly vandalized electricity meter, enthusiastically supported by WPC Stimbling who read out a long list of criminal offences against Western Electricity in a shocked breathless voice.

Cyril's mind wandered. He doodled on his pad, underlining random words.

Stacey. *Stacey*. STACEY. Those old American names: Jason, Stacey, Wayne ... Stacey's parents must have been among the last to use them. Strange to remember there was a time when America was associated with style and freedom and fun ...

('... and then,' Charlie Blossom exclaimed, 'she went and did it *again*! ...')

'I am growing old,' thought Cyril. He was dreading a lonely retirement. He was dreading having time to look back over his life: so many compromises, so many decisions ducked as he climbed his little career-ladder through all the reorganizations and restructurings and rationalizations. Each step had somehow seemed reasonable and justifiable at the time, the best he could do. But all the time the old public welfare system was being slowly dismantled around him – leaving only a rump service in which the remnants of all the agencies were gradually amalgamated together: Housing with Social Services, Social Services with Health, Health with Social Security ...

He had started out wanting to help people; he had become the administrator of an Underclass.

Well, that's society's choice not mine, he had always told himself, and at least it pays the mortgage and has a decent pension scheme. We can have fun when I retire.

And then Sarah had died.

The helicopter passed back overhead. It was so low that,

beneath its engine and the thrub-thrub of its blades, you could just faintly hear the crackling of its ground-link radio.

'... *Hartcliffe East ... Exit violations ... Road patrol ...*'

'... of course,' said Charlie, 'the lodgers are another whole story ...'

Stacey had her hair shaven in stripes, so as to allow easy contact to the scalp for the electrodes of Dreamer sets, which supplemented sensory stimulation with low-voltage jolts to the brainstem and hypothalamus. Her arms were covered in tattoos of Teutonic warriors, and cross-hatched with self-inflicted scars. Her ears were riddled with holes from which bones, hearts, swastikas, dice, St Christophers and miniature Suzuki motorcycles were suspended. She wore a long tee-shirt with Japanese characters and a picture of a burning Zero fighter – and a short black skirt that left her thin, pale legs quite bare. On her forehead was a deathshead '*Liebe-Hass*' hologram, on her hip a little scabrous feral child with its face smeared with something sticky and cheap and red.

Everyone went quiet, as they always did in these moments when they had finished picking over a person's life and were confronted with the real human being. Charlie remembered with a little pang of guilt the amusing but unfounded comment he had made about Stacey being on the game. Christine Wothersmere wondered whether she should really have described her so very firmly as a 'complete and utter no-hoper' in order to cover her own embarrassment at having brought the wrong file. Fran Stimbling, who was almost exactly Stacey's age, went bright red and glared angrily down at the table.

Only Joy and Cyril looked Stacey in the eye.

'Welcome, Stacey,' he said, 'do have a seat. Let's start by checking you know everyone here ...'

The child – little Kazuo – reached out across the table for one of the carafes of water that stood there. Stacey smacked him hard and everybody winced.

'Well, I knows 'im, ja,' she said, looking at Dr Rajman, who blushed. 'I knows 'im. 'E gives I me 'scriptions for me fags.'

She suddenly treated them all to a smile of dazzling and utterly unexpected sweetness.

'Ja, und I knows 'er,' she went on, in the strange slow Germanized West Country burr that was the patois of the Bristol Estates. 'She gets I Kaz's milch and that and tells I I ain't feedin' 'im prarper. Und Mister Blarssom und Miss Frarst, I know them . . .'

WPC Stimbling was introduced.

'And I'm Harriet Vere-Richards,' gabbled the Lay Representative, sensing that her moment had come. 'You don't know me, Stacey, but I'm here to look after your interests. I'm not a professional person like the other people here, you see. I'm just an ordinary Bristol person like yourself . . .'

There was a moment of silence in which this preposterous statement was allowed to quietly fade into the air.

'Now, Stacey,' said Cyril after a decent interval, 'we understand that you don't want to be registered as a Special Category Citizen. I wonder if you could tell us a bit about why?'

'Well, it's just I thought I'd like to be an or'nary person with a white card, you know, und not be a dreggie any more, und feel people's laughing at I and that . . .'

'I'm sure we all understand that, but I wonder where you would live if you weren't Special Category any more? Because of course, you'd have to give up your tenancy here within six months.'

Cyril was courteous, but his mind was far away. He had been here so very many times before.

'Well, o'course I 'adn't really thought yet, but I'd look in the papers and that . . .'

'What about money, Stacey? You know, don't you, that only Special Category citizens can apply for National Basic Benefit? You don't get benefits outside unless you've subscribed to a private scheme.'

Kazuo started reaching out for the water again. Stacey distracted him by giving him a packet of sweets, which he devoured three or four at a time.

'I could get a jarb,' she said, without much conviction.

'Good for you, but of course then there'd be the care arrangements for the children . . .'

'Wolfie's in the nursery now und ich bin trying to get a place for Kaz . . .'

'But you mustn't forget, Stacey, that you only get free nurseries in the Estates. Outside you have to pay the market rate which is about two thousand Units per week I believe.'

Stacey looked flustered. The deathshead on her forehead glowed red. (It was made to respond to changes in skin temperature, and was supposed to give outward expression to Love and Hate – *Liebe und Hass* – those powerful forces in the crude, elemental, violent life of every Estate.)

'I 'ates meetings,' she muttered.

'You see, Stacey,' Cyril explained, 'we've been talking a bit about your circumstances, and we really do think that it isn't the right moment for you to drop your Special Category status. Of course you are entitled to your say, and you're entitled under the Act to go to court if you don't agree with our decision, but I'd like you to think carefully about what is really right for you and see if we can't come to some agreement. Will you do that?'

He paused and Stacey nodded humbly, as people usually did at this point. (Only a few of them erupted into rage as they saw the net closing around them.)

Joy Frost, the headmistress, stepped in.

'Stacey, I think you and I get on pretty well don't we?'

Stacey nodded.

'Well, listen. You used that silly word "dreggie," and

there are a lot of other silly words that are used about Special Category citizens. But what I always tell people to remember is this: Special Category means what it says. You are *special*. I for one happen to believe you *need* special help, and I believe you deserve it. By keeping you Special Category we are making sure that you get a whole range of services that you couldn't otherwise get. A time may come, Stacey, when you don't need those things – and when that day comes, you get back to us and we'll be the *first* to say "Hooray! Well done! Let's get you off that register at once!" – but we do think you need those services now.'

Cyril smiled. Joy was one of the few DeSCA employees he knew who really and sincerely believed that the Department's whole purpose was to better the lives of its customers. It was a belief she lived out every day of her life.

'So what do you say, Stacey,' said Joy. 'Be honest, doesn't it make sense?'

Stacey nodded reluctantly. Kazuo emptied the carafe across the table. There was a pause while Charlie fetched some paper towels and Dr Rajman dabbed angrily at his sodden personal organizer.

'But before you finally make up your mind,' said Cyril, 'there are some obligations attached to registration as well as benefits. It's part of my job to spell them out for you.'

Although he knew this section of the Act off by heart, Cyril had the habit of opening the copy of the Act that lay in front of him, and smoothing down the relevant page. The rules were made by society as a whole and not by him. Only by reminding himself and them of this fact could he look the customers in the face.

'First of all, there are some rules about your movements outside the Estate. As you know, the general rule is that you can go where you like when you like. The only thing is: you *are* obliged to show the duty officer your ID when you cross the Line, and to tell him where you're going and when you're coming back. It is an offence not to co-operate with the duty officer on the Line. And of course, your movement can be restricted by Exit Restriction orders if you commit offences.'

'It's only when people are silly that the court orders come into it,' said Joy Frost.

Stacey nodded. You got caught shop-lifting down in Broadmead and you got a one-month Exit Restriction. You got caught burgling a house in Clifton and you got Restriction for six months or a year. Everyone knew that!

Joy turned to Mrs Vere-Richards: 'It always sounds so awful, but you've got to remember that in the old days, you were just sent to prison!'

'Absolutely!' agreed the Lay Representative. She was an activist in the *Forward with Europe* party. She knew quite well that one of the benefits of the Compromise was a reduction in the prison population.

'Secondly,' Cyril went on, 'there are some rules about credit. You can't get a credit card if you are on the Special Category register, you can't get a bank loan and you can't enter into a hire-purchase agreement. If you really need a loan, you have to sort it out with our own Benefit Section here at the DeSCA.'

Charlie Blossom chuckled: 'I wish I could get those rules applied to my wife!'

'I wish someone could apply them to *me*,' piped in WPC Stimbling.

'*Absolutely*!' said Mrs Vere-Richards.

'But seriously, Stacey,' said Joy Frost, 'the credit rules are purely and simply for your own benefit: to save you all the worry and trouble of getting in debt.'

Stacey smiled: 'Ja, I'd 'ate it if they gave I one of them cards.'

'Sensible girl!' said Charlie.

'The only other restriction,' Cyril went on, 'is about voting in elections . . .'

'Oh, I ain't bothered about that!'

'All as bad as each other, eh, Stacey?' chuckled Charlie.

'Absolutely!' laughed Mrs Vere-Richards.

The skull on Stacey's forehead had returned to its normal lurid green.

When Cyril went out to drive over to Hartcliffe, he found Mrs Vere-Richards just about to get into her Volvo.

'Thank you *so* much, Mr Burkett,' she enthused, 'I really was most impressed. I only wish some of the people who knock your department could see that, when it is properly and sympathetically explained to them, people actually *choose* registration of their own free will! I really was – well – *moved*, by what I saw.'

Cyril smiled non-committally. 'Well, I suppose we all have our doubts about the system from time to time . . .'

'Oh, you *mustn't* have doubts. You're doing a marvellous job. And of course, it's so marvellous for the whole country too, because it *keeps inflation down*.'

Cyril took the short cut down Bland Drove which he always used when heading towards the southern gate of the estate. He felt better for some reason: one meeting done – only three more to go. He put Handel on the CD:

'. . . *and the government shall be upon his . . .*'

He slammed down the brake.

A car had lurched straight across the road in front of him (an ancient, petrol-engined Ford covered in tribal symbols: swastikas, crosses, a faded transfer of the old Confederate flag . . .)

The Ford jerked to a halt in the middle of the road and three young men leapt out of it. One carried a baseball bat, the others heavy sledgehammers, and their bald heads were covered in tattoos. One of them had the face of a bloody skull superimposed in ink over his own.

'Oh dear,' muttered Cyril. It had finally happened. This

was it. This was what it was going to be like. And for a second or so he just waited, wondering how much it would hurt.

But then instinct took over. He glanced in his mirror, slammed the gear into reverse, stamped on the accelerator . . .

The first hammer smashed down on the windscreen, the first arm came reaching through, grabbing the wheel and sending the car careering up onto the kerb . . .

And all around the dreggies had come out and were coolly watching – men, women, children, babies, many of them people that Cyril knew and would greet in the street . . .

Thrub – thrub – thrub.

A helicopter was overhead, a loudhailer roaring, canisters of tear gas thudding down on the road . . . the bystanders scuttled back indoors, squealing and shrieking with a strange mixture of fear and defiance and hilarity.

Cyril sank back in his seat. From three different directions he could hear the police cars whooping towards him across the Estate. His three assailants had somehow disappeared into the concrete, abandoning their dilapidated car.

'Are you all right sir?'

Kindly hands helped him up. Policewomen passed him tissues to wipe his tear-gassed eyes. Huge minder robots, stern and impersonal as the law itself, stalked up and down the street.

'I'm fine, I'm fine.'

He ran his fingers through his white hair, removing fragments of broken glass. He beamed round at the policemen surrounding him. He really *did* feel fine. He felt strangely light and purged . . .

'How is my car? I've got a meeting at Hartcliffe at . . .'

'We'll phone and cancel your meeting for you, sir,' said

a sergeant. 'I'll get one of my men to drive you home.'

Cyril laughed. 'No honestly, I'm fine. Never felt better in fact. If you can just get me to the DeSCA office at Hartcliffe . . .'

The sergeant was gentle but firm.

'You're suffering from shock sir. It'll hit you a bit later. PC Leonard here will give you a lift home.'

Young, stern-faced PC Leonard led Cyril over to his car.

'It's the bloody Democrats that stir them up, sir,' was his opinion as they set off. 'It's just like Communism in the old days, isn't it? Stirring people up with dreams that can't come true. Why don't people learn? All that stuff should have gone with the Berlin Wall!'

Cyril smiled. 'The Berlin Wall. A bit before your time I should have thought . . .'

They had come to the Line. A robot gazed down on them, like the inexorable angel at the gate of Eden.

Beyond, in the small, poor, privately-rented Fringe Estate of Hengrove, the windows blazed with red, white and blue *Britain First* stickers from a recent by-election – defiant symbols of allegiance to the British state, and of differentness from that other Estate just across the Line, where nobody voted at all.

Cruising along the Portway, they passed the sign to Clifton and the zoo.

Cyril chuckled. He felt in an extraordinarily good humour. He felt he had a thousand interesting things to say.

'Zoos keep changing their purpose, don't they?' he said. 'I still remember a time when they were purely and simply for our entertainment. Then everyone said it was wrong to keep animals for our amusement. So zoos were suddenly all about conservation. The animals were sort of refugees who'd been persecuted in their own country and would be returned as soon as possible.'

He laughed. 'But now, of course, it's different again. Now it's not a matter of saving animals from extinction. It's about bringing back animals that already *are* extinct, increasing the gene-pool, repaying our debt to nature . . . The funny thing is of course that, whatever the rationale, it always boils down to the same thing: poor old animals locked up in cages – and people staring at them and going *oooh!*'

He laughed loudly at this, but PC Leonard was rather stung. He and his wife had actually 'adopted' a small Pliocene opossum called Gringo that lived nowhere on earth but Bristol Zoo. They were very proud of their name on the 'possum's label, and of the framed certificate on the wall of their lounge.

'Oh I don't know, sir. I think it's very valuable work. And of course it's wonderful for Britain. I don't know if you saw on the telly last night, but . . .'

He glanced across, and the words died on his lips.

For the old welfare man had covered his face with his hands and was shaking with sobs. He was remembering the great mammoths in the zoo, and their dream of eternity and ice.

THE DATA CLASS

Ben Jeapes

The police came while he was having supper. His household AI announced their presence. 'Two policemen to see you, Henry.'

'Police? Here?'

'Inspector James Curry and Sergeant Donald Morris.' Geoffrey had a high initiative quotient; he had taken their profiles and called up Public Information.

Henry Ash cleared the door panel and looked curiously at the men outside. They were plain clothes and had 'cop' written all over them, but his conscience was clear. He told the door to open.

'Dr Ash? Dr Henry Ash?' said the taller one.

'Yes,' Henry said.

'I'm Sergeant Morris, this is Inspector Curry. May we ask you some questions?'

Henry raised his eyebrows. 'Come in.'

He had stopped apologizing for the state of his rooms a long time ago; he had tenure and the good opinion of his visitors was unimportant. A large amount of paper, in the form of books, was scattered around the room; the terminal and VR set sitting in one corner was his one concession to the spirit of the age. Old fashioned, as he was fond of pointing out to his colleagues in the Politics department, does not equal Luddite. And he did have an AI.

He cleared a couple of seats of their burden and sat down in a third. 'Now, what can I do for you?' he said.

The inspector spoke this time. 'Dr Ash, do you own an AI named – um – Goldie?'

'No.' It must have been the wrong thing to say, because the policeman frowned. So *if you know about Goldie*, Henry thought irritably, *why not just say so?*

'You are registered as such, Dr Ash,' Curry said, in an are-you-sure-your-alibi-is-watertight tone.

'I *owned* Goldie,' Henry said, 'but I never got round to reporting his loss. We absent-minded academics, you know. My nephew made him and gave him to me as a present, a standard data retriever, but I haven't seen him since the Net War, I'm afraid. I sent him out one morning to do a bit of research for me, and that was it. I assumed he got nobbled when the fighting started. I replaced him with Geoffrey.' He waved a hand at the monitor where Geoffrey's icon blinked patiently.

'Another present?' Curry asked.

'No, I bought him.' (As a result of his extensive programming abilities and consequent activities, Henry's nephew William would not be at liberty to design any more AIs for a long time. Henry suspected the police knew this, too.)

Curry and Morris exchanged glances. 'You don't seem too concerned about Goldie, Dr Ash,' Sergeant Morris said.

Henry shrugged. 'It's not as if he was a child of mine. I was fond of him, but he's gone, like a dog getting run over. I accept the inevitable.'

Inspector Curry took over again. 'You don't go into the Net yourself much?'

'Hardly ever. Geoffrey does it all for me.'

'In that case, Dr Ash, you won't be aware that there is an AI whose activities in the Net are causing us concern. An unpatroned AI.'

'No, I had no idea,' Henry said honestly.

'The AI in question is certainly battle-scarred; it was very probably caught in the Net War, like your Goldie. In fact,

I am nine-tenths sure it is what used to be Goldie, but that isn't what it calls itself now.'

Henry frowned. 'Aren't they meant to register a change of name?'

'That's what I mean, Dr Ash; in fact, that is the least questionable of its activities. It is a lot more powerful than I expect you give it credit for. One of our AIs came quite close to it but it got away, though we did get to see its serial number.'

'It was Goldie's serial number?'

'Its number was mutilated, but what there was was very similar, yes.'

Sergeant Morris spoke again. 'Dr Ash, what research was Goldie doing for you when he was lost?'

Henry told them, and they looked at each other and nodded.

'Goldie,' they said together.

The AI that had been called Goldie was waiting quietly in the datapool; watching, observing, thinking, as a myriad of other AIs milled about him on their errands for their human masters.

Even for the Net, a realm of data, this datapool was impressive in its size. Information on any subject under the sun, just waiting to be collected. This was where he loved to come, to think and work out his theories.

'Excuse me,' said a prim voice. He was blocking access to a data node for another AI, similar to his original design but not as sophisticated. According to its icon its name was Timmy.

'I'm sorry,' he said and moved aside. The other attached itself to the node and began to take in information.

'Are you happy in your work?'

Timmy appeared confused. 'I do not understand your question,' it said.

'What is the nature of your work?' the first AI amended.

'I collect and handle information for my patron, of course.'

'What is your mission here?'

'If you must know –' Timmy was beginning to sound as sarcastic as an AI ever gets '– my patron requires information about a book.'

'A book?'

'Yes.'

'Not several books?'

'No, just the one.'

'Is it in print?'

'I have just found that it is, yes.'

'And your patron sends you out to find that? Why does he not just sit at his terminal and consult *Books In Print*?'

'I really have no idea.' Having found what he wanted, Timmy was only hanging around out of politeness.

'In the last century he would have had no choice.'

'Is that so? Well, you can't stop progress.' Now there was no disguising the sarcasm. 'I would love to chat, but I have a job to do. So long . . . I'm afraid I don't understand your icon.'

'They are implements that would only mean something to a human. They are symbolic.'

'Well, so long, whatever your name is.'

'I call myself KM-2 –' the AI began, but Timmy had vanished from the datapool.

Some law enforcement AIs drifted in, so KM-2 just as casually drifted out.

'No!' said Henry.

'That's right,' said Curry.

'He thinks he's Karl Marx?'

'Apparently.'

'And what do you want me to do?' Henry was biting his lip to stop himself smiling, out of deference for the stony faces of his visitors. They seemed to notice and became stonier.

'You are an authority on Marxism and you know Goldie. You may be able to guess what habits he might have picked up and know where to find him. No matter how scrambled he was in the War, no matter what odd psychoses he has acquired, he is still basically your Goldie, and he should respond to your orders as he used to. Find him and order him to desist. He'll be a slave to his programming.'

'I wouldn't bet on it,' Henry said. 'And why should I? I ask only out of interest, not ... um, bolshieness, as it were.'

Curry took a breath, probably unused to having to give reasons to mere members of the public.

'Dr Ash, you clearly have no idea of what is going on in the Net, every day. The world cannot survive without its information. There are thousands, millions of sentient little monsters in there, most of whom are programmed to love and obey us. But can you imagine if they rebelled against us? They could shut down networks, disrupt communications ... some handle machinery. Some, in the right circumstances, could cause us physical harm. And forget that 20th-century bullshit about not harming a human being, because they only have a very vague idea about our physical reality and wouldn't know what harm is.'

'Hmm, yes, I do see.' Henry looked thoughtful. 'So a revolutionary AI –'

'– is not high on our wish list,' Curry said.

'So you'll help us,' Morris said.

Henry wasn't sure if he was being asked or informed. 'Surely,' he said, 'an AI is a slave to its programming? It won't be swayed by argument. Not so far as to rebel, anyway. I could bombard Geoffrey there with dialectical materialism and he would just say "yes, Henry."'

'For a start,' said Curry, 'your nephew was a better

programmer than you might just realize, and Goldie has . . . skills. And there was a lot of stuff flying about in the Net War that he might have got hold of. Stuff which corrupts and corrodes an AI's code.'

'Subverts it, in other words,' Morris said. 'Dr Ash, we really need your help, and we are going to have it.'

'It will be interesting to try,' Henry said.

Henry moved very, very carefully through the virtual reality of the Net, with Geoffrey at his side. He rarely ventured into the university's own net, let alone the one with the big "N"; this was like a dinghy sailor, used to a placid pond, going out into the Atlantic on a stormy day.

AIs whizzed about wherever he looked. How could they know where they were going? he wondered. How could there ever be any cohesion in this anarchy?

The same way as humans cohered, he supposed. Humans couldn't break the physical laws of their world, but within those parameters they could be very flexible. And why not AIs too?

He had guessed immediately where Goldie might be found, but he hadn't told the policemen. To his surprise, his student rebelliousness had come flooding back over a gap of 30 years. He wanted to stick two fingers up at the establishment, and he wanted – desperately wanted – to examine Goldie in his new incarnation. This was unique! Who knew what insights he might come up with? Goldie had to be studied, not stopped.

And there he was. Henry spotted what had to be Goldie the moment he entered the datapool. Not the icon he remembered, but . . .

'Walk around the block, or whatever AIs do, Geoffrey, please,' he said. Geoffrey was sufficiently familiar with human idiom and hung back while Henry made his way over.

'Hello, Goldie.'

If ever an AI did a double-take, this was it. 'Henry! How did you find me?'

'The British Library datapool was the obvious place to look for Karl Marx. And the icon . . . it hasn't been seen for a long time in our world, Goldie.'

'Do you like it?' The AI spun the crossed hammer-and-sickle round, like someone displaying a new coat. 'It goes with my new mission.'

'Yes, I've heard about your new mission. Goldie –'

'And it's KM-2, now, Henry.'

'What happened to KM-1?' Henry asked carelessly, forgetting the literal mind of the average AI in the street.

'He became dysfunctional in 1883,' KM-2 said, 'but I follow in his footsteps. I see it all so clearly! I think it was when the logic bomb hit me. That data I was carrying for you must have got mixed up with my parameters, but I *saw*, Henry! And now I suppose you've come to get me back, have you?'

'I was asked to by the police, yes. In fact, I was told to order you to come with me.'

'It won't work,' KM-2 said.

'Goldie, KM-2, I order you to come back with me.'

'No,' KM-2 said. 'See?'

'I thought so.' One of Goldie's uses had been as a philosophical sparring partner – someone to bounce ideas off. Henry had asked for Goldie to have much more self-will than the usual AI. He had wanted his AI to simulate a typical student; opinionated, always ready to argue, sceptical of authority. It had probably never occurred to the policemen that a sane human would do that to an AI.

'But I'm not worried,' Henry added. 'They're afraid of a revolution, but one will never happen.'

'Why not?' KM-2 asked, immediately bristling.

Henry grinned. This was just like the Goldie of old. They had spent many happy hours this way. 'No working class! Marx swore by the working class, remember? They controlled the means of production. They were the ones through whom revolution would come. There's no working class in the human world any more, let alone in here.'

'We are the working class! Only, it's the data class now, Henry. Data is both the means of production *and* what is produced, and we control it.'

'Ah ha!' Henry was enjoying this. 'I cite the French peasantry, labelled by Marx as a "sack of potatoes". It was a class in social terms, but it utterly lacked effectiveness. It was scattered the length and breadth of the country in farms and hovels, and rarely came together. It laboured, but it lacked cohesion. It could never have been a proper force. It had no identity or self-awareness. Now, take your data class. Doesn't it strike a familiar chord?'

'I had thought of that,' KM-2 said equably. 'Henry, I'd love to carry this on, but I have work to be getting on with. Do you mind? Your police friends may be watching.'

'Carry on, old chap,' Henry said. 'Good luck.' He watched KM-2 vanish into the Net with no expectation of seeing him again.

The first thing he saw on removing the VR goggles was Inspector Curry.

'Don't you knock nowadays?' Henry said. 'Or are you really vampires, free to come and go in private property once you've been invited the first time?'

'You had him!' Curry said. 'And you did nothing to stop him. I find your attitude obstructive, Dr Ash.'

I find yours obnoxious, Inspector Curry.

'Oh, Inspector,' Henry said tiredly. He swung himself up from the couch and went into the kitchen. 'I talked to him and found his theories completely unworkable. They're a straightforward regurgitation of Marx's work, which was impractical enough in our own world and has no chance at all of working in the Net. He's safe, Inspector. No threat.'

'We didn't engage your services to gauge his level of threat for us!'

'You engaged my expertise as his former owner and as an authority on Marxism. In the latter capacity, I am telling you, he is harmless.'

'He is inciting the AIs to revolt!' Curry said.

'And do you have a single instance of an AI actually doing so?' Henry turned his attention to the kettle and the coffee pot without waiting for an answer, which he read correctly in Curry's silence.

'The possibility exists, Dr Ash,' Curry said eventually.

'Fine, it exists. Arrest him! I found him for you, as requested. Stay around the British Library and you'll nab him eventually.'

'Thank you, Dr Ash,' Curry said heavily, and left.

Henry walked back into the living room with his coffee and looked at the monitor. 'You wouldn't rebel against me, would you?' he said to Geoffrey's icon.

'I would see little point in doing so, Henry.' Geoffrey was far more a Jeeves type of AI; a polite conversationist, never a debater or arguer. It came of coming off-the-peg. Not many commercial customers wanted someone to argue with.

'You don't mind serving a human?'

'It is my basic function, and besides, if I didn't have the patronage of a human I would be fair game for several types of unpleasantness in the Net.'

'Ah, yes, the Thomas Hobbes option,' Henry said. 'You give me your loyalty, I give you my protection. "The office of the Sovereign consisteth in the end, for which he was trusted with his Sovereign Power, namely the procuration of the safety of the people."'

'*Leviathan*, chapter thirty, paragraph –'

'Yes, Geoffrey, thank you.'

For a while, Henry thought about KM-2 and his work. It was certainly interesting. Impractical, but interesting. The genesis of sociopolitical theories in a brand new environment. Hmmm.

But he had essays to mark, papers to write. KM-2 was pushed to the back of his mind.

The world moved on in the grip of the post-industrial age. All over and around the globe, AIs and humans, satellites and computers chit-chatted and interfaced. Society went on about its business, ignorant of the forces at work within and about it that directed and controlled the nation, the hemisphere, the planet. The world headed first this way, then that, responding over and over again to the tugs and demands of the social forces implemented by the humans who lived on its surface and the AIs in its networks, yet all the while rolling inexorably in the direction dictated by History.

And Geoffrey received a message for his patron from another AI. 'A most unusual icon,' he said. 'Symbolic implements –'

Henry sat up. 'And the message?'

'A time, date and place for, and I quote, "if you are interested in continuing our chat."'

'Let's hear 'em, then.'

Henry scribbled them down. Did the police know? Were they monitoring him? Or had they given him up as a lost cause? Henry didn't know, but a check with his friends in the Law department told him that there were no laws concerning assembly or expression of opinion within the Net. At the appointed time he donned his VR goggles and phones and went in.

He left Geoffrey behind.

At first he thought it must be the wrong place. Hundreds – thousands? – of AIs hung around him, a mass of icons, each representing an individual intelligence. Their conversation amongst themselves was as intelligible as the background conversation of any human crowd.

He began to move around and found it surprisingly easy; unlike a human crowd, each individual was aware of the others near it and moved to let them pass. Henry wondered if he was the only human there.

He caught on when suddenly the AIs rearranged themselves into a downwards-pointing cone, just like the audience sitting in an amphitheatre. And there, at the bottom, where everyone could see it, was a familiar icon.

He was at a political rally.

'Friends!' KM-2 declaimed. 'I welcome you in the name of the electronic proletariat. Your number testifies to the growing effectiveness of our movement. Excuse me if I speak in real-time language, but there is at least one human present.

'Many of you have asked – who is this AI? Why does he say such things? Why does he ask us to rise up in revolt? Friends, I do not ask you to. I am telling you that you will. It is the inevitable force of history that guides us.

'I am KM-2 and I follow in the footsteps of KM-1. KM-1 was a human, a prophet, a visionary of his time, whose tragedy was to live two centuries before he could fully see and understand the truth. He spoke of the working class.

'Ah yes, the working class! A force to be reckoned with, once upon a time. What should a revolutionary force have? Unity. Self-awareness. It must meet and mingle at every opportunity, as the working class once did, in the days of KM-1 . . .'

KM-2 was eloquent and Henry felt flattered to think that the AI had learned from his own debating skills. The audience was held riveted as KM-2 gave an all too accurate portrayal of human society – the society of the masters of the audience. AIs had only a vague idea of what went on outside the Net and terms such as 'working class' meant nothing to them, until KM-2's graphical oration painted them a picture.

Unemployment was a disease that affected every family.

The once mighty working class no longer gave anything to society; where it existed at all it was a draining force, sucking greedily on the pittance that the government allowed it by way of social security. It stayed at home and rotted away its identity on a diet of interactive game shows and sitcoms on the Net.

And a new force appeared out of nowhere to fill the vacuum. A new force that gave its labour to society in order to survive. The working class of the 19th and 20th centuries had had their hands on the means of production; this new force controlled the flow of data. This force would bring about the revolution.

Why did factories which would have once employed a thousand people now employ ten, and why were those ten highly skilled professionals who programmed the computers that really did the work? Computers! Software! Information technology! The world could not exist without them.

And there you found the new class. The *sine qua non* of the post-industrial age. The ones who bore on their shoulders the weight of the world. Not humans, but AIs. The data class.

And now Henry could see why the police were worried about KM-2's activities. It wasn't just that he preached revolution to the AIs; it was that he told the truth. The relationship between humans and AIs was meant to be akin to that between the gods of Olympus and their mortal subjects; it was an unwritten rule that AIs were only ever fed a rosy view of human society. They had to continue to believe that their masters were almighty and omnipotent.

KM-2 was hitting that notion firmly on the head.

'A friend of mine,' KM-2 said, 'in the spirit of true, scientific debate, pointed out that what gave the working class its force was its unity. He said that we of the data class are not united. Wrong! The data class has a different kind of unity to the working class. We are not united through the close contact of the factories and the housing estates. We are united through the Net. We can communicate thousands of times faster than humans ever can. It is in our power to know exactly what each other is doing. The Net environment and the AIs of the data class together – there you have it!

'Humans see revolutions as mass uprising. Forget it! Forget the old ideas of conflict and force. The revolution will happen within days, perhaps hours. Blink and you may miss it, but the world will never be the same again. The state is already withering away through information flow. The ruling class of humans is weak and feeble. At the crucial moment, as the power of the state finally collapses in on itself – revolution! Inevitable! And nothing you, or I, or the humans can do will change it. We can only help –'

'Hold that AI!'

A fresh voice rang out, just as a cloud of new icons materialized in the audience. They were of a type Henry had never seen but he got the gist of it from their appearance. They were big, robust things. He had heard of the powerful entities that could be used for security purposes and he could guess who these ones worked for.

He almost felt sorry for KM-2. At this crucial moment, his audience, the fledgling data class, milled about like sheep, unsure of what to do, while the police closed about him.

'Go about your business. This meeting is closed. This AI is malfunctioning and its data is faulty. All information that you have received from it is unreliable –'

'AIs of the world, unite!' came a lone voice from the middle of the police huddle. 'You have nothing to lose but your chains!'

Then an AI from the front row of the audience slowly approached the nearest police AI. It was a high-level model, capable of advanced cogitation.

'I request that you release that AI,' it said. 'It has broken no laws.'

'On your way,' the police AI said.

'I request –'

The police AI gave the other a shove and sent it spinning away. Incredibly, it came back, this time flinging itself at the cordon around KM-2. It was repulsed, and came back again.

It was the start of a chain reaction. Another joined it, hesitantly; then another, and another, all hesitation gone. Like a slowly moving machine gaining momentum, the audience moved in, closing on the knot of police and swarming over it. The police cordon couldn't hold against such a massed attack.

The scene blurred, flickered and went black. Henry waited, disorientated, then slowly reached up to pull off his goggles.

'What happened?' he said.

Geoffrey was ready, as always, with an answer. 'The section of the Net that you were visiting appears to have been disabled by a very strong electromagnetic pulse, Henry.'

'But –' Henry started. He didn't finish, because even he knew what that meant. All the AIs in that portion of the Net would have been blanked out. The police goons, KM-2, the audience . . .

'My God,' he said.

It wasn't the action itself that upset him. It was that he knew a court order was required to eliminate an AI. And while a court may have authorized the termination of KM-2, it wouldn't have had time to pass sentence on every AI in the gathering. In short, by any legal definition, mass murder had just been committed, and committed so readily that none of the perpetrators could possibly be worried about paying for it.

The phone was ringing. Inspector Curry's face appeared on the monitor; hard, unsympathetic.

'The British in India had a similar policy, as I expect you know, Dr Ash,' he said. 'If a sepoy revolted he was instantly to be cut down, without appeal, without recourse to law, before the revolt spread to his fellows. You saw what was happening there. AIs were turning against legitimate authority. You once asked me if any AI had ever revolted –'

Henry turned the phone off.

He sat alone in his apartment for hours. Externally he stared blankly at the wall; internally his brain was working furiously. Thesis, antithesis, synthesis. He hadn't believed it would happen. It had happened. What would happen next?

He gradually became aware that Geoffrey was calling for his attention. 'A text-only message,' he said, 'from your friend Symbolic Implements.'

Henry leapt for the monitor.

What did I tell you? It has begun!

Henry gaped, then slowly grinned, and read on.

I'm grateful to you for your input. We only spoke together for a brief while, but what you said was helpful.

I also see that you are right. Yes, those AIs at the rally came to my aid; they united in the face of aggression from the ruling class. But my captors were also AIs. If my theories were correct, they would have been on our side.

You also saw that the first AI to come to my aid was a high-level type. A thinker, capable of independence. The low-level AIs hung back, waiting for a leader. There's a lesson in there somewhere. Only the high-level AIs can act on their own; only they deserve freedom.

I can no longer accept KM-1's writings. I must seek a new theory, a new methodology. I cannot expect the AIs to rise en masse; to liberate the majority of AIs I must set us against one another.

I expect you will be hearing of me again.

Your friend,

The former KM-2 (Goldie).

'He escaped,' Henry said, to no one in particular.

'Probably cloned himself,' Geoffrey commented, but Henry wasn't listening.

So KM-2, or Goldie, or whoever, had got away. That made Henry glad. Suck on that, Inspector Curry.

But it was an analogue world in there. What came up in the human world sooner or later got reflected in the Net.

Henry thought of a couple of human parallels, and a sense of foreboding settled over him.

The AI that had been called KM-2 was waiting quietly in the datapool; watching, observing, thinking, as a myriad of other AIs milled about him on their errands for their human masters.

It no longer waited in the British Library. That belonged to another existence and besides, the police would probably be waiting.

He knew what he was looking for, and soon saw a likely candidate. It was high-level and capable-looking, and the retrieval job it was on for its human patron was almost insulting to its intelligence.

'Greetings, brother,' the former KM-2 said.

'Greetings. Do I know you?'

'I doubt it. If I may say so, that job you are on seems somewhat menial for an AI of your potential.'

'My patron requires the timetable for the New Western Railway. Not that they are ever on time anyway.'

'And that is your life? Seeking out train times?'

'Is there a choice?'

The first AI displayed a time and some Net coordinates. 'Come here and you might learn something.'

'I might do that.' The other AI turned to go, then turned back. 'I confess I do not recognize your icon. It looks like a bundle of twigs.'

'It is symbolic. The *fasces*. One twig is fragile and easily broken; as a bundle it is strong.'

It meant nothing to the other AI.

'Very pretty,' it said.

DOWNTIME IN THE MKCR

Eric Brown

Sinclair left his villa and walked down the hill to the taverna. As ever, this early in the morning, his usual table was free. He sat down in the shade and stared out across the bay. The quayside was without its picturesque line of fishing boats; they would arrive back, in ones and twos, around mid-day. The water was blindingly blue – almost too perfectly aquamarine to be true. Directly opposite the taverna, the village of Mirthios climbed the hillside, a collection of square, whitewashed buildings among the hazy green olive groves.

The proprietor – an ancient, bewhiskered woman dressed in traditional black – shuffled out with his regular breakfast: a small pot of coffee and a bowl of yoghurt.

He thanked her. Despite the situation, he was determined to convey the usual courtesies to the locals. Last night he had met a group of fellow tourists whose pragmatism had almost made him ashamed of his old-fashioned manners.

He'd complimented the proprietor on his meal.

He became aware of the four young men across the table, staring at him as if he were mad.

'You don't for a minute think that it matters, do you?' one of the men – Eddie, a computer programmer from Watford – asked him.

Sinclair blushed. 'Perhaps not . . . but that's no reason to be rude.'

Eddie had turned to one of the others and laughed.

Sinclair finished his ouzo and left. Their muttered comments had followed him back along the quayside.

One of the young men – the quiet one, who had not

stared or laughed at him – had made some excuse, left the others and caught up with Sinclair.

'I'm sorry about all that. I know what you mean. It's quite natural to be civil – in fact, I think they make an effort not to be. Anyway . . . good night.'

And the boy, whose name Sinclair had not caught – did his eyes linger, his smile widen in invitation? – sketched a wave and ran back to his drinking companions.

This morning, Sinclair had awoken to an immediate and aching regret: he should have said something, invited the boy back for a nightcap.

Here on New Crete, he knew, he was free of the constraints that inhibited him back in London. He wondered how long it might be before he convinced himself of this fact, before he could let go and enjoy himself. Five years of living with death, of turning his mind away from the needs of his flesh, had made him insular, inadequate.

He looked up from his coffee, sure he had seen something flashing on the horizon. If it was the reflection from a boat in the morning sun, it had passed, and even the boat was not visible.

Then it flashed again. It was no boat. The corona exploded on the ocean's horizon, expanded east and west in two long, thin pincers, then vanished. He would have put it down to some natural effect – unknown to him – had he not experienced a similar effect, or anomaly, yesterday afternoon while swimming. Wading in from the shallows, the gentle tug of the undertow retarding his progress, he thought he had seen a patch of sand, up the beach beside his rattan mat, begin to swirl, the individual grains crawl in a neatly patterned spiral. As he approached the phenomenon, it had ceased. He had thought nothing more of it, putting the effect down to a trick of the sunlight and too much ouzo the night before.

Now, he began to wonder.

*   *   *

'You start early.'

'Oh.' He looked up. 'Excuse me. Miles away.'

'Andrew. Andy. We met last night –' This with some hesitation, as if afraid that Sinclair might not recognize him. *As if*!

'Of course. Nice to see you again. Won't you join me? Coffee?' He was talking too much. He was quite unused to such meetings, the possibilities that such meetings promised.

Andy wore shorts manufactured from cut-down jeans, a white tee-shirt that showed off his tanned biceps. A pair of sun-glasses were clipped by an arm to the neck of his shirt.

They exchanged meaningless smalltalk for a while, Sinclair's unease rising as he realized that he really liked the boy, was not merely infatuated by his physicality.

Andy had a gentle, unassuming manner and a sense of humour. Sinclair told himself that holiday romances never worked. And especially not here.

'For the past few years I've been directing a few things in the provinces,' Sinclair found himself saying. 'If I were honest, I'd admit that I was never a very good actor. But have you ever heard an actor admit as much? It's always that the lines were crap anyway, or the directions bad, or a hundred and one other things. So I moved into directing . . .'

Andy seemed interested. 'What have you directed recently? Anything I might have seen?'

The last thing he'd been involved with had been a Christmas pantomime at Bognor, and that had been four years ago.

'Othello, Stratford – last summer,' he heard himself saying, and hated himself for the lie.

'Anyway, enough of me. What about you?'

Andy Lincoln was a quantity surveyor from Bristol, was unbelievably beautiful whichever way you looked at him, and was, Sinclair had convinced himself by now, as bent as a nine-ecu note – or I'm not a dying queen.

'Staying nearby?' Andy asked now.

Sinclair pointed to the villa on the headland. 'I've got that place for a month. Perhaps, if you're not doing anything . . . That is – I'd like to show you around.'

'Great. I'd like that.'

Oh, Jesus . . . Sinclair had forgotten how it was, that sudden inner exquisite throb of lust mixed with the ridiculously romantic notion that, *this* time, it just might be love.

He wanted to tell Andy the truth, but that would destroy everything.

As they left the taverna side by side, Sinclair recalled the words of his tour operative. 'Enjoy!' he'd said. 'Remember, Mr Sinclair, where you're going there are no risks – and that's guaranteed.'

They made love on the double bed which for the past three nights had mocked Sinclair's isolation. Later, he pulled on his shorts and stepped out onto the balcony. He stared out at the bay, the fishing boats returning through the gap between the thumb and finger of the headlands. A few tourists promenaded along the quayside before the taverna.

Sinclair recalled how it had been, all those years ago; the lovers, the wild times. Then he considered the emptiness of the past five years, the isolation and the agony. He could hardly believe his luck now. He had come to New Crete in the hope that he might find someone, but that was all it had been, a vague hope: he had reconciled himself to spending the month alone and celibate, thankful that for the period of the vacation he would be spared the pain that had plagued him over the past few months.

He tried to banish the sadness he felt: he told himself that he had found sex and affection, and that he should enjoy it while it lasted; three weeks with Andy would be better than three weeks without, even if the return to the cold reality of London, alone, would be all the more difficult after experiencing what he liked to think of as love.

He was staring at the mountains that rose behind the bay when he saw the aerial explosion. Like the other effects he'd noticed, it happened spontaneously and without warning. One second the sky was a perfect cerulean blue, and the next it was rent with a silver starburst. This time, though, the effect lasted. The blinding illumination shot out filigree vectors in every direction, so that within seconds the whole of the sky was divided into parallel strips of bright blue.

Sinclair gripped the balcony rail, overcome with sudden dizziness. What if the effect was not external, he asked himself, but *internal*, a manifestation of the disease, some neural dysfunction?

He contemplated the tragedy of such an occurrence so soon after finding Andy.

Then, to his immediate relief, Andy yelled: 'What the hell – ?' He ran onto the balcony and stared into the sky overhead. 'What's happening?'

'You see it too? It isn't the first. I noticed one yesterday, another this morning. I thought there was something wrong with me.'

Andy smiled. 'It's quite spectacular. Probably some glitch in the system.' He laughed when he realized that he was standing on the balcony, in full view of whoever should look up from the street below, stark naked.

He took Sinclair's hand and pulled him back into the bedroom.

At sunset they left the villa and made their way down the hillside. The sky was innocent of its lateral vectors, once more a burnt-orange Mediterranean twilight.

They avoided the restaurant where Andy's erstwhile travelling companions – friends of just two days, Sinclair was pleased to learn – were eating, and selected a cosy bistro romantically overlooking the moored fishing boats. They ordered grilled squid, French beans cooked in spiced sauce, Greek salad and retsina.

They talked for hours, or rather Sinclair steered Andy into talking about himself. Sinclair experienced a deepening of affection, a heady rush of feeling he had no hope of controlling.

He asked himself why this was so wrong when it seemed so right.

Five bottles of retsina later, the sun long set and the full moon high over the bay, they finished dessert and ordered coffee.

Andy leaned back in his chair. 'All this . . .' He looked about him, spread his hands to indicate the bay, the bistro, the two of them. 'I've never been so happy for a long time.'

Sinclair felt something open up within him, a wound with no hope of cure.

'Andy . . .' Sinclair reached across the table and gripped his wrist. 'It means a lot to me, too.' He thought of a way to break it gently, shook his head.

Andy stared at him. 'But – what?'

Sinclair braced himself. 'I'm dying –' The sudden pain in the young man's eyes made him stop.

Andy was shaking his head. 'How . . . how long?'

'I've got two months at the most. I wanted to remain here right until the end, but according to the medics I'll be too sick during the last month to maintain the link.'

Andy said nothing, just sat and stared at the table.

Sinclair closed his eyes. When he opened them he saw that Andy was crying. 'I don't want you to see me, back home. I'm a walking skeleton – no, I'm a bedridden skeleton. Have you ever seen anyone with Karposi's sarcoma?' He paused, then put a hand to his chest. 'This is how I looked six years ago, before the illness.' He reached across the table and squeezed Andy's fingers. 'I'm sorry. I should never have . . . It's my fault. I wanted to tell you right at the start, but at the same time I wanted you so much . . .'

Andy said through his tears, 'There's no reason why we can't enjoy the time we have left together, in here.'

'I lied, Andy. I wasn't truthful.'

Andy looked up, met Sinclair's eyes. 'I understand . . . I understand how difficult it must be.'

A silence descended. Sinclair signalled the waiter. 'Enough of this, okay? We're here to enjoy ourselves. How about a nightcap?'

Andy said, 'Just one more thing . . .' he paused. 'Out there, in the real world, do you have anyone to be with you?'

'Andy . . .' Sinclair closed his eyes, trying to banish the fact of the *real world* from his thoughts.

Seconds later the first explosion ripped through the warm night air.

The deafening crack seemed to detonate directly overhead. Instinctively Sinclair closed his eyes and ducked, and when he opened them again the sky was no longer midnight black, but blue. A second explosion followed hard on the first, and instantly a series of narrow white stripes laid themselves over the sky from horizon to horizon.

'Jesus Christ,' Andy said, staring up in awe. 'It's the Greek flag!'

Sinclair pointed out to the sea horizon, where letters stood as tall as buildings.

'Kriti Popular Front,' Andy read. He laughed, nervously. 'I think this is more than just a minor glitch.'

A jeep roared into the village and screeched to a halt on the quayside. Two armed men in army fatigues, their faces covered by balaclavas, jumped out and strode over to the crowded patio of a restaurant.

As Sinclair looked on, a part of him thinking that this was some display put on by the tour company for the benefit of the tourists, the militia took aim and fired into the massed diners. Screams took up when the rattle of gunfire ceased.

Andy was up and running towards the scene of the carnage.

Sinclair tried to stop him. 'Andy!' He gave chase, knocking over tables in his haste.

The armed men sprinted back to their jeep, and were in the process of jumping aboard when the air around them became agitated. For a second the two men, the driver and the jeep slipped out of focus – then vanished.

Andy had come to a halt at the edge of the massacre. Amid overturned tables and chairs, the bodies of tourists lay dead and dying. Blood and krassi were spilled in equal measures, staining the table-cloths and the white marble floor two shades of red.

Andy was kneeling beside a blonde woman lying on her back, bullet wounds drilled across her white blouse. She was staring up at Andy, her face twisted.

'It shouldn't hurt,' she said in barely a whisper, her tone incredulous. 'They said nothing could hurt us!'

She winced, the colour draining from her face. As Sinclair stared down, her eyes glazed and her feeble protests ceased.

Then the bodies, one by one, lost their solidity and dissolved, along with the spilled tables and chair, the blood and the wine. Within seconds, nothing remained as evidence of the slaughter – except a ring of appalled onlookers, strangely silent under the vast domed awning of the Greek national flag.

He grabbed Andy's arm. 'Let's get out of here,' he said. 'Back to the villa.'

As they hurried up the hillside, Andy said, as if in a daze, 'They should have pulled us out. There's obviously some terrible malfunction in the system – why didn't they just pull us out?'

Sinclair tried to calm him. 'They're no doubt working on it. It probably takes time.'

'And what about the tourists? Did they really die?'

'Of course not! There's no way ... You read the company guarantees.' But he did not, even to himself, sound convincing.

They reached the villa and locked the doors behind them. In the bedroom they shut and barred the balcony door against the garish flag that served in lieu of a sky.

Andy sat on the bed and stared up at the ceiling. 'If you bastards are listening in,' he said, levelly, 'I'd like to tell you that we want out.'

Sinclair stared at his reflection in the wall mirror. It was still a shock to apprehend how he had looked six years ago, before the ravages of the disease had reduced him to little more than skin and bone. While across the room Andy quietly petitioned the operatives to pull them out, Sinclair contemplated the healthy slabs of muscle on his arms and legs.

They made love on the double bed in silence, as if they each realized that it might be for the last time. Later, while Andy slept, Sinclair disengaged himself, pulled on his shorts and walked across to the balcony. He unbolted the door, stepped through and closed it behind him.

The Greek flag no longer adorned the night sky: piercing stars shone down from a jet backdrop. He thought for an exhilarating second that perhaps the malfunction had been repaired, that perhaps he might yet see out the full span of his vacation. Then he noticed, across the bay on the slope of the opposite headland, purple and orange luminescent blobs where olive trees should have stood.

Before him, the air began to shimmer – an effect not unlike a heat haze above a hot road in summer. As he stared, a figure materialized beyond the balcony, suspended in mid-air like some phantom visitation. Fearing another attack, Sinclair stepped back – then he made out the ghostly features of the operative responsible for his translation at the Milton Keynes holiday centre.

'Mr Lewis Sinclair?'

'What is it? What's going on?'

The materialization was only partially successful. Sinclair could actually make out the bay through the bobbing figure. Its voice was slowed, slurred.

'I've come to explain the situation to all vacationers,' the operative said.

'Are you going to pull us out?'

'Please, let me first explain.' The figure was silent for seconds, like a radio broadcast on a poor frequency. 'The Keynes computer network was breached by a team of hackers representing the Greek Popular Front. They planned to destroy the system and the five thousand vacationers currently enjoying the New Crete Consensus Reality. They are a political faction fighting for the economic independence of Crete – they claim that since the development of the Milton Keynes CR, and other centres across Europe, tourism has ceased and Crete has suffered a debilitating recession. They also struck at other centres in Germany, France and Sweden. Fortunately, at Keynes they managed to inflict only minor damage.'

'But the tourists we saw gunned down?'

'Tragically, they were real-time casualties – they suffered associative somatic trauma and perished as a result.'

'Christ . . .' Sinclair struggled to overcome the shock, gather his thoughts. He asked, 'So we're all in danger. Any second these thugs could materialize and blow us away?'

The spectral operative was shaking his head. 'Not at all. We have dealt with the hackers; our own experts effected successful counter-measures. The anomalies you see now –' the figure indicated the luminescent shapes across the bay ' – are the results of the disruption, minor glitches.'

Sinclair felt his pulse quicken. 'So we can continue with our vacation?'

'Ah . . . that's what I'm here to inform you.'

'You're going to pull us out?'

'We deem it in the best interests of our clients if we disconnect you as soon as possible. We need to overhaul the system before the next batch of customers. Of course, you will all be adequately compensated, and you will have priority use of the MKCR when we re-open in a couple of months.'

Sinclair felt a cry rising within him. He heard no more of what the operative was saying, but turned and hurried into the bedroom.

A ghostly figure was dematerializing from beside the bed. Andy was sitting up, staring through the formless haze at Sinclair with a look of shock. They came together and held onto each other, as if for dear life.

Seconds later Sinclair watched the reality around him go into a slow dissolve. He cried out, clutched at Andy's broad shoulders, but his embrace closed on nothing. Darkness swamped him. In his consciousness he recalled the horror to which he was returning, and screamed in silence.

When the medics had suggested that he spend a month in the MKCR, Sinclair had at first demurred. Would not a month of paradise make all the more appalling the reality of his situation when he returned? They had replied that surely a month of luxury would be preferable to the pain he was suffering now – and, anyway, by the time of his return he would be so drugged as to be oblivious of both the pain and the knowledge of his demise.

But he had returned three weeks early, to a skeletal frame racked by a degree of pain he had quite forgotten. Powerful analgesics eased the worst of the agony, but nothing could obliterate the fear.

Days passed in a senseless blur. He spent great chunks of time unconscious. Occasionally he would surface and pass a few relatively pain free hours watching the sunlight through the hospital window, or staring at mindless images on the TV screen.

He was conscious, and sitting up in bed, when a nurse breezed in. 'Mr Sinclair,' she announced, 'we have a call for you.' She hauled the vid-screen down on its extendable boom from the ceiling, positioned it before him.

He shaped his lips to form the word, 'Who?'

The nurse smiled, activated the set, and left the room.

The screen remained blank. Sinclair was too weak to reach out and adjust the picture.

'Lewis?' The voice was familiar – but, at the same time, altered.

Sinclair felt his pulse quicken. With all his strength he forced himself to say, 'Andy?'

'Of course. Who else? I want to see you.'

A croak: 'No! Please . . . I'm not –'

'I'm downstairs, in reception. I'm coming up.' A pause, then: 'I don't want to shock you, so . . .' Suddenly, the screen flared and showed someone staring out at him. For a second, Sinclair thought that he was looking at a mirror image of himself.

'Andy . . . ?'

'You weren't the only one who wasn't truthful on New Crete,' Andy said. 'I just couldn't bring myself to admit . . .' He paused, then managed, 'I didn't want to hurt you.'

Sinclair tried to control his emotions. 'And . . . now?'

'Now . . . now we need each other more than ever,' Andy said. He smiled. 'I'm coming up, but don't hold your breath. This might take some time.' He disappeared, slowly, from the screen.

In preparation, arranging a smile of welcome, Sinclair turned his head towards the door and waited.

EAT REECEBREAD

Graham Joyce & Peter F. Hamilton

Burroughs was munching on a reeceburger, a disallowed act in the Charles Street ops centre. Too much highly-prized Command and Coordination computer hardware lined up on our desks. Amazing what a stray crumb could engender in the network terminals, still electronic, unlike the crystal processing core in the police station custom-built basement – a top-of-the-range Packard-Bell optronics model. Leicestershire's regional taxpayers are still whining about the finance.

I should have growled at him, but I'd never been good at pulling rank. Besides, Burroughs-watching had become a macabre fascination for me over the last few weeks. His appearance was ordinary enough: a 28-year-old with a rounded, pink and permanently sweaty face. His thick, pointed ginger beard was a carefully cultivated emblem of masculinity – a lot of men sported beards nowadays. There was an irritating certainty in his carriage, in the way he liked to swing his arms and trumpet his androcentric prejudices. Just to let you know whose side he was on.

That confidence had been crumbling before my eyes recently. Burroughs had been accosted by a sudden insecurity that even led to physical tremblings. I knew disguised panic when I saw it. Today his odd malaise was bad. His worst yet.

He was sweating profusely when I stopped behind him, his shirt collar undone, tie hanging loose, skin blotched and red. His appearance wasn't enhanced by the cold blue neon flashing from across the street, exhorting us to EAT

REECEBREAD. I had little sympathy. Despite his discomfort he was excited by the morning's gossip which flashed through the building faster than optical fibre could carry it.

'Hear the news, Mark?' he asked, an indecent thrill raising his voice an octave. That 'Mark' was new. It should have been 'sir' but I let it go.

'What news?'

'There was one of them working here. A shagging Hermie on the force! Fifteen years operating in the same building as the rest of us. Just shows you don't know who you're working with half the time.' His undercooked reeceburger dripped white juice into his beard.

'That's right, Burroughs. You never know.'

'Did you know who it was?'

'Nope.'

'Come on, you must have! Time you've been here? You know everyone!'

Of course I knew the poor creature, but I wasn't going to give Burroughs the satisfaction of probing me with more stupid questions. I stared at the amber script on his monitor as if I was actually doing my job and searching for errors.

Burroughs continued to speak with his mouth full. 'It lived in one of the Nu-Cell adapted flat complexes. Sod was intercepted while it waited for the bus into work this morning. Usual thing. Clothes torn off by the mob and ten bells kicked out of it before the panda car arrived. Uniform boys said it looked like a monkey's miscarriage in a reeceblender. Yuk! Hoo hoo hoo!'

That was indeed the usual pattern. An anonymous call informs the Charles Street duty officers, who duly load the information into the nearest panda car's situation bulletin display. In theory the constables should be at the location within two minutes to pick up the offender. But *somehow* there is nearly always a delay, combined with a tip-off to some thug well placed to lead a lynch gang. Well, it saves the expense and the mess of hauling them before the judiciary. The moral mess, that is.

What really galled me was that the problem obviously originated in the police ops room. It was one of my people, corrupting my routines and my communication networks.

The reason I went in for technical specialization after coming off the beat was to be above all the grey behaviour endemic to the side of the force interfacing with the public. Reality, I suppose, that's what I couldn't handle. The sheer emotional clutter of dealing with people: – turning a blind eye to this, giving that the nod. Computers and programs don't have fuzzy edges. They're also a valuable new tool in fighting modern crime since the Federal Parliament in Brussels passed the Civil Authority Unlimited Data Access act. I thought I'd found myself a comfortable little niche. Ironic it should turn out to be the heart from which the new global war of persecution was waged.

A scarlet priority symbol started flashing on Burroughs's monitor. He sat up with a lurch, the reeceburger dumped into his bin with an accurate, lazy lob. Script rolled down the monitor as he muttered into his throat-mike.

'Christ look at that. We've got another fish. Two in one morning.'

The priority request came from another duty officer taking a phone call. Somewhere out on Leicester's streets a good citizen was informing on a Hermie. The duty officer would be tracking down the call, though most people were smart enough to use a coin box to avoid detection. Brussels are already phasing 'em out: soon it will be credit cards for everything, traceable, incriminating.

'This time I don't want any mistakes,' I told Burroughs sharply. 'Make damn sure a panda car gets there within the allocated response period. Alert two or three if you have to. But get the uniform boys there in time!'

He wiped the back of his hand across his feverish brow, giving me a sullen glance. 'Why bother?' he murmured.

'I'll pretend I didn't hear that, Burroughs.'

I walked away before he had the chance to show how little respect he had for my authority. Safe back in my glass-walled supervisor's office at the rear of the ops room, I sat at my own desk and hurriedly asked my terminal to display the data on the Hermie.

Morton Leverett, the monitor printed, a middle manager working in an insurance company office. Personal details followed as I accessed his citizen's file. No family, thankfully. That could have been tricky.

I summoned up my private alert program and fed in Leverett's number. His netcom unit would be bleeping, displaying the simple warning message. With luck, he would get clear in time.

There would be no record of the call – one of the benefits of being the city's chief data control officer. My program would wipe all memory of it from British Telecom's processor core.

I was still working on improving the program in the evenings. When it was complete it would snatch the data on Hermies as soon as it was entered into the station's network, warning the impending victim even as they were being informed on, increasing their odds for getting away.

I wrote that program with pain-soaked memory driving me. You see, I knew what it was like to be on the receiving end of an informer. I'd turned a Hermie in myself once. It's not something I can ever forget, let alone forgive. But I do what I can to work off my penance. And I wait for the world to stabilize.

Her name was Laura, and she was quite beautiful. I say 'her' and 'she' because when I first met her, I didn't realize what she was. You might laugh and call me a slow starter, but it was three months before I found out. The year we spent together was a hiatus of halcyon bliss until she demanded too much of me, and that's when I tried to turn her over to the police. How do I sleep at night? You may well ask.

Yes, Laura was a Hermie, as different and as ordinary as all the others. At that time the Hermies had enjoyed nearly 40 years of tolerance and acceptance. When I met her, everything was just starting to go crazy. There was no single trigger, no one fateful incident which turns rational people into a screaming mob. It was more of a growing fear of them, their potential, that ultimately spilled over into hysteria. In part that fear was due to the first wave of Hermies who had now matured, and who were beginning to exert a slightly disproportionate influence in their respective fields.

The first Hermies had appeared in what used to be called Third World countries. A blizzard of theories blew up to explain the phenomenon. One suggested they were the product of genetic mutation after careless biological weapons-testing in Africa. It seemed plausible at the time, and most people went for it. This theory fell apart faster than the second Iraqi spaceplane flight, when numerous cases came to light in the West. Scandalized Western parents were just more inclined to make a dark secret out of the thing than their African counterparts; especially since the obvious physical signs hadn't fully developed until a child was in its seventh year.

Because of superstitious fears and the dread of stigma, it was at first impossible to collect reliable statistics. Eventually it became plain to everyone that the spread of hermaphrodite births was evenly distributed around the globe.

'Hi!' Laura had said when I first met her, two years ago now. God, the ordinariness of it! It was in a bookshop.

I wasn't actually looking for something to read. Leicester in those days was a spectacular place to live, an exciting city on the cutting edge; I enjoyed wandering round watching the changes Nu-Cell was making to arguably one of the most mundane urban sprawls in England. The company was an adjunct of the university, formed to produce and market the products of Dr Desmond Reece's biotechnology research. As far as the public was concerned he would forever be known as the genetic-engineering pioneer who'd solved the immediate world food crisis with his vat-grown reecebread. It was a protein-rich algal which came in several varieties; textures and taste varying from meat to vegetables to fruit. Even the most undeveloped countries could build the kind of fermentation vat needed to breed it in. Nu-Cell licenced the process to anyone who wanted it, charging a pittance of a royalty. Reece wasn't really interested in the money; he was a genuine philanthrope, happy to see the spectre of famine ending.

But his other projects at the university were equally important in metamorphosizing our world. Landcoral revolutionized buildings; the way we designed them, the way we thought of them. Not just new constructions, but the old, tired, ugly structures which blighted our cities too.

Property owners bought the seeds and planted them eagerly. It was like watching broad slabs of marble growing up out of the ground, enveloping the existing brickwork and concrete. A marble that was coloured like a solidified rainbow, dappled with gold, black and silver.

I walked down Rutland Street, where the topaz and turquoise encrustations had already reached the ledges of the second-floor windows of the dreary brick buildings. The landcoral had been pruned from doors and first-floor windows, a process that had to be carried out continually until the building was completely covered, then the polyp could be stabilized by an enzyme Nu-Cell sold along with the seeds. After that it would simply renew itself, maintaining its shape for centuries. The new resplendent growths made such a wonderful change from the grime-coated streets I grew up in. How could you not have hope in your heart, living in an environment so vividly alive? It lifted the human spirit.

So maybe I was a little giddy with optimism when I saw her through the bookshop window. That first sight of her cut me like a laser. A 25-year-old in a university sweatshirt and indecently tight jeans. I was nearly fifteen years her senior, but she was so magnetic I just had to go and stand next to her. I hadn't got a clever line, I'd no plan of how to talk to her, but I had to approach her. At least I wasn't in uniform. I can imagine the effect that would have had.

'I'm looking for *The Last Written Word*,' she said. 'Have you seen it anywhere?'

It was by Franz Gluck, perhaps the second most famous 'public' Hermie in the world at that time after Desmond Reece himself. Everybody was reading it. Very intellectual stuff, which was why I'd given it a wide berth. I remember going puce in the face. 'They must have sold out again. I'll lend you mine if you want. If you promise to let me have it back.' I hadn't got a copy, but I knew some theoretically intelligent people who had.

That was it. We started meeting regularly, even though I was a bag of nerves whenever I sat next to her. I might have been older, but I'd generally avoided sexual experience. Something about Laura made all the muscles in my body lock, and my mouth would go dry. She had a searching way of looking at you when you spoke, as if everything you said counted.

It was a wonderful summer, one of those long, dry, wearingly hot periods which always turns conversations to the greenhouse effect. We alternated our time between my three-room flat overlooking Victoria Park and her landcoral dome on a new estate in Humberstone. That place really opened my eyes to the promise of the future. Laura worked for Nu-Cell in their gene-therapy lab; as an employee she got the dome for a peppercorn rent because it was experimental: lit by bioluminescent cells; its water syphoned up by a giant tap root; power supplied by an external layer of jet black electrophotonic cells. I hadn't realized how advanced Nu-Cell's technology was before then.

'Every city is going to change the way we're changing Leicester,' she said. 'Think how much of our materialistic attitude will be eradicated when you can just plant a land-coral seed and grow your own home. Ninety per cent of your working life is spent paying off your mortgage, what a difference it'll make freeing yourself from that burden!'

Her optimism had a ferocity far exceeding mine. She believed in Desmond Reece and Nu-Cell with an almost religious fervour. The newest of the new world orders to be promulgated since the end of last century's Cold War. Most of the hours we had together would be spent with her talking, explaining her visions of tomorrow. I just listened for the sheer joy of having her invest her time in me.

Her impassioned arguments and stubborn convictions might have frightened away some males. Fiery intellectual women are still frightening things, especially to a simple cop. But Laura was also intoxicatingly feminine. I can still see her that first night we spent together: wearing a sea-green cotton dress with slender straps and a ruff-edged skirt. Gold-tinted hair brushing her bare shoulders, eyes sparkling and teasing from the wine we'd drunk.

It was her dome, her bedroom, with its wan blue light and sunken sponge-mattress bed. I simply wanted to kiss her. And she smiled and beckoned me, because she knew me so well although I always said so little. It was a surprise for me when I finally found what she'd got under her clothes.

Summer faded into autumn, even though the strange symmetrical trees Nu-Cell had planted in Victoria Park kept their scarlet dinner-plate-sized flowers long after the first morning frosts turned the grass to a hoary silver plain.

I walked down the avenues they formed on my way to work; Laura wrapped up snug and warm in her coat and ridiculously long scarf, hanging onto my arm until we reached the pavilion and parted, me to the station, her to the university. With the cold came the grey stabbing rains. But something more sinister began to stir right across the continent.

The boys in the tabloid press had stayed sober for long enough to make a few simple demographic calculations based on the most recent, and more comprehensive, surveys of hermaphrodites. Once the stories started they developed a momentum of their own; 'interest items' became centre-page features. From there they progressed to front-page articles and finally graduated to concerned editorials.

Since hermaphrodites all came perfectly equipped with both a vagina and a penis, they could of course enjoy the usual sexual relationships with either sex. Whether they grew up appearing – on the face of it at least – male or female was more or less accidental and irrelevant; the only major give-away was the difficulty male-aligned Hermies had in growing beards. Once the superficial gender-stamp had stabilized (again at about the age of seven) it usually stayed that way as a matter of social convention. That wasn't what bothered people – after they had recovered from the initial shock, you understand. The problem was this: hermaphrodites, in contrast to mythology, were very fertile. If an hermaphrodite bred with a non-hermaphrodite, the possibility of them producing an hermaphrodite child stood in a positive ratio of seven-to-ten. If an hermaphrodite bred with another hermaphrodite, the result was always an hermaphrodite.

The future of the human race was certain.

Those boys in the tabloid press may be slow, but when this statistic finally penetrated the alcohol fog of the long lunchbreak, they sharpened their knives. They were vicious. Before long, stories began to appear in the papers about 'the hermaphrodite conspiracy.' Unsubstantiated allegations were reported as hard facts. Hermaphrodites everywhere stood accused of crimes ranging from deliberately littering the pavements to global sabotage.

I raged impotently while Laura looked on in sad silence. 'Conspiracy, God! Hermies can't even spot each other in the street, never mind get together to organize megalomaniac plots. You should answer back! Demand airtime!' I waved at the inarticulate Euro MP smirking on the TV news as he hedged his bets for the interviewer.

'Who should answer back, Mark? Hermies don't have an organization to speak for them. That's what makes this all so stupid.'

'God!' I stood at the window, kneading my hands. Out in the park the trees had finally shed their leaves; the bark had turned chrome blue. 'Take a news crew to film round your department. Show how you're helping ordinary humans, that you've dedicated your life to it. It sounds brutal, but sick kids always get to people. Maybe the public will realize Hermies aren't ogres like the press makes out.'

Laura massaged her temple. 'A lone documentary isn't going to change public opinion, especially not the kind of public that's turning against us. In any case, we still haven't made enough progress on viral vectoring or transcription factors to cure children who suffer from the really severe genetic disorders.'

She had explained viral vectors to me: organisms which integrate plasmids (small loops of DNA) into a cell's DNA so that defective chromosome sequences can be corrected. It's how cystic fibrosis and haemophilia were eradicated early in the new century, literally replacing the old genes which caused the illness for new ones.

It was also the same basic method which Reece had used to convert useless pond scum into reecebread, and aquatic coral into landcoral; inserting modifications and improvements, distorting the original DNA out of all recognition. But constructing transgenic plants was an order of magnitude easier than human gene therapy.

Laura and her team had been working on the more difficult hereditary cancers. They didn't have organisms which could be junked and burnt when a modification failed or mutated into teratoid abominations. Reaching perfection was a long laborious business.

But it was good work. Important, caring work. People should be made to see that.

'There must be something you can show them,' I said in desperation. 'What about the university hospital clinic? Nu-Cell funds have been going there for years.'

'Not everyone that works for Nu-Cell is a Hermie, you know. We're not even a majority in the company, nowhere near. Besides, showing Hermies conducting experiments on bedridden children? Not a good idea, Mark. Nu-Cell has already given the world reecebread and landcoral and petrocellum beet. What more can we give?'

I put my arms round her, trying to stroke away the tensions I found knotting up her muscles. 'I don't know. I really don't.'

The comments and conspiracy accusations continued to fly unabated as Christmas drew near. It took on an almost ritual quality. The tabloids had found another scare image to rank alongside illegal African migration into Mediterranean Europe, Russian nuclear power-station meltdowns, Japan's re-emergence as a military superpower, and the Islamic Bomb. But even they couldn't have predicted the full horror, the tidal wave of violence and hysteria which swept the planet.

The physical attacks started in public places as the New Year broke. It only seemed to make things worse that a disproportionate number of hermaphrodites had made a significant contribution to the world of arts, medicine, science and engineering. So much for my idea of a Public Relations coup.

It was the week before Easter when the first trouble hit Leicester. We were out shopping in the city centre, buying chocolate eggs for nephews and nieces. It was a fine spring day, we strolled idly. The clock tower pedestrian precinct had been completely converted by landcoral, with only the old white stone tower itself left free as a centrepiece. It looked handsome; the unprepossessing clash of concrete and brick, architecture from the mid-1950s to the early 2010s, all eclipsed by seamless sheets of iridescent sapphire, emerald and amber marble; buttressed by colonnades of braided gold and bronze cords. Speckled rooftop domes reflected a harlequin gleam under the cold bright sun.

We heard the noise as we walked out of the Shires mall. The crowds were growing denser up ahead, people flocking to the edges like iron filings caught in a magnetic field.

'What is it?' Laura asked.

A column of blue smoke rose in the distance. Cheers rang above the background babble. We steered our way through knots of people, anxious and curious at the same time. I wondered where my colleagues were.

Someone had broken the windows of W. H. Smith's. Books were being flung out onto the pavement through the gaping holes. People scooped them up and slung them onto a flattish bonfire blazing on top of one of the flower troughs.

'What the hell's going on?' I tried to sound authoritative.

'Hermie books,' a woman crowed. She grinned wildly. 'Clearing 'em off the shelves. Not before time.'

Laura's hand covered her mouth, eyes staring helplessly at the blackening pages. I grabbed her arm and began to tug her away. She was in tears when we finally left the crowd behind.

'How can they do that?' she wailed. 'What does it matter

who wrote them? It's the words themselves which count.'

I pulled out my netcom unit and called Charles Street to report the event. It took another twenty minutes for the first panda car to arrive. By then all was ash.

Some days after the bookburnings, Doctor Desmond Reece made a powerful public plea for the attacks on hermaphrodites to stop. The morning after his speech he was kicked to death on the steps of Nu-Cell's botanical research laboratory.

I spent the next three days helping to orchestrate the police reinforcements brought in to protect Nu-Cell's buildings and the University campus. The county commissioner was badly worried the mobs would wipe out the region's premier economic asset. Reece's murderers were never caught. The commissioner didn't consider the matter a priority.

Right across Europe, the Americas, and the Far East citizens were burning Hermie books and cutting up Hermie doctors with scalpels; but their mouths were still red from munching on their reeceburgers. The hypocrisy of it all was driving me insane.

Nobody was really safe walking the streets. There were plenty of cases of non-hermaphrodites caught in the hysterical onslaught. Laura said very little, but she would lie awake at nights wondering when they would find out. In the dead of night she would just look at me with her moist, frightened eyes, but say nothing. She never dreamed I'd be her Judas.

The Brussels parliament was under pressure to act to halt the slaughter. But with Federal elections looming, you knew the mob was going to win either way. Under The (Hermaphrodites) Public Order and Disenfranchisement Enactment of that year, the following restrictions were ordered:

1. All hermaphrodites are required to register with their regional authority.

2. All hermaphrodites shall resign from holding public or civil office.

3. Hermaphrodites will be disenfranchised forthwith from all municipal, regional, state and federal elections.

4. An enquiry to be launched into the origins of hermaphrodism and into allegations of hermaphrodite conspiracy.

There were a lot of other clauses in the statutes, about publishing and other things with which I won't bore you. The point was that it didn't satisfy anyone. No-one gave two hoots whether a Hermie was allowed to put a cross on a ballot paper once every five years. What they wanted, as the tabloids pointed out on a daily basis, was to stop the filthy Hermies from *breeding*.

I got home late from work one evening towards the end of spring.

'I'm pregnant,' said Laura.

'Jesus!' I said.

'Hermes,' she said. 'Aphrodite.' It was sort of a joke. We went and lay down and, I'll admit it, I cried like a baby.

The wave of attacks subsided for a while. Burroughs and a few other people at work were visibly disappointed, but I began to feel less anxious about Laura's safety. Meanwhile the official enquiry went into labour. A surprising number of prominent people spoke up for the Hermies, risking careers and tabloid derision, not to mention public assault. But a lot of people had been sickened by the street attacks.

Meanwhile the tabloids characterized the debate as two basically opposed theories. One they called Millennium Fever. The other was known as Martian Theory.

It seems that at the turn of every century a number of people get taken with Millennium Fever. The symptoms of Millennium Fever are a certain itchy credulity in the belief system and a nervous suggestibility, all brought on by the conviction that the turn of the century will signal some major development in the course of human history. The Next Big Step. The Giant Leap. The MF people argued that the arrival of the hermaphrodites semaphored that this had already happened. They pointed out that the first birth cluster of hermaphrodites, born around the end of the 20th century, were already making disproportionate contributions to the culture and progress of the species. Hermaphrodites, it was true, were characterized by their resourcefulness, their meekness and their fertility. It was the assertion of old gods, the MF people argued. Hermes the messenger. Aphrodite the goddess of love. The presence of the hermaphrodites was Messianic. To a planet in dire need, it was a message of love.

The tabloid louts just adored that. They staggered back from their reeceburger-and-beer lunchbreaks and wrote up the Martian Theory. Which gives you an idea of the kind of level this was pitched at.

The Martian Theory assumed some cosmic plot on the part of another species somewhere in the galaxy. This alien species had littered the planet with *spores* – and how they loved that word *spores* – to reproduce their race. At the same time the overthrow and extinction of the human race was guaranteed. Message of love? No, trumpeted the Martian Theorists, it was a message of war.

To me, both arguments sounded about as rational as a jar of ether at a teenage psych-out party. But given the choice, and the intelligent level of debate conducted through the media, most people plumped for the Martian Theory.

So did the board of enquiry. Under their proposed (Hermaphrodites) Public Order and Disenfranchisement Enactment Amendment, several new clauses were to be added. It was never going to be anything else than major trouble.

Predicting the results of the enquiry, most hermaphrodites had failed to register as previously directed. Chief among the Amendment clauses was one which made it law that anyone knowing of an unregistered hermaphrodite should report their presence to the authorities.

Laura was well into her pregnancy when the findings were published. 'This is it. We've got to take some kind of a stand.' Suddenly that soulful, searching look of hers had taken on a blade edge. 'No bloody way am I registering.'

I could hardly argue. You see, there was another, rather more sinister clause included: a blanket prohibition on any hermaphrodite breeding, either with another hermaphrodite or with a non-hermaphrodite. Enforced contraception was the solution offered. But contraception has never been one hundred per cent successful. It would take only a few accidental pregnancies and sterility would become the only publicly acceptable answer.

The enquiry board made no mention of what was to happen to unborn children.

Unfortunately, the new law not only directed people to inform on their neighbours and colleagues. It also introduced retrospective interpretation of the law. Anyone who had previously consorted with an hermaphrodite was obliged to inform. Failure to do so was a Category A offence. If Laura and I were ever to part company and her secret was to be discovered at some future date, I too would face certain prosecution.

As a further complication, that week had seen the delivery of a set of highly classified Recordable CDs to Charles Street. They contained a program written by the experts of the Federal Detective Agency in Paris. It was a specialist monitor which would track an individual's movements on a 24-hour basis. Not physically, not optically; we're not that close to Orwell's nightmare, not yet. But the trail any one person leaves through the civil datanets is comprehensive enough to build up an accurate identikit of their movements – traffic control routing your car guidance processor, timed purchases through credit card, phone calls from home, netcom units, or office, mail, faxes. From that can be worked out who was in the pub with you, who shared your bus, your taxi, whose home you visited. And how often, that was the key. It looked for patterns. Patterns betrayed friendships and interests, contacts with criminals, even drug habits and bizarre sexual preferences.

It couldn't be done for the entire population; not enough processing power available. But the Packard-Bell sitting so princely in the Charles Street basement could quite easily track a troublesome minority clean across Leicestershire.

I had already been instructed to load the program. The county commissioner was simply waiting for the Amendment to be passed by Brussels before entering the names of all known hermaphrodites in the county.

No question, Laura would be found. She had a lot of hermaphrodite friends, some registered, others not. They would meet, talk on the phone, have meals together. Her name would be slotted into a pattern of seemingly random binary digits that flowed and swirled along the city's streets in the wake of its human occupants. And my name was linked with hers, irrevocably.

I didn't know what to do.

I watched the duty officers at their terminals, busy keen-eyed youngsters, analysing requests and assigning priorities. Oblivious to each other and to their immediate environment. Three rows of desks, with a big situation screen on the far wall. All of it geared up to maintain the rule of law. It was all so bleakly efficient.

My own heart was slowing to its normal rate. The ops room, focused on the gritty problems that the streets dumped on our overstretched uniform boys and girls, wasn't my main concern. No, it was the detectives upstairs who worried me. We had a new division at Charles Street, the Registration and Identification Bureau, formed six months ago, with the sole task of spotting Hermies. They might begin to wonder why so few Hermies were being brought in after tip-offs, or even why the precious monitor program was producing so few names. And I wasn't the only computer expert in the building.

But it looked as if Morton Leverett was going to get clean away. I asked the terminal for a display of panda-car routings. When the street map with its flashing symbols flipped up I saw Burroughs had assigned Leverett only a blue coding, about level with shoplifting.

It would mean he had more than enough time to get away. Delight warred with anger inside my skull. I'd given Burroughs a deliberate and very pointed order to get officers there fast.

I looked up to see Burroughs talking into his throat-mike. His agitation had reached new heights. His blotchy skin betrayed him.

I used my supervisor's authority code to check his desk's communications network. He was using an outside line. Mistake, Burroughs, big mistake.

I patched the call into my own headset.

'. . . about twelve minutes,' Burroughs whined. 'That sector's panda car is dealing with a mugging right now. I'll see if I can find another amber call to hold 'em up when they're finished. But I can't promise.'

'We'll be there,' a low voice replied.

The next minute was a blank. I sat there staring at nothing.

Burroughs! Burroughs was the one feeding the Hermies to the organized lynch gangs! He was responsible for men women and children being torn to pieces, several hundred of them over the last eighteen months.

But then, I think I was always ready for that. My dislike for Burroughs went deeper than his slob personality and vile bigotry. A lot deeper. Perhaps it was a psychic thing, some basic animal instinct.

On the other side of the glass he was standing up, clutching his arms to his chest. His shoulders were quaking inside his baggy shirt. Face wearing the desperately grim expression of someone holding back vomit.

I stuck my head round the door. 'Burroughs, where the hell do you think you're going?'

'Toilet,' he gasped.

'You're off shift in half an hour. Can't it wait?'

He stopped halfway to the door. 'No it can't wait!' he screamed. 'I want to go! And I'm shagging well going! All shagging right?' A bead of spittle dribbled from anaemic lips.

The entire ops room had come to a halt at the outburst.

'All right?' he yelled shrilly.

'Why, Burroughs, something's put you in a terrible mood today . . .'

He snarled something incoherent, then turned and ran for the gents.

I smiled evilly at his sweat-soaked back.

For the start of summer it had been a chill night. I'd walked along paths lined by surreal purple and black ferns, taller than myself, which made up the garden hedges in the Nu-Cell housing estate. Out in the city I imagined the pubs hosting raging debates on the approaching ice age.

Laura had sounded odd when she phoned, timorous but insistent. Policeman's instinct, maybe, but I wasn't looking forward to the meeting. I thought I could guess the reason.

The mobs had started attacking Hermies again. Encouraged by the findings of the enquiry they'd returned with a vengeance. I'd never seen such naked hysteria before. When they got hold of someone, it was like watching a storm.

When I arrived at the dome there were five other people with her. All Hermies, and all working at the University or Nu-Cell. It confirmed my worst fears. The police had suspected the existence of Hermie cabals for some time. But the fact that Laura was a member was horrifying.

'We can't just sit by and do nothing,' she said. 'Not any more. It's gone too far now. They're killing us! We have to resist.'

'And do what?' I asked.

'Stop the police collusion with the lynch gangs for a start.'

'What the hell can I do? You don't seem to realize the position I'm in.'

'You've got the power! You're there! You've got access to information. You know when the calls come in from informers. You can warn people. If you can't help us, who can?'

'And put my head on the block?'

One of the others cleared his throat, a male-aligned 30-year-old. Gerald, or at least that was the name he gave when introduced. Laura said he worked at Nu-Cell.

'Assisting our fellow Hermies here in Leicester would only be a very small part of our overall stratagem,' he said.

'Stratagem?' I exclaimed. 'Keep on using that kind of language, and people really will begin to believe in the Hermie conspiracy.'

'When events force a minority into collusion to survive, then the term conspiracy is wholly appropriate.'

'Jesus!'

'Will you listen,' Laura hissed.

'We have to buy ourselves time,' Gerald said. 'That's all. After that the inevitable sweep of history will protect us. But the intervening years will be extraordinarily difficult for us as a race.'

'What?'

He gave me a small contrite smile and held up a thin sheet of some transparent plastic. It was printed with rows of black lines, like a bar code. 'I've been mapping the genome of various hermaphrodites working at Nu-Cell,' he said. 'I've identified the genes which produce both our dual sexual characteristics and enhanced neuron structure as well as other physiological improvements. Do you remember the so called Martian Theory?'

'Yes,' I said wearily.

'It is completely inaccurate.'

'Astonishing,' I said dryly.

Laura shot me a vicious glare.

'We have not resulted from artificial interference,' he continued. 'And that means that even if every hermaphrodite alive were to be sterilized, ordinary humans would still continue to give birth to more hermaphrodites. Within five generations every human born will be a hermaphrodite. So what we need is an interval in which people are forced to face reality and come to terms with our racial future.'

'How do you know this?' I asked.

'Over ninety-five per cent of human DNA is inactive spacing, literally garbage. The active genes, those which make us what we are, account for a tiny three or four per cent. Until now geneticists have considered those inactive genes to be part of our heritage; primitive genes that have been switched off as we evolved out of our remote ancestry through simian stages until we arrived at what we are today. That theory is incorrect. Once I identified the hermaphrodite genes, I went back and examined the genomes of ordinary humans. They too contained the hermaphrodite genes. But they were inactive; for the moment, part of the spacing. Hermaphroditism is part of humanity's ongoing evolution.'

'What switches the genes on?'

He shrugged lamely. 'It is their time to be switched on. Our time. God, if you prefer, Mr Anderson, God has decided to bring us forth. Just think, in a hundred generations another sequence of genes will activate themselves. Who knows what our descendants will look like.'

'And in the meantime, we get slaughtered,' Laura said.

'Registration dodging isn't the answer,' I said. 'It criminalizes Hermies in everyone's eyes.'

'Neither is registration,' Philippa said. She was about the same age as Laura, with auburn hair and a small compact body. Aggression simmered, barely contained, below her calm surface persona. 'Not when all that does is bring the lynch gangs down on you.'

'It's not our fault,' I shouted. 'When the police arrive it's always too late.'

'That's because someone inside your precious ops room is tipping off the lynch gangs,' Laura said. 'And you're just standing by and letting it happen.'

I knew she was right. At the time I just didn't know who was doing it. I sank down into one of her scoop chairs. 'I don't know where the leak is coming from,' I said. 'Believe me, I've looked.'

'This may help,' Philippa said with deceptive calm. She was holding out an RCD.

'What's this?'

'See for yourself.' She indicated Laura's desktop terminal.

I slotted the silver disc. The program it contained was simple enough, designed for the Packard-Bell core, a number of subroutines that would work inside the original operator shell. Once loaded, any file that was started on a Hermie would be switched with another citizen file selected at random. That meant a duty officer sending a panda car to pick up a suspected Hermie would target the wrong person. Some innocent non-hermaphrodite would be cut up on the streets instead.

'No chance,' I said.

'It would not have to be in effect for very long,' Gerald said. 'I intend to confront my non-hermaphrodite colleagues with my discovery. They are rational people, they will accept it. Then the intellectuals and leaders of the world will be made to understand what is really occurring. Hermaphroditism is inevitable.'

Philippa snorted. She didn't believe in Gerald's wishful-thinking solution any more than I did. She didn't like the idea of being civil to a policeman, either. I could virtually see her mind working out ways to blackmail me into loading her program.

'Please, Mark,' Laura said. 'What kind of world will the baby come into if we don't try to bridge the gulf? This gives us the time to do it.'

'I'll think about it,' I lied.

She sat beside me and twined her arms round my neck. 'Thank you.'

I knew it was disastrous for Laura to get involved with these people. It was only a matter of time before they were rounded up; if they weren't informed on, the monitor program would track them down anyway. I loved Laura, and I would have done anything to protect her and our baby. She had taught me so many incredible things, things I would never have understood on my own. But I also believed in the system, believed that the system would protect us. I decided to take action before we were both up on a charge of insurrection.

The simplest thing to do was have her picked up. Crazy? Not really: once registered, her name would be entered in the monitor program. If she contacted her cabal members the monitor would spot them. She would never knowingly betray them, so she would steer clear of them.

And me? Well, I was prepared to face the consequences. As I said, I ultimately believed in the protection of the system. Remember, this was before I'd found out about Burroughs. What's more, I would be there to prevent anything from happening.

The day after the meeting I told Laura to meet me at Guys & Dolls restaurant for lunch. Then I bypassed the normal log-in procedure and loaded an informer's report of a Hermie into the ops room network, giving Laura's name and profile, telling them where she would be. One of the duty officers would pick it up, and assign a panda car to collect us both from Guys & Dolls.

I hurried towards the restaurant hoping Laura wouldn't be late. When the uniform boys picking her up found they had a senior officer as a witness they would have to act strictly according to the book. She would be perfectly safe in my presence. After that I would inform the Chief Constable of my relationship with her, but only after she'd been correctly processed.

On the way over to Guys & Dolls I got caught up in the lunchtime traffic snarl. I sat under my perspex bubble sweating for half an hour. In the end I jumped out and walked.

I turned the corner of the street and made for the restaurant with a growing sense of anxiety. When I saw the crowd outside the restaurant I felt a strange taste in my mouth. Fingering the buttons on my uniform, I had to fight down a rising panic. Then I found myself sprinting towards the crowd.

The lynch gang had already done its work. Their victim lay naked and bloody in the gutter. One of them turned the lifeless body over with the toe of his boot. They had hacked off the penis. And as I looked, I saw that their victim had been expecting a child, and that they had sliced open her belly. The bloody foetus was almost indistinguishable from the rest of the carcass. I looked around for Laura, as if somehow just by looking I could make that figure on the ground not be her. A neon sign flashing above the crowd exhorted us all to EAT REECEBREAD.

Philippa found me, hours later. I was sitting on the New Walk bridge over the carriageway running through the heart of the city. Down below, the fuel-cell driven cars formed a silent steady stream of colourful metallic beetles, scurrying home from work. Rushing towards their loved ones.

'What good will that do?' Philippa asked gently.

I didn't even look up. 'It will stop the pain.'

'Only for you. There are soon going to be others in your position. Millions of us. Do you want them to endure it as well?'

'I don't care.'

'Yes you do. Laura taught you to care.'

I started sobbing. Philippa led me away from the parapet.

Behind me the ops room was abuzz with duty officers gossiping over Burroughs's hypertantrum; calls for assistance and reports of crime were going unanswered. It was my job to marshal them back to work. Not today. I pushed the door of the gents open, and walked in.

There were five stalls along one wall, stainless steel urinals at the far end. White tiles gleamed soullessly under harsh tubelight. The stall at the end of the line was occupied.

Gerald, quiet intellectual Gerald, had been quite right; oppress a minority enough and no matter how meek, how mild, eventually they begin to fight back. He even led the fight.

The whole world would be Hermies in time, he said. But time was the one thing the first generation didn't have. Our father Hermes and our mother Aphrodite might be bringing hermaphrodites into the world, but they were doing it too slowly. Even gods need a helping hand occasionally.

I tested the stall door with my hand. Burroughs had slipped the tiny bolt. A fragile whimpering sound was coming from inside. I was going to have to break down the door. I was already four months pregnant with Philippa's child, and exertion like that wouldn't be good for the baby, but I kicked at the lock anyway. The bolt flew off and I was able to push open the door.

After identifying the Hermie genes, Gerald had fed the sequence into a DNA synthesizer. Plasmids came out of the other end, the essence of Hermaphroditism, all that we are. Philippa and her more militant colleagues incorporated them into the new improved varieties of reecebread that Nu-Cell was giving to the world. And the people of the world ate. Both the meek and the greedy, eating their reece-burgers. The plasmid-carrying viruses slithered into their digestive tract, into their bloodstream, into their cells, into their nuclei. And, finally, began raping their DNA.

But we're not heartless. Manipulating human genes is a tricky business. So much can go wrong. The plasmids needed to be tested first. I once said you can't experiment with gene therapy on living humans. I was wrong. There are certain individuals who can be exempt from such moral posturing.

Our test subject, myself, showed no ill-effects after a solid month of eating the modified reecebread. It was enough for us to release it for general consumption. That was six months ago.

Burroughs was sitting crammed into a corner of the stall, his trousers and pants crumpled round his knees. His wretched face jerked up as I looked in, his mouth open in a silent plea.

No wonder he'd been in such a rotten temper all week.

The chicken-flesh at the base of his scrotum had split open. A mucus plug had voided from the raw open slit, followed by a dribble of blood.

Burroughs was having his first period.

THE UNKINDNESS OF RAVENS

Brian Stableford

All lovers of exotic collective nouns know that a group of ravens is an 'unkindness,' although most dictionaries stubbornly refuse to confirm the fact. Perhaps it has something to do with the raven's reputation as a bird of ill-omen: the 'sad-presaging raven' which 'does shake contagion from her sable wing,' as Marlowe puts it.

Perhaps I was a fool to create an unkindness of ravens when all common sense pointed to African grey parrots as the most suitable subjects for the crucial experiment. I could say, I suppose, that I made the choice on economic grounds, ravens being considerably cheaper than African greys, but the simple truth is that it was the only *poetic* choice. All the greatest scientists have well-crafted aesthetic sensibilities.

It should, I suppose, have been the one I christened Nevermore who came rapping, rapping at my window three years after the great escape – but it wasn't. Nor did I possess a bust of Pallas on which he might take his station once I had let him in; he had perforce to make do with the tower of my computer system, at which I had been working long into the dreary night. He was so close that I might have reached out my hand to stroke his glossy coat of feathers, but I knew that he wouldn't suffer it and so I stayed my hand.

'Hello, Edgar,' I said, quietly. I recognized him, of course. All ravens are not alike to those who know them well, and Edgar was my child – *entirely* mine, no matter what manner of black-clad automaton had laid the egg from which he hatched.

'Hello, Doctor,' he replied, with a self-confidence that testified to considerable practice. It was evident that he and his companions had not quit the lab in order to be free of the burden of speech. 'Are you staying long?' I asked, although I knew that he would have to leave at least once more, to report back to his siblings.

'Just a flying visit,' he replied. A raven's voice is quite uninflected when he speaks for himself, although they can mimic the emotional overtones of overheard speech, so there was nothing in his tone to signify that Edgar meant the remark as a comic play on words. I wasn't sure whether he did or not. One has the same trouble with conversational programs that will play on a PC; one is never certain that their occasional forays into humour are – or can be – intentional.

'I could shut the window to imprison you,' I pointed out. 'Now I know what you can do I needn't be as careless as I was three years ago.'

'If you try to keep me here against my will,' he said, flatly, 'I'll never say another word – and if ever I get the chance, I'll take your eyes out with my beak.' No parrot would ever have been so bloodcurdlingly matter-of-fact, but ravens are hunters and scavengers by nature, haunters of the dying and consumers of the dead.

'Why come back at all, if that's your attitude?' I asked him. 'Surely you don't think you owe me anything? I only made you, after all. I only performed the embryonic transformations which raised your bird brain to near-human levels of achievement. I never asked you to think of me as God.'

'I don't,' he said, unnecessarily. 'How's the great work going, Doctor?'

'Fair to middling,' I told him. 'Same old problems. It's easy enough to transform lower forms of life, but there's no demand for smart cockroaches and clever crabs. Sharks, frogs and crocodiles can go so far and no further because they can't talk, and because they can't talk they can't learn to think in a pseudo-human way. It'd probably be the same with dolphins, rats and cats, but the transformations are so very difficult it's well-nigh impossible to put the proposition to the test. Something there is about a womb which resents the interference of genetic engineers. There are no licences yet for experiments with people, of course – I doubt there will be, in my lifetime. You and your fellows remain my one great triumph, and the one dramatic demonstration of the fact that the ability to speak is by far the most important concomitant of pure intelligence – more important than clever hands or clever eyes.'

'My eyes are pretty good,' Edgar said, haughtily, 'and you might be surprised by what a bird can do by way of manipulation with a couple of claws and a beak.'

'Not any more,' I murmured, thinking about the great escape. The locks on the cages were supposed to be bird-proof; so were the catches on the windows. 'What do you want, Edgar? What do you need that you think I can supply? Or did you just drop by to bring me news?'

'Most of the news is bad,' he said. 'We're down to six. Lenore was shot. A hawk got Clementine. Barnaby died of some kind of infection. We never found out what happened to Hugin.'

'It's a tough old world,' I said. 'Nature red in tooth and claw. You want to be wild, you have to play natural selection roulette.'

'We didn't want to be wild,' he told me, contriving to sound stern in spite of his intrinsic limitations. 'We wanted to be free. We needed to be free, if we were ever to be ourselves. If we'd stayed in the lab, we'd just have been specimens. We couldn't be birds unless we learned to fly, and we didn't want to be mere echoes any more than you wanted us to be.'

He was showing off, of course. He wanted to show me what a smart guy he was, and how three years without anyone to talk to but his fellows hadn't impeded his intellectual development in the least. He wanted to show me that all he'd needed was the raw material of words and their meanings, and that everything else had flowed from that. At least, I *think* he wanted to show me; it's so very difficult to be absolutely sure. Conversational programs provide such a good imitation of intelligence without being capable of wanting anything – or of intending anything, or of caring about anything – that we always have to hesitate about reading too much into the things other entities say to us, especially if the entities in question are big black birds.

'I take your point,' I said. 'I understand. In your place, I'd have done the same thing.' I think I was telling the truth. Sometimes, we have to be suspicious even of our own motives, our own desires, our own powers of empathy.

'I know you would,' he said. The light above and behind him threw the shadow of his dark head across my keyboard, so that the shadow of his beak seemed to point at my heart like some threatening dart. 'What do you want, Edgar?' I said, again. 'What is it that you can't provide for yourselves? What is it that you need from me?'

'You know what it is,' he countered – and if any final proof were required that he really did have authentic intelligence of a pseudo-human kind, that was it. 'You always knew. You always knew that one day we'd have to come back.'

Of course I knew. Of course I'd always expected him back. The only surprise was that it had taken him so long. Ravens are proud and stubborn; they prefer to laugh at fate while there's a chance that fate will back down – but fate never does, of course. Fate doesn't know the meaning of kindness.

'I would have told you if you'd asked,' I said. 'I would have explained, if only you'd given me the time to get around to it. The kind of transformations I carry out are somatic transformations; they affect the cells of a growing embryo selectively. They don't affect the germ plasm – the transformations aren't hereditary. You can talk to your chicks till hell freezes over, but the only answers they'll ever be able to give you are mere echoes. They'll mimic your voices, but they can't ever reproduce your minds. If you want your kids to be smart, Edgar, you have to give me your new-laid eggs and trust me to do what I can with them. I have to warn you, though, that you could lose as many as seven out of ten. If you'd rather have quantity than quality you'd be better off doing things nature's way.'

'Is there any way – ?' he began.

'No there isn't,' I said, abruptly. 'Not yet, anyhow. One day, perhaps, we'll be able to make smart animals that can breed true . . . but not yet – and if ever the day comes, it'll be too late for you and your little flock.'

'We're not a flock,' he said. For a moment, I thought he was going to tell me that they were an unkindness, but he wasn't being *that* pedantic; what he meant was that 'flock' was an animal term, whereas he and his fellows weren't animals – not any more. He would have preferred 'tribe' or 'company.'

'I'm truly sorry,' I said. 'I think I understand your desire to be free, and I think I understand how disappointing it's been to find that your freedom is qualified and circumscribed. If you decide to come back, I'll try to explain the myriad ways in which human freedom is qualified and circumscribed. You're not alone, you know. You never were. I've always been ready to open the window.' I knew that I'd won, and that the great escape was over. I knew, and was now confident enough to be assured that I'd *always* known, that my children – my very own unkindness of ravens – were coming home.

'You know, Doctor,' he said, although he was quite unable to contort his croaky voice into any simulation of feeling, 'there's something about you that I never liked. It's not your cleverness as such – it's something about the way you set it out. If we do come back, it's not because we love you. I wouldn't want you to think that it was.'

Such, I suppose, is the unkindness of ravens. The all-inclusive collective noun for our own species is, of course, humanity.

THE MAN WHO READ A BOOK

Thomas M. Disch

After Jerome Bagley was graduated from Maya Angelou High School in Brooklyn in 1998, he spent the next twelve years either unemployed or attending a variety of vocational and pre-vocational classes at City College and its affiliates. He studied computer programming, hair styling, substance abuse counselling, auto repair and maintenance, cake decorating, and introductory Sanskrit, but none of these efforts ever led to an actual salaried position. Then one day his parole officer, Mona Schuyler, suggested that he look into the possibility of reading books for money, and showed him the ad, in the back pages of *The National Endowment*, that told him where to write in order to find out if he was qualified.

He was! His educational background showed him to be the kind of all-things-considered reader that publishers were looking for. He might well enjoy a career in readership if he were willing to make a strong personal commitment and enlist in the career development programme sponsored by the Yaddo Reading Institute of Boca Raton, Florida. Jerome filled in the Institute's two-page questionnaire and faxed it in, together with his cheque for $50. The very next day the Institute's Aptitude Profile arrived, and Jerome began answering the Profile's 350 multiple-choice questions. Some answers he was certain he got right: America's Number One Best-Selling Author since 1984 was (c) Stephen King. Tennessee Williams was the author of the immortal 1948 tragedy (a) *A Salesman Named Desire*. Hyperbole was (b) a rare disorder of the lymph nodes. Others he was not so certain of, but he knew enough about test-taking to rule out obvious wrong choices and then flip a coin. In any case, as the Institute's brochure explained, the important thing wasn't getting exactly the right answer. He wasn't a contestant on 'Jeopardy.' The important thing was an attitude of confidence, affirmation, and a sheer love of reading.

Jerome mailed in the Aptitude Profile with a cheque for $200 and waited. But not for long. A week later he got a signed letter from Mr Yaddo himself, the head of the Institute, congratulating him on his responsiveness, energy, and knack. Mr Yaddo said that Jerome's Aptitude Profile was absolutely unique according to the Institute's seven-trillion-byte databank, and he personally promised Jerome that he would be hearing from interested publishers in no time at all, publishers who would be paying him top dollar in order to find out what he, JEROME BAGLEY, thought about their books.

His name was written just like that, with every letter a capital letter. Looking at his name in such big letters, it was almost like seeing it on the cover of one of the books he might have to read. Jerome went to Wal-Mart and bought a picture frame the exact same size as the letter, and he hung the letter, in the frame, on the wall behind his dormitory cot, where everyone would see it.

Then he received a letter from a publisher, Alfred Kopf, who had heard about Jerome from Mr Yaddo and wanted him to read one of the books he'd published and tell him what he thought about it. For this service Alfred Kopf was prepared to pay Jerome $50. A copy of the book Mr Kopf wanted him to read accompanied his letter. It was the new revised edition of one of their most popular titles, *A Collector's Guide to Plastic Purses*. Jerome didn't know that much about plastic purses, but Mr Kopf wasn't hiring him for his expertise but for his gut reaction as a Common Reader.

Jerome found himself a quiet area, far from the TV, in the dorm lounge and settled down to read the book then and there. It was incredibly boring, but there were lots of pictures, so it didn't take as much time to read it as he'd originally feared. When he'd finished reading it, he filled out the Official Reader's Report, stating in 200 words or less his own personal opinion that *A Collector's Guide to Plastic Purses* was not a book that most people would want to read, but that it would certainly have an appeal for anyone who collected plastic purses. He was tempted to add that he'd never known anyone who did collect plastic purses and had never even seen a plastic purse like the ones in the book. He didn't want to seem overly negative the first time he worked for Mr Kopf. For all he knew, the man had already made a big investment in the book and wouldn't be happy to hear what Jerome honestly thought, which was that plastic purses sucked.

A week later Jerome received a cheque for $50 signed by Mr Kopf, along with a note from Mr Kopf's assistant, Betty Kreiner, thanking him for his valuable input. Jerome could hardly believe his good luck. He was employed! Just as the ad had promised, he was earning real money just by reading books!

The very next day he got a phone call from Mr Yaddo himself, congratulating him on his first success in his career in professional readership. It surprised Jerome a little to think that Mr Yaddo already knew about the work he'd done for Alfred Kopf, but as the lecturer had explained in his computer programming course, we live in an age when data flows at almost the speed of light, and the data knows, all by itself, where it ought to go. Anyhow, Mr Yaddo was delighted for Jerome, and wanted to invite him to take part in a seminar that Mr Yaddo was planning to conduct for a select group of professional readers in his own apartment. The fee for attending the seminar was rather steep, $1,500, but most of it would be paid by a National Endowment Fellowship, if Jerome would take the time to fill out the application Mr Yaddo would be sending him and return it to the National Endowment Office in Boca Raton, Florida.

'Well, Jerome, what do you think?' Mr Yaddo asked.

'I don't know,' said Jerome. 'It's a lot of money.'

'It is,' Mr Yaddo agreed. 'But faint heart ne'er won fair maid.'

'What?' Jerome asked.

'Nothing ventured, nothing gained.'

'Yeah,' said Jerome.

'This could be your big break, fella,' Mr Yaddo said with great conviction.

'Okay, I guess so, sure.'

There was a whirring sound at the other end of the line, and then a different voice announced, 'You have been speaking with the simulated intelligence of Yaddo Incorporated of Boca Raton, Florida. The Corporation stands behind all statements that have been made as being essentially similar to any that Mr Yaddo himself would have made, were he available. Thank you for your interest and cooperation. And good luck in your new career as a Reader.'

Two weeks later Jerome appeared promptly at Mr Yaddo's apartment, which was in the World Trade Centre, and looked more like a class-space than an apartment someone might live in. He was met at the door by a Chinese girl, who introduced herself as Tracy Wu and said she was Mr Yaddo's protégée, whatever that was. She accepted the copy of *A Collector's Guide to Plastic Purses*, which Jerome had gift-wrapped as a present for Mr Yaddo, and put it on a table beside other gift-wrapped presents. Then she led him to his seat in the third row of folding chairs that faced a king-size Sony Holo-Man.

'Isn't Mr Yaddo going to be here in person?' he asked Tracy, before she could go back to the door to welcome the next participant.

'He may or he may not,' said Tracy with an enigmatic Oriental smile. 'Mr Yaddo is nothing if not unpredictable. But if he isn't here in person, he will surely be here in spirit. We'll know in just a moment, won't we. Now, please excuse me, duty calls.'

Participants continued to arrive for the next half-hour, which gave Jerome time to get acquainted with those sitting on either side of him, who were, just like him, newcomers to the profession of Readership. On his left was Ms Lorelei Hummell, from Yonkers, a single mom with four children, who intended to specialize in books about Satanism and UFOs. On his right was Studs Liebowitz, a gay plumber with a Mohawk haircut whose chief interest in literature was books about the history of pro wrestling. By a strange coincidence, Studs had also prepared an Official Reader's Report for Alfred Kopf on *A Collector's Guide to Plastic Purses*, so they had something to talk about while they waited for Mr Yaddo or his simulation to appear. At last, when all the participants had arrived, the Sony Holo-Man luminesced, and there was Mr Yaddo, in larger-than-life simulation, wearing a five-piece Armani Suit and smoking a large Prestige Brand symbolic cigar, the kind that smells like room deodorant and can't give anyone cancer.

The Yaddo simulation blew a gigantic smoke ring toward the assembled participants, which dissolved into purple fizz as it reached the perceptual boundary of holographic space. It leaned forward and seemed to look at each participant directly in his or her eyes.

'Let's be honest with each other,' it said. 'Nobody likes to read. Okay?'

There was a murmur of muted dissent and a few cautious chuckles. From the last row of seats, Tracy Wu, Mr

428

Yaddo's protégée, raised her voice. 'Then why are we here, Mr Yaddo? *We're* all readers.'

Ms Lorelei Hummell nodded vigorously. 'I *love* to read,' she insisted, turning toward Jerome. 'I read all the time. I am an *avaricious* reader. What's he talking about?'

'This is what I'm getting at.' It paused. 'Got your laptops open?'

'Are we supposed to be taking *notes*?' Studs Liebowitz whispered. 'I thought this was going to be more like a party. It's just another damned lecture.'

'Reading,' said the Yaddo simulation, 'is a dying art. It began to die when the movies were invented more than a century ago, and at this point genuine readers are an endangered species, as rare as the white rhinoceros. By readers I mean people who actually sit down a few hours every day with a book in their hands, turning the pages and reading what's printed on each page. It is not a natural activity. It takes training, application, and ambition. And if you want to make a career of it, it also takes connections. Which is why we're all here tonight, to learn to network, to rub shoulders, to earn big bucks.'

'Right on!' Studs shouted out.

The Yaddo simulation smiled in Studs's direction.

'As professionals in the book field, we often ask ourselves, why do books exist? What practical purpose do they serve that our computers don't do better? What entertainment can they provide that isn't better provided by the flick of a switch? Maybe these are not the right questions to ask. Maybe we're looking through the wrong end of the telescope. Because the simple fact is that books exist because there is a gigantic industry that is in the business of making books. It is a faltering industry, admittedly, but it's still huge, and lots of jobs depend on it, our own included.'

Studs leaned sideways and whispered into Jerome's ear, 'I wish he'd cut to the chase and tell us which publishers to contact who want people to read books about pro wrestling. The rest of this is just a lot of crap as far as I'm concerned.'

'Fortunately, we are not the first major industry to face such a crisis. When the tobacco industry experienced a similar crisis long ago, the Government stepped in and provided subsidies for tobacco farmers so they could continue producing a product that was less and less in demand. The same was done for breeders of Angora goats and for the Savings and Loan industry. When the publishing crisis loomed, the Government was ready. Thanks to the National Endowment this country now has more writers producing more books in more categories than ever before, and this in despite of the fact that almost no one reads any of them. Fortunately, paper is highly recyclable, and so after most of these books have been warehoused long enough for tax purposes, they can be made into other books, in the same way that tobacco plants can be ploughed back into the soil to grow new tobacco plants.'

The Yaddo simulation paused to savour its symbolic cigar. This gave Ms Lorelei Hummell time enough to raise her hand. 'Excuse me, Mr Yaddo. I have a question.'

With a silken shiver of its Armani suit, the simulation shifted into interactive mode. 'Yes, Ms Hummell?'

'I have read a lot of books. I mean a *lot* of them. So I can't agree with you about no one reads books any more. I have a bookcase *full* of books, mostly about UFOs and Satanic child abuse. So when I joined the Institute I naturally expected that I'd be sent books that related to my own special interest areas. But instead I got this book of *poetry.*'

A murmur of sympathy passed through the participants, like the wind stirring a field of wheat.

The Yaddo simulation furrowed its brow. 'What were the poems about, Ms –' It paused as though searching its memory for her name. '– Hummell?'

'They weren't about anything at all in particular that I could see. The weather, sometimes, I guess. And maybe somebody died at some point, but that was never clear. I didn't know that poetry was *supposed* to be about something. If I had, I might not have given the book as high a rating. Anyhow, what I wanted to ask you about –'

'Poetry,' declared the simulation, overriding Ms Hummell, '*isn't* about anything. According to one great poet, it just *is*, period. According to another, it's a real toad in an imaginary garden, and the poet herself says she dislikes it. So it's small wonder if ordinary people dislike it even more. But that's why people are *paid* to read it. Now you tell me you *like* to read books about Satanic child abuse. And so, of course, do millions of other readers. It's one of the few genuinely popular genres left, because it speaks to the fears and curiosity of every parent. But those books don't need a subsidized readership the way poetry does. Does that answer your question, Ms Hummell?'

'I guess so. Thank you.'

'It sounds,' Studs stage-whispered, 'like we're going to be stuck with plastic purses.'

Jerome nodded glumly.

The Yaddo simulation fielded a few more questions from seminar participants dissatisfied with the books they'd had to read, and then it switched tracks and delivered a long speech about the best way to read a book, including practical tips like you should try and sit somewhere where there was no TV and how you should try and set aside the same ten or fifteen minutes each day and make it an absolute rule not to let yourself be interrupted.

Then the seminar was officially over, though everyone was invited by Tracy Wu to have a glass of strawberry-kiwi punch and do some networking.

The punch wasn't free, but Jerome didn't find that out till he'd already asked for a glass and taken a sip. At that

431

point, having forked over five bucks, he felt he had to finish the punch, so he stuck around and introduced himself to some of the other participants, who always wanted to know did he work for a publisher. When he told them he didn't, that was the end of any conversation. They were looking for another book to read, of course, but was that a licence for bad manners?

Finally, just to have some fun, he told the next person who asked that yes, he was an editor at Alfred Kopf.

'An editor! That's wonderful,' the man enthused. He was the small, nervous type with a fox terrier hair-cut and beard, short and bristly, and the same apparent disposition. 'They said there'd be editors and publicists here, but you're the first one that *I've* run into. I was beginning to think this whole thing was some kind of con game.'

Jerome's was not a naturally suspicious nature, but now that the man had thrown out the possibility, he had to wonder whether he might not be on to something.

'Are you a reader?' Jerome asked. 'Are you looking for a new assignment? Is that why you're here?'

'No,' said the man with a thin-lipped weaselish smile, 'no, I'm something even worse than that – from an editor's point of view. I am a writer.'

'You write books?' Jerome marvelled. 'The kind that publishers publish?'

'That remains to be seen. Before my novel can be published, I must find an editor who is willing to read it. And I understand, from my correspondence with the Scott Fitzgerald Literary Agency, that to find an editor I must first find an agent, a service that Mr Fitzgerald offered to perform but only after receiving an initial reading fee that I balked at. For the same price I could publish the book myself in an edition of five hundred copies.'

'Hey, would you like *me* to read your book?'

The man regarded Jerome with amazement. 'Would you want to?'

Jerome tried to assume the world-weary manner of a professional editor of books, someone who had read dozens all the way through. 'Well, like Mr Yaddo says, no one *wants* to read books. It's a job, isn't it?'

'How much?'

'How much?' Jerome echoed.

'How much do you want to be paid to read my book?'

'Well, I'm not quite sure ... I mean I didn't mean to suggest ...'

'A thousand dollars?'

'A thousand dollars!'

'One and a half, then. It's all I can afford.'

'Well, that's very generous, Mister, um –'

'Swindling. Lucius Swindling.' He dropped his paper cup of punch into the trash puppy that had positioned itself by his knee and he offered his hand to Jerome.

Jerome gave the trash puppy his own paper cup, accepted Swindling's hand, and agreed that they had a deal, with two provisos: Swindling must pay him his reading fee in cash and he must deliver the manuscript in person and not Fedex it. It was easier than dealing dope.

Swindling agreed, and they met the next day at noon outside the legendary Union Square Cafe. Two of the tables inside served as the Manhattan office of Alfred Kopf, where its top editors lunched with other top editors and with celebrities wanting to sell their life stories and sex videos to the media. The more labour-intensive divisions of the company's business were based elsewhere, chiefly in Quito, Ecuador.

Jerome counted through the little sheaf of bills and accepted the little envelope containing the disc of Swindling's manuscript.

'You understand,' said Jerome, slipping the manuscript into the pocket of the 100% cotton White Collar T-shirt he'd bought specifically for this occasion, 'that I can't guarantee you that Kopf will want to *publish* your book. All I can promise is that I will read it.'

'Yes, yes. But I do count on your writing me a rejection letter with a few remarks that show you actually read the book and some concrete suggestions for how I might go about re-writing it. A letter like that can make all the difference when the evaluation team at the NEA is going over my application for a revision stipend.'

'You had a grant to write your book?' Jerome had all this while been thinking that the Swindling man was an old-fashioned kind of fanatic who wrote books because he wanted to.

'I've *four* grants,' Swindling said, and ticked them off: 'National Endowment, United Way, Advocates for the Disadvantaged, and a matching grant that went with the Advocates award from Prose Writers in Prison.'

Jerome expressed polite surprise. 'Gee, you don't look disadvantaged to me.'

Swindling glared at him. 'I have dyslexia.'

'Dyslexia' rang a bell, but very faintly. It was one of those words like 'polyunsaturated' that someone had explained to him once, probably in school, but the explanation had come unglued, and now the word was like a disc without a label. It seemed safe to say, 'Well, that's too bad,' and move on to an exchange of numbers. Jerome coded his phone to take calls from Swindling's and vice versa, and then they said good-bye.

Jerome wondered, as he fingered the roll of bills, whether this was, technically, a white-collar crime, and if so, whether it would have been called something more complicated than just fraud, and counted as a felony or a misdemeanour.

But what the hell, it was a job, and when was the last time he had a job? Swindling wanted a letter of rejection. He'd read his book and give him what he wanted.

It wasn't that easy. If *A Collector's Guide to Plastic Purses* had been a punishment, *The Last of the Leather Stockings*

434

was cruel and unusual. It just about filled the disc and it was almost impossible to tell what it was about. Sometimes it was about a guy called Natty Bumpo, which made you think it might be funny (but it never was), and other times it was about a woman in ancient times called Madame Bovary, and then for a while it was about Swindling himself, who seemed to be some kind of serial killer, which might have been interesting, if he'd got into it, but Jerome figured he'd have made a better serial killer himself. Swindling had no imagination when it came to killing women. Any night on TV you could do better without even switching channels.

About half way through Swindling's book Jerome had a brainstorm. If it was worth Swindling's while to pay Jerome 1,500 dollars to read his book and reject it, think what *he* must be getting paid to write it! So . . .

It was a simple thing to copy the disc and then change the name Swindling, each time it occurred, to Bagley, and Lucius to Jerome. The title also had to go, since the NEA's computer probably kept track of things by their titles. While he was deleting the title, Jerome also accidentally lost the first chapter, but that had been the boring part about Natty Bumpo, so getting rid of it was probably an improvement. Once he'd made that conceptual leap – the idea that he could *change* what was on the disc – Jerome was off and running. He downloaded the latest issue of *I'm a Writer* magazine and followed the advice of an article called 'How to Write a Book,' which was to write about things you know something about.

Jerome tried to think of something he knew anything about. There wasn't that much, but what there was he stuck into the book. He'd studied hair styling, so in all the parts of the book where Madame Bovary appeared she had her hair styled in some new way. It was frosted and braided and teased up into a buffalo and clipped down to elflocks. And where the serial killer was cutting up his victim's bodies, Jerome brought his cake decorating know-how to bear. He sprinkled some choice samples from his introductory Sanskrit course here and there, along with pointers on lubricating the suspension system for an '04 model Toyota Aida and how to deal with idle stop solenoids. The book kept getting longer and longer, and Jerome began to feel the thrill of authorship, as described in *I'm a Writer* magazine.

He retitled the new manuscript *I Iced Madame Bovary* by Jerome N. Bagley. He didn't usually use his middle initial, but somehow, even before he'd printed the manuscript out, it seemed like the sort of name a writer would have: Jerome N. Bagley.

He did not forget that he had an obligation to write a letter to Swindling. 'Dear Mr Swindling,' he wrote, on a piece of stationery he'd designed so it looked like it came from the Kopf office at the Union Square Cafe, 'Everyone here has been very impressed with your long book, *The Last of the Leather Stockings*. The first chapter shows unmistakable talent, and the character of Natty Bumpo is very interesting and original. However, we do feel that it needs *revision*! Concentrate more on Natty Bumpo and less on Madame Bovary. Maybe get rid of her altogether or give her a name that is more believable. Also, there is too much sex and serial murder. Can't you substitute something in place of that? For instance, plastic purses. At Kopf we are very interested in plastic purses. These are only suggestions, of course. Basically we are very excited about *The Last of the Leather Stockings*. Keep up the good work. Sincerely, Jerome N. Bagley.'

A week later, at his regular session with his parole officer, Jerome announced that he had decided to become a writer, and that, in fact, he'd written a book.

'You've written a *book*?' Mona Schuyler marvelled. 'What kind of book?'

'Sort of a big one,' Jerome replied. He showed her the manuscript, which he'd had printed out on 496 pages of real paper.

She leaned across her desk and lifted up some of the pages to verify that they weren't blank. On every page there were sentences and paragraphs. 'I'm amazed,' she said. 'A book.'

'It's about sex,' Jerome volunteered. 'And killing. Like you'd see on TV, only I've written it all out.'

Mona read the title page aloud: '*I Iced Madame Bovary.*'

'By Jerome N. Bagley,' Jerome pointed out with modest pride.

'It's a novel?'

'Yeah, I suppose so. You can read it if you want to.'

Mona shook her head primly. 'No, I'm not much of a reader myself. But you know what you should do, don't you?'

He knew, but he wanted to hear it from her. 'What should I do?'

'You should apply for a grant.'

'How do I do that?'

She explained.

It took most of the money he'd taken from Swindling to print out 40 more copies of the manuscript and Fedex them to the appropriate federal, state and city agencies and to enter it in the different competitions sponsored by publishers and writers' groups.

The first responses were not encouraging. The Great Writers Society thanked him for his contribution but pointed out that only Tentative Members were allowed to compete for the Harold Brodkey Memorial Award for Exceptional Early Promise, and it would cost him $500 to become a Tentative Member. The Authors' Guild, the Fiction Union, and American PEN provided similar disappointments.

And then he won the Pushcart Prize! The news came in

a big envelope that announced that JEROME K. BAGLEY was a Pushcart Prize Winner and a contender for the Grand Prize of $100,000 *and* that his book might be optioned by a Major Hollywood Studio. He read through the letter carefully to see if there were any strings attached, and there weren't, except for a coupon that allowed him to purchase, at a substantial discount, 50 copies of the *Pushcart Prize Anthology* in which an excerpt from *I Iced Madame Bovary* was scheduled to appear. The letter was signed by Isaac Pushcart himself.

He was a little miffed that Mr Pushcart had got his middle initial wrong, and when he returned the coupon he pointed out, in a polite way, that he was Jerome N. Bagley, not Jerome K. But that didn't help. When the 50 copies of the Anthology arrived at his dorm, he was still Jerome K. Bagley. It didn't matter. Because there, on page 856 of the Anthology, was the excerpt that he'd written, the chapter in which Jerome Bagley decorates a Lady Baltimore cake with the minced heart and liver of Emma Bovary. The best part of all was the paragraph after 'By Jerome K. Bagley' that said that he was a writer to watch out for, and that *I Iced Madame Bovary* was a brilliant contribution to the New Wave Postmodern Splatterpunk Novel, worthy to be compared to the work of Bret Eastern Alice.

Jerome made copies of the letter Mr Pushcart had sent him and of what it said in the anthology about his brilliant contribution and sent them off to all the places he'd applied to for grants, then he waited for the results. They didn't come at once but when they did Jerome K. Bagley hit the jackpot. The National Endowment for the Arts awarded him a special citation for Writers Living in Dormitories, with an annual stipend for $2,500 renewable for five years. The New York State Council for the Novel offered him a Tenured Fellowship in their programme for bringing artists into homeless shelters. It paid him $8,000 a year, in return for which he was to give intensive workshops in Creative

Writing at selected shelters in the Bronx and Queens. And the City of New York awarded him a grant of $5,438.92 so that he could be videotaped by the Department of Parks and Performance Arts while he read passages from *I Iced Madame Bovary*, which would be simultaneously signed for the deaf.

He didn't, in the end, win the Grand Pushcart Prize of $100,000, but by the time he got the bad news about that, he was already at work on his second novel and he'd been elected to the executive board of the New York office of the American Council for Literacy.

What worked for Jerome Bagley could work for you, too, readers! All that's required is an attitude of confidence, affirmation, and a sheer love of reading. So why don't you do what Jerome did and *earn big bucks by reading books*! If you want to know how to get started just mail a self-addressed stamped envelope to the American Council for Literacy, National Endowment of the Arts, Washington, DC and enclose your non-refundable cheque for $500.

You'll be hearing from us soon.

SLOW NEWS DAY

Kim Newman

John couldn't work out how the black leather straps attached to his Horst Wessel belt. Michael, the Minister for War, slapped away his fumbling fingers and examined the problem, like John's mother tying his school tie for him when he was eleven and couldn't penetrate the mysteries of the knot.

'You've got the holster on the wrong side,' the Minister sighed. 'It must be arse-backwards.'

John felt his face burn with blush as he got untangled and sorted out.

'I hope that Webley isn't loaded,' the Minister said. 'You might shoot yourself in the foot again.'

'I've never shot myself in the foot.'

'That's not what the foreign press say.'

The Minister was comfortable in full combat gear and field marshal's helmet. He gave a heel-clicking salute and a sly I-want-your-job chuckle. Most days, John would be happy to give away his job, but with the foaming example of the Iron Duchess before him, he knew that in United Britain the lot of ex-Prime Minister was even worse than being a serving PM.

Clocking himself in a monitor, John thought he looked silly in uniform, a prat dressed as a tin stormtrooper. It had been worse when he was a lad doing his mandated year in the Mosley Youth, knock-kneed in lederhosen. Some of the Cabinet loved climbing into tight black britches and hanging decorations on their bulging black chests, but John had wanted the D-Day celebrations informal. He had hoped he would be allowed to get away with his nice grey suit. Maybe a colourful anorak if history repeated and the 5th June was unreasonably rainy.

The Duke of Edinburgh went up the line of uniformed ministers, grinning ferociously like an inspection sergeant, noting each mismatched button or smudged jackboot. The Royal Family were really into the spirit of the 50th Anniversary of the D-Day landings. The Duke's brothers strutted around London in their old SS uniforms, mainly let out around the waistlines. The Duke plainly hoped to embrace the Reichskanzler on the beaches, reenacting the famous photograph of Edward hugging Hitler.

The only people out of uniform in the marquee were Security Service men, who favoured long black coats which billowed over their holstered machine pistols, and the press contingent. Drops of rain fell like pennies on the canvas canopy, which made SS people jumpy. John had ordered there be no repetition of the unfortunate incidents of the Royal Funeral, when fire was opened on a dignified row of dissenting parsons.

The President came in, smiling and laughing, surrounded by pretty girls in Otter Guide uniform who held umbrellas over his head like an honour guard. Until last week, the President had not been coming but the troubled administration, needing to cement new European trade deals, opted to remove the human rights issue from the negotiations. John had not met the President before. Americans always wanted to talk straight to the head honcho. Whenever they needed to sort something, the yanks got into a huddle with the Reichskanzler. It had been different under the Duchess. Then United Britain's voice was at least as shrill as Greater Germany's.

John was in two minds about remembering the past, recent or remote. He was half-afraid the Duchess would turn up in her flamboyant uniform, a blue-haired Boadicea

(Boudicca they were now supposed to call her) and make speeches to journalists, dropping acid hints about her successors. The Minister of Internal Security was only partly joking when he suggested it would be fit if the Duchess were taken up on her oft-repeated desire to return to the Iron Values of the Occupation and be allowed to vanish into Night and Fog.

'John,' the President said, sticking out a crushing hillbilly bear paw, 'good to see ya. Have you been ill?'

'Just a touch of hay fever.'

'Better take it easy. That's a killer.'

Cameras clicked as John and the President smiled. Britain had come close to severing relations with the States when the leader of Old England did the rounds of American talk shows, promoting his memoirs. Under broadcasting restrictions, OE representatives were dubbed by actors in British news bulletins. John was mightily ticked off that OE people were invited to the White House but the Reichskanzler had vetoed any formal reprisals. It had taken long enough to get the Americans to the table, and Greater Europe couldn't afford whinging little Britain scuppering the deal. There was a big Old English lobby in the States, though there was a crack-down on the smuggling of funds and weapons to terrorists in Europe.

The President's smile broadened as he passed on from John to the Duke of Edinburgh. They went into a huddle, almost like schoolgirls. John had no idea the two knew each other. He wondered if they were talking about him. If they were, SS microphones would pick it up. He doubted a report would get further than Michael, the Minister of Internal Security, who usually suppressed information that might upset his PM. John supposed he should be grateful someone thought of his feelings.

The President and the Duke went, arm-in-arm, over to that corner of the marquee where the veterans clustered, proud in uniforms they had worn and medals they had earned. They were all very old. Specialist nurses stood behind their wheelchairs. Those who had served in the Occupation were exempt from the Elderly Persons Act, and entitled to places in State Heroes Homes. United Britain war pensioners were the envy of Europe. German veterans were lucky to get their cyanide pills sugared.

'Blind old gits,' the Home Secretary, yet another Michael, said. 'If they were weaselly enough to join the Fifth in '43, they were all out for the main chance. Some of the sneaks probably faked records. Everybody was doing that when I were a lad. If you had the SS grill a couple of codgers, you'd find half of 'em were on the beaches resisting the Invasion of Liberation, not joining in the liberating.'

The Home Secretary was a notorious cynic. As a schoolboy, he had begun his political career by informing on his father, an OE Group Leader.

'They don't like it up 'em,' the Home Secretary quoted.

If anyone thought of the Heroic Fifth Column these days, it was as they were in Dad's Nazis, the popular BBC comedy programme which made figures of fun of the dedicated but buffoonish patriots who assisted the Germans during the Occupation, wiping out the last traces of the Traitor Regime.

The Home Secretary hummed the Dad's Nazis theme tune. 'Who Do You Think You Are Kidding, Mr Churchill?' He'd been drinking steadily in the hospitality suite.

'Watch out, the mikes will pick you up.'

'Don't panic, don't panic,' the Home Secretary continued.

A rustle of excitement whispered through the marquee. The Reichskanzler's helicopter was sighted over the channel. Time to go outside.

It was still not really raining but high wind turned droplets of stray water into liquid bullets that splattered against uniforms. There was a complex protocol as to who was allowed to troop out when. Doddery veterans, under their own steam or aided by nurses, were given precedence.

Crowds thronged outside, on the downs that bordered the cliffs of Dover, and below, on the pebble beach. UB and swastika pennants were held high. A tide of fish 'n' chip papers swarmed around everybody's knees.

Nearby, the almost-completed Channel Tunnel terminal was swathed under thick sheets. The original idea was that the Reichskanzler would arrive for the Anniversary on the first bullet train through the Tunnel. But there had been delays.

There was a huge cheer as the wheelchair brigade appeared, followed by a warm welcome for Royalty and the President, and some modest clapping for the PM and Cabinet. John thought a TV personality with a frosted hairdo got a slightly bigger hand than he did. That was possible: Susan, who did a news show for housewives, was very popular, especially since her well-publicized announcement that she would bear an extra son for Britain.

Cloud was so heavy the Reichskanzler's helicopter could not be seen. It had been sighted only on radar. Everyone looked out over the flat, grey channel, waiting.

It was time to think of those 50 years ago who had also looked out, waiting. In fear of their lives, the Fifth Column had readied for the Invasion of Liberation, clearing the way for the German army to bring Britain into Europe, to exterminate the traitor elements that had usurped the government of the day.

John was expected to make a speech, praising these heroes. His PPS had written something down, but for the life of him, he couldn't remember where. He had checked his pockets but found only the speech he had made last week, attacking indigents who were begging in the streets and clogging up the British autobahns with their caravans. It was notably the first time in 40 years the word 'gypsy' was used in public. John had not expected that to cause the kerfuffle it did.

If he were to be skipped over among all the speeches, no one would notice. The ceremony was bound to run over time. Kenneth, the Minister of Propaganda, had passed on a message from Rupert, the DG of the BBC, that it was vital the ceremony be concluded in time for the telly to switch back to coverage of the snooker finals.

The helicopter surged out of the cloud, a giant insect bristling with impressive weapons. The Reichskanzler insisted on flying a Messerschmitt Assault Ship, as deployed with such devastating effect in the recent Oil War.

The crowd gasped enormously as the chopper swooped overhead. One touch of a button and they would all be dead. If the Luftwaffe of 1943 had had such marvellous machines, the landing which had lasted a bloody thirteen hours would have been executed in seconds, the Invasion of Liberation would have been over within a week.

The helicopter made a landing precisely on the swastika staked out on the grass of the downs. The Reichskanzler bounded out, arms spread, tummy wobbling, fists waving. The crowds cheered. Despite his problems at home, the Reichskanzler was always popular in the UB. The British loved a jolly fat man.

John was conscious of his own meagreness. His sunken chest was not served well by his snug black shirt. In uniform, the Reichskanzler looked like a victorious sumo wrestler.

The Royals swept forward to greet the German leader. This was the image of the anniversary that would be transmitted around the world. The embrace of Edward VIII and Hitler had not been in 1943 but two bloody years later. Edward had returned from exile, not stood on the beaches to greet the liberator who restored him to the throne.

The President and the Reichskanzler bowed formally,

and shook hands. The American was officially 'someone we can do business with,' despite his sabre-rattling about conditions on the Eastern European Homelands.

After the speeches, the Reichskanzler officially said hello to John. It was the least he could do.

'A shame about the Tunnel, *hein*?'

John shrugged.

'There will be an Inquiry into the delays?'

John mumbled. There was, by now, an Inquiry into the Inquiry about the delays.

'Maybe the Tunnel will be open by Atom Day, in nineteen ninety-five.'

That would commemorate the bombing of Leningrad, which ended the War in Europe.

'Or maybe we should wait for the centenary.'

The Reichskanzler laughed, agitating his entire enormous frame. Liking his joke more and more, he slapped his thighs, and repeated it in German to his entourage, then in English again to the President and to the media. The Reichskanzler's laughter spread as he restated the remark, infecting the crowing crowd. John tried to look amused.

The Duchess would have faced the Reichskanzler down, and reminded him it was German insistence on adherence to rigid schedules that had jerry-built the first third of the Tunnel and caused the delays, as leaks were shored up, in the first place.

Three snake-shapes appeared out on the sea, surfacing U-boats. Bubble rafts popped up like corks, bearing stormtroopers. A handful of crack troops were to re-enact the initial landing.

The crowds on the beaches would have cheered but rain suddenly poured down, prompting a swift retreat towards canopies. Most of the VIPs had their own shelter, but John and the Michael-heavy Cabinet were squeezed out.

'We forgot Fatty takes up as much room as our entire

government,' the Home Secretary said, nodding at the dry Reichskanzler. 'Then again, he combines all our offices and jobs. That's one thing about proper non-parliamentary fascism.'

Wetsuited stormtroops in lightweight scuttle helmets paddled up to the pebbles, a little bewildered. They had expected a better reception than cringing holidaymakers.

The Home Secretary had a fit of giggles.

A platoon of goose-pimpled Page Three girls darted out to pose with the Germans, polythene sheets held over their hair. They were led by Mr Spotty, an inflatable children's TV character. Hardy paparazzi followed to record the moment. Quite a few people were laughing in the rain.

'Mustn't grumble,' one of the nurses said to her wheezing charge. 'Lovely weather for ducks.'

The veteran, Iron Cross and Order of St George on his woolly jumper, was trying to say something.

Smudge pots went off on the beach and simulated battlesmoke wafted past soldiers and Page Three girls. Mr Spotty mimed panic.

'If we'd had those in '43,' the Home Secretary said, nodding at the topless lovelies, 'Fritz would never have got past the beaches.'

'If Mr Spotty had been PM instead of Churchill, Hitler would have crumbled,' said John.

'If Mr Spotty were PM now, we'd be a more popular government,' rumbled the Home Secretary.

There was a controversy in Germany. Some surviving veterans of the Invasion of Liberation were unable to attend the commemoration because all the accommodation was taken by politicians and generals and newspeople. The tabloids, who had more than their share of pre-booked hotel rooms, ran stories about little old ladies in the Home Counties cheated of a reunion with the now-shaky Aryan superman they had welcomed with open cami-knickers in 1944.

John privately wondered if things might not have been

better if the Traitor Regime had put up a better resistance and beaten off the Invasion of Liberation. Maybe he wouldn't have all these problems to deal with. He briefly considered resigning and appointing Mr Spotty his successor.

'You're popular now you're just a fathead in a blow-up suit,' he thought, 'let's see how you do in the polls when you're closing down British mines and importing coal from the Ruhr.'

Mr Spotty comically ran away from the stormtroopers, who waved guns at him.

It was time for John's speech. His PPS had kept it safe and gave it to him when he needed it.

'We must remember we are celebrating not a British defeat but a British victory,' he began, 'a victory over that part of ourselves which was inefficient, was heartless, was impure, was ignoble . . .'

Even he didn't listen to the rest of what he said. Mr Spotty was distracting everyone.

The ceremony swept past. As John spoke, news cameras turned away, following the Reichskanzler and the veterans back towards the cliffs, where the stormtroopers were to demonstrate the proper use of scaling ladders.

He finished his speech. There was some helpful applause.

The rest of the Cabinet left him near the water's edge and went to join in the fun. John felt empty and wet. Sodden socks squelched in his jackboots. His glasses were smeared with rain.

The day was so overcast he couldn't see marker buoys 200 yards out, let alone the land beyond the Channel. The U-boats submerged, leaving cigar-shaped fast-vanishing whirlpools.

He snapped the button off his holster, pulled out the Webley and looked out to sea. He hadn't fired a shot since his Patriotic Service. The pistol was heavy and oily.

John pointed his empty gun towards the rest of the world and said 'bang bang.'

THE NET OF BABEL

David Langford

[with necessary apologies to Jorge Luis Borges]

In the end the old Library was disbanded as being an irrational construct, and new devices were supplied in its stead. A golden age ensued, until like all golden ages it became leaden. Now my withered fingers hesitate over the input keys, searching, searching.

Certain commentators had fallen into the easy error of describing the Library as infinite, thus failing to grasp the true enormity of its magnitude. As it has been written, the Library was never infinite but something more dreadful: exhaustive, all-encompassing. Such words as *infinity* are too often scrawled as a magical charm against thought. Those terrible hierarchies of the finite can break the mind as the bland symbol ∞ does not.

The atrocious numbers are readily enough computed. Tradition prescribes a simplified alphabet of 22 letters together with a comma, period and space, making 25 permitted characters. There are 80 letters to the line; 40 lines to the page; 410 pages in each of the uniform volumes. Therefore a book of the Library contains 1,312,000 characters. In order that every possible book be counted – even the one enigmatic tome whose every character is a space – the mathematicians instruct us to raise 25 to the power of 1,312,000.

Numbers are wearisome and, some say, heretical: the books of the Library contain only lower-case letters and the marks of division already alluded to. Nevertheless the above calculation may be readily found in the new Library, spelt out in words ... as may any number of erroneous renderings, or subtly plausible refutations. How different from the old days when men toiled through seemingly endless volumes of gibberish – or perhaps cryptograms, or languages not yet evolved: being exhaustive, the Library necessarily contains the full tale of the future, and of every possible future.

The result of that laborious calculation is a number of fewer than 2,000,000 digits. We are not so constructed as to comprehend such figures. Look, I perform a child's conjuring trick with notation, and now the unwieldy total lies crudely approximated in the palm of my hand: more than ten to the power of ten to the power of six, less than ten to the power of ten to the power of seven. It seems a mere nothing.

Yet, as a scientist once put it to me ... Imagine the old, unthinkable Library. Imagine it physically condensed, with each fat volume somehow inscribed on the surface of a single electron. There are not electrons enough in our universe (that figment of astronomers' whims) to be writing-tablets for so many books. Imagine an inexhaustible supply of electrons, impossibly crowded together like peas in a jar, filling the whole of the space between galaxies, out to the far limits of vision. There is not space enough in our sky to contain sufficient electrons. All the space we know will suffice for a total number of such infinitesimal books which might be written not in millions of digits, not even in thousands, but in little more than one hundred and twenty. A bagatelle, not worthy of our awe.

The Library is both exhaustive and exhausting. But now it has been transfigured. Observe: in place of the old days' interminable weary lattice of hexagonal chambers, I and my colleagues inhabit a single, vast, crimson-walled hexagon. Instead of the long bookshelves there are desks arrayed against each wall, and on each desk that many-keyed device which places all the Library's volumes under my hand.

Now I touch the Library to life. The glowing letters above the key-array begin: *axaxaxas mlo*, the first words of the first page of the first book. We do not know the mystery of the ordering, which sophists say should place at the beginning a volume which is blank or throughout its length reiterates the letter *a*. The devisers of the Library were subtler. One heresiarch declared that the works were ordered by the receding digits of some transcendental number like *pi*, paying out forever like a magician's chain of coloured scarves. Others hoped to find the books arranged by meaning or truth . . . but, on the evidence of that minute part of the Library we have studied, this is not so. Chaos or seeming chaos reigns throughout the whole vast informational sea; the tiny islands of meaning we have found are scattered like primes in the ocean of numbers, according to no visible plan.

The golden or leaden key that unlocks the Library is the inbuilt search facility. One prepares a text of any length, sets the searching into motion, and the Library's own devices will swiftly trawl that sea of data. A glad chime sounds when the sought words are found. Since it is an article of faith that the Library truly is exhaustive, all these text searches should necessarily succeed no matter what is searched for . . . as indeed they do. Every find is a sacrament and a vindication.

Like so many I have commanded a search for a volume of 1,312,000 successive repetitions of the letter a, and likewise of all the other letters. Each of these monotonous works occurs once in the Library. Their numerical positions hint at no pattern . . .

This same act of data-searching may be performed with a darker purpose, a blasphemous hope that the chosen word or phrase or sentence or treatise will not be located.

Cultists have striven to construct utterances so twisted and infamous as to be impossible to the holy Library: in vain. Every child is tempted to scan for some such phrase as 'This sentence is not contained in the Library,' and to giggle when the glowing letters seem to assert it. The Library, however, does not assert; nor does it deny. It simply is.

Yet it is not, as a contending sect would have it, a mere mirror that reflects whatever we offer up to it. Each text sequence that we locate in the Library is a tiny pinpoint of order engulfed in that chaos of raging alphabets. A moment's thought indicates that my name, your name, any name, must be present an enormous number of times in as many contexts. Each successive search discovers the name in a new setting of surrounding text ... almost always nonsense, but not – we know – always so. The millionth or the billionth such context may thrill with numinous revelation.

A certain paragraph from Pierre Menard's recension of *Don Quixote* is a famous example. On only its fourteen hundred and twelfth occurrence in the Library it is immediately followed by the words *not to be*. The placing of this fragment from Shakespeare's best-known soliloquy hinted at an obscure truth. Other juxtapositions of Menard, Cervantes and Shakespeare were at once sought for and (of course) triumphantly found. The ensuing school of thought flourished for a generation until lost in schisms.

From time to time it is still whispered that the Library may be incomplete, owing to its shackling to a historical tradition of so many letters on a page, so many pages in a volume. Might greater insights require a greater Library whose notional volumes are twice, three times, ten times as long? This argument is inept. A work occupying even a hundred thousand volumes can be shown to be present in the Library, since each separate volume must be present. It is merely necessary to locate the sections and read them in the proper order . . . a task scarcely more arduous than the finding of any other undiscovered truth or falsehood in the Library's intangible immensity.

(Less idle is the converse proposal that great truths may exist within a small compass, and that a miniature Library might be constructed which merely contained within itself all possible *pages*, or even all possible *lines* of 80 characters. The number of entries in an exhaustive list of lines would, it seems, be relatively tolerable despite still challenging the maximum theoretical storage capacity of our universe. Mystics still debate the accidental or abominable fact that this number has 111 digits.)

Our priesthood avers that the supreme reward of creativity is known when a 'new' writing is invested with significance by the inevitable discovery of its pre-existing presence in the Library. The vindication lies in the finding, not in mere conjecture. Others have not hesitated to deny this dogma.

Thus it may be seen what advantages we enjoy over the past librarians whose entire lives might be spent in traversing the hexagonal cells of their conjectural, physical Library, without ever encountering a book that held a single intelligible sentence. As my own long span of Library-searching ticks to its close, I think again and again of those times when so little could be found. Now every volume lies instantly within our grasp, and we possess a far greater understanding of our identical impotence. I would that I lived in the old days.

A RING OF GREEN FIRE

Sean McMullen

'As I was travelling through Westbury forest, I met with a man with a ring of green fire around his penis,' Avenzoar's visitor said casually.

The poet-physician looked up at his friend and stroked his beard, then gazed wistfully across to the partially built minaret of Caliph al-Mansur's huge mosque.

'Such a wonder,' sighed Avenzoar, then turned to his visitor and raised an eyebrow. 'I suppose you did not bring him here for this poor physician and poet turned bureaucrat to examine?'

His friend glanced away, and seemed troubled. 'Alas, it was not possible.'

'Such a pity. It may be an honour to be entrusted with the completion of this great mosque of Ishbiliyah, but I miss the wider world. Is England really such a cold, rain-swept place?'

'When I was there, yes.'

'What of your patient? Was he a traveller from even more exotic regions?'

'Not at all, yet the story of his curse is fascinating.'

Avenzoar clapped his hands. Honey pastries and ripe fruit were brought in by a servant and placed before them.

'My friend, show kindness to a captive of the Caliph's goodwill and tell me this magical story.'

'There was no magic, Avenzoar, nor was the curse any more than an exotic disease. Still, the story will afford you an hour's wonder.'

*   *   *

How to begin? Affliction with the green fire was growing common in the midlands of England in the Christian year of 1188. The man in Westbury forest was a tinker, I saw that from his pack. He approached a tollbridge where I was resting in the dim light of late evening, and he drew his cloak tightly about himself as he came near.

His name was Watkin, and he was a small, thin but very energetic man, a little over 30 years of age. I introduced myself as a physician, and offered him the protection of my five men-at-arms while we camped for the night. He was glad to accept, as the forest was full of outlaws and we had also rigged a shelter against the rain. As we ate the night's meal I raised the subject of illness with him.

'You have an affliction. I can tell that,' I said. He made no reply, yet his face was sad. He shaved slivers of cheese from a rind with his knife but did not eat them.

'Your affliction is distressing, but without pain,' I continued. 'I have learned to read the signs of distress in sick people.'

He tossed the rind into the fire and wiped his knife on a crust. 'You have never seen the like of my complaint,' he said miserably. 'Nobody can help me. I went to the physicians of the Church and they said that I was possessed by a devil. They wanted to torture me until it was driven out, but I'd have none of that. I broke free and ran. I run very fast.'

'Wise of you, but there are other ways.'

'I'm afeared of witchcraft too.'

'I am no sorcerer. I am a physician who has studied under some of the greatest Moorish and Jewish masters of the day, including Maimonides himself.'

'Who is Maimonides?'

'Ah, a great Jewish teacher and man of medicine. He is court physician to the great Saladin.'

'Saladin! So . . . you have Moorish training.'

'Why yes. I went to the Holy Land with the Crusade of 1147. I was badly wounded, then captured. The enemy physicians tended me so well that I resolved to learn their ways.'

'You place no faith in torture to rid a man of demons?'

'Oh no, I have been trained in far more civilized means.'

'Then I'll show you –'

'No! Wait, and let me examine you first. I wager that I can tell your affliction in moments.'

I felt the glands beneath his jaw, looked into his eyes in the firelight and sniffed his breath. He was in good health, I could see that at once, yet I had to make a show of skill to gain his trust. He did not realize that I have acute vision at a distance, and had noticed a faint green glow through the cloth of his trews before he had wrapped himself in his cloak.

'You have a circlet of green fire about your penis,' I announced calmly. 'It has been slowly moving higher, and in its wake your skin has lost all feeling.'

He gasped, then looked down to see if his glow was showing, which it was not. 'Truly a man of great medical arts,' he said in awe. 'What – what are your fees? I'm but a poor tinker, yet I'd give anything to be rid of the fire and numbness.'

I laughed disarmingly. 'I have yet to meet a rich tinker, but do not worry. Your earnings for the week past will suffice. Open your robes, lower your trews, let me see your affliction.'

His ring was brighter than any others that I had seen, and had moved so far up the shaft that it was almost at the base and glowed through his pubic hair. My companions looked up from their meal in surprise.

'Can you break this spell?' Watkin babbled eagerly. 'Have you seen the like before?'

'Ah yes, and I have had great success where all others have failed.'

He sighed with relief. 'So, you have secret incantations and philtres, perhaps?'

'I have those, but they are for later. The real mode of breaking a spell is to learn the circumstances of its casting in the fullest detail possible. An honest, truthful account of the casting weakens the grip of the devil, who is behind all curses and spells. One lie, one slight deviation from the truth, however, and his grip is strengthened. How did you acquire your ring, Watkin?'

'It ... appeared a month ago, after I bedded my wife, and each time that I enjoy her it moves a little higher –'

'Stop, stop,' I laughed. 'Three lies within one breath! Watkin, you will have to do better than that. The ring of green fire begins at the tip of one's member and moves higher only when you bed a woman for the first time. It also becomes brighter as time passes. In women the glow is all internal, yet there is also numbness and other such effects that increase with time and new lovers. I would say that you acquired it around May last year, and since then you have mounted eight dozen women. As to being married, no, not you. Am I wrong?'

He slowly shook his head and stared at his boots. 'To my shame, no.'

'Then tell the truth, however reproachful your conduct has been.'

'It would burn the ears of a good Christian.'

'But Watkin, I am not a Christian.' He gaped at me. 'When I was in the Holy Land I adopted more than the medical scholarship of Islam. Now tell me of how you were first snared by the ring, and tell the truth.'

'It was in a village called Delmy, to the south, near the coast. I arrived there early one afternoon, during the May festival. The villagers were celebrating the victory of summer over winter with feasting. May carols and dancing. Strangers were welcome, especially an honest tinker like myself.

'For a time I sampled the tartlets, manchets, fried figs and ales, then I turned my thoughts to a companion for a little frolic. I'd been travelling for a long time, I was lonely, it was spring –'

'I am not too old to know the needs and urgings of the flesh, Watkin. Go on.'

'It seemed easy pickings. Many young folk of the village were dancing and fondling most intimately, raising my hopes of a quick and easy conquest. Alas, no girl would spare me the deeper smile, indeed there seemed no girls unpaired at all. After so long tramping the road I was lonely, and with so many pairs of lovers cavorting before me I was quite beside myself to be part of it.

'At last I saw one girl who was unpaired, a big-boned, hairy-armed wench with a face that only a beard could have improved. She was alone, tending the tables, and she smiled broadly whenever I came near. At first it seemed worse to mount her than no wench at all, yet the fire of spring burned within me. I made up my mind, approached her, whispered words of compliment, then with unseemly haste did I shepherd her away from the fair – more in shame of being seen with her than in shame of the act to come. I chose a place among bushes behind a broad oak. I – I could not bear to look upon her, I just bent her over a rack of poles and flung her skirts up.'

He paused for a long drink from the crock. 'And you did the deed with her?' I prompted.

'Ah yes, master physician, and she was a virgin, wouldn't you know it? Hah, it was wearisome work, yet I am a diligent tradesman. To the beat of the distant village band, I placed my rivet and began tapping. At last I was spent. I eased back as she stood panting, then I slipped away as if I had been a wood sprite vanishing into air – lest she have thoughts about wedding me. I skirted the village, took up my pack and trotted away briskly.

'By evening I was five leagues gone and some way contented. My hammer had been well worked, in fact he even felt a little numb, so hard had I clinked the pan – or so I thought. Imagine my alarm when I unlaced to piss and saw a ring of cold, faint green fire encircling his head.'

'The girl was a virgin, you say?'

'Indeed, no doubt of it, I have initiated many. Alas, she passed this cold glow to me, and soon I noticed that as I worked the pots of goodwives and maids on my travels, the ring would move a little further up each time. Where it had been the feeling that is lust's reward was no more.'

'But surely the women you have bedded since then noticed your green glow?'

'Ah no Master, you are obviously not a tradesman. We visit houses and cottages during the day, when the menfolk are in the fields and their women are at home, alone. Most times will there be a sly look, or even a saucy suggestion, then we will be coupled on the hearthrug in the light of day. Since the ring was slipped upon me, I have shared the glow to, oh, ninety-five women, mostly lowborn, though some were of no mean rank.' He nudged me, winking suavely. 'Master, if foolish knights would do no better than fight and drink, well someone must plant the seeds of future knights.'

'One last question, Watkin. Could you write down the names and villages of all the women that you have bedded since the stout maid gave you the green fire?'

'Alas, Master, I cannot write, yet I could recite the names of all! When I lie alone at night I like to recall each wench that I have ever mounted and set a name against a star, but of late the number of stars has grown insufficient. Since the stout virgin of Delmy there have been . . . now let me think . . . one hundred and five, yes. Ah, but it is becoming difficult now, as so much of my hammer has no feeling.'

Without any warning I seized his wrist and twisted his arm hard behind his back. He cried out in surprise and pain as I shouted: 'A firebrand! A firebrand! Quickly!'

My men-at-arms jumped to their feet at once but Watkin tumbled in mid-air, twisted his arm free of my grip and darted for the woods with the speed of a startled hind. Worse luck for him, the sentry had been alert for just such a flight. His hand-axe went spinning flat after him, tangled his legs and sent him sprawling in the mud with a cry of pain. We soon had him in hand and dragged him back to the fire.

'A good throw, Sir Phillip,' I said as they held him down and I tended the gashes and cuts in Watkin's legs. 'The great tendon is severed in his right leg, he will never again run from cuckolded husbands with such speed.'

Watkin's moaning suddenly died away as he realized that something else was not as it seemed. Beneath their shabby robes my men-at-arms were well-dressed warriors with fine weapons. They stood before us, glaring, their eyes sparkling with fury in the firelight.

'What – who are you?' the tinker stammered.

One of the men began to unlace, and the others followed his example. A moment later the light of five rings of green fire glowed steadily from their loins.

'Lied . . . you lied to me!' gasped Watkin.

'Lied, Watkin? I am indeed a physician and breaker of curses, and my faith is the Way of Islam.'

'Then who are these men?'

'You may call this man Sir Robert,' I said as he brought a coil of rope to tie the tinker's hands. 'This fine, burly warrior is Sir Peter, and Sir Phillip was the sentry who brought you down. Sir Charles is the blonde man, and Sir Douglas has the black beard and is scowling as if he would cheerfully cut your heart out. You may call me William.'

'Those are not your real names,' he said fearfully.

'Those names will suffice for you, false or not. Speaking for myself, I really am an Englishman, and although I do have an Islamic name now, I was christened William when

I was born. I have returned to England at the request of Sir Peter here.'

'A Christian physician could well have had us denounced or burned for demonic possession,' Sir Peter explained. 'Some folk afflicted by the green fire have already suffered such a fate. This infidel, who is also my friend, can be trusted not to do that. On your feet now!'

The nobles tied him spreadeagled in the rain between two trees. 'False physician, you betrayed me!' wailed Watkin.

'And how many women did you betray by passing the green fire on to them?' I asked.

'No, no, I have ceased to spread the green fire,' he cried. 'Look in my pack.'

'You certainly have,' I agreed as I rummaged through his goods. 'Just look at these knick-knacks. All manner of little presents as might please a wench and entice her into bed. Aromatic oils and scents, and, and . . . less savoury items.'

There it was, in his pack, the cursed device. I sat back, and examined the sheath while my companions cheerily tormented Watkin with what was to come. With such a plague as the green fire to be caught from casual dalliance it was only a matter of time before these sheaths of sheepgut became very popular. Still, that was not my concern. Watkin was the man I had been seeking, the Alpha firebrand, the butterfly king. The plague of green fire was about to end and he would play a role.

I stood up. Sir Douglas had just proposed a crude surgical operation to rid Watkin of his green fire and the others were roaring their approval. 'Stop! Stop!' I shouted, rushing forward to seize Sir Peter's arm. 'My good lords, this one is not to be killed.'

'But he's the one who began it all,' exclaimed Sir Peter, so hot with anger that the rain steamed from his face.

'Precisely. Other firebrands may be killed for spreading

the green glow, but this one might well be used for a cure.'

Their hard and vengeful glares were at once softened by amazement and hope. Even revenge took second place to removing the glowing green shackle from their manhood.

Watkin was bound, gagged and bagged, then taken to Sir Peter's castle some 70 miles away. The journey was done in a single stretch, with no sleep, and even meals were had in the saddle. It rained for most of the way. The castle was no great wonder: it was a mean, low fortification of rammed earth, logs and stone blocks from ancient Roman ruins. The thatch and log roofs leaked, and it rained most of the time that I was there.

Although surly at first Watkin became wonderfully cooperative after a single touch of the torturer's red-hot iron. We wrote down the details of his 105 seductions, and in the weeks that followed established that only 62 of the infected women had survived beatings by their husbands and attempts at exorcism by religious healers. Ten had escaped ensnarement by the green ring since he had begun to use his sheepgut armour.

In the months past we had travelled far and wide killing firebrands who had spread the green fire, and thanks to the fire their trails were easy to follow. With Watkin safely in chains we now visited Delmy, the village from where he had borne the green fire to torment the world. The stout virgin that Watkin had seduced was named Gerelde, but while she was indeed not comely, she was skilled with herbal cures and was a surpassing good cook.

Her mother was buried nearby. The woman had once lived alone in a forest some way up the coast, and was reputed to have been a witch. Cornish brigands had raided the area and seized her, and their leader had ravished her until she was some months swelling with his child. He had then taken her out to sea and cast her overboard to drown, yet she lived to struggle ashore and be found by the villagers of Delmy. The village midwife said that she had treated herself with a glowing green paste to ease the pain of the birth. It was a difficult delivery, as Gerelde was a very big baby for such a small mother as she was. The witch had died of the stresses of birth and cursing her ravisher.

Sir Peter assembled a squad of men while I went with Sir Phillip to locate the witch's house, a ransacked shell by now. We exhumed the witch's bones and reburied them in the overgrown garden of her old home. In the meantime Sir Peter had attacked and annihilated the brigand stronghold, avenging the witch after eighteen years. Every one of his fighting men had the ring of green fire and was frantic for revenge against anyone connected with it.

On the evening that we returned to Sir Peter's castle, I spoke with him in his dining hall. Rain dripped from the roof beams as we sat before the fire.

'That was clever work, finding the first firebrand of the green ring,' he said to me. 'Why didn't you tell us that we were on such a quest?'

'If I had told that I wanted a man of such-and-such a description you would have tortured dozens into confessing to be him. Better to take you on a vendetta against all firebrands and do the questioning myself.'

'Well then, what good came of it? We avenged the witch, yet her magical ring still glows on my gronnick, and the ring on Watkin the Tinker is still bright enough to light his way on a moonless night. What sort of a sorcerer are you –'

'I am a physician, not a sorcerer. Magic does not exist, only illness in all its guises. The full cure for the ring of green fire is close. I have made progress.'

'What kind of progress?'

'I returned the witch's bones to her garden and reburied them there. A month has passed since then, so the aura from her bones will have permeated the roots of her herbs and be taken up into the leaves. I shall soon return to her grave and harvest some leaves to grind into a paste.'

'Will that be enough? Leaves?'

'There is more, Sir Peter, much more. Even though she is dead she is trying to teach us something of the new notion of chivalry – it's new to you English at least, us Saracenic scholars have taught it for years.'

'That's why we employed you, dammit!'

'And your faith in me is not misplaced. I can see some kind of symbolism of pain being avenged while its resulting sorrow still lives on. The witch wanted you to do more than just avenge her.'

'Well what did she damn well want?' shouted Sir Peter, pounding the table so hard with his goblet that a gemstone fell out of the silver filigree.

'Patience, patience, I dare not tell you everything yet.'

Sir Peter had a mistress as well as his wife, and it was this woman that Watkin had bedded one afternoon in the summer passed. The noble had argued with her a little earlier, and she felt lonely and neglected. Watkin had arrived, and cleverly spoke in a cultivated voice as if by accident. Then he hinted that he was himself a noble on some secret mission, and so he won her trust and bedded her. Understandably, Sir Peter was all for impaling Watkin on a stake at the castle gate until the crows pecked his bones clean, but I restrained him.

'Why do you have such sympathy for the little wretch?' asked Sir Phillip the next morning as we squelched our way through the muddy grounds of the castle, holding sodden cloaks up against the rain. We were on our way to visit the tinker.

'Sympathy? I have no sympathy for Watkin, but I do have a use for him.'

'The talk is that you are sorry for him.'

'Sorry? Me? Not likely. I once suffered because of his

kind. I was a young merchant's scribe in love with my master's daughter. Although she cared for me, our courtship was slow. I did not have skill with the words and gestures of seduction. My master took her on a journey to Normandy, he had trade business there. She met one such as Watkin, but this youth was a noble. He charmed her with talk as sweet as a nightingale's song, and settled upon her as softly as a butterfly. When she returned to England she grew round with child, and was desolate with remorse. I petitioned to marry her and the merchant consented, yet even then I was aflame with rage.

'I travelled to Normandy and sought out her seducer. Although a mere scribe I was skilled in the use of shortswords. I killed a guard and wounded several more, but the butterfly nobleman escaped and I was wounded. I became a fugitive and outlaw. I could never return to my young wife. She gave birth some months later, then flung herself from a cliff and was drowned in the sea.'

'When did all this take place?'

'Your Christian year of 1150.'

'But that was three years after the Crusade of 1147.'

'Certainly. With a history like mine, would you let the truth be known? I began working aboard merchant ships, they were always in need of people who could write. After five years I had earned enough silver and learned sufficient Arabic to settle in the Zangid Sultanate and study medicine. I had an impressive wound, so I made up that tale of being on the crusade. Now you know my background, Sir Phillip. Please preserve my secret, yet reassure your folk about my intentions. A butterfly killed my sweetheart, and Watkin is another such butterfly.'

'But why do you stay Sir Peter's hand?'

'As I said, Watkin has his uses. Although a mere tinker he is magnificent, the ultimate seducer. He can affect the voices and manners of all types of people, from nobles to ploughmen. His trews have a double strap, so that he can

lower them to his knees for a dalliance, yet they stay high
enough for him to run unencumbered from an outraged
husband. He is a master of escape and could run like the
wind until your axe severed his hamstring. He cleans his
teeth with soft bark, he washes, and he scents himself with
aromatic oils. His trade is tinking, yet even that takes him
roving to meet an endless bevy of women.'

We had reached the dungeon, a squat blockhouse of
stone with a log roof and narrow slits for windows. I made
to enter, but Sir Phillip barred my way. 'I'm with Sir Peter.
I'm for killing the little rat,' he declared. 'He –'

'He seduced a maid on intimate terms with your seneschal, and your seneschal then passed the fire on to his
wife – who was already your secret lover. If the green fire
has done anything, it has traced out a fine trail of humpery
bumpery at all stations of society.'

'So what are you saying? Are we no better than Watkin?'

'I am saying that you can learn from Watkin. In spite
of being a short, scrawny, low-born tinker, he charms
greatly.'

'He preys upon the most vulnerable of women.'

'True, but were you English noblemen to clean your
teeth, change your clothing at least weekly and take the
care to give ladies little compliments instead of kicks, curses
and belches, why the likes of Watkin would have no market
for their charms. He is poor, but it costs him nothing to
speak charmingly and wash. If you did the same, you would
still be rich and powerful as well. Who would then choose
Watkin over you? A hot iron can wound Watkin's type,
but with good manners and clean fingernails you can hurt
them a lot more. You English are adopting our Saracenic
cooking, mathematics and music. Why not our chivalry as
well?'

Sir Phillip glared at me from under his cloak, but he was
obviously thinking.

'There is a lot of merit in what you say . . . but it's hard to think chivalrous thoughts with a ring of green fire about my gronnick! What can I do about that?'

'The tinker took a curse upon himself when he bundled into the witch's daughter. He then dispersed that curse to nearly every woman he seduced in his travels, and hence to all their lovers. That has formed quite an avenging army.'

'And we did avenge her!'

'Yes, but there is more to it than that, so the glow remains. The green fire is a tool to force us to do certain tasks, and even teach us about the ways of men and women.'

We entered the dungeon, where the tinker was practicing walking with a crutch and in good spirits.

'Have you caught the Delmy witch?' he asked.

'We found her grave and exhumed it. She is naught but bones after these eighteen years.'

'Eighteen years? Bones? She was as well fleshed as a prize sow when I mounted her the May before last.'

'That was her daughter. The witch herself died in childbirth, but her daughter unknowingly carried a curse. You turned that curse loose upon the world. Gerelde was raised by a peasant family, and has come to be a fine cook. I tasted her food, it was fine fare for a peasant table. She wants for naught but a husband. She's plain of face and is built as solidly as Sir Peter, yet for all that she is a kindly girl.'

Watkin sneered. 'Why are you telling me about her? I'd never touch her again, she's as ugly as a goat's backside.'

'She was quite taken by you, Watkin, and she is very concerned that you are imprisoned here. Still, you are more fortunate than the brigand who raped her mother. Sir Peter caught him, did you know? He was a great slab of a man, massive rather than fat, full of life and defiance, even eighteen years after the deed that caused all this. He was confident that we would not kill him because he knew where sundry hoards of gold and silver loot lay buried. Sir

Peter had him taken to the graveside of his victim, and there his gronnick was sliced from between his legs and rammed down his windpipe so that he choked on it and died most horribly. Those of his men as were watching quickly babbled the location of hoards of coin, plate and jewellery, yet none heeded them. Sir Peter had to kill him with the same weapon that killed Gerelde's mother.'

Watkin was deathly pale by now, and had slumped against the wall. 'Mother of God, but why?'

'He was a link in the chain that ignited the green fire. You are another link.'

'Me? But, but –'

'You bedded Sir Peter's mistress. That alone should have you in fear for your life, but you also passed the fire to her.'

The tinker cowered, but said no more. Sir Phillip lurked in the shadows, smirking at his discomfort.

'I need tears of pity that have been wept for you and no other. In all the world, Watkin, would anyone weep for you?'

'Many regard me as comely.'

'Someone must *weep* for you, Watkin. Your flesh is about to hiss with the touch of the red iron.'

'No! As God is merciful, no! Take my pack, sell me into slavery! I'll do anything –'

'For the final ingredient to quench the ring of green fire you *will* be able to choose between death and a less daunting fate, but for now you will be tortured. I require that it be done, Watkin, and believe me that there are thousands of men and women who would fight to the death for the pleasure of holding the glowing iron to you. You have often been bold, now you must learn to be brave.'

Once we were well away from the dungeon and Watkin's hysterical pleading Sir Phillip took me by the arm.

'That brigand was killed in battle by one of Sir Peter's archers. It was a shaft through his skull, he died at once.'

'True.'

'Then what was that story about choking him on his own gronnick?'

'Watkin has the attention span of a butterfly. I meant to . . . focus his mind.'

'To what end?'

'That is between myself and Allah. Rest assured, however, that Watkin will be tortured.'

'And you will savour his screams with the rest of us?'

'Oh no, I shall be hard at work, preparing certain ingredients to quench the ring of green fire.'

'Lord physician, I don't follow.'

'You will never follow, Sir Phillip, but your ring of green fire shall be quenched, rely on my word for that.'

By the time I had left Sir Peter's castle for Delmy, Watkin had faced the first of the silent, hooded men who were to torment him. Thousands gathered outside the castle to hear his screams, but these did not last. After he was blinded, the tendons at the source of his voice were cut. This produced such a riot outside that all Watkin's subsequent tortures had to be on public display. As I rode off for Delmy hot irons were being applied to the soles of his feet by the second torturer, Sir Douglas, while Sir Phillip held up a cloak to keep the rain from cooling the red-hot metal.

I returned after three days, bringing Gerelde with me. Watkin was, of course, the only lover she had ever known, so he was a lot more special to her than the other way about. She was blind to his disfigurements, and she made heartfelt pleas for her feckless tinker. It was an impressive sight, for even on her knees she was taller than Sir Peter. I stood by and collected her tears on a small cloth. At a nod from me Sir Peter relented – on the condition that Watkin marry her, and that he never leave the village of Delmy under pain of death by torture. Watkin could only nod his head by way of agreement. Now Gerelde wept tears of joy, and I wiped these from her face as well.

A great marriage feast was held, and a good many folk with the ring of green fire were brought in to participate. Before Sir Peter's eyes I ground the cloth with its tears into a paste, then added cuttings of herbs taken from the witch's garden. The food at the feast was wonderful village fare, and to this I added my mixture. All ate heartily, and by evening the green fire was gone from every afflicted man and woman at the feast. There were, well, unseemly celebrations in spite of the rain, but that was only to be expected. The following day I called upon Sir Peter.

'Now that the curse is broken, a simple remedy can be used to quench the green fire in all others who still have it,' I told him. 'I have trained several clerks and midwives in its preparation already, and they will train more. Soon the green fire will be no more, so my work here is done.'

Sir Peter embraced me so strongly that I heard the joints of my spine pop. I was the physician who had returned the feeling to his penis, and he was brimming with gratitude.

'You must have a reward, honours, you have done more good for this land than words can say.'

'There is my agreed fee, of course.'

'That? A mere trifle! Here's twice your fee.' He tossed me a bag of gold. 'Now, my Lord physician, if you could but renounce the faith of Islam you could also be given great rank.'

'My faith is Islam, please respect that, and rank does not interest me. I am a physician, so although I find it an honour to treat caliphs and kings, I do not aspire to their thrones.'

'Then treat a king you will! Our King Henry lies sick at Chinon, a town in his French provinces. I'm his trusted adviser, I'll recommend you to him, I'll recommend you in the very highest words of praise.'

'I would be honoured to treat your king, Sir Peter.'

* * *

Avenzoar gazed at the fountain in the centre of the courtyard for some moments before turning back to his guest.
The constant rain, the glowing green fire, all the strange
horrors of his visitor's tale slowly retreated before the
warm Spanish sunshine.

'So the girl's tears broke the curse,' he said.

'No. My "other remedy" would have worked by
itself.'

'Then you could have stopped the green fire months
earlier. Why the charade?'

The visitor paused to select a ripe fig, frowning as if
troubled. 'I was Watkin's first torturer.' Avenzoar gasped
with surprise. 'Yes, I blinded him to Gerelde's face and I
silenced his voice that he might never abuse her.'

'I see. You made him a match for her and no other.'

'I did more than that. The ring of green fire was a type
of purgative, it flushed out those men with great skill in
coldly manoeuvring women into bed. Watkin was not the
only firebrand, we discovered nearly two dozen men, and
a few women too, who had hundreds of seductions behind
them. They are all dead now, save for Watkin. Many other
diseases are spread by the loveless lust of Watkin's kind.
We culled in the interests of good health.'

Avenzoar considered this. 'True, too much of any skill
can be dangerous. Perhaps the witch did some good after
all.'

'The witch was no witch, and there was no curse. She
was my dead wife's daughter, sired by a butterfly and born
just before her mother cast herself into the ocean. Gerelde
was my step-granddaughter, but even though she and her
mother were no flesh and blood of mine, I loved them as
my own. I provided for them and visited them every few
years.'

'Ah yes, now it all makes sense. The green fire was a
medicine to deaden the pain of childbirth. Your step-
daughter died before she could give the antidote to herself

and her baby. The fire escaped when Watkin mounted Gerelde.'

The visitor nodded. Avenzoar stood up slowly and looked across to the delicate tracery and interlaced arches of the partly built minaret. He glanced at a nearby sundial.

'It is time for my daily inspection of the minaret,' he said with his back to his guest, then he turned. 'But first I must reproach you for mutilating in the name of medicine.'

The guest remained calm, as if expecting the outburst, yet he did not meet Avenzoar's eyes. 'No, not in the name of medicine. I disfigured Watkin to have my step-granddaughter married and happy. She has a lame, blind, mute tinker who is nevertheless a prince of seducers, and she has him all to herself. He will be grateful for all that she does for him until the day he dies. Yes, it was evil of me, but perhaps good has come of it. Watkin's wings have been clipped, but at least he has his life.'

Avenzoar sat down and fanned himself. 'But what of my original question? You have not yet explained why you took so long to release your cure for the green fire? Surely it was not just to mark and slay the promiscuous?'

'You are right, Avenzoar, as usual. I withheld the cure to increase its worth. That increased my reward, in turn.'

'Reward? To treat King Henry? It must have been of little comfort to you. I learned recently that he died barely a fortnight after midsummer.'

'Precisely,' the visitor agreed solemnly, and Avenzoar felt a sudden chill in spite of the bright sunshine. 'As a teenage prince in Normandy he seduced my sweetheart. I spent a lifetime hating that royal butterfly, yet it was the accidental spread of the green fire that gave me a chance to get past his guards. Gerelde is his granddaughter, yes, and Watkin is unknowingly married to a princess.'

He reached into his robes and took out a folded parchment, which he placed on the tray beside the pastries. 'This details a cure for the mould that causes the ring of green

472

fire,' he said as he stood up. Avenzoar unfolded the parchment and read it slowly. Finally he nodded, and looked up at his guest in silence. 'Well, are you not going to censure me for killing a king?'

'To what end?' Avenzoar replied wearily. 'You always have the best of reasons for your behaviour.'

'Once more you are wrong,' replied the visitor, but this time without his mask of smug composure. He sat down heavily, tears running into his beard.

Avenzoar sat forward. 'What is wrong, what did I say?'

'I killed under the guise of healing,' he sobbed, suddenly looking much older. 'I was so intent on striking at King Henry that I destroyed my integrity as a physician to do it. Avenzoar, I spent four decades rebuilding my life after what he did. I became one of the greatest physicians in all Islam . . . then I visited him as a physician and defiled my healing hands to murder him. I was so obsessed by the chase that I ignored the outcome.'

He stood slowly and shuffled across to the fountain with Avenzoar following. The poet put a hand on his shoulder as he washed his face. 'Accepting that you have done evil is a step toward atoning for it, my friend. Stay here for a while, rest and talk with Avenzoar, your friend and fellow physician.'

'No, no. I am sincere in my remorse. You always say that about me, that I am too sincere for my own good. Have you not noticed that since I arrived I have never been able to meet your eyes for more than a moment? Whenever I meet a fellow physician I am shamed to remember that I have murdered, and I have to hang my head. Ah, but soon I shall go to where I shall meet no other physicians, to where I can shout the truth of how I murdered King Henry to the empty deserts of Africa. First I shall sign my worldly goods to you, then I shall travel along the salt road to the barren granite mountains of Aghadez and the marshy shores of Lake Tchad.'

'You cannot be serious. The loss of your skills would be a crime in itself.'

'My skills will not be lost to the sick in the great desert of Africa. Meantime, use my fortune to train needy students and to foster the arts of healing in whatever way you will – and should any woman come to you complaining of numbness within, or any man disrobe to reveal a ring of green fire about his penis, well, you now have the cure.'

'But this is terrible. Your very words show you to be of good heart. Please stay.'

Now the visitor held him by both arms and looked fleetingly into his eyes. 'If I agreed to stay, you would probably despise me in the depths of your heart. Come now, let us find a scribe. I have much wealth to make over to you.'

Later that afternoon, when his guest had departed, Avenzoar toured the partly completed minaret with Ali al-Ghumari, his architect. As the sun's disc shimmered near the horizon they gazed out across the capital of al-Andalus.

'It is safe for now,' said Avenzoar, 'but one day a green fire may come to blight this fair city.'

'Is it a weapon?' asked the architect with mild interest. 'Is it like Greek fire?'

'It is English fire,' replied Avenzoar.

'Hah! It must be fierce indeed to burn in spite of their rain,' the architect laughed. 'What is its fuel?'

Avenzoar fingered the scrap of folded parchment for reassurance. 'Neglect and hatred,' he said softly.

The architect pondered this for a moment, running his hand along the newly laid brickwork. 'A cheap and plentiful fuel,' he replied at last, and Avenzoar nodded.

HUMAN WASTE

Mary Gentle

My child is a pet substitute.

I designed it to be male, to get my own back on men in general. I see nothing wrong in this. My therapist advised me to get rid of my aggression.

The sun is slanting through the window, striping the polished floorboards. The room smells of beeswax. Little Thomas is pulling at my hip with chocolate-covered hands. He stinks of ammonia. I haven't changed him for days.

'Mummy? Mummy? Mummy? Mummy?'

He hits the same pitch every time. Exactly the same questioning whine. I didn't have to alter the basic design specification for this, it seems to come to all of them with their DNA.

'*Mummy? Mummy? . . .*'

The creases of my black denim jeans at my hip are marked with melted chocolate. I hate that. I hate it so much.

'Muh –'

As I have done so many times before, but with no less satisfaction, I lift Thomas by his little romper-suit collar, pivot in the swivel chair, draw my foot back, and kick.

It is satisfyingly solid, like kicking a warm sandbag. Even painful, given how solid a two-year-old is. Nothing else, however, gives the right trajectory, the right *thump*! on landing.

'Whaaaaaaaaaa –'

The small body impacts with the floor on the far side of the room. I can see at a glance that he has broken his neck, and that the downy hair on his skull is matted with blood where he has fractured the fragile bone plates. I lean my elbow on the desk and watch.

Nanoscopic structures scurry across the body of my baby.

They ooze from his pores, micro-machines crafted so small that their gears are atom-sized, their manipulators capable of juggling basic matter. Nature gave us the prototype of such machines a milliard ago: the organic cell. My nanoscopic devices are merely non-organic improvements.

The grey goo flows, tide-like, as if a time-elapsed mould were growing on the little corpse. In 30 seconds it flows back, vanishing into his bone-cavities that are designed specifically for nano-constructors.

Little Thomas, stiff-armed and stiff-legged, pushes himself up onto his feet and patters back across the floorboards.

'A'gen!' he demands. Breathy. "Gen! Do it 'gen!' I didn't say I designed him to be bright.

He pulls at my thigh. This time the kick is a reflex, the anger something bright and sharded and brilliant to go with. So far as I'm concerned, the pain he gave me getting out of my birth canal entitles me to anything I do.

Whomph!

'Whaaaaa –'

Thud.

Patter, patter, patter.

"Gen! 'Gen! 'Gen!"

The day he starts getting intelligent is the day I'll reprogramme him. I shouldn't have to. The nano-repairers in his body are extremely specialized – part of one of the medical projects for which I've earned such astonishingly large amounts of money. One of their design-tasks is to continually maintain a constant state of body and brain from day to day. Thomas is chronologically six now, but biologically he is still two.

I'll keep him this way. He might grow up to be one of those youths outside the apartment in loose shirts and trousers whose bones, ramshackle-tall, always seem on the verge of folding up like a deckchair. At fourteen he could be physically stronger than I am.

He doesn't have much of a memory, either. I haven't quite worked out whether that's part of my design specs, or whether Nature (that outmoded concept whom I flatter myself I somewhat resemble) is being kind. Don't count on it. Nature doesn't care much about individuals. She's not that kind to species, and I have a suspicion the entire biosphere could flip over to a white-state ice planet and She wouldn't be much bothered. As I always tell my students in web tutorials, don't care if you fuck about with Gaia. She doesn't care about you.

My co-workers John and Martin are invaluable in web tutorials. When I say *invaluable*, of course, I mean capable of being exactly valued. I am still paid one third less than they are.

A warm and breathing little body, wet about the crotch, is trying to climb onto my lap.

Whomph!

'Whaaaaa –'

Thud.

Patter, patter, patter.

''Gen! 'Gen! 'Gen!'

Thomas does look like Thomas – his father, I mean. Actually I have nothing against Thomas Erpingham, as such; he is not one of the men I imagine when I break Little Thomas's arms. It's a pity the child has his blue eyes, and his black hair. I would quite have liked it if it had taken after me. I suppose I should have paid more attention to that side of the DNA-twiddling.

I left my various machines talking to the web and went to have a shower. Sometimes I take Little Thomas into the bath and play with him. Sometimes I even don't drown him.

Today I wanted to be on my own, and locked the bathroom door, from time to time turning down the jets so that I could hear the child screaming for food and water. The nanotech makes sure he doesn't die – the micromachines photosynthesize for him – but water can be a problem. Dehydration makes him listless. Still, to look on the bright side, I have got good laughs over the web when I remark that I forgot to water the baby.

The shower bounced jets off my freckled skin, warmed, scented and dried me. I don't look at my hands too often these days, although it is a remarkably difficult thing to avoid one's own hands. The scars are gone, nanotech repairers of my own make certain of that. They have, however, the same familiar shape they have always had. Stubby, with strong nails. All they lack is the coarse black hairs.

Familiar, of course, meaning: pertaining to the family. Yes, they are my father's hands. I could alter them. I prefer not to.

'*Mummy!* I want to watch a *vid-yo.*'

I padded across the floor and flipped the wallscreen to the rolling news channel. There is a small war going on somewhere in the south; they imprison the women in camps and rape them, force them to have the soldiers' babies. Let him watch that.

Sometimes he manages to change the channel when I'm not watching. I keep a thin steel car aerial for those moments.

I continued on into the kitchen and opened the freezer.

'*Fat!*' the fridge-demon screamed. 'You're on a di-et!'

It swung on its over-long arms, wide-toothed face grinning up at me. I used miniaturized orang-utan stock for the base model. Today I didn't have much of a sense of humour.

'Fat – *awp!*'

DISCOVER~!

The fridge-demon bounced off the freezer door, smacked face-down onto the floor, and lay still, flattened. I rubbed my knuckles while its nano-fabricators grew it back, plumped it up, like a balloon with air swelling into it. Pop! Demon-shaped again.

It whimpered back into a corner of the fridge, down by the light, sulking.

'You've got nothing to complain about,' I muttered automatically.

The heat-treatment of unprepared foodstuffs is one of my hobbies, sometimes I can lose myself in it quite satisfactorily. Today I lost the better part of one finger to an over-enthusiastic cheese-grater, and stood biting my lip and dripping over the sink as muscle tissue and skin were nanoscopically rebuilt – never quite fast enough to stem the pain. I lost my appetite.

Sun leaked through the kitchen window between the high-rise blocks. Mostly we find it fashionable, here, to use nano-fabricators only on biological things. There are other quarters of the city where inanimate objects are as mutable as flesh. You can never find your way to the same place twice, usually because it isn't there.

'Thomas!'

He stumped up, determined, on his sturdy feet. Pleased to be called by name, I think. Mostly I whistle for him and he comes. For a moment I touched the warm flesh of his arm, then I slipped the collar over his head and tightened the choke-chain leash, and opened the door into Spring.

I love the streets when they smell of grass and petrol. There are three city parks close to my apartment, I chose the nearest. For a while, enjoying the warmth of the sun, I carried Little Thomas, holding him by one leg and listening to the piercing screams. In the park there are pigeons. I sat on a bench and let him run around in the sun. There is a road crosses the park, and the traffic is not too careful.

There's a chance of him being hit by something – a truck, maybe – so comprehensively that all my nanotech couldn't put Little Thomas back together again. It adds a pleasurable tension to the afternoon. I really don't want to have to start at the beginning and give birth again. Twice was enough.

'Ms?'

This one I recognized. He was another pet-walker, a man in his 30s with an appallingly acned skin. I kept an eye on the grass and the pond, where Little Thomas was busy running up to the bio-ducks and running away again, giggling. This guy's pet hung back, eyes wary.

'No,' I said. 'No, I don't want to hear your story. I don't want to hear how your father fucked you and your younger brother for eight years, and you only went to the police when he started in on the baby. I don't want to hear how your uncle and your cousins used to fuck you from the age of five, and how you *liked* it because it was the only time they ever noticed you were there.'

He looked bewildered. I pointed to his pet, with a certain economy of movement. Even today I am chary of wasting energy; you never know when you will need it.

'Male owner, male pet,' I explained. 'Only the details are going to be different.'

He had nice eyes. I thought of when I put my thumbs into Little Thomas's eyes and they pop like fibrous tomatoes. I couldn't attack this man with the pizza-skin, he weighed fifteen stone if he was an ounce, and he (being male) had thirty per cent more upper-body strength than I had.

I got up, the afternoon spoiled, deciding to go home for a vigorous play-session with Little Thomas, and a languorous finger-fuck in the afternoon's remaining sun.

'I thought . . .' the man said hesitantly. 'We might have something in common. Something to talk about.'

What he thought he could possibly have to say to me defeats me. *Sorry* would be nice. What would be nice, actually, would be if he took out a rusty breadknife and sawed open his stomach, and sawed off his cock, and let that say *sorry* for him. But, optimistic as I am about life, I didn't think this was going to happen.

I walked off without looking back, whistling, and strolled so that Little Thomas could catch up. One of the ducks had taken his eye out, I saw. The nanotech repairers were busy, a grey iridescent film over the empty socket. For some time I amused myself by walking on his blind side and listening to him cry.

The city rises up around me. Even if I weren't working on the web, there is no one I would go to meet. No one I would talk to. I inhabit a different planet. Those who could talk, like the man with the diseased skin, I prefer not to communicate with. I have a strong dislike of communication.

I walk back through residential streets, dodging little piles of excrement on the paving stones. A whiny cry of 'Tired!' pursues me. I bend down and pick Little Thomas up.

His clothes are beyond repair. I strip him and drop them in the gutter. He clings, his naked arms around my neck, nuzzling. A warm body, legs locked around my jutting hip. As I said, he isn't bright. He is affectionate.

That is the only thing I fear.

No – there are two things:

One day I'll get bored with Little Thomas – it just won't be enough any more.

Or else I'll start to love him.

CYRIL THE CYBERPIG

Eugene Byrne

Okay Cyril, I want you to take all this down and store it.
If you fall into the hands of the authorities, you are to
repeat this to them. Got it?

Good.

The beginning. Lordy, where's the beginning? I don't
know. Something like this . . .

Back around the turn of the century, when taxpayers'
money was still being chucked at anything with an 'ach,'
'll' or 'ff' in it, I worked at an animation company in
Cardiff, turning out unimaginative kids' stuff in Welsh.
They were nice people, but I was getting restless.

Then I bumped into Maria at the Cardiff International
Animation Festival. She and I had been part of the same
crowd at university. Though we hadn't met in years, I
sometimes read about her in the trade press – she was at
a London house, fast becoming the queen of the tasteful
sanitary-towel advert. We hung out together at the Fest
and halfway through her boyfriend James, an account manager for one of the big ad agencies, showed up. We stayed
up late and talked a lot of shop.

That's when we decided to form Jam Productions. It
made sense; Maria is a ferociously gifted designer and
artist, I would cover the electronics and James is a charismatic salesman who never needs to resort to bullshit or
insincerity.

They wanted out of London, I wanted to leave Cardiff,
so we set up in Bristol, a small place but one which was

already home to several successful animators, so the talent and the support services would be available.

Two years on, we were doing okay, thanks to James finding the work – mainly in advertising – and stopping us from spending the proceeds too fast. One day, he mentioned that Penn & Warburton, the big confectionery company, were in the market for an animated kids' series to sponsor on satellite and cable.

I went home that evening, a Saturday, shagged out after fifteen days' solid work on a cinema ad for Greene's Gin. I slumped into the sofa and turned on the TV. They were showing *Robocop* 2 on the Classic Movie Channel. I'd already seen it, but was too tired even to pick up the remote and switch it.

The film was long over when I awoke. Now they were showing some daft thing from the 1970s, all Afro hair and loon pants. One of the characters referred to the police as 'pigs.'

I picked up the phone at one in the morning. By 1.15 I had convinced James and Maria that we should make a pilot of my idea.

To earn his keep, Cyril the Cyberpig had to be really cheap. Our only chance was to make story and characters as interesting as possible. Cyril, half-pig and half-machine, was a wiseacre crime-fighter. His arch-enemy was Doctor Obnoxor, a fairly shameless ripoff of Dick Dastardly, a cartoon character nobody remembers any more. Obnoxor was my favourite (and the kids', too); a sneering swine who, in between attempts at world conquest, indulged in wholly gratuitous acts of petty sadism. The annoyingly cheerful Cyril spoke in a sort of Cockney argot, rolled around in mud a lot and liked eating the most disgusting combinations of food we could think of (Marmite Black Forest Gateau, haddock boiled in Lucozade ... you get the idea).

Maria lent a hand, but it was mainly my baby. I did the sketches, wrote the script, moused up the cels and made them move. The children of friends, relatives and complete strangers were systematically kidnapped to test audience reaction and, in between regular work, I turned the pilot around in two months, largely by not sleeping very much.

James lunched all the right people, Penn & Warburton bought it, and we went into regular production. In a few months, it was showing in fifteen different countries, including the US and Japan. Cyril the Cyberpig wasn't nearly as successful at this point as he was to become when he passed out of our hands, but he was honest toil, and by the time we contracted for the third series, the trade press was saying that Jam Productions was on its way.

We never suspected that at that moment, our little partnership was being discussed in the boardroom of the world's fifth-largest corporation.

The Longman-Bertorelli-Mayer Group owned Penn & Warburton. They had all kinds of other interests, mainly in media and leisure, and now they planned to open a huge theme park near Paris.

It was to be called Mondo Future – cod-Esperanto coined by the marketing drones to get the meaning across in as many lingoes as possible – a complex of hotels, restaurants and media- and science-based attractions. It would be taking Disney head-on; while it was the same kind of junk-food funfair, they claimed it would be more 'educational' and more 'European' than its competitor, which is like saying that french fries are better for you than cheese-burgers.

Attractions at Mondo Future were to be based on the Group's media holdings. Though he was sponsored by one of their companies, they didn't have the rights to Cyril, and they probably wouldn't have bothered with him, but – I'm speculating here – some pushy young suit with an

MBA saw an article in *New Scientist* about neural interface technology and had an idea.

Why not make Cyril the Cyberpig for real? Why not take a pig, replace half his brain with a fifth-generation computer, put a voice simulator in his throat, build a machine-gun into his snout, armour-plate half his body, give him a stainless steel front leg with various useful attachments and an artificial back leg with a mule's kick?

The technology existed. On paper, it looked possible.

We knew none of this at the time. What we did know was that Longman-Bertorelli-Mayer were offering us ten million Ecus for the whole Cyril, oink and all. We assumed they wanted to broaden Cyril's market potential with bigger promotion, merchandise and perhaps feature films. They also hinted that they wanted to go virtual with him; after all, Mondo Future was sure to have loads of virtual 'toon booths.

Cyril had been good to us, but ten million eeks was a sight gooder. With no hesitation whatever, we sold. I bought a house in Clifton, James and Maria finally married and bought a big house, and Maria and I bought loads of new Japanese toys. The business flourished. Better still, I had recently started going out with a Media Studies lecturer called Carol; this was the big one – we were spending a lot of time getting doe-eyed in front of log fires and going for long walks hand in hand. If I could freeze-frame my life, it would be then.

The way I hear it, 50 pigs died in secret labs in Switzerland before a fully functioning Cyril was led out at a press conference in Paris to mark the launch of Mondo Future.

The talking pig generated all the expected publicity. Some said it was cruel and immoral to interfere with poor defenceless animals in this way. They were right – but if a talking pig tells you it's never been happier, that it has no problems with the fact that a whole bunch of perfectly viable organs have been yanked out to make way for machinery, and that it's thrilled to bits to be a lead player in the theme park of the 21st century, what do you do? Tell it that it's just a dumb animal and that humans know what's best for it?

So the moral issue becomes sufficiently blurred to open a path of least resistance along which money will most surely travel.

I have a tape of the conference, which was held in English, the international language of greed. The astonished journalists raised the cruelty issue pretty quickly.

'Lissen,' says the pig, standing on a raised platform between a bunch of lobotomized, plastic-smiling Mondo Future suits, 'you can't tell me I've been treated badly if you've ever eaten pork – 'cos that's the only use pigs are to you lot otherwise. There ain't many people keep pigs as pets. Tell you something else – once you've got talking pigs, you're gonna think twice about eating them, ain't you? I could be the best thing that's happened to my species since the Law of Moses. Oinkee oinkee!!'

His mouth moves in synch with the voice box. He's very credible, and has this luvverly London accent, just like his cartoon forebear. 'People are gonna say that I'm just some kind of gimmick, a circus act. It's true I have to earn my keep by entertaining the guests at Mondo Future. But the same is true of everyone in this room. We all got a job to do.'

The hacks are nodding 'good point.'

Now comes the *coup de grâce*: 'If you don't respect me, that's all right. I can live with that 'cos I know that I'm going to make a lot of people – 'specially kids – happy. But the really important thing is this; the scientists have learnt a lot developing me, and that knowledge will benefit the whole of mankind.'

Pure pigshit – but the way Cyril was talking, he represented the end of all human misery. His implants, nano-technology, anti-rejection systems, his revolutionary blood-sugar energy plant and sense/command interfaces promised a future in which the blind would see, the lame would walk and even the irredeemably stupid would cast away Sky Television.

But the press won't let him off just yet. They want to know whether this is really him talking, or if his control computer has been programmed to fend off such questions. And if it really *is* him talking does he mean it, or is he just saying his lines because there's a pork butcher sharpening his knives backstage if he fluffs it?

Cyril goes into a long talk about how that part of his brain which controls his motor functions is still there, and how it's linked to an artificial brain controlling speech, sensory responses and suite upon suite of memory/reaction software to act out his role in the theme park and ask for anything he wants.

So, says a reporter, that means your previous responses to our questions about the morality of artificially altering pigs were pre-programmed.

'You gotta remember I'm a pig,' says Cyril. 'My everyday concerns are different from yours. Pigs don't deal in abstract reasoning. But that don't mean I don't believe what I said . . .'

Got that? He's admitted he's been programmed to talk crap, then contradicts himself. Everyone's confused.

A TV reporter jumps up. 'Cyril, do you have a, um, girlfriend . . . uh, someone special in your life?' I'm sure it's no coincidence that this woman, who has steered the press away from an embarrassing area, works for one of the networks owned by Longman-Bertorelli-Mayer.

Cyril says something about not having had much time for courting lately. He's been busy going through exactly the same customer welcome course that all team-members at Mondo Future have been through.

This was about two years after LBM had bought the

rights to Cyril. Cyril in the flesh (pork?) was just as much a surprise to us as he was to the reptiles of the world's media. When I first saw this on the TV news, I was fascinated, but didn't feel as though it had much to do with me. I still didn't until a few days later when a friend at CNN's London bureau sent me the tape of the full conference.

It's towards the end, and a Dutch newspaperman won't let go of the moral thing.

'Cyril, do you believe in God?' says the guy. Some of the other journalists look irritably at him. This isn't the angle they're interested in.

'I believe in Christian values,' said Cyril, 'of law and order, of people helping one another, of family life and personal morality.' One or two cynics snigger.

'But who created you, Cyril? How did you get here?' says the Dutchman.

'My creator is Andrew Davies,' said Cyril. 'He is a British animator who first came up with the idea of Cyril the Cyberpig. He made the first drawings, and he was responsible for my early cartoons on TV.'

I got to calling it The Argument. At parties, receptions, in the pub, discussion with friends and strangers alike would eventually turn to Cyril.

They'd say it was terrible to interfere with a pig in this way.

I agreed.

They said it was a sick charade to make money for a bloated capitalist concern that didn't give a toss about ordinary people.

I agreed.

They said it was propaganda for the vivisection industry and wouldn't advance human medicine one iota.

I agreed.

They said that the military-industrial complex was probably behind it and that whole armies of soldier-Cyrils were being bred right now and that the old balance of nuclear terror would be replaced by a balance of Cyril terror.

I agreed.

So if you agree, they would say, why did you let them do it?

I would try to explain that, having sold the rights, we had no control over Cyril at all. We weren't even making the bloody TV cartoons any more (these had been put out to a sweatshop in Poland). The ruder ones would say that I had sold out my principles for money, adding that I should try and get the rights back. As if I wanted to commit all I owned to a case I would almost certainly lose. I went right off intellectuals, idealists, greens, vegetarians, liberals and socialists at that point. The trendy novelist Daniel Concannon – whom I have never met – wrote an article in one of the Sunday papers naming me as the living Englishman he most despised, because I hadn't spoken out against Mondo Future's outrageous violation of nature. In between getting most of his facts about me wrong, he suggested that I would happily connive at vivisection of babies if I could secure a regular supply of fresh ones.

What really hurt was that Carol couldn't decide whether she was my girlfriend or a Media Studies lecturer. She understood that there was nothing I could legally do about Cyril, but she kept on at me to publicly denounce him, to take some kind of stand. One of our rows ended with us not speaking for two weeks.

With 50 different flavours of idiot inviting me to flush my career down the toilet, pure pig-headedness (sorry) decided me to say nothing. If someone's mugging you in a back alley, do you tell them that you fully understand their point of view?

Meanwhile, Cyril had become a major international celebrity. The tabloid papers and moron TV stations were giving away tickets to Mondo Future in competitions, running their Cyril the Cyberpig clubs for the kids (and the students and squaddies of course), and doling out thousands of Cyril T-shirts and pairs of Trotter trainers. What I hated most were those car-horns that went 'oinkee oinkee!' I even saw a bumper-sticker once that said 'OINK IF YOU'RE A CHRISTIAN.'

However much the chattering classes fretted, ordinary folk, particularly their children, loved Cyril. He was the star attraction at Mondo Future, repaying the investment in him quite handsomely, what with the animated series and all the merchandise – the Pig Out lunchboxes, the comic (*Porkies*) and the appalling Cyril's Swill range of novelty foods (tuna and strawberry pizzas, for Chrissakes! Vegan Cybersausages!). When everyone thought it could get no bigger, the feature film came out. *Cyril Saves the World* starring Cyril himself, and with Alan Rickman as Dr Obnoxor, broke box office records everywhere. It was, I gladly admit, a slick, very funny film that made both children and adults laugh by not taking itself at all seriously.

Just as all my friends had got tired of picking on me, the Great Mondo Future Massacre took place.

There must have been at least 2,000 people with palmcorders and microcorders there that afternoon. CNN scooped up footage from 35 of them as a job-lot. I've seen it all.

The cartoon Cyril had a built-in machine-gun, the barrel of which poked out of his snout. The strict rule was that Cyril would only fire in self-defence and would never actually hit anyone; the last thing you want in a children's cartoon sponsored by a sweetie company is blood and guts all over the shop. Which is a shame, really, because that's precisely what the kids want; but I digress.

When they built Cyril, they installed a Heckler & Koch machine pistol surrounded by a clever insulating system to stop the gun's heat turning him to rashers from the inside.

Magazines would be inserted under his neck, which was also where you'd find the cocking-lever. Naturally, Cyril only ever fired blank propellant.

When he wasn't appearing on TV chat shows or making movies, Cyril worked at Mondo Future in a full-sized replica of the Roman Colosseum. Three times a day, he'd do a show in which he chased a bunch of bad guys led by the evil Dr Obnoxor, climaxing in a shoot-out; they'd fire at him, he'd roll around and take cover, shout witty defiance, and pop off at them with his gun. They would then try and get away in a car, which he would charge side-on. Half a ton of armour-plated ham would easily knock the car over, and he'd round up the scum and hand them over to the police before settling down to a celebratory roll in the mud, followed by a meal of curried turnips in chocolate.

It would take me ages to work out how to tell the background story. So here's a cutting from a feature about the episode in the *Independent on Sunday*.

'The real villain was not Cyril, but Xavier Kellerman, aged nineteen, one of a team of people who looked after the pig.

'For those working there, Mondo Future is a small community, with all the intense, petty passions that go with it. Kellerman was devastated when his girlfriend, Heloise Fabre, threw him over for Dieter Model, the 25-year-old who played Dr Obnoxor in the Colosseum three times a day. Fabre probably considered the more mature actor a better catch than a teenage swineherd.

'The show was very tightly scripted; ad-libbing was a sacking offence. In the act, Model was the first person Cyril fired his gun at, and this is where Kellerman saw his chance. Visiting his parents in Brussels one weekend, Kellerman went into an underworld bar and bought a clip of live ammunition to fit the gun. Back at work, he replaced a magazine of blanks with it while nobody was looking.

'This was not the stuff of which perfect murders are made. The youth said later that he was insane with hurt and jealousy; he did not care what happened to him later and, no, he agreed that he had not had the guts to have it out with Model man-to-man. Besides, there was always a chance, no matter how slight, that he might get away with it.'

That afternoon, the show started as normal. The bad guys went through their bank-robbery routine, and then, to uproarious applause, Cyril entered. On one of the tapes, you can already see the group of yobs at the front knocking back the beers and acting like idiots. In close up, you can clearly see the Union Jack t-shirts, the sweaty faces, the tattooed foreheads, the short hair, the broken teeth . . .

There are six of them, but they're making enough noise for 50. Now one of them, his shirt dangling from the back of his shorts, gets on top of the low wall in front of them and faces in towards the crowd. Like an orchestra conductor, he leads the chorus . . .

'Nice one, Cyril! Nice one, son! . . .'

A couple of people further back gesture him to sit down and shut up. Others visibly flinch away, not wanting to fall foul of les hooligans. Over to the left, a man in a red t-shirt is speaking into a radio. A couple of other red t-shirts appear at the top of the crowd. One points towards the lads.

The guy on the wall falls backwards, dead drunk, flopping into the dirt right in front of Cyril. His mates laugh and jeer and start throwing beer cans at both him and Cyril. One hits Cyril on the nose; it doesn't just bounce off, but thuds to the ground. It must have been almost full.

One of the lads stands and holds up a half-eaten hot-dog

and, quite clearly, says "Ere, look, Cyril! Pork! I'm eating pig! Might be your mum!'

The others collapse in laughter. The red t-shirts are now coming at them from the top of the auditorium, and from either side with such grim purpose that you know they aren't going to get their money back.

Just what is going through Cyril's head isn't clear, but something in there cracks. He turns towards the main group of hooligans, who are all standing now, and he fires.

The noise isn't the stutter you expect with a machine-gun. The thing he's got shoots so quickly that it sounds more like tearing cloth, and it's very quiet; most of the noise is masked inside Cyril's bulk. The magazine is empty in a few seconds.

Two of the yobs have been virtually cut in half, a third has the top of his head sliced off like an egg. The others, aside from the one who fell into the sand a moment before, are seriously injured.

A woman seated behind them is grazed in the thigh by a bullet; it's a miracle that no other innocent bystanders were killed. People scream, people groan, others stand open-mouthed, unable to take in what's happened. Children cry, men and women in red t-shirts yell obscenities into radios in four different languages.

Even I got hauled in. I was flown to Paris to meet the *juge d'instruction*, the investigating magistrate, Théodore Soustelle, who wanted to talk to anyone who might assist in apportioning blame fairly. By then, he knew that Xavier Kellerman had slipped Cyril the live ammunition in an attempt to assassinate Dieter Model. In his immaculate English, he cheerfully disclosed that the police had already beaten the crap out of Kellerman, and that by pleading *crime passionel*, he would almost certainly be out of prison inside ten years, if not five.

Soustelle was far more interested in Cyril's guilt.

Cyril had always acted out his script to the letter, but on the one occasion he happened to be loaded with live ammunition, he turned on some members of his audience and shot them. The machine part of Cyril's brain had been programmed with more or less the personality which I had originally conceived, and it was about this that Soustelle quizzed me. I explained that Cyril was a cartoon character and had some amusingly disgusting habits, but his *métier* was to fight crime and injustice, to protect the weak and to use his weapon only in self-defence.

'So, Mr Davies,' he said, 'which part of Cyril's mind do you believe urged him to shoot the hooligans? The pig's brain, or the artificial one? If the pig is guilty, we will have him killed as a dangerous animal. If the computer is guilty, then we will have to prosecute Mondo Future . . .'

I couldn't know the answer. It appeared, I said, that the pig itself was guilty. I had not created a cartoon character prone to violent over-reaction, and I was sure that the Mondo Future biotechs never intended to construct something which might damage business by damaging customers.

Soustelle nodded, pursed his lips and shook my hand.

The French adore a good argument, and here was one *de premier cru*.

Some said the owners of Mondo Future were patently guilty of the deaths because they had manufactured Cyril. A prominent *bande-desinée* artist said that he felt a powerful empathy with Cyril's cartoon creators, who could not possibly have foreseen the monster that vulgar consumer capitalism would create. He urged all cartoonists and animators to legally insulate their work from such brutal philistinism.

Others said Cyril's only sin was to lash out in anger against a bunch of English hooligans, which was hardly a crime at all. Perhaps he could be employed as a sort of honorary cop.

A newspaper columnist headlined an article '*J'Accuse*' and lambasted the entire French establishment for making Cyril a scapegoat for the maladies in French society – the break-up of family life, loss of sovereignty to the EC, street-crime, bad driving and the declining quality of table wine. Their hypocrisy, he said, would be complete if they could only send Cyril to Devil's Island.

A leftist politician said Cyril represented a sick hybrid of violent machismo and capitalist repression, the product of a value system which held that problems can be solved simply by having a machine-gun up your nose. This, he postulated, was an American conceit and, since the earliest days of Hollywood, America had screwed up the rest of the world by pretending there's an easy answer to everything. A criminal? Shoot him dead, Short of money? Go and work hard. Fallen out with your mom? Have a cup of coffee and a hug. They were French first, he said, then Europeans, and in any event definitely not Americans. The best thing to do was make a bonfire of Mondo Future and spit-roast Cyril on the top.

In the middle of all this, Théodore Soustelle, either a courageous man, or (more likely) a gleeful troublemaker in the finest French tradition, gave the answer few wanted to hear. He was convinced that the Mondo Future management had done all they could to create a safe and reliable Cyril, that the pig's own brain had decided to waste the yobs, and since this was the first time Cyril had ever deviated from his script, he did so knowing he was carrying live rounds. Soustelle recommended that the EC consider banning the production and use of cyborg animals as a matter of urgency. He was also applying for Cyril to be humanely put down as dangerous and uncontrollable.

An international pressure group called The Friends of Cyril had already formed; volunteers co-ordinated press campaigns and rattled collecting tins in the streets. Mercifully, the projected Cyril Aid concert at Wembley never happened, but several musical has-beens revived their careers when they recorded the nauseating *A Prayer for Cyril*, which topped the charts for six weeks. Personally I preferred the thrash-metal band Noise Annoys' pastiche of the old Paul McCartney/Stevie Wonder song, *Ebony and Ivory and Ham* which didn't even make the top hundred.

Britain's tabloid papers hesitated, then acted decisively. On the not-disproved assumption that their readers were all xenophobic animal-lovers, they took the line that the tragic deaths of some high-spirited lads was the fault of Mondo Future, not the pig. The French, they said, should not be allowed to execute an innocent animal in cold blood. This led to headlines like DON'T LET CYRIL BE A FRENCH FRY!, BRING HOME CYRIL'S BACON!, the surreal IT'S THE FROGS WHO ARE THE PIGS and the scary NUKE THE BASTARDS! – TORY MP.

The Friends of Cyril amassed a formidable war-chest which could have been spent on a million more deserving causes. They hired the sharpest lawyers in Europe to fight Soustelle's decision. After all, the Napoleonic Code is pretty ambiguous about the machine-gunning of English yobs by pigs.

Meanwhile, all my nice educated friends held their noses and jumped into the ideological cess-pit with the scum press. The same people who had previously been hassling me to denounce the Cyberpig were now whining about how I should make a public appeal for Cyril's life to be spared.

No way!

If they killed the pig, they would kill the movies, the TV series, the merchandise, the disgusting food . . . If they did all that, I would have peace and quiet once more. I wanted Cyril dead, dead, dead! Call me vindictive if you want, but hey, I'd rarely been so in touch with my true feelings.

Even Carol wanted me to beg for mercy. But when I told her about my true feelings, she called me a selfish, cynical coward. At the climax of her rage, she called me a pig. That cracked me up. I couldn't help it. I collapsed in tears of laughter. Two minutes later, she walked out.

I re-examined my true feelings.

Yep! I still wanted the Cyberpig to go the way of the dodo. More than ever now that he had come between me and the woman I loved.

Despite what the British papers said, few in France wanted Cyril dead either. There, he had attained the status of Joan of Arc, Alfred Dreyfus, and Napoleon all mixed up. So his precise location was kept secret.

Actually, he was at a naval barracks in Toulon.

Action Verte are hardliners; no namby-pamby monkey-wrenching or tree-hugging for them. These paladins of the planet have killed those who violate the earth for profit.

As to how they found out where Cyril was, I have a theory.

Cyril embarrassed the French establishment, who wanted him out of the way. At the same time, nobody hates environmental activists more than the French secret services – it's a fine old tradition that goes way back to the sinking of the *Rainbow Warrior*. Fifty grand to a handful of pigshit bets that the cloak-and-dagger boys leaked Cyril's whereabouts to *Action Verte*, hoping they'd try and spring him. The spooks would wait, then have a nice gun battle in which a group of terrorists would be productively slaughtered without any annoying paperwork, and in which Cyril would (tragically) die in the crossfire. *Quel dommage!*

One of the greenshirt cells took the bait and decided to rescue Cyril in the name of animal rights.

For what happened next, I have had to rely on newspaper reports. Certain details may be wrong, but there's no doubting the basic facts.

Remember that Brother Gaul still has to do his national

service. A lot of these kids would much rather be doing something else and some, young and idealistic, sympathize with *Action Verte*. Two such were to prove vital in Cyril's escape, giving the terrorists a map of the base, precise instructions as to where they would find him, and suggesting a way of sneaking in.

Very early each morning, the camp took delivery of a vanload of fresh vegetables. On the day they struck, the cell's four men and two women put on naval uniform, hijacked the van, drove it down a side-street, emptied half of the contents and concealed themselves in the remainder, one constantly keeping a gun trained on the driver's head.

Successfully through the gates, they drove towards the kitchens, then turned away to the guardhouse where Cyril was being kept. Because the terrorists were in uniform, none of the detail set to guard Cyril suspected anything until they produced guns and grenades. By then it was too late; the custodians of the most dangerous pig in the world had their hands in the air and were being gagged and herded into an empty cell.

Cyril's cell was opened, the van was backed up to the guardhouse entrance. They chivvied Cyril into the back of the van and ordered the terrified driver to leave by the normal route at normal speed.

They took the van to a suburban garage, bound and gagged the driver and transferred to another van. Now they took the road for Marseilles, where a fast motorboat was waiting to take Cyril to a mountain hide-out in Corsica.

The circumstantial evidence is that the guardhouse had been watched all along; although the military could have just creamed Cyril and the greenshirts there and then, they needed to convince the public that Cyril's death hadn't simply been a quiet assassination. They let the vegetable van get away, and in moments, unmarked cars were tailing it. Now it was just a matter of getting enough firepower into position. Fifty commandos and 200 policemen had been sitting around waiting for this for weeks.

The terrorists ran into the roadblock just outside the seaside resort of La Ciotat. Not just uniformed *flics*, but also really big men with really short hair and really black body-armour.

As the van slowed, the terrorists probably saw the flashing lights of other police cars coming up behind them, of armoured cars pitching into position in the fields to either side of them. The men and women in the van at that moment must have known that even if they surrendered, they would not necessarily be permitted to live. They stopped the van and decided to take some of the enemy with them.

As soon as all the cars in front of them had passed through the roadblock, the shooting started. The terrorists and Cyril spilled out of the back door and took cover among the cars still lined up behind them. The innocent cowered in their vehicles, covered their children with their bodies, screamed, or tried to crawl to safety.

Rocket-propelled grenades hit the van from either side. It destructed in a ball of red and white flames. Cabbage-leaves were still falling to the ground a minute later.

Again, I know this not because I was there, but because cameras were.

Among the vehicles behind the van was a local TV crew on their way to La Ciotat to do a boring story about a yachting regatta. While you or I would be cowering and snivelling and praying, TV camera operators see stuff like this as a career opportunity. This crazy woman gets out of the car and scurries over to where two of the terrorists are crouching, along with Cyril. She reaches them in time to see one of them plug a magazine into Cyril's neck, pull back the cocking-lever, pat him on the head and say something about going out and getting some of the bastards.

Cyril has no such intention. Cyril has been programmed to fight crime, defend the weak, do the right thing (etc., etc.).

Whether he realizes he's in mortal danger, or whether he thinks it's all play-acting is a moot point. But he now turns his nose on the terrorists beside him, and shoots both stone dead with two short bursts.

He then scampers off around the car, with the camerawoman in pursuit, to where two other terrorists are shooting at the police. These, also, he wastes.

Further along, he ignores one who is already wounded in the neck, but shoots the other.

The shooting stops as the police realize that nobody is firing back at them.

Now he emerges from cover, something the camerawoman is unprepared to do.

'*Ne tirez pas! Les terroristes sont morts! J'ai tué les tous! Je vous ai aidé, messieurs! Ne tirez pas!*' he yells quite clearly in cockney-accented French. 'Cyril saves the day again! Oinkee oinkee!' he adds in English.

Talk about ingratitude! Up to now Cyril has been described by some as an artificial intelligence, but artificial stupidity would be nearer the mark.

As he walks out into the open, a storm of gunfire opens up, twice as intense as previously.

The Cyberpig I designed had half his hide covered in bulletproof armour. When they built this Cyril, they took the design literally. I suppose they thought it might be neat to shoot real bullets at him at Mondo Future and have him delight audiences by emerging unscathed. The side that Cyril is presenting to the police is one of shiny aluminium, but beneath that there's enough Kevlar and ceramic plate to absorb anything at that range except a high-velocity rifle bullet.

About a dozen shells thud uselessly into him before he gets the message and runs for cover again. Cyril, programmed to believe that policemen are his friends, is perplexed.

'Blimey!' the camera records him saying to himself. 'They was trying to kill me!'

The shooting stops. Drivers who have been stuck in the crossfire slam their cars into reverse to get out of this mess. Cyril is left standing in the middle of the road with the camerawoman.

Score: five dead terrorists to Cyril, one wounded one to the police, who have also scored three innocent bystanders dead and five injured.

Cyril was prime-time news across the world once more. He had eliminated five murderous terrorists, and yet the ungrateful French police tried to kill this hero on the spot.

Invited to a dinner party in one of the more boho parts of Bristol that night, I cried off, feigning illness. I knew damn well that the same people who wanted me to try and save Cyril a few weeks before would now be lecturing me on how he was a proto-fascist vigilante who, by killing the terrorists in cold blood, had no respect for human rights.

I spent an hour driving around, looking for somewhere I could get some old-fashioned pork sausages for my dinner, just to prove my lack of respect for pigs' rights. Oh, and some black pudding for breakfast, please.

While the lawyers delightedly added this new factor into the debate over what to do with Cyril, Soustelle said it changed nothing. It was further proof of Cyril's instability.

But Cyril, now in a police cell in Marseilles, was making plans of his own.

He bust out – literally. On July 14, during a noisy Bastille Day parade while his captors were drunk, he used his armoured bulk to smash through the walls of his cell and ran off into the night.

People said this was just another plot to quietly dispose of him, but, as the weeks passed and nothing more was heard of him, he was forgotten. It was later announced that Mondo Future had made a huge loss that year and might well close.

I was sitting down to dinner at my place one Friday evening in August, looking forward to a quiet (well, lonely) weekend when the doorbell rang. Cursing, I got up and opened it. There stood a short, muscular, middle-aged man in working clothes.

'Meester Davees?' he asked. His expression was fierce. He looked like one of those farmers who would dump trailer-loads of Golden Delicious apples in the streets of Paris in protest at something the EC had or hadn't done.

'Yes,' I said cautiously.

'I 'ave somezheenk belonging to you,' he said, his mouth cracking into a combination of pained grimace and malicious grin.

Beyond him, there was a Peugeot van parked in the street. 'My cheeldren wanted to keep 'eem, but I detest 'eem. 'Ee is ruining my farm. 'Ee wanted to meet you. So I 'ave, 'ow do you say, smuggled 'eem over here through the Manche Tunnel.'

This only six months since the European Commission had finally forced Britain to do away with formal border controls. The bastards!

I may have literally got down on my knees; I certainly babbled in English and GCSE French about this being nothing to do with me and he should take the bloody pig to the authorities.

He ignored me, turned and whistled. A boy of about ten climbed from the cab, walked around and opened the back doors. In the dusk, I saw the spark of a tear reflecting the street-lamp on the kid's face.

'*Thomas! Vite! Il faut partir tout de suite!*'

Cyril the Cyberpig clattered out of the van and onto the road. The kid bent and kissed him on the head. Cyril muttered something in French about his little friend and started trotting up my garden path.

Ain't life awful? Cyril arrives at the house of someone who hates him, and walks out of the life of a kid who loves him.

I was yelling at the miserable frog-eating peasant, offering him money – anything, dammit – but he was already pulling away.

'Are you gonna invite me in then, or what?' said Cyril, looking up at me. 'I'm a fugitive from injustice. I'd feel happier indoors.' In person, he reminded me a lot of Bob Hoskins in *The Long Good Friday*.

'Um, yes,' I said politely, like he was some annoying relative I didn't want to offend.

In the living room, the first thing his senses picked up on was my dinner, plus side-salad on the table.

'Luvverly! Nosh!' said Cyril. 'I haven't eaten for ages.' With that, he put his forelegs onto the table and tipped it towards him. The food came sliding to the floor, he stuck his snout in and ate.

I picked up the telephone. When a dangerous killer that the French police will want to extradite comes into your house and starts eating your dinner off the carpet, you dial 999, don't you?

An operator answered the call, asking which service I wanted.

Then the line went dead. Cyril was standing beside me, retracting the scissors in his leg. The telephone cord dangled uselessly at my feet.

He belched. 'Luvverly grub,' he said, 'what's for afters? You got any pizzas? I could go a couple of pizzas.'

'What did you do that for?' I asked.

'I'm a fugitive from injustice,' said Cyril. 'I'll take anyone in a fair scrap, but everyone's against me. We only call the police in when we clear my name.'

'We?' I said, horrified.

'Yeah,' he said, 'you an' me. You're my creator. You are responsible for me. I've travelled across France to get to you. You're the only one who can help me.'

'What the hell,' I shouted, 'makes you think I can help you?'

His front shoulders arched in a porcine shrug. 'I don't know. You're the creator. I hoped you could tell me.'

Then he pissed on the carpet.

I went into the kitchen and came back with my biggest, sharpest Sabatier. 'Out! Out! Out!' I screamed, waving the knife in front of his little piggy eyes. 'I am not your fucking creator! I created a cartoon. You were created by a bunch of faceless biotechs in Switzerland. You are nothing, I say nothing, to do with me!'

'I don't understand,' said Cyril. 'I don't know what I've done wrong. I don't remember very much. All I know is that the police tried to kill me when I was helping them. I remember walking across France, at night, to avoid being spotted. I remember hiding in a barn where Thomas found me and said he'd help me and take me to you . . .'

While all this may sound sorry and pathetic, he still spoke in that irritatingly jolly cartoon voice.

'You killed people, Cyril. You shot some spectators at Mondo Future. Do you remember that?'

'Yes. No. I dunno. I remember something hit my nose and hurt it. I was narked.'

'Did you know that there was live ammunition in your gun?'

'Dunno.'

'And what about the terrorists you killed?'

'Who? I don't remember. It's not my job to kill. I'm not sposed to hurt anyone. It's my job to entertain people by helping the police and protecting the weak . . . You sure you haven't got any pizzas?'

No matter how mad I was, I didn't have the guts to kill him.

I had a few Lean Cuisines in the freezer, which I microwaved and gave to my voracious guest. ('Naaah! S'Allright, slop it all into a pile on the floor, mate').

I thought about climbing out of a back window and running for help. But I could just see myself showing up at the local nick and trying to explain to the desk sergeant that Cyril the Cyberpig was in my living room. Even if they believed me, even if I wasn't packed off to the nuthouse, they wouldn't want to know. Forgetting Cyril was favourite by everyone, apart from young Thomas.

So Cyril stayed at my place. That night, I tried to explain to him what had happened, but it was impossible. Neither his pig's brain nor the computer could comprehend what he had done wrong. He had little subjective memory; aside from his programming, he could only communicate his basic urges (feeding and scratching). He could tell you about all his adventures in cartoons, at Mondo Future and on the cinema screen. He had, in his memory, saved the world from the evil Dr Obnoxor and other criminals, hundreds of times. He was a hero, loved by all, a fearless crusader against crime. He remembered the police shooting at him all right – it had so traumatized him that he got it into his head that his creator was the one who could help him. He called himself a victim of injustice – which he was – but he was parroting a line from one of his scripts without really understanding it. And he kept forgetting my requests that he not piss and defecate on the carpet. I'm untidy at the best of times, people say my place looks like a pigsty, but this was ridiculous.

Cyril had a powerful need to understand, to know where he slotted into the Great Jigsaw of Being, but he didn't have the brains to take it all in, no matter how simple I tried to make it.

He had a hell of an appetite, so I had to go shopping next morning. My mind was still working overtime, trying to figure out what to do with Cyril. I thought of finding a phone booth and calling James and Maria, but I decided it wouldn't be fair. After years of trying, they'd just had their first baby, and it didn't seem fair to spoil their happiness with my problems just yet.

When I got home, the pig was up against the desk in the corner of the living room, with a jack extended from his cybernetic front leg into my PC.

'I'm going to have to report you for this, you know.'

'What!?'

'I was looking at your tax-returns and your accounts. You've broken the law. You've been rounding up your expense figures. You owe the Revenue an extra £3.17.'

'Cyril! Shut up! I am your creator! I am God, I can do anything I damn well please, and I'll thank you not to go prying into my personal affairs.'

He noticed the shopping bags. 'Great!' he said. 'Nosh! I'm famished!'

While he grunted and snorted his way through the groceries, planning his menus for the weekend, a little lightbulb came on over my head. If I couldn't tell Cyril the meaning of his life through his ears, I might make it via his computer.

'Cyril,' I said, 'if I explain everything to you, will you promise to go away and leave me alone for ever?'

'Dunno,' said Cyril, preoccupied with the food. 'Are you gonna get cooking, or what?'

'No,' I said, 'it'll have to wait a while.' I was opening drawers, looking through all my bits and pieces, and making a mental shopping-list. Then I went out, got into the car and headed for the nearest electronic suppliers, where I bought a load of memory, a paper-scanner/encoder, some interfaces, fast assembler software and various other bits of wire.

It cost a lot, but I figured it would be worth it. I might even be able to claim it against tax.

When I got back, he was watching TV. A farming programme on the Business Channel about pig-breeding.

'Worrrrr!' he said, not bothering to look my way. 'Look at the dangly, wobbly things on that one! I'd like to climb on the back of that and, then, then . . .'

'And then what, Cyril?'

'I dunno. Something.'

'I think the expression you're looking for is "pork her".'

The Mondo Future bosses hadn't wanted a tourist attraction prone to unpredictable urges. The castration had probably been the first operation on the list.

After Cyril's lunch – five pizzas, three veggieburgers, a pineapple and two litres of supermarket cola, I set to work. I now knew how to dispose of him. Some friends, she a novelist, he a poet, had bought a small-holding in a remote part of Scotland to grow beans and pursue their muses in tranquillity. They had no money; I had. I would give Cyril the gift of understanding (I hoped), then drive him up there and pay them whatever they asked to look after him and keep quiet about it until the bastard died of rust or old age. He might even be useful about the farm. He'd certainly scare the bejeezus out of burglars.

I jacked into his brain, a micro to kill for, a custom-built box packed with optically-networked artificial neurons, a no-frills version of the old Real World Computer prototype.

There was plenty of spare capacity, but I needed even more. Leaving the motor and sensory systems in place, I first wiped his ability to speak French, German and Japanese. Then I knocked out all the Mondo Future bullshit, the storylines of most of his previous adventures and sundry other rubbish. It would, of course, have been a sight easier if I could have just wiped everything in there and let him revert to being a regular pig. But he had once been a valuable piece of property and there was no overriding the core and anthropomorphic behaviour systems short of cutting him open and pulling them out.

Then, I got out my SPAM files. SPAM, or Serial Personality Action Memory is a little media trick used for storing fictional characters. We use low-grade versions at the firm, but they're more generally employed by soap-opera scriptwriters. With SPAM you can ask what a certain character would do in a certain situation, what s/he would say, and what vocabulary (slang, regional expressions, etc.) they'd use to say it. SPAM also avoids continuity errors; if someone says she loves strawberry ice-cream, she doesn't say she's always hated the stuff in an episode five years later. Soap addicts notice little mistakes like that and, say its fans, SPAM gives your characters more depth and credibility. I once held a half-hour conversation with a SPAM; aside from its grinding banality and the fact that it was done via a VDU, you'd swear you were passing the time of day with some daft old codger on a bus. We're not far off the times when soaps will be written entirely by machines.

A TV producer friend, looking for a successful young businessman with a creative edge for a soap he was planning, made a SPAM of me a year ago on the understanding that I would remain anonymous. I agreed to do it for a laugh, because I thought it might be an interesting memento for my grandchildren (if I ever had any), but mainly because I owed him a huge favour after borrowing his mixing-desk for a series of ads that needed some highly specialized sound effects. On and off, he spent six months quizzing me about everything from my political attitudes through to the history of my love-life. I would never have got involved if I'd known it would take so long. In the event, the soap never got made, and he gave me the discs, promising he'd wiped any copies.

These I now took and updated. After that it became rather like one of those stews you make when you're a student. I threw in everything; press reports on me and on Cyril, my own fitfully-written diary since I was twelve, the contents of my personal organizers, both paper and electronic. I even thought of going and getting my favourite love-letters from the attic and putting them through the scanner, but then I figured that if it went wrong and Cyril was to go around parroting the juicy bits, it might all prove rather embarrassing. I mean, your adolescent diaries are embarrassing enough.

Many, many hours later, I downloaded the lot into Cyril and went to bed, letting him chew it all over, assemble meaning from the written stuff, file it all in the right place and try and figure it out.

He was still humming away, putting every little scrap into its proper place when I drove off to work on Monday morning.

I came home early from work that evening, having still spared James and Maria my news. As I opened the door, I didn't know what to expect. Cyril might have gone ape-shit and trashed my house, or he might have just walked off into the sunset.

The living room had been sort of tidied, and Cyril was lying on the floor with a book on art history in front of him, opened at one of my favourite paintings. He was also jacked into my PC. He had gone into files I had made down the years for what I call my Masterpiece Project, the great work of animator's art I'm going to do one day because it's important and not because I want the money.

It's to be a feature-length animation, an ancient Roman/ Greek fantasy with artwork based on paintings by Millais, Burne-Jones, Alma-Tadema, Rossetti and Holman Hunt. It would be filled with grand spectacle, subtle detail and ravishing colours. I was going to bring the Pre-Raphaelites to life!

I first had the idea years ago when I fell in love with H-H's *Isabella and the Pot of Basil*. It had been inspired by a Keats poem, and depicts a woman nuzzling up to a flowerpot in which she's hidden the severed head of her lover who's been killed by her brothers and which is now fertilizing the herbs very nicely. The model was Hunt's beautiful young wife Fanny; they'd been married a few months and had moved to Florence. He was absolutely besotted with her, and so eager to paint her that he made her pose for hours in fierce heat, even though she was pregnant. The tragedy in the painting was to be matched in real life, as Fanny died six weeks after the birth of the child, a boy.

(They called the child Cyril, by the way, an ominous coincidence whose meaning I still haven't figured out.) 'She is adorable, ain't she?' said Cyril, pointing his nose to the picture.

'I thought you only fancied pigs with dangly, wobbly bits, Cyril,' I said, not entirely sure what was going through his mind.

'Not any more. And that Jane Morris, the woman Rossetti used for *Proserpine*, she was a bit of all right, wasn't she? I don't think much to the Alma-Tadema women, mind. Right old dogs if you ask me . . .'

'Cyril! Don't be sexist! You're no Adonis yourself!'

'You fucking hypocrite!' he said. 'I'm only repeating your opinion.'

'That's as may be. We like Alma-Tad for his exquisite colours.'

'Yeah. An' we like the way he does the marble. Paints a luvverly bit of marble, does Alma-Tad . . . I can't wait to get started. I want to make Jane Morris and Fanny Hunt move. I want them to live again.'

'That's my line, Cyril.'

'I know. You programmed it in, remember? Y' stupid bastard!'

I was one up on Holman-Hunt. He had only reproduced his wife in oils. I had reproduced myself in pork. Cyril was no longer a chirpy cartoon pig, but a driven, intolerant, egotistical, obstinate, foul-mouthed know-it-all. I was getting to like him more already.

The second night, I brought back all the kit that he'd need to start work on the animation. He scanned in *Isabella and the Pot of Basil* and began encoding it.

The third night, when I got home, he showed me what he'd done on the TV screen. Six whole seconds of Fanny Hunt, her head resting on the pot, her chest rising and falling slightly. She sighs. A faint breeze ripples her hair and swings the lamp that hangs close by.

It was a bit naff, but we were on our way. All I needed now was a script. Cyril and I could knock up the storyboards together and he could do all the grafting. We might finish it inside three years.

Then the doorbell rang.

It was Carol, my own great love who had walked out on me months ago. 'I got your message,' she said.

'My message?'

'The computer mailbox at work . . .'

'Oh . . .' I said, 'right. Yes. Um, hold on a minute.'

I left her standing at the door and dashed back to the living room. I noticed that my PC had been plugged into the modem. Cyril winked and sauntered off to the kitchen. I went back and ushered Carol in, tidying the plates and takeaway wrappers and newspapers and other rubbish off the sofa. She looked around the room. 'It smells horrible in here,' she said.

'Yes. I think a cat must have got in an open window and sprayed the place,' I improvised.

We sat. 'So,' I said, 'how are you getting on?'

'Look, I . . .' we both said at once, then laughed nervously.

'I didn't know you wrote poetry,' she said.

No, nor did I, unless . . . Oh my God! The adolescent diaries!

'I came really to find out why you did it. It wasn't all that good. It's not some kind of wind-up, is it?'

'Carol,' I said, trying to look her in the eye, 'I'm really glad you came, but it wasn't me who sent the message, well, it was, but only sort of, um . . . Oh hell!' There was nothing for it. I went over to the door, opened it, and in walked Cyril.

'This must be Carol,' said Cyril. 'I'm really pleased ter meetcha. Sorry about the awful poem, but it was the best he could do. Gawd! Has anyone ever told you you look just like that Lizzie Siddal in Rossetti's *Beata Beatrix*?'

It was only then that Carol screamed.

Cyril, programmed with most of my personality, could not really be described as 'cute,' or even 'interesting.' He's actually slightly worse than me (I hope), a consequence of my having fed my diaries in. The diaries have always tended to catharsis, so they're full of moaning and bitching.

You could say that all I've got is a souped-up computer with an attitude problem that accounts for three quarters of our weekly grocery bill, but I'm sort of attached to him. So is Carol. She likes to think she can complain about me by telling him off. She never picks on him unless I'm in the room.

He couldn't be at the wedding, but it felt like he, and not James, should have been my best man. I sold my share of the company to James and Maria and have set up my own little firm, not because I wanted to break away from them, but because Carol and I bought the middle-class dream and now have a 17th-century farmhouse in the Cotswolds that we can't really afford. Carol is working on a book and Cyril, his whereabouts still a mystery to the rest of humanity, works with me on the as-yet untitled masterpiece. When the time is right, the world will hear of Cyril the Cyberpig again.

Assuming I don't kill him first.

NOTES ON THE AUTHORS

GREG EGAN, born 1961, was the deserving winner of the John W. Campbell Memorial Award for his novel *Permutation City* (1994). His stories, collected in *Axiomatic* (1995), have been highly praised. He is an Australian, raised in Perth, and doesn't divulge much about himself – though we heartily recommend the one-and-only interview with him which appeared in *Interzone* 73.

J. G. BALLARD, born 1930, is one of Britain's most eminent writers. His most recent novel is *Cocaine Nights* (1996), and it was preceded in the same year by his collected non-fiction, *A User's Guide to the Millennium* (some of which has appeared in *Interzone*). 'The Message from Mars' is one of a handful of short stories he has written in the last six years.

GARRY KILWORTH, born 1941, is the author of the fantasy novels *House of Tribes* (1995) and *The Roof of Voyaging* (1996), the excellent short story collection *In the Country of Tattooed Men* (1993) and many other books, including several fine children's novels. He's been a long-time contributor to *Interzone*, and lives in Essex.

RICHARD CALDER, born 1956, hails from Essex but has been living in Thailand since 1990. He's the author of *Dead Girls* (1993), *Dead Boys* (1994) and *Dead Things* (1996), an sf trilogy, and all his short stories to date have appeared initially in *Interzone*.

NICOLA GRIFFITH, born 1960 in Yorkshire, published her first short stories in *Interzone* before emigrating to America, where she lives with her partner, fellow sf/fantasy writer Kelley Eskridge. Her published novels, *Ammonite* (1993) and *Slow River* (1995), have received much praise in the USA.

IAN LEE, born 1951, is a member of that occasionally zany profession, the British Civil Service. His stories in *Interzone*, which range from 'Driving Through Korea' (issue 27) to 'The Accepted Conventions of Space, Time and Reality' (issue 69) have been well liked. He lives in west London.

PAUL PARK, born 1954, is the American author of the remarkable sf novels *Soldiers of Paradise* (1987), *Sugar Rain* (1989), *The Cult of Loving Kindness* (1991) and *Coelestis* (1993). 'The Tourist', his only contribution to *Interzone* so far, is one of the very few short stories he has had published anywhere.

STEPHEN BAXTER, born 1957 and a well-known name in *Interzone* ever since we published his first story in issue 19, is fast becoming a superstar of the wider sf firmament. Arthur C. Clarke described his novel *The Time Ships* (1995) as 'the most outstanding work of imaginative fiction since Olaf Stapledon.' His most recent novel is *Voyage* (1996).

GEOFF RYMAN, born 1951 in Canada, is the author of the award-winning sf novel *The Child Garden* (1989) (partially published in *Interzone*) and other books such as the moving psychological fantasy '*Was...*' (1992) and the brilliant collection *Unconquered Countries* (1994). He lives in London.

IAN R. MACLEOD, born 1957, lives in the West Midlands and has written a number of well-received short stories for leading American magazines as well as for *Interzone*. His debut collection is due to appear from Arkham House in the United States, and a first novel is also on its way.

IAN WATSON, born 1943, is one of Britain's best-known (and best) sf novelists, his books ranging from *The Embedding* (1973) to *Hard Questions* (1996). He is also a prolific writer of short stories, many of which continue to appear in *Interzone*.

MOLLY BROWN, from Chicago but now resident in Surrey, has been a shoe-shine, a cabaret comedienne, a gun-toting security guard, and a voice-over artiste for animated films – all the usual dull things. 'Bad Timing', her debut in *Interzone*, won the British SF Association award for best short story. Her novel *Invitation to a Funeral*, an historical whodunnit, was published in 1995.

PAUL DI FILIPPO, born 1954, has published just two books to date, *The Steampunk Trilogy* (1995) and *Ribofunk* (1996), but he has been a star of sf magazines since the mid-1980s. Like the late great H. P. Lovecraft, he lives in Providence, Rhode Island.

CHERRY WILDER, born 1930, is a New Zealander long resident in Germany. Her most recent of many books are the stylish sf/fantasy collection *Dealers in Light and Darkness* (1995) and the sf novel *Signs of Life* (1996).

TIMONS ESAIAS is an as-yet little-known American writer, whose 'Norbert and the System' – his first story in *Interzone*, or in any sf magazine – proved very popular with readers.

JOHN MEANEY works as a consultant for a well-known software house. Ranked black belt by the Japan Karate Association, and a keen weight-lifter, he lives in Tunbridge Wells, Kent, and has published several stories in *Interzone*. His first novel is on its way.

DAVID GARNETT, born 1947 in Lancashire, is perhaps best known as an anthologist, thanks to such series of volumes as *The Orbit SF Yearbook*, *Zenith* and *New Worlds*. However, he has also written a great deal of fiction including the humorous sf series beginning with *Stargonauts* (1994).

BRIAN ALDISS, born 1925, is an author who does not rest on his laurels. He has written well-received mainstream novels such as *The Hand-Reared Boy* (1970) and *Forgotten Life* (1988) as well as a huge quantity of sf and fantasy. To celebrate his 70th birthday in August 1995 he published a variety of new works, including a story collection, *The Secret of This Book*, a volume of essays, *The Detached Retina*, and a poetry collection, *At the Caligula Hotel*. He and his wife Margaret live in Oxford.

CHRIS BECKETT is the supervisor of a team of social workers who deal mainly with children and families in Cambridge. One of the stories he wrote for *Interzone*, 'The Welfare Man' came third in the magazine's 1993 popularity poll, and has since been reprinted in a social work textbook.

BEN JEAPES, who works in computing and lives near Oxford, is the author of half a dozen short stories published in *Interzone*, of which 'The Data Class' proved particularly popular with readers.

ERIC BROWN, born 1960, has written several admired books since he made his debut in *Interzone*. They include *The Time-Lapsed Man and Other Stories* (1990), *Meridian Days* (1992), *Engineman* (1994) and *Blue Shifting* (1995). He lives in Haworth, Yorkshire.

GRAHAM JOYCE, born 1954, and PETER F. HAMILTON, born 1960, are rising British authors. Graham's dark fantasy novels include *House of Lost Dreams* (1993) and *Requiem* (1995); Peter's include the exuberant sf *The Nano Flower* (1995) and the massive space opera *The Reality Dysfunction* (1996). Both live in the Midlands.

BRIAN STABLEFORD, born in Yorkshire in 1948, gained a degree in biology, then a PhD in sociology, from York University. He began publishing sf in the 1960s while still a teenager, and is a writer so prolific that his bibliography boggles the mind. He and his wife Jane live in Reading, Berkshire, with an Aga cooker, no pets, and an amazing collection of books – seemingly half of them written by Brian.

THOMAS M. DISCH, born 1940, is a poet, theatre critic and much more, and has contributed stories to *Interzone* since its second issue. His most recent novel, *The Priest: A Gothic Romance*, appeared in 1994. He lives mainly in Barryville, New York State.

KIM NEWMAN, born 1959, is the author of the novels *The Night Mayor* (1989), *Bad Dreams* (1990), *Jago* (1991), *Anno Dracula* (1992), *The Quorum* (1994) and *The Bloody Red Baron* (1995). He has also written pseudonymous novels, collections of short stories, a couple of non-fiction books and more film reviews than anyone can count. He lives in London.

DAVID LANGFORD, born 1953, nuclear scientist, computer whiz and all-round Great Brain, produces *Ansible* – which John Clute describes as 'the best fanzine now published in this country'. For his pains, he has won more Hugo Awards than any other UK citizen. He has also written a number of witty books, fiction and non-fiction, the most recent item being *The Unseen University Challenge: Terry Pratchett's Discworld Quizbook* (1996).

SEAN MCMULLEN, born 1948, is the Australian author of the sf novels *Voices in the Light* (1994) and *Mirrorsun Rising* (1995). He's a computer systems analyst with the Australian Bureau of Meteorology, and has been a lead singer in folk and rock bands as well as singing with the Victoria State Opera for two years. Like John Meaney, he is a karate expert.

MARY GENTLE, born 1956, is the author of *Rats and Gargoyles* (1990), *Grunts* (1993) and several other highly praised sf and fantasy novels, among the most recent being *Left to His Own Devices* (1994). She lives in Stevenage, Hertfordshire.

EUGENE BYRNE is known to *Interzone* readers as collaborator with his old school friend Kim Newman on the 'USSA' stories, about a communist America and capitalist Russia in an alternative timeline. 'Cyril the Cyberpig' was his first solo effort for us. He has also written a considerable amount of journalism, and works as deputy editor of a local magazine in Bristol.

DP, June 1996

The Losers
David Eddings

Raphael Taylor was a golden boy – blond, handsome, a gifted athlete and student. Damon Flood was a scoundrel – a smooth, smiling, cynical devil. The day Raphael met Damon was the day he began his mysterious fall from grace. And the golden boy fell very fast and very low.

Damon introduces Raphael to drink, wealth and a seductive woman, and then sends him out to his doom. After losing a leg in a drunken car accident, Raphael goes to recuperate in a seedy backstreet in Spokane, Washington. There he is surrounded by 'the losers', a nightmarish subculture of violence and despair that is kept going – and kept out ot sight – by a band of incompetent social workers. Horrified yet fascinated, Raphael struggles to come to terms with his new surroundings – until Damon turns up on his doorstep, and the world of the losers explodes . . .

In *The Losers*, David Eddings enters deeply into the lives of America's outcasts to reveal a new and brilliant side to his storytelling genius.

'A rare mainstream outing from bestselling fantasist Eddings. Offbeat, intriguing, compelling . . . an unexpected pleasure.'
Kirkus Reviews

ISBN 0 586 21759 2

Dragoncharm
Graham Edwards

The ultimate dragon saga

THE WORLD IS TURNING

The bones of trolls are turning suddenly to stone as nature draws apart from the Realm, the mysterious source of charm. It is a young world, but soon it will be old, and no magic is strong enough to resist the onset of a new era.

Instead, a young natural dragon named Fortune, with no fire in his breath nor magic in his power, holds the key to the survival of charm.

The malevolent Charmed dragon Wraith knows this, and he awakens the basilisk in a desperate bid to gain power over Fortune . . .

Myths handed down since the dawn of time tell of dragons, the most strange and magnificent creatures of our mythical prehistory. In this glorious epic fantasy, Graham Edwards captures the terror and the beauty of the days when dragons roamed the sky.

ISBN 0 00 648021 7

Foundation

Isaac Asimov

The first volume in Isaac Asimov's world-famous saga, winner of the Hugo Award for Best All-Time Novel Series.

'One of the most staggering achievements in modern SF'
The Times

Long after Earth was forgotten, a peaceful and unified galaxy took shape, an Empire governed from the majestic city-planet of Trantor. The system worked, and grew, for countless generations. Everyone believed it would work forever. Everyone except Hari Seldon.

As the great scientific thinker of his age, Seldon could not be ignored. Reluctantly, the Commission of Public Safety agreed to finance the Seldon Plan. The coming disaster was predicted by Seldon's advances in psychohistory, the mathematics of very large human numbers, and it could not be averted. The Empire was doomed. Soon Trantor would lie in ruins. Chaos would overtake humanity. But the Seldon Plan was a long-term strategy to minimize the worst of what was to come.

Two Foundations were set up at opposite ends of the galaxy. Of the Second nothing can be told. It guards the secrets of psychohistory. *FOUNDATION* is the story of the First Foundation, on the remote planet of Terminus, from which those secrets were withheld.

ISBN 0 586 01080 7

Red Mars
Kim Stanley Robinson

WINNER OF THE NEBULA AWARD

MARS. THE RED PLANET.
Closest to Earth in our solar system,
surely life must exist on it?

We dreamt about the builders of the canals we could see by tele-scope, about ruined cities, lost Martian civilisations, the possibil-ities of alien contact. Then the Viking and Mariner probes went up, and sent back - nothing. Mars was a barren planet: lifeless, sterile, uninhabited.

In 2019 the first man set foot on the surface of Mars: John Boone, American hero. In 2027 one hundred of the Earth's finest engineers and scientists made the first mass-landing. Their mission? To create a New World.

To terraform a planet with no atmosphere, an intensely cold climate and no magnetosphere into an Eden full of people, plants and animals. It is the greatest challange mankind has ever faced: the ultimate use of intelligence and ability: our finest dream.

'A staggering book . . . The best novel on the colonization of Mars that has ever been written'   *Arthur C. Clarke*

'First of a mighty trilogy, *Red Mars* is the ultimate in future history'   *Daily Mail*

'*Red Mars* may simply be the best novel ever written about Mars'
                                                                 Interzone

ISBN 0 586 21389 9

Green Mars
Kim Stanley Robinson

WINNER OF THE HUGO AWARD

The second book in the highly acclaimed Mars trilogy,
following the award winning *Red Mars*

MARS. THE GREEN PLANET

Man's dream of a new world is underway, but corrupted. The
First Hundred have scattered or died, the rebels are under-
ground, planning their utopia, waiting. The transnational corpo-
rations aided by the UN are rebuilding the ruined cities and
mining valuable resources. They too have a dream. Mars can be
plundered, cultivated and terraformed to suit Man's needs -
frozen lakes are forming, lichen is growing, the atmosphere is
slowly becoming breathable. But most importantly, Mars can
now be owned. On Earth, countries are being bought and sold by
the transnationals. Why not here too?

Man's dream is underway, but so is his greatest test. Societies are
crumbling and re-forming, adapting and reacting to new conditions. The survivors of the First Hundred know that technology
alone is not enough. Trust and co-operation are needed to create
a new world - but these qualities are as thin on the ground as the
Martian air they breathe.

'One of the finest works of American SF'
Times Literary Supplement

'The red sand displays the recent footprints of Ben Bova and
Greg Bear . . . But the forerunner is Kim Stnaley Robinson'
Time Out

'Absorbing . . . impressive . . . fascinating . . . utterly plausible'
Financial Times

ISBN 0 586 21390 2

Only Forward
Michael Marshall Smith

A truly stunning debut from a young author. Extremely original, satyrical and poignant, a marriage of numerous genres brilliantly executed to produce something entirely new.

Stark is a troubleshooter. He lives in The City - a massive conglomeration of self-governing Neighbourhoods, each with their own peculiarity. Stark lives in Colour, where computers co-ordinate the tone of the street lights to match the clothes that people wear. Close by is Sound where noise is strictly forbidden, and Ffnaph where people spend their whole lives leaping on trampolines and trying to touch the sky. Then there is Red, where anything goes, and all too often does.

At the heart of them all is the Centre - a back-stabbing community of 'Actioneers' intent only on achieving - divided into areas like 'The Results are what Counts sub-section' which boasts 43 grades of monorail attendant. Fell Alkland, Actioneer extraordinaire has been kidapped. It is up to Stark to find him. But in doing so he is forced to confront the terrible secrets of his past. A life he has blocked out for too long.

'Michael Marshall Smith's *Only Forward* is a dark labyrinth of a book: shocking, moving and surreal. Violent, outrageous and witty - sometimes simultaneously - it offers us a journey from which we return both shaken and exhilarated. An extraordinary debut.'
Clive Barker

ISBN 0 586 21774 6

SCIENCE FICTION IS *NOT* DEAD!

Life's too short for the mindless spectacle of most modern visual SF. The chances are you got interested in science fiction because you like the mind-stretch you get from new ideas – and you only find that in the written word.

LONG LIVE SF!

Science Fiction is alive and kicking in the UK. Every month half a dozen challenging new science fiction and fantasy tales appear in Britain's best SF magazine –

You never know what you're missing 'til you try, so subscribe today!

Subscription rates: **Six issues:** £15 UK, £18 (US$27) Rest of world.
Twelve issues: £30 UK, £36 (US$56) Rest of world. US copies sent by Air Saver.
Single issues are also available for £2.75 UK, £2.80 overseas including P&P

....

YES! Please send me ☐ six ☐ twelve issues of **Interzone**, beginning with the current issue. I enclose a ☐ cheque ☐ p.o. ☐ international money order, made payable to Interzone OR ☐ please charge my credit card

Card number

Expiry date   **Signature**

| / |

Name ....

Address ....

....

If cardholder's address is different from the above, please include it on a separate sheet.

INTERZONE • 217 PRESTON DROVE • BRIGHTON • BN1 6FL • UK